A GALAXY UNKNOWN

CASTLE VROMAN

Book 6

BY

THOMAS DEPRIMA

Vinnia Publishing - U.S.A.

Castle Vroman

A Galaxy Unknown series – Book 6
Copyright ©2004, 2012 by Thomas J. DePrima

ISBN-10 : **1619310120**

ISBN-13 : **978-1-61931-012-4**

1st Edition

Amazon Distribution

Cover art by: Martin J. Cannon

Appendices containing political and technical data highly pertinent to this series are included at the back of this book.

To contact the author, or see information about his other novels, visit:

http://www.deprima.com

Acknowledgements

Many thanks to Ted King for his technical expertise and encouragement, and to Michael A. Norcutt for his suggestions, proofreading, and for acting as my military protocol advisor.

I also want to thank James Richardson and Adam Shelley for their beta reading and invaluable suggestions, and Myra Shelley of Independent Author Services for her wonderful editing work on this novel.

This series of novels includes:

A Galaxy Unknown…

A Galaxy Unknown
Valor at Vauzlee
The Clones of Mawcett
Trader Vyx
Milor!
Castle Vroman
Against All Odds
Return to Dakistee

Other series and novels by the author:

AGU: Border Patrol…

Citizen X

When The Spirit…

When The Spirit Moves You
When The Spirit Calls

A World Without Secrets

Table of Contents

Chapter One
~ October 1st, 2277 ~

"Is this rumor true?" Emperor Maxxiloth roared with all the intensity his body could produce. One of his four tentacles darted out and clenched a portable electronic pad so tightly the device began to warp. He smashed it down onto the table with such force that the officers and ministers, most of whom had averted their four eyes to avoid his stare, jumped in their seats. "Did our First and Second Fleets, the pride of the Milori Empire, run away from a fight with a convoy of merchant ships?" he bellowed. "Have we sunk so low that we fear to have our finest warships engage lightly armed food merchants and baggage handlers?"

Considered by most Terrans to be the ugliest sentient species so far encountered since first moving off Earth, just looking at a Milora could make a person's skin crawl. Terrans often referred to them as giant cockroaches because of their stringy body hair and four bug-like eyes. However, placement of the single-colored eyes offered them peripheral vision far superior to that of Terrans. Generally about the same height as Terrans, they had what passed for two arms, but instead of hands, the arms terminated in claws. When a claw was open, two opposed digits, like fingers on a Terran, were visible. The digits provided dexterity not possible with claws, while the claws could clamp down onto something like a vise.

A Milora also had four tentacles, and it was probably those appendages that upset Terrans so much. The body hair and loose cloaks they wore completely concealed their tentacles when at rest, but eyewitness reports indicated that they could dart out to coil around a person and then crush them to death, as would a boa constrictor on Earth.

"My Lord," Exalted Lord Space Marshall Berquyth said softly, hoping to calm the emperor, "the intelligence information appears to be accurate, but Supreme Lord Space

Marshall Dwillaak couldn't have known they were freighters. They were positioned behind a line of Galactic Alliance warships of the highest caliber and so far distant that they were barely registering on the scanners. Space Command's senior officer in the area, an Admiral Carver, tricked Dwillaak into believing the convoys were fleets of warships, and the ship sizes, as recorded by our own DeTect systems, certainly made them appear to be battleships, cruisers, frigates, and destroyers.

"This Carver," Berquyth continued, "is their most able admiral. It was she who annihilated our Third Fleet. Although outnumbered seven to one, she suffered only minor damage to her task force. Her exploits have become legendary throughout the Galactic Alliance and she is generally credited with forcing the giant Raider organization to its knees. Even *they* admit to that. At one time, they had placed an astronomical bounty on her head. Two armed assassins died trying to earn that reward— one by her own hands and the other by a bite from one of her pets."

Berquyth turned to face the enormous wall monitor in the War Planning Chamber where an image of Admiral Jenetta Carver jumped into focus. Taken during an awards ceremony, the image showed her receiving her third Space Command Cross. "We've obtained a picture of her from one of their news broadcasts," he said.

"Is this the most recent image we have of her?" the emperor raged. "Surely someone of such importance must have her picture taken regularly. My regal visage is captured dozens of times every day."

"This image is just a few weeks old, my Lord. It was part of a live broadcast from one of their news services at the ceremony where she was decorated for defeating our fleets. I know you're unfamiliar with their military insignia, but if you'll notice her shoulders, you'll see two stars on each. They mean that she's risen to the second level of five in Space Command's topmost ranks. Her rank and seniority place her sixty-seventh in their top hierarchy of two hundred seventeen flag officers."

"But from what I know of the physiology of these ugly, almost hairless creatures, she looks like a mere child," the emperor said, speaking a bit more rationally now that he had become intrigued.

"She's the youngest admiral in Space Command history by quite some measure. Chronologically, she's forty-two Earth years old, but she was in stasis for eleven of those years following an accident aboard her ship while she was a junior officer. Space Command, for purposes of calculating years to retirement, records her age as just over thirty-one Earth years."

"Thirty-one Earth years? Isn't that the equivalent of about twenty of our annuals?"

"Yes, my Lord. Twenty-point-seven-seven of our annuals."

"How could someone so young rise to such a powerful position? Is her clan so well connected that she has received special promotional consideration?"

"No, my Lord. While her ancestry chart evinces a proud lineage of military service, her sire is a mere ship's captain. She was captured by the Raider organization nine or ten Earth years ago after sneaking into one of their bases to gather intelligence information and was subsequently slated for servitude at one their brothels. She managed to escape. During the process, she destroyed the entire Raider base, along with dozens of warships and tens of thousands of Raider personnel. But our agents have determined that she never attempted to exploit new political connections for favorable treatment. I distinctly remember hearing that Space Command promotes on some strange sort of merit system instead of the time-honored tradition of clan ascendancy. She still carries the slave brand and is officially registered as the property of Resorts Intergalactic in many systems within the Uthlaro Dominion."

"And this young escaped slave is responsible for destroying one of our fleets and greatly humbling the others?"

"Yes, my Lord. The Space Command task force was under her direct supervision and one of the battleships that faced Dwillaak served as her flagship."

3

"And she only had twelve warships, not the hundreds Dwillaak thought?"

"It certainly appears that way, my Lord. She is incredibly clever."

"Then she is indeed a worthy opponent, despite her young age," the emperor said. Beaming as if he had already defeated Carver, he said, "Her mounted head will fit in well with the other trophies in my study. You will issue orders for Dwillaak to immediately reverse course, engage this child and her fantasy force again, and bring me her head."

"Uh, there is a difficulty, my Lord."

"What is it?" the emperor asked angrily. "Is Dwillaak afraid to take on this child again?"

Calmly, Berquyth said, "Not at all, my Lord. He is most anxious to restore his clan's honor. But our spies report that at least nineteen more warships have arrived at Stewart since the confrontation. Carver now has at least thirty-four first-class warships in her command."

"Only thirty-four? We'll crush them to space dust. Dwillaak has almost two hundred left of his invasion force."

"We also know that Space Command has scrambled its entire fleet. We estimate that as many as two hundred more warships are underway to the border at top speed. We've definitely lost the element of surprise. We can still engage Space Command, but it's extremely unlikely that we could even get *near* Earth now. At best we might only succeed in destroying much of their force at the expense of our own."

"But wouldn't that accomplish most of our goals?" the emperor asked. "We already intended to let privateers run wild in the territory until it was time for us to take full control. The privateers will keep Space Command bottled up and their systems in turmoil while we consolidate our territories."

"But we didn't intend to lose the three fleets we sent. That might make us much more vulnerable to attack by our other enemies. And there's still the matter of the unknown weapons Space Command used against us. Our Raider contact, Commandant Mikel Arneu, has explained the construction and operation of the energy cage and Dwillaak figured out

4

how Carver made it appear that the cage was causing ships to explode upon contact. She had positioned proximity mines in positions coincident with the array pattern of the generated electronic fields. But we still don't know anything about the invisible bombs that explode with the force of a hundred nuclear mines. That one weapon makes their forces several times more lethal than their ships would be on their own."

"So you recommend that Dwillaak not reengage her at this time?"

"That would be my recommendation, my Lord."

"Where is Dwillaak now?"

"The First and Second Fleets are still over one hundred twenty-five light-annuals inside the Alliance's Frontier Zone, headed back towards our territory as we speak. They could turn around now and be in position to attack Stewart Space Command Base in a quarter of an annual if that is your wish."

"And if they don't turn around, they travel three-quarters of a light-annual further away from this Admiral Carver each day. Perhaps we should simply halt the invasion force and have them maintain position until we learn more about these new weapons."

"We know Admiral Carver has spotter ships watching for our fleet at irregular intervals because we were given specific course instructions for leaving their territory so they could monitor our exodus. If we fail to pass the hidden spotter ships, they will know we have stopped and could declare us in breach of the treaty that Dwillaak endorsed."

"I didn't agree to that treaty and I don't recognize it," Maxxiloth said angrily. Defiantly, he added, "*Let* them declare us to be in breach."

"But they might then begin making preparations to invade *us*, my Lord. With half our fleets still in their territory, we are ill prepared to stop a major invasion force in our space should they get past our borders undetected."

Emperor Maxxiloth growled ominously in frustration. "Very well, allow our fleets to continue as if they are headed home— but I want a detailed report on the status of our remaining forces by the end of this day. I want to know how many additional ships we can free up from other duties to send against the Galactic Alliance. The record of this inglorious defeat must not be allowed to stand any longer than necessary."

Chapter Two
~ October 1st, 2277 ~

Admiral Vroman entered the Captain's briefing room as the doors parted to admit him.

"Good morning, Admiral," Captain Halmar Lindahl, captain of the destroyer *Lisbon*, said as he stood up. "Won't you have a seat, sir? Would you care for a beverage?"

"Thanks, Hal, I'm fine," Vroman said, as he settled into one of the oh-gee chairs facing Lindahl's desk and adjusted the control for the chair's height. "I hope I'm not interrupting anything important. I'm just feeling a little antsy. I won't have much to do this trip except study the latest status reports filed by Admiral Carver and continue to acquaint myself with every aspect of the operations at Stewart. My only break in the dull routine has been reviewing the vids of her encounters with the Milori."

"The vids make for very exciting viewing," Lindahl said.

"The first dozen times," Vroman said. "After thirty or more viewings they start to lose their edge."

"Thirty, sir?"

"Yes. Everyone, including Admiral Carver, expects the Milori to return once they've replaced the warships she destroyed. It's almost a given that they'll attempt to seize our territory again. I must be prepared for that day in case it happens during my tour there. I've been studying every aspect of their tactics, and Admiral Carver's."

"Since she sent the Milori packing back to their own empire, things have really calmed down out there. Given the distance to Milor, the time it will take to build a hundred-plus new ships, and the return time, I doubt they'll be back before your tour is over. The large fleet Admiral Carver commands is providing Stewart's sectors with unparalleled patrol coverage. I've heard it's been as quiet out there as it is in the sectors around Earth."

"I expect that by the time we arrive at Stewart in fifteen months, Admiral Carver should have all the trouble-making elements in her sectors under firm control. I'm hoping all I'll have to do is follow her blueprint through to the end of my tour."

"Other than a few smugglers now and again, I doubt you'll have much to worry about, sir."

* * *

Jenetta had sufficient time to prepare a mug of coffee, check her mail, and think about the day ahead before her first appointment in the pristine and spacious headquarters section of Stewart Space Command Base. The tall young officer, with a face and body like that of a blond Aphrodite, sported the two gold stars on each shoulder proclaiming her an admiral in Space Command.

But for the fact that there were no windows and stepping outside for a breath of fresh air wasn't an option, the command base was indistinguishable from a military base on Earth or some other planet. Positioned near the inner edge of what's called the Frontier Zone, a hundred-parsec-wide band of space that surrounded much of Galactic Alliance space, Stewart was the farthest StratCom base from Earth. Housed inside a hollowed out hundred-twenty-kilometer-long asteroid in permanent orbit around a Type F5 blue/white MMK class IV star with an asteroid belt but no planets, the base was well protected from both enemies and natural phenomena.

Commander Barbara DeWitt, the fifty-year-old head of the Weapons Research section, was always punctual, and Jenetta's aide, Lt. Commander Lori Ashraf, sent the attractive brunette in after first advising the admiral of her presence.

"Come in, Barbara. Coffee?"

"Thank you, Admiral," DeWitt said, smiling as she walked towards the beverage dispenser mounted in a sidewall. "I could use a cup. We've spent the early morning disassembling one of the Milori laser weapons in a clean room."

"Find anything interesting?" Jenetta asked after DeWitt had prepared her coffee and taken a seat.

"Nothing I've felt obligated to immediately report to Weapons Research at Supreme Headquarters, but the Milori do things a little differently than we do and we're documenting everything for our regular weekly report."

"Good. If you have some time, I have a little project I'd like you to look into."

"Of course, Admiral, anything."

"We were seriously impacted, no pun intended, by Milori torpedoes in the battle with their Third Fleet. Our gunners did a magnificent job, but far too many torpedoes got past them, and I've been giving it a lot of thought. Throughout most of Space Command's history, opponents who haven't immediately surrendered have tried to run. The Raiders might fire a torpedo or two before showing us their ship's stern, as is the case with the Tsgardi, but neither ever believed they had a chance of beating us in a fair fight and usually took off as soon as they saw an opening. But during the past decade, we've found ourselves increasingly facing opponents who stand and fight."

"Yes, Admiral?"

"I remember from my studies at the Academy that during the late twentieth century the U.S. Navy had a special cannon system designed to automatically protect a ship from incoming surface-to-surface or air-to-surface rockets. Have you heard of the Phalanx?"

"Yes, I have. It was a fast reacting, rapid-fire, twenty-millimeter Gatling gun, providing a last chance defense against missiles. It automatically detected, tracked, and fired upon any incoming threat using an advanced, forward-looking infrared detector with a unique search and track radar system. As I recall, the later models fired four thousand, five hundred rounds per minute using a pneumatic gun drive, although the magazine only held fifteen hundred fifty rounds. The rounds were armor-piercing with a depleted uranium sub-caliber penetrator initially, but were later changed to a tungsten penetrator. The weapon's name comes from the fighting method developed by Philip II of Macedon where a formation of infantrymen, sixteen wide by sixteen deep, would overlap their shields and project their very long lances,

9

called sarissae, through the defensive shield barrier. That defense made it almost impossible for warriors of the day to breach the square. The technique was used quite effectively, and quite often, by Alexander the Great."

"I guess that means you're familiar with it," Jenetta said, smiling.

"Yes, Admiral," Barbara responded with a grin.

"Why don't we have something like that on Space Command vessels?"

"It's a thorny issue. There's a faction in Weapons Procurement that wanted it, but another faction at Supreme Headquarters was strongly opposed to it."

"How could anybody be opposed to a purely defensive weapon?" Jenetta asked.

"It's because of the laws of physics. The opposing viewpoint centers on the fact that we're in space, not on Earth. Any kinetic rounds fired from such a weapon would keep traveling at a constant velocity until they struck something, as opposed to the naval situation on Earth where expended rounds drop harmlessly into the water after their velocity is sufficiently diminished. The planetary atmosphere and gravity prevent them from becoming a permanent threat to innocent shipping."

"The obvious solution seems to be the use of a laser pulse. Even at full strength, alignment and optical phenomenon means that it's rendered harmless a few meters beyond the target."

"The problem there has always been with the rapidity of fire," Commander DeWitt said. "We can't fire a laser array forty-five hundred times a minute because of the time needed to build the pulse charge and the need for heat dissipation. The last time the two factions locked horns on this issue, we could only fire twenty-eight times a minute. SHQ Weapons Research decided that a human gunner who could also use the same cannon for offensive purposes was a better use of resources than having the array dedicated only to defense."

"And what's the normal fire rate of a human gunner manning a laser weapon now?"

"Oh, no more than thirty pulses per minute if they're trying for a target lock, but it's extremely difficult to maintain a lock on a torpedo because they're usually sheathed in an energy-dampening material. Normally, the gunners just fire as rapidly as the cannon allows, so figure on the full hundred pulses per minute."

"But even if a computer can't maintain a lock, once it's established an initial lock it's still got to be better at projecting a track than a gunner who's just firing wildly."

"I see what you mean," Commander DeWitt said. "The improvements in laser array technology since this idea was last debated have perhaps made it a bit more feasible now. Unless being 'flown to the target' by one of our experienced specialists who can make slight course alterations until impact, most torpedoes follow a somewhat predictable trajectory. The newer automated systems might stand a much better chance of getting and maintaining a lock. That should be true even with stealth covering and controlled flight activity."

"If we allow the human gunner to retain control of the array unless a specific level of torpedo threat is detected," Jenetta said, "we can have the best of both systems. Upon detection of an incoming torpedo, the weapons control system can override gunner control. Once it eliminates the threat, it relinquishes control to the gunner. Since movement of the guns is already controlled by servos, we only have to develop the sensors and computer tracking system."

"*Only*, Admiral?" Commander DeWitt said, smiling.

"I never said it was going to be easy, Barbara," Jenetta said, chuckling. "Perhaps you can get the data for the tracking system used with the Phalanx system from the archives and work from there."

"Okay, Admiral. I guess the Milori laser cannons will have to wait."

"Not necessarily. Perhaps their system can fire more pulses per minute than ours can. If you have sufficient staff, it's worth pursuing both."

"Okay, I'll divide my people into two main teams and we'll work on both projects."

"If your teams can find a way to track and destroy the enemy torpedoes without operator intervention, you'll be giving us an extremely potent weapon in our future engagements with the Milori. It was the torpedo strikes that caused so much damage and death aboard our ships, not the laser strikes."

"It sounds like you expect them to return any day."

"Let's just say I won't be *too* surprised when I receive word that they've been spotted heading this way again. They're bound to find out how I tricked them and they're going to be damned angry about my making them look so foolish. They won't succumb to mere trickery again, so we must have sufficient ships and weapons to stop them with brute force next time. It's going to be a fight to the finish— perhaps ours, unless your section can develop some super weapon we can use."

"I can't promise that, Admiral, but we'll do our best. We do have a few ideas for new weaponry we've been kicking around."

Jenetta nodded. "I know you always do your best. Thank you, Barbara. Dismissed."

Jenetta had time to prepare another mug of coffee before her next appointment.

"My recommendation would be to follow the same basic prioritization list that Commander Cameron established at the battle scene," recently promoted Commander Derrick Jacoby, chief engineer for Stewart SC Base, said. Older than his appearance suggested, the forty-three-year-old engineer with boundless energy had held this important position since Admiral Carver had commandeered the base from the Raiders and turned it into a first class Space Command base. The five-foot, nine-inch officer with sandy hair and light brown eyes ate, slept, and breathed engineering.

"We should concentrate most of our efforts on the battleships *Prometheus*, *Chiron*, *Thor*, and *Bellona*, first. Then we'll move to the cruisers *Song*, *Plantaganet*, *Romanov*, and *Mentuhotep*. The destroyers *Geneva*, *Ottawa*, *St. Petersburg*, and *Beijing* would be in the third group, and we'll tackle the destroyers *Asuncion*, *Buenos Aires*, and *Cairo*, the three ships needing the most work, last. The hull damage to those last three is extensive, but we have a formidable engineering staff right now with our own base and repair-dock engineers, the engineers from the ships under repair, and the engineers you borrowed from the ships already sent out on patrol. It would be great if we could keep it intact until all the work is done."

"The ships going out on patrol must have at least half their normal engineering staff aboard when they leave this base," Jenetta said. "As soon as the four battleships are ready, they'll also be sent out, taking half their engineers with them. I'm afraid your workforce will shrink with each ship successfully completed, but we need those ships out there on patrol, Derrick. And they must have a minimum level of support personnel when away from the base."

"I understand, Admiral. Some of the new reinforcement forces should arrive soon, so perhaps we can borrow some of their engineers."

"I'll see that you get as many as we can free up when the ships arrive. What's your best time estimate for the work, Derrick? I won't hold you to anything."

"The heaviest part of the repair work was tackled immediately after the battle with the Milori, so we should be able to have the battleships completed within three months. Now that we have our new foundry in operation, we can reforge damaged tritanium plating ten times faster than they can do it aboard ship. When we're done, you'll never know they just fought a major battle. We'll complete the cruisers in six months and the first group of destroyers in nine. We should be able to complete the last group in a year's time if I assign a small crew to work on each of the three ships, beginning immediately. In nine months, we'll have the major structural repair work completed. When the full crew finishes on the other destroyers, they'll take over and complete the engine work, electronics, and interior work."

"Okay, Derrick, let's get started."

"We're already well underway, Admiral. If you wished to follow a different plan, we'd halt what we were doing and follow that instead. But nobody wanted to waste any time while the assessment was completed and presented to you for evaluation. It all has to be done anyway."

Jenetta smiled. "Okay, Derrick. Is there anything else?"

"Uh, yes ma'am. I wanted to speak to you about those Milori ships we took in battle."

"What about them?"

"That's my question, Admiral. Should we plan on repairing any of them and putting them into service for Space Command as the Raiders used to do with ships they defeated?"

"Are any salvageable?"

"Oh, yes, ma'am. I estimate that twenty-three are beyond any possible hope of repair. They were the ones closest to the detonation of our WOLaR weapons. But of the remaining ninety-two, I think we could put at least sixty back together using the other fifty-five more seriously damaged ships for parts."

"Sixty ships?"

"Yes ma'am."

"Would they be worth the effort?"

"From what I can glean from their engineering manuals, their slowest ships are capable of Light-375, with the newer ships capable of Light-412 to Light-450. Their design isn't bad. The interior and life support systems are suitable for anthropomorphic creatures up to eight feet in height, so they'll even accommodate Nordakians, and the hulls are a *lot* more solid than those Raider ships we captured. They use a double layer of thousand mil Tritanium with self-sealing membrane for the entire skin, with the usual armor protection on the sides and keel. That's pretty similar to our own destroyers and frigates, and they're a lot faster. We also have twenty-six Tsgardi-built Raider warships in the yard, at least half of which could *potentially* be repaired and placed into service, but it might be a little difficult finding crews willing to staff them given the severe shortcomings of their design and construction."

"I wouldn't send any of our people out to fight in a Tsgardi-built warship, but they could be used for transport or light patrol duties in a pinch." Jenetta leaned back in her chair

14

and stared at the ceiling for a few seconds. Sixty more warships as powerful as her Space Command destroyers and frigates could make a significant difference when the Milori returned. Even if they didn't return, it would substantially improve Space Command's ability to provide patrol coverage in the Frontier Zone. She straightened her chair up and looked at Commander Jacoby again. "We're already talking a year for repairs to the fifteen warships we used to defeat those Milori ships in the first place. How long would it take to make them useful again?"

"I estimate that it could take several years to get all sixty operational, but we can begin putting some into service within a few months after beginning work. The twelve ships damaged in the second confrontation aren't that bad at all; the damage looks far worse than it is. There was no laser fire. The minefield caused major breaches in the hull that depressurized large sections of the ship, overloaded electrical systems, and took out forward maneuvering thrusters. If the Milori had won the day, they definitely would have repaired them and put them back into service fairly quickly."

"What about training crews to operate them?"

"We'll have to change the signage over to Amer, of course, and adapt the controls for Hominidae hands instead of Milori tentacles and gripper claws, but that's about it. The control systems are compatible throughout, so once we design an adaptation for the first one we can mass-produce the rest. Then it's just a matter of learning the systems and the ship. Of course, you're going to need at least fifty thousand new officers and enlisted personnel to fully man the repaired ships if we go ahead."

"We also have the problem of their design configurations. They don't look anything like Space Command ships. It could be difficult to discern who the enemy is if we use them to engage the Milori."

"Outwardly, that's true, Admiral, but the adapted Milori ships would all be fitted with transponders that emit a Space Command vessel signature. They'd be immediately identifiable by other vessels in a battle and the emitted signature would prevent our gunners from even firing at them if they were using the proper code."

"Okay, Derrick, I'll approve the work on the condition that you get our fifteen SC ships completed first. Then you'll be free to tinker around with the Milori ships as much as you want, as long as all other normal repair work continues to receive top priority."

Derrick smiled. "Absolutely, Admiral. I know every engineer in the station is eager to get their hands on the Milori ships, but it won't prevent them from doing the best possible job on our own ships first. In the meantime, we'll continue to have our engineering bots measure and evaluate every millimeter of the Milori ships. By the time we're ready to work on them, we'll have such complete plans that you'd think we'd designed and built them ourselves."

Jenetta nodded and said, smiling, "Dismissed."

Chapter Three
~ November 30th, 2277 ~

"The next group of topics concern Stewart SC base," Admiral Moore said to the nine other admirals sitting at the horseshoe-shaped table in the Admiralty Board's large meeting hall. The gallery seating was empty for this regular business session, and only the usual assortment of clerks and aides sitting dutifully behind their admirals were witness to the proceedings.

Still fit at eighty-nine, Admiral Moore didn't have a spare ounce of fat on his five-foot, ten-inch frame. Straight silver-grey hair of regulation length still covered his head. Although he had always been a little vain about his hair, hating the color and texture it had adopted over the past thirty years, he still refused to dye it back to his original color of dark auburn. The Admiral of the Fleet normally projected the benign look of a loving grandfather, but people knew it wasn't smart to trifle with him. Those who made that mistake lived to regret it. They'd either finished their career through early retirement or at some remote location in the most inhospitable of places.

"We should first discuss the request by Admiral Carver," Admiral Moore said, "for additional personnel needed to man the sixty Milori warships she expects to repair and retrofit for our use. Her projected timetable for the completion of repairs is three years, although some will be available for use before the end of this coming year."

"That is an absolutely preposterous request," Admiral Hubera said. Now in his early nineties, Hubera had long ago misplaced his sense of humor. A permanent scowl defined the face beneath a mat of silver-white hair. "We've already assigned ninety-six Space Command warships and three Nordakian warships to her command. Including her base staff and the crews of all her support ships, she commands over two hundred ten thousand Space Command personnel. Now we're supposed to send her another fifty thousand?"

"We're not talking about sending them to *her*, Donald," Admiral Platt said, exasperation clearly noticeable in her voice. Unlike Admiral Moore, the eighty-eight-year-old Director of Fleet Operations had never hesitated to use the aids available for restoring her light brown hair to its original color. She was a little vain about her appearance and worked hard to maintain a trim figure. "We're talking about sending personnel to Stewart Space Command Base to man a fleet of ships that Admiral Carver has captured. She won't even be the base commander when these personnel arrive. Don't forget that Admiral Vroman is already on his way to Stewart to assume command when Admiral Carver's five-year duty tour is up next December. And sixty-five of the warships currently assigned to Admiral Carver's command won't arrive until the third quarter of next year, just a few months before she's relieved."

"I support the proposal a hundred percent," Admiral Hillaire said. The ninety-year-old Director of Academies had always been among Jenetta's staunchest supporters. "If Admiral Carver can do as she says, and I don't doubt that she can, the sixty warships will expand our fleet by almost twenty percent. Our current ship construction schedule, even with the new emergency appropriation for ships that the Galactic Alliance Council passed after we learned of the Milori invasion plans, will only add twenty-five new warships per year, and it will take us six years to reach *that* level of output. This year we'll launch just sixteen new warships. Admiral Carver is exceeding our entire new ship-building capability for the next three years."

"And just *where* do you propose we get the fifty thousand personnel necessary to man this vaporific fleet, Arnold?" Admiral Hubera asked.

"We must increase the number of graduates we accept from the Academies for shipboard duty. If we raise the percentage taken from each class from fifty to sixty percent and accept reassignment applications from all similarly qualified graduates previously passed over for shipboard assignments because they weren't in the top fifty percent, we might be able to provide enough officers to man the ships. The *senior* line officers for this new fleet can come from the line officer ranks aboard the ninety-six ships already assigned to Stewart. We'll still have a sufficient number of new positions aboard the ships we're constructing to keep the rest of the officer corps satisfied. And, since the Milori invasion, service recruitment numbers are way up, so our crew complement can come from the new recruits. It will take time to get them trained and out there, so we must act quickly."

"Recruitment numbers may be up," Admiral Hubera said, "but they're not up fifty thousand a year. We're going to fall far short of the number we need for immediate training."

"Then we'll clean out every base in Galactic Alliance regulated space and assign them to shipboard duty. We can't afford not to have every available ship manned and ready for the Milori invasion we all know is coming."

"I'm sure that we can work out the crew complement situation," Admiral Moore said. "Is there any question that we should accept this— gift of sixty ships that Admiral Carver is holding out to us? No? Okay, we'll begin preparing to receive the ships into Space Command fleet operations as they become ready for duty. The next topic is Admiral Carver's suggestion for an automatic weapon system that will assist in the protection of a ship from enemy torpedoes. The design and operation will be along the lines of the Phalanx used on Earth's naval vessels, although it will fire laser pulses instead of solid projectiles."

"I've read the proposal and initial research that Commander DeWitt at Stewart has done since Admiral Carver ordered her to work on this idea," Admiral Plimley said, "and I'm intrigued by the possibilities. As Director of Weapons Research and Development, I support the work completely. It addresses all of the previous concerns that were raised about a similar kinetic projectile weapon and could offer a significant improvement in ship protection if we can make it work effectively."

"As long as the weapon is restricted to laser pulse, I wholeheartedly support it as well," Admiral Ressler, the Director of Budget and Accounting said.

"All in favor?" Admiral Moore said, looking around the table for a show of hands. "Passed. We'll put our full support behind the research and incorporate it into all warship weapon systems if it's proven effective. Admiral Plimley will see that all research sections coordinate their efforts with Stewart's, who will lead the project." Admiral Moore paused to clear his throat. "The final topic for today concerns the posting of Admiral Carver herself at the end of her present duty tour. It's previously been proposed that she be assigned the onerous task of merging the Nordakian Space Force into Space Command, and we've discussed that task at length. Because of her dual citizenship with Earth and Nordakia, her fluency in Dakis, her rank of Senior Admiral in the Nordakian Space Force, and the fact that she's a member of that planet's nobility, she's ideally suited to handle the post. I recently discussed this again with King Tpalsh of Nordakia and he's prepared to name her Admiral of the Fleet of the Nordakian Space Force for as long as the Space Force remains a separate entity. Admiral Yuthkotl, their present Admiral of the Fleet, will take the Space Command oath and become the eleventh member of this board with the rank of Rear Admiral, Lower Half. He'll remain on Nordakia until Admiral Carver relieves him and assumes his duties."

"You feel confident that she'll accept the position?" Admiral Hillaire asked.

"Her initial orders will only direct her to proceed to Higgins and report to Admiral Holt. I'm hoping he can convince her that this job is so important she should put aside her personal feelings of wanting a ship and accept the posting."

"What about her rank?" Admiral Burke, the Director of Intelligence asked.

"I feel it's imperative she remain as an Upper Half if she's to carry out the duties of her new posting. She'll be responsible for coordinating *everything* between the new Space Command Academy on Nordakia, the Nordakian

Space Force Academy, and the Nordakian Space Force itself. She'll need her two Space Command stars to outrank Admiral Rensiller and the officers of the new Academy, along with the five-moon cluster she'll receive for her Nordakian uniform when appointed Admiral of the Nordakian Fleet. As senior ranking officer over all military personnel in the Nordakian system, she'll have the authority to take whatever actions she feels necessary to accomplish our goals. I'm sure there will be some resentment from senior Nordakian Space Force officers who won't be able to make the transition to Galactic Space Command. They'll just have to transfer to the Nordakian agency that supervises civilian freighter services."

"She's expecting to return to her permanent rank of Captain at the end of her current tour," Admiral Ahmed, the Director of Quartermaster Supply said. "Won't the retention of her two brevetted stars alert her that we're not being completely open?"

"It can't be helped," Admiral Moore said. "I don't want to inform her that she's not getting her own ship just yet because I'd rather the news of the new posting didn't fester like an open sore during the year-long trip to Higgins. I believe she'll take the news better from Admiral Holt in a direct contact meeting because of their close friendship; then she's just three months from Nordakia and her new post. Perhaps she'll simply believe she's being honored by the extension of extra pay and privileges during her voyage to Higgins."

* * *

"Is this the best plan you can come up with?" Emperor Maxxiloth shouted, his voice echoing off the fine wood and stonework of the large meeting hall. Like every room in the palace, it had been constructed with the finest materials available. Short decorative stone columns with carved stone busts of former emperors lined the walls. "I could have done this in just one solar. What have you been doing all this time?"

The dozen senior military officers and twelve ministers sat stone-faced, staring down at the table in front of them.

"My Lord," Exalted Lord Space Marshall Berquyth said calmly, "we've spent many solars reviewing every minute detail. The ships that will make up the two new fleets are the best we have left. We had already sent all of our newest ships as part of the first three fleets. These ships aren't as fast, so it will take them a little longer to reach Dwillaak, but the crews are just as eager to fight for you and the glory of the new Empire."

"But there are only two hundred fourteen ships in this plan. Combined with Dwillaak's existing forces, we'll still only have four hundred fourteen ships to move against Carver."

"As you've ordered, my Lord, every ship available is being prepared for the voyage. We're holding back just eighty-eight ships, and they are the oldest and slowest still in service. We dare not send any more or we shall be leaving the Empire much too vulnerable to attack by our other enemies. I greatly fear what the Hudeeracs might do if they were to learn just how limited our remaining forces are once these ships have deployed."

"Bah! The Hudeeracs are sheep! We destroyed their fleets and drove them out of two full sectors, losing only a dozen ships ourselves. They cower in their own solar system now, afraid to risk travel beyond their small cluster of planets. The Galactic Alliance is another matter entirely. We must crush them before they become so strong they'll be dictating terms while in orbit around our home world."

"But our fight with the Hudeerac occurred when we had a full armada of warships to support our advances. I must beseech you once again not to proceed until we've built enough ships to replace those we lost to Space Command. In three or four annuals we can produce three hundred new warships as fast and powerful as the ones we lost. We won't be leaving ourselves in such a precarious position. With less than a single fleet of warships to protect the Empire, even the Tsgardi might get designs on part of our territory."

"Bah! More sheep! Moreover, the Tsgardi are not just sheep, they're complete imbeciles. They would never attempt to annex part of our territory because they know we'd crush them in an annual if they ever dared."

"But, Excellency, what if the Tsgardi were to join forces with the Hudeerac?"

"Impossible! The Tsgardi are too stupid to ever conceive of such a plan, and too disorganized to ever carry it out."

"But the Hudeerac aren't. If they were to ally themselves with the Tsgardi, or possibly the Gondusans, our eighty-eight ships might not be enough to protect us."

"Enough, Berquyth! I've made my decision. By now, word of our defeat at the hands of Carver must have reached our enemies; I can hear their laughter ringing in my ears. We mustn't allow them to start thinking we've grown soft or we invite attack. We'll show them the Milori Empire is stronger than ever. I've already given word to our shipbuilders that they must double production. All new ships will be used to bolster the fleet that remains behind."

"Yes, my Lord," Berquyth said humbly. He had pushed his position as forcefully as he dared.

"Since you fear the Hudeerac and Gondusan sheep, move all our remaining warships, except for our core protection group, to those parts of the empire. When the fleet returns in glory from Galactic Alliance space, they can reinforce the undermanned bases throughout the empire."

"Yes, my Lord."

"How long before we'll be in position to launch our attack?"

"It will take almost a full annual for the replacement fleets we're sending to meet up with Dwillaak's main force just outside of Galactic Alliance space, but as soon as we notify Dwillaak, he'll begin splintering off some of his retreating forces and sending them to pre-designated locations. We're counting on the ability of our DeTect distortion equipment to confuse the spotter ship sensors. Unable to count the passing ships properly, they should only be watching for the passage of the two main fleets. If they notice that ships are missing, we'll tell them they stopped to make minor repairs and will be resuming their exodus shortly. The separated ships will then travel independently, so as not to attract any attention, and wait quietly in their hidden locations until they receive word to unite for their attacks. We believe that with the help of

Commandant Arneu of the Raiders, we should be able to place as many as thirty of our best warships within the sectors controlled by Stewart SC Base. Arneu suggested that we hide our entire fleet inside one of their camouflaged asteroid bases, but the Imperial Military Council doesn't fully trust him and doesn't want our ships bottled up inside an asteroid if Space Command attacks."

"I agree with that assessment. Space Command has already found and commandeered two of their asteroid bases, and destroyed another. We'll work with him, for now, but never trust him. He's a Terran, after all."

"I've allowed him to believe we'll turn Carver over to him when she's captured."

"No!" the emperor shouted, "I want her head for my collection."

"Of course, my Lord, but to ensure his complete cooperation, it's been necessary to let him *believe* he'll get his escaped slave back."

"Tell him what you must, but her head comes to me. I *will* have my trophy for the embarrassment she has caused the Empire. He may have the rest of the husk if he wants it."

"As you wish, my Lord."

* * *

Jenetta leaned back in her office chair after viewing the message from Admiral Moore. She had received approval for her proposals to repair the Milori ships and work on the development of the new defensive weapon, but the rest of the message was confusing. Admiral Vroman was already en route to Stewart to assume command at the end of her tour in one year and she was to proceed to Higgins where Admiral Holt would brief her on her next posting; however, she was to retain her brevetted rank during the trip. She had expected, or at least hoped, to receive orders directing her to revert to her former permanent commissioned officer rank of captain when her tour was up and to proceed to a place, most likely the Mars shipbuilding facility, where she would assume command of a battleship.

The more she thought about the message, the angrier she became. She couldn't force the Admiralty Board to give her a ship, but she had earned the right, hadn't she? She was the most highly decorated officer in Space Command. That had to mean something, didn't it? She had proven herself repeatedly. Just what did it *take* to get a ship anyway?

"They're up to something," she said aloud, with only her two Jumakas as an audience. They purred contentedly from opposite sides of the room in response to the sound of her voice. The hundred-sixty-pound animals, resembling Terran Jaguars with fur as black as space, had provided both companionship and protection since she had gotten them from an Alyysian trader years ago. When Jenetta walked through the station, the two cats walked at her sides, unleashed but never more than a half meter away. She was able to defend herself, but powerful people make powerful enemies. She slept better knowing that her pets, always alert in a heartbeat, were near the bed each night.

Jenetta rose to prepare a mug of coffee at her beverage synthesizer, then carried her beverage to the SimWindow. She sipped at the hot liquid as she stood staring at the image of the port.

"What aren't they telling me?" Jenetta asked herself aloud. "I've done everything they asked of me, and more." Jenetta reached out and adjusted the controls to zoom to the shipyard area where several GSC battleships floated at their moorings. As soon as all hull repairs were complete, engineers removed ships from the enclosed docks and moored them at normal shipyard docking piers. Looking at their external appearance, one couldn't tell that they had fought a life-or-death battle just months ago. Unseen hordes of engineers were currently hard at work inside the battleships now, completing internal repairs and testing or replacing equipment.

In a few weeks the work would be finished and the ships would join the nineteen ships already on patrol in the hundreds of thousands of square light-years that was the territory assigned to the base commander of Stewart. When the sixty-five ships reassigned to Stewart arrived, Jenetta would finally feel that she could adequately cover the territory. Facing the center of the galaxy, the sectors assigned to Stewart were the most dangerous along the many thousand light-years bordering the perimeter of Galactic Alliance space. Stewart's sectors would be a tempting target to any of several warlike empires or dominions that might one day look to expand their territory towards the Galactic Alliance. The Milori was the only race to attempt it so far, but they might not be the last.

Jenetta moved the control again and looked over at the other GSC ships. Dozens of EVA-suited engineers, specialists in hull repair, were working on several cruisers with the assistance of hundreds of bots, and smaller groups were working on the several ships nearly destroyed in the battle. Months of structural framework repair efforts were still required before the mounting of new exterior plates could even be considered for the latter group. Jenetta panned across to the rows of Milori ships tethered to the far wall. Even there she saw activity, but it was only the engineers, weapons people, and dozens of robots examining the ships, documenting their construction and condition.

Returning to her seat, the message from Admiral Moore receded quickly into the back of her mind as she dedicated herself to getting through a number of reports before her next appointment.

* * *

In early January, Space Command Supreme Headquarters on Earth forwarded a promotions list to Stewart. Personnel officers announced over six hundred promotions at a ceremony in the convention center. Quite a few were for personnel attached to the base, but most were shipboard postings to replace crewmembers lost during the engagement with the Milori. The largest concentration reestablished crew rosters on the two ships that had suffered devastating losses. Many more posts existed than available people to fill them, but they managed a basic complement for each ship. New personnel would be arriving at Stewart over the next year to complete the staffing for individual vessels. The captain of each ship presented the promotions for his or her crewmembers, and Jenetta presented the promotions for station personnel.

Commander DeWitt, Head of Weapons Research, received a promotion to Captain, as did the heads of several other sections. It was clear that Supreme Headquarters was creating an entire new level of bureaucracy beneath Jenetta to handle a lot more of the day-to-day matters she had previously handled personally. She hadn't requested the changes or complained of the workload, so she felt sure the purpose was to establish the same formalized structure found on all other StratCom-One bases. Being fairly new, the command structure on Stewart had developed slowly and un-evenly as base personnel arrived, but Admiral Vroman would expect it to be a fully matured operation when he arrived to assume command. Captain Gavin had advised Jenetta to expect such changes, and he was correct once again. Originally anticipating that she would resent losing direct control of each of the operational areas, she found it didn't bother her now that the end of her duty tour was growing closer. Until relieved by Admiral Vroman, she was still in command of—and therefore responsible for—everything that occurred within three-hundred light-years or more in almost every direction from the station.

Jenetta's sisters, Christa and Eliza, received promotions from Lieutenant(jg) to Lieutenant at the ceremony.

* * *

Following a private celebration dinner in Jenetta's dining room, Jenetta, Christa, and Eliza continued the celebration in Jenetta's quarters. Billy had congratulated both his sisters at the ceremony, but his duties as the Captain of the *Mentuhotep* prevented him from attending the small party on this evening.

"It's going to feel very strange having a different base commander after you leave, sis," Christa said. "I'm really going to miss the wonderful dinners in the base commander's dining room."

"Perhaps you can trade your boyfriend, Adam, in on a two-star admiral," Eliza said jokingly, "and then continue to dine in the base commander's dining room each evening."

Christa giggled. "No thanks. I don't want an octogenarian until I'm a little closer to that myself. And speaking of octogenarians, will Hugh be near Higgins when you get back, Jen?"

Jenetta looked at her sharply and feigned anger. "You know Hugh is only ten years older than I am. I don't want to hear any 'old man' jokes." Softening her voice she said, "I don't know where he'll be. He wanted to rejoin Space Command when we first called for retired line officers younger than the mandatory separation age to return to active service, but his company held him to the new four-year contract he'd signed. When he gets back to Higgins next week, the contract will be up and he's going to submit his application to re-join Space Command."

"It's difficult having a boyfriend who only drops around every four years," Eliza said, "but it might be more difficult having a boyfriend you outrank by four grades."

"Hugh was a lieutenant commander when he separated after twenty years of service. With the need for experienced line officers, he might be commissioned as a full commander, so when I revert to my permanent rank we'll only be one level apart. Hugh would surely have made captain by now if he hadn't retired when he did."

"*Will* you revert to your permanent rank?" Christa asked.

"Of course. I was only *brevetted* to a two star."

"But you told me that your orders are to retain your rank after you leave here."

"Yes, I'm a bit confused about that. I can see having me remain as a flag officer while I'm here, but once I leave for Higgins it doesn't make sense."

"Perhaps they're only extending the honor for the duration of the trip," Eliza said. "Admirals are treated differently than mere captains when traveling as VIPs. Perhaps Admiral Holt will formally return you to your permanent rank when he gives you your new assignment. Do you think you'll be getting a new battleship? Maybe one shielded with Dakinium?"

"I have no idea, and they haven't given me a clue yet. As far as Dakinium is concerned, I haven't heard anything about it since the *Colorado* returned to Mars for additional testing. Perhaps an almost indestructible hull is just a pipe dream."

28

"Pipe dream?" Christa said incredulously. "The *Colorado* was *very* real. The Raiders didn't leave a mark on you when they targeted you with their laser arrays."

"But what's the value of being impervious to laser fire if you can't move? We found ourselves in hostile space unable to re-engage the Light Speed drive. If they had resolved the problem, the *Prometheus* would surely have received its scout ship back by now and the *Chiron* would have received *its* new scout ship. We could have really used them in our fight with the Milori."

"But the *Colorado* also used a radical new engine design," Eliza said. "Perhaps that was the problem and not the Dakinium?"

"I don't know. I suppose we'll find out eventually."

"Think you'll have a chance to go home and visit Mom?"

"If I get anywhere near Earth, I'm going to make the time. I have a lot of leave coming because I haven't been able to use any during my tour here, and by the time I get to Higgins I'll have a full six months of time owed to me."

"That's not enough," Eliza said. "It's three months' travel time from Higgins to Earth at Light-375. You'll need six months just for the trip, *if* you travel by battleship."

"Not if I'm getting a *new* ship. I'd have to travel to the Mars shipbuilding facility to pick it up. From Mars to one of the orbiting Earth Stations is just a fourteen-minute ride at Sub-Light Ten, and then another half-hour for docking and such."

"But what if you're not getting a new battleship?" Christa asked. "New captains are supposed to pay their dues by starting with a destroyer and working their way up."

"I've paid my dues by performing jobs I didn't want. They owe me. Besides, the rules only state that a newly promoted captain receive a destroyer for his or her first command. My first command was the battleship *Prometheus* and my second command was the heavy cruiser *Song*. I should be exempt from the normal progression plan, shouldn't I? But if they ignore that, then I'll work my way up. With the number of new ships being built, the list should move pretty fast for the next decade."

"What if you're not getting a ship at all?" Eliza asked.

"I won't even contemplate that. Admiral Holt as much as promised me a new ship when my tour here was up and I feel I've earned it by spending five years doing a job I didn't want. I won't accept anything else."

"Are you saying you'll resign your commission if you don't get it?" Christa asked.

"I— don't know. I don't know what I'll do. Hugh told me I couldn't be happy as a freighter captain, and I think he might be right. I'm too used to military life now. If they don't give me a ship, I don't know what I'll do. Now that I'm a senior admiral in the Nordakian Space Force, I can't even get a ship *there*."

Arriving back at her quarters two weeks later after an arduous day of work, Jenetta found a message from Hugh among her personal messages. She played his first, smiling as soon as his face appeared on the com unit.

"Hi, honey. Well, I did it. I re-up'd with Space Command. From now on, I'll have to salute you when we meet, but I'll be saluting you as Commander Hugh Michaels. Space Command upgraded my rank, as you thought they might. I'm to report aboard the GSC destroyer *Bonn*, commanded by Captain Marie Simpson, when they dock in a couple of weeks. I met Captain Simpson when she was just a lieutenant, and I'm sure we'll get along well. I'm replacing Commander Jessica Billsworth as the ship's first officer. She's receiving her own ship as soon as she can hitch a ride to Mars.

"Since the *Bonn* is one of the older ships in the fleet, I expect that we'll stay in this sector and handle patrol duties. When you get here, I should have some leave time accumulated and maybe we can get together. Have you received any clarification on your orders yet? Are you getting a ship? I know you won't quit the service if you don't, but don't tell them that. Let them continue to think you might leave if they snub you another time.

"I can't wait to see you again. Do you realize it will be more than three years since we last touched? I guess my stasis sleep has dulled the edge on that a bit, but I sure do miss you and I can't wait until we're in the same sector again, or better yet, the same sub-sector. And if we can't get together, at least it won't take two weeks to exchange messages.

"Time to go. I love you and I'll be counting the days until you get here. Take care of yourself until then." Hugh kissed his forefinger and then pressed it to the vid lens in the com unit.

"Commander Hugh Michaels, message complete."

Chapter Four
~ May 24th, 2278 ~

The combined engineering staffs, under the direction of Commander Jacoby, completed repairs on the destroyers *Geneva*, *Ottawa*, *St. Petersburg*, and *Beijing* a full month ahead of schedule. As they had with the battleships and cruisers, the engineers had eradicated all visible signs of battle damage. Also as with the battleships and cruisers, a number of newly designed sensors graced their hulls. Incoming torpedoes would now be automatically detected, tracked, and destroyed by a special computer module installed in the weapons control system, that is, once the Weapons Research section completed and perfected the systems software.

Tests of the new system had been promising. From the very beginning, the system was almost as good as the best gunners. With each computer code upgrade, the success rate improved against torpedoes fitted with dummy warheads. Captain DeWitt and her team were striving for a one-hundred-percent kill rate, although that might not be technically feasible. The system still tended to get confused when three or more incoming torpedoes received the same threat-assessment value. At least one of the torpedoes always got through to the target because an array would try to divide its fire among the targets instead of concentrating on each one until destroyed. This was very similar to what human gunners did as trainees, but with stringent training they learned to overcome this tendency. Captain DeWitt promised to resolve that software problem soon.

The destroyers *Asuncion*, *Buenos Aires*, and *Cairo* were the last to receive the attention of the entire engineering group. The small work parties assigned to the three ships had worked every bit as hard as the full teams assigned to the other ships. They had managed to complete most of the structural framework repairs. With the full attention of the main workforce now focused on the ships, the work would speed up immensely. With luck, the engineers might complete the work on the three destroyers by the end of September.

As Jenetta's time on the base grew shorter, she found herself with more and more time on her hands. The new bureaucratic layer of captains insinuated immediately beneath Jenetta was functioning effectively now, but Jenetta was having trouble letting go. She had to force herself to place some distance between herself and the lower officers. She remembered the lessons she had taught others about micro-managing and now strove to follow her own advice.

Most of Jenetta's workday now consisted of reviewing reports from her senior officers or having meetings with them or visiting dignitaries. Her promotion to Rear Admiral, Upper Half, brought with it full responsibility for all ships in her sectors. Where before she could alter patrol routes that originated with Space Command Supreme Headquarters, given sufficient cause, her office was now fully responsible for establishing all patrol routes and all ship captains reported directly to her as the Supreme Military Commander for this entire area of space.

The number of ships on patrol presently numbered twenty-eight, with more than half assigned to patrol routes in the Frontier Zone. In years past, the number of ships patrol-ling in the Frontier would have represented only a small percentage of a command's available warships, but Jenetta used her authority to change the policy in *her* sectors. Taking a page from the Raider handbook, Jenetta dispatched most of the small ships captured in engagements with the Raiders or seized during interdiction activities and established them as a network of spotter outposts to watch ship traffic and report suspicious activity. Their hull plating was not up to Space Command warship standards, so they had standing orders to avoid any confrontations. If challenged, they were to disable their ACS and go to FTL at the first opportunity. They moved frequently so the Raiders wouldn't be able to identify their positions and simply avoid them.

In the coming months, the warships re-assigned by Supreme Headquarters would begin arriving at Stewart. Once they restocked their supplies and rested their crews, they would join the other ships on patrol. Jenetta had already established patrol routes that would utilize all but five of the ninety-nine ships assigned to Stewart, giving substantial coverage to its assigned territory. The Stewart Base Protection group would always consist of five warships. Ships returning from patrol duty would immediately become part of that group, freeing up a ship for patrol. When the system was operational, no ship would sit in the base for longer than thirty days. That would give adequate time for personnel to enjoy some R&R and get them back out about the time they started getting bored and antsy.

* * *

In early September, a message from Admiral Vroman aboard the GSC Destroyer *Lisbon* appeared in Jenetta's message queue. As she tapped the play button, the image of a very distinguished-looking octogenarian in a Space Command uniform filled the screen on her com unit.

"Hello, Admiral Carver. I've heard your name so much and seen your picture so often that I feel like I know you. But since we haven't met, I'm still a stranger to *you*. I hope that will change, and that we'll become friends. We expect to arrive at Stewart in mid-November, so I'll have a few weeks to adapt to the base operations before I assume command. I'm very much looking forward to meeting you.

"Thaddeus Vroman, Rear Admiral, Upper Half, aboard the GSC Destroyer *Lisbon*, message complete."

Leaning back in her chair, Jenetta smiled. This certainly didn't fit the image of Admiral Vroman that she'd created in her mind. She'd seen pictures of him and heard stories of how he could turn an ensign into a quivering mass of jelly with just a look. Admiral Holt and Captain Gavin had this ability, and she wondered if she'd ever manage to perfect such a look. She certainly had a long enough time ahead of her in which to work on it, she thought with a giggle. She sent a quick reply telling Admiral Vroman that she was looking forward to personally welcoming him to Stewart's sectors.

A few days later, Jenetta was reviewing a performance report on the newly repaired ships when her aide, Lieutenant Commander Ashraf, informed her that a Wolkerron was requesting a few minutes of her time. As surprised as she was to have a Wolkerron visitor, Jenetta was also curious, and she immediately said to send him in.

The Wolkerron entered confidently, smiling widely in the toothy grin of his species that appeared so ominous to the uninitiated, until he spotted Jenetta's two Jumakas. His momentary hesitation and change of facial expression was enough to make both large cats rise to their feet and assume a stance that clearly announced they were prepared to spring if they detected the slightest hint of a threat. Black as space, with yellow eyes that seemed to glow, a steady gaze by the potentially dangerous duo was normally enough to halt any visitor in his or her tracks.

"Cayla, Tayna," Jenetta said, "down. Come in Ker. That is the usual salutation for your race, isn't it?"

"Quite so, Admiral," the tall, gaunt, anthropomorphic creature with yellow skin and large black eyes said. "I'm Ker Sopherra, and it's my pleasure to make your acquaintance."

"I'm pleased to meet you, Ker Sopherra. What can I do for you?"

"I have a gift for you, Admiral," he said, holding out a very small package.

"A gift? From whom?"

"The sender did not reveal himself. Another courier delivered it to me. My task is only to deliver the parcel to you. I naturally checked it for dangerous chemicals and contaminants before I accepted it, as did your security personnel before I was permitted into this part of the station."

Jenetta reached out and accepted the tiny parcel. "Is there a card or a message?"

"Nothing else, Admiral, just the package. That concludes my business. Good day."

"Good day, Ker."

The Wolkerron turned and left as Jenetta sat back down at her desk. What he had said about security was true. Base security would no doubt have scanned both him and the package thoroughly before allowing them through, so there was no obvious threat. Unwrapping the parcel revealed a clear acrylic jewelry box containing a ring. A close examination of the wrapping paper turned up no clues about the identity of the sender. Since the box wasn't hermetically sealed, it should be safe to open, but she took a small sensor device from a desk drawer anyway and checked it once just to be certain. When the sensor indicated that it was perfectly safe, she opened the box and took a closer look at the ring.

The simple silver band with a delicate filigree lattice around the outer surface had a smooth interior without any visible inscription. Jenetta ran the sensor over it once again, but the readings remained the same, proof that the metal band offered no chemical or biological threat. The sensor device further confirmed the absence of chemicals in the paper that would cause a message to remain hidden to the naked eye until some condition such as a temperature variation occurred.

Satisfied that there was no danger, Jenetta removed the ring from the box and examined it from every direction. Her scrutiny revealed nothing untoward. About to return it to the box, a thought occurred to her, so she opened the media drawer on her desk and touched the ring to the data spindle used to read and write information to data rings. Her com screen immediately filled with garbled bits of data. "Ah-ha," she said, recognizing that her hunch was correct. The ring was definitely a data ring. Undoubtedly, the sender would have encrypted any message, but there was no indication of where she might find the key needed to view it.

It had been a long time since she'd used her skills as a hacker to break encrypted messages, but she couldn't pass up such a challenge. Forgetting the report she'd been working on when the Wolkerron arrived, she began to work on decrypting the message. She ignored lunch, only pausing for scheduled appointments and meetings during her efforts to crack the code.

It took her six days to break the cipher that protected the message; it was the most difficult decryption Jenetta had ever worked, requiring every bit of her math and computer skills. Engineering had since analyzed the packaging and box, and had found nothing dangerous. The wrapping paper came from a genus of trees not recorded in the SC database and the structure of the acrylic like box was actually crystalline. Apart from those anomalies, there was nothing unusual or noteworthy. The ring appeared to be the only puzzle that required solving.

When an unscrambled image finally appeared on the com screen, Jenetta knew she had cracked the code, but now she faced a new puzzle because the image on the screen appeared to be that of an alien species known as Hudeerac. The Hudeerac were borderline anthropomorphic, using the broadest definition spelled out in the Space Command Handbook. Their average height was between six and seven feet, but their mottled greenish-brown skin was scaly, like that of a reptile. They had two arms, a torso, and two legs, but their hands only had three thick fingers, plus a smaller opposing thumb, and the males always had a short reptilian-type tail. Although she had seen pictures and art representations, Jenetta had never met one. She wondered why a Hudeerac would be sending her a message, especially in this unusual manner.

Tapping the play button, she leaned back to watch the message, not even knowing if the translator would be able to handle the Hudeerac language. Apparently it could, because she heard, "Greetings, Space Command. This message is for Admiral Jenetta Carver only. Please forward it to her immediately because it will play only once and then be erased. Stop your machine *now*."

Jenetta quickly stopped the playback and set the com unit to record a copy before restarting the message. There was a long pause before the Hudeerac appeared again.

"Greetings, Admiral Carver. If you're receiving this message directly from the encrypted ring, then you are the only one to have seen it. As a safeguard, this message will self-scramble after one playback, making it unrecoverable.

Although the messenger, Ker Sopherra, is reputed to be most trustworthy, the self-scramble feature of the playback is our guarantee that neither he nor anyone else has viewed it. Since we don't have retinal scan data for recipient verification, we must use this extreme method. The encryption algorithm is acutely complex and it was felt that only a highly sophisticated organization such as Space Command would be able to crack the encryption code in time to view it. A second protection scrambles the message if it isn't played within a limited timeframe that commences when first access is attempted. I applaud the efforts of your decryption people.

"Allow me to introduce myself. My name is Vertap Aloyandro, and I'm the Minister of Intelligence for the Hudeerac Order. I'm sending this message on behalf of our Sovereign, King Jamolendre, who feels that it might be advantageous for us to work together against our common enemy, the Milori. News of your outstanding victory against them has greatly buoyed the spirits of our people. Until a decade ago, the Hudeerac lived in relatively peaceful co-existence with our space neighbor, despite the fact that Maxxiloth's great-grandfather seized much of our territory during his reign. But when Maxxiloth killed his father and proclaimed himself Emperor of Milor, the state of affairs changed again. He's revived the old ideas of galactic conquest originated by his great-grandfather and has systematically waged war against us, driving our people out of most of our remaining territory. We tried to resist, but his fleets have been too strong for us. We've pulled back, abandoning planets, moons, and space stations to consolidate our forces within our home solar system. The Milori haven't yet come to believe that our final eradication is worth the potential losses to the Empire, but we don't expect that sentiment to prevail forever. Maxxiloth will eventually decide to finish us off. If he had sent those three hundred ships against *us*, they would surely have destroyed us. Maxxiloth has enslaved the people on the worlds that we can no longer defend and they suffer greatly under his heavy hand.

"With Maxxiloth's attention now turned towards the Galactic Alliance, it's hoped that we'll have time to better prepare our forces for what we know is coming. Currently, we are directing all our efforts to building powerful ships that will stand a better chance against the Milori. Since our home world is almost twenty-five hundred light-years from your base, it's unlikely that we shall ever meet, but I propose that we agree to share intelligence about the Milori. The data ring that you now possess is capable of encrypting or decrypting messages using a different algorithm than the one your people cracked. Simply place the ring in your media tray whenever exchanging data with us. Please guard the ring well. We have intentionally disguised it to appear as an ordinary, decorative piece of jewelry so that it might fit in with other rings you possess. Please respond to this message with a retinal scan encrypted video message so we'll know you've received the ring with the message intact. This ring contains a file with my retinal scan data. I ask that you always preface it to any message so the correspondence will only be viewable by me.

"Minister Vertap Aloyandro. End of message."

Jenetta stared at the screen for several minutes after the image faded. The Milori didn't normally tolerate Terrans in their Empire. That was true even before they began hostilities, so intelligence data was scarce. Having an ally able to collect and report information about the Milori could be extremely useful. Of course, it could be a ploy and the minister could actually be someone trying to learn what information Space Command possessed. Lack of direct contact made that even more plausible. As an SC captain, Jenetta could not have agreed to a proposal that she share information with a foreign power, but as a flag officer, her decision-making authority had widened exponentially. She decided to play along for now. The ring data was still loaded in the temporary file area of the spindle. Outgoing message software would look for an encryption scheme there if she didn't specify any of the stored algorithms. Jenetta leaned towards the com unit and recorded a retinal scan for the outgoing transmission.

"Greetings, Minister. I've received your message and I agree to a sharing of information about the Milori. Following our second confrontation, they agreed to leave our territory and never return, but we don't really believe this will prevent another invasion in the future, and we're preparing for that eventuality. It's been fifteen months since the remnants of their forces left, and by now they should be clear of the new one-hundred-light-year-wide Buffer Zone that our treaty with the Milori established. Spotter ships located along their route have verified passage of their two fleets, but I have no other information that I can forward at this time.

"Jenetta Carver, Rear Admiral, Upper, Commander of Stewart Space Command Base, message complete."

The message didn't contain anything the Milori didn't already know, so it provided nothing if the received message was fraudulent. If the message was genuine, it might be data that the Hudeerac could use and might cement an alliance. She would play along, providing general but useful information until she could trust this contact. Picking up the ring from her desk, she examined it again, concurring that it did appear to be just an ordinary piece of jewelry. She tried it and found that it fit the middle finger on her left hand, so she left it. It was as good a place to hide it as any other. Space Command regulations allowed one simple ring, or engagement and wedding bands, in addition to a personal log ring. Officers were also required to wear their Space Command ring at all times, except to bed or while on leave. Most rarely took it off.

Jenetta hadn't gotten very much regular work done during the past six days, so she turned her attention back to neglected tasks and devoted herself to catching up, after first sending an encrypted copy of the message and her reply to the new head of the Intelligence section at Stewart. As one of Captain Kanes' chief deputies at Higgins before receiving his promotion and posting to Stewart, Jenetta had known Captain Lofgren for some time. She trusted his judgment, and his opinion would carry significant weight as she decided whether to continue sharing information with the Hudeerac.

* * *

In early October, the base held a sort of re-christening party to celebrate the completion of work on the destroyers *Asuncion*, *Buenos Aires*, and *Cairo*. The speeches evoked memories of the intense battle in which so many brave SC personnel had died and which had left the ships so badly damaged that doubts about their reparability had been common. At one point, SHQ suggested Jenetta scrap the *Asuncion* and possibly the others as well. But she had supported her engineering staff completely, and the result was three more ships back in service, every bit as good, both cosmetically and operationally, as their brother ships.

Even before his people had applied the finishing touches to the three GSC destroyers, Commander Derrick Jacoby had begun work on the captured Milori ships. After compiling survey data, Jacoby established an order of priority for repairs. As engineers moved the three last destroyers to normal airlock piers in the shipyard area to have their interior work completed, three pre-selected Milori ships were being detached from the cavern wall and towed to the vacated enclosed docks. Jacoby had very early on identified which ships they would repair and which ships they would only use for replacement parts.

* * *

As November approached, engineers were completing the fifth Milori ship selected for repair and retrofit. They had selected the least damaged ships for their first attention. The months of examination and evaluation work by bots had given the engineers such complete construction plans that any piece of hull plating on the former Milori ship could be produced by computer simply by identifying it's location on the ship, as was done for Space Command vessels. After a machine cut a plate to the right dimensions according to the specifications in the computer, enormous presses took the flat piece of Tritanium and heated it until it glowed. The presses then shaped it and allowed it to cool. When brought to the ship for welding into place, it fit perfectly.

The space trials of the first four former Milori ships had gone extremely well. Jenetta was pleased to christen each with names and official ship designations from a list sent by Supreme Headquarters. The assigned names followed the standard naming protocol for the ship's type, but the designation included an 'M' to denote the reason for the ship's design differences. Among the first ships completed were one battleship, a cruiser, and two destroyers. Although the battleship, now identified as *Pholus*, GSC-B376M, only had two layers of tritanium in its hull, it was the equal of SC battleships in all other respects. A few design modifications, not visible externally, addressed some minor vulnerabilities found by the SC engineers.

* * *

Captain Lindahl entered the bridge a few minutes after 0100 GST. Commander Fannon, his XO, had turned command over to the ship's Second Officer, Lt. Commander McCloud, at midnight and gone to get some sleep. McCloud, as watch officer, had been occupying the Command Chair. He immediately yielded the chair to the Captain and moved to the First Officer's Chair, then gave Lindahl a full update on the current condition of the ship.

Lindahl didn't take command of the bridge. He was there because the astrogator had estimated they would reach the reported location of a stricken freighter at about 0118. When the call for assistance had come in, the *Lisbon* had been the nearest SC ship, and it required just a slight deviation from their course. On Lindahl's orders, the com chief had notified Stewart that they would assist the freighter.

"We have the freighter on long-range DeTect," the tactical officer announced as soon as the large object showed up on his scans. "She appears to be max'd out with ten kilometers of cargo containers."

"You're relieved, Commander," Lindahl said to McCloud.

"I stand relieved, sir," McCloud said.

"Helm, bring us alongside the freighter, two kilometers' distance off their larboard beam," Lindahl ordered.

"Captain, we're less than fifteen kilometers from the Frontier Zone," McCloud said.

"I'm aware of that, Commander."

"Yes, sir. But regulations require that we maintain a twenty-five-kilometer distance from any ship until we verify they have no hostile intent."

"That's been established, Commander. They called for assistance from any Space Command ship. They would hardly do that within five light-years of Stewart SCB, a base with the largest fleet of warships in Space Command, if they had hostile intentions. The ship registry file shows that they have a top speed of Light-150. They can't run away, and with ten kilometers of cargo, they can't hide."

"Yes, sir, but the regulations…"

"I've given my orders and they stand."

"Shouldn't we at least go to General Quarters, sir?"

"Drop it, Commander," Lindahl said calmly, but with a hint of irritability in his voice."

"Yes, sir," McCloud said.

As the helmsman cancelled the temporal envelope and engaged the sub-light engines, a slight lurch was noticeable. It only lasted as long as it took the inertial compensators to kick in and correct for the acceleration. As the *Lisbon* reached the freighter, the helmsman reversed the sub-light power to slow the ship, then used thrusters to maneuver it alongside the small freighter at the head of the long cargo section.

"Chief, hail the freighter," Lindahl said.

"Aye, Captain," the com chief said.

"Captain," the tactical officer said loudly. "They've launched torpedoes."

"The freighter?"

The ship shook violently before the tactical officer could respond.

"Sound GQ," Lindahl practically screamed.

Emergency lights began flashing throughout the ship as a GQ message sounded over public address speakers and via CT and ID cranial implants. In seconds, officers, NCOs, and crewmen were leaping from, or falling from, bunks as they groped for clothing before running for their battle stations.

Lindahl stabbed at a button on his chair's right-hand monitor that would allow him to address the crew. "Attention, this is the Captain. We're under attack by a freighter off our starboard beam. All gunners fire at will."

Before the first torpedo left the *Lisbon*, or the first laser gunner sent a beam of coherent light towards the freighter, the *Lisbon* was rocked a second time.

43

"Helm, get us out of here," Lindahl shouted.

"The FTL is offline, Captain, and the Sub-light engines are non-responsive. All we have is maneuvering thrusters."

"Captain, warships approaching on the larboard beam," the tactical officer said with urgency.

Lindahl leaned back in his chair. He knew he had been suckered. Without mobility, they didn't have a chance against three Raider warships. Lindahl stabbed at the 'ship wide' announcement button again and said, "Larboard weapons gunners, there are three warships approaching. Light them up. Fire at will."

The doors to the bridge slid apart and five tactical officers rushed in to take their places at the tactical station. Within seconds, they were targeting the freighter and warships. Torpedoes began to belch from all tubes as quickly as the systems could load and ready them for launch.

Lindahl just sat back and watched. There was nothing he could do. The weapons specialists knew their job and would do it until their weapons were rendered useless by enemy fire, the supply of torpedoes was exhausted, they were ordered to stand down, or they ran out of targets. The latter seemed the least likely.

* * *

Awakened in the middle of the night on November 3rd, Jenetta fumbled to open the com on the nightstand next to her bed. A head-and-shoulders image of Captain Wavala, the officer now in charge of the Communications and Computing section at Stewart, filled the screen as it brightened. Obviously agitated, judging from the tone in his voice and the quickness of his speech, he began by apologizing for the interruption.

"Sorry to wake you, Admiral, but we have an urgent problem!"

"What is it, Bernie?" Jenetta said sleepily.

"We received a distress signal from a freighter several days ago. They reported a problem with their FTL drive but stated they weren't in any immediate danger. They requested that any Space Command vessel stop to assist because their engineers weren't able to correct the problem."

"Yes, I saw that report. The ship was the *Galadvia*, wasn't it?"

"Yes ma'am. That was the name given."

"And did you contact the nearest GSC ship?"

"Yes, after verifying the identity of the freighter, we asked the *Calgary* to assist, since they were the closest ship on patrol, but then we received a message from the *Lisbon*, which had also picked up the distress call. Since they were only half a day away and it wouldn't take them far from their course, they offered to handle it. We told the *Calgary* to continue on their normal patrol."

"Fine, what's the problem?"

"We've just received a message from the *Lisbon* that they're under attack from the *Galadvia* and several warships. They'd barely stopped their ship when the *Galadvia* loosed a broadside of torpedoes that caught the *Lisbon* by surprise. The initial barrage knocked out their temporal field generator, and as they were attempting to return fire, three warships showed up. That was all we got. The message wasn't completed."

Jenetta was wide awake now. "Contact the *Calgary* and any other ships within ten days and tell them to go to the aid of the *Lisbon* at top speed! I'll be down there in fifteen minutes. Carver out."

Chapter Five
~ November 3rd, 2278 ~

Jenetta dressed and made it down to the Base Operations Center in less than twelve minutes. "Anything more from the *Lisbon*?" she asked of Captain Wavala.

"Nothing, ma'am."

"Let me see their message."

After viewing the urgent call from the *Lisbon*, Jenetta knew that help wouldn't get there in time. The freighter's distress call was obviously phony, but who would be foolish enough to attempt the entrapment of a Space Command warship? The Tsgardi? The Raiders? No answers would be forthcoming until one of the four ships proceeding to the location of the attack arrived and investigated. A number of ships would be able to respond quickly because the attack had taken place just five light-years from the base. But who would be so bold as to risk an attack practically on Stewart's doorstep?"

The *Calgary* arrived on the scene the next day. Jenetta had returned to bed after listening to the *Lisbon's* message but revisited the Station Control Center in time to hear the first report from the *Calgary*.

"To Stewart Base Ops Center from Captain Charles Hoyt of the GSC Destroyer *Calgary*.

"We've arrived at the location of the attack. The *Lisbon* is still here, along with the freighter. Both ships have suffered heavy damage. We're at GQ and standing off twenty-five thousand kilometers in case someone on either ship is waiting to attack whoever shows up. I've dispatched fighters and shuttles to investigate, and I'll transmit another report as soon as our boarding parties have had a chance to look around.

"Captain Hoyt of the *Calgary*, message complete."

Shuttles filled with Space Marines approached the *Lisbon* first. An escort of six fighters accompanied the shuttles and continually circled the vessel as the Marines entered the destroyer. Captain Hoyt waited anxiously on the bridge while they searched for any sign of life. The huge monitor at the front of the *Calgary's* bridge was a patchwork of small images transmitted from the helmet cameras of the sergeants leading the squads of searchers. They found no survivors, although they should have been numerous because the interior of the ship was largely intact and the life support systems were still operating throughout the sealed areas of the ship.

What the Marines did find were the lifeless bodies of crewmembers unfortunate enough to be working in areas where the hull had been breached soon after the battle commenced. Several huge gaping holes were evidence of torpedo strikes. The number of crewmembers sucked out into the vacuum of space was unknown. The *Calgary's* first officer, Commander Hilton Rowell, was in almost constant communication with the ship as he directed the search effort, but the monitor provided a complete picture without the need for words.

"That completes the sweep, Captain," Commander Rowell said after several hours of effort. "The enemy must have docked with the ship and taken the survivors away, unless they spaced them. I'm pretty sure that none of the crew is left alive aboard this ship, but we'll complete another sweep using sound sensing equipment now that we're sure the ship hasn't been booby trapped."

"Okay, Commander. I have another group ready to leave for the freighter. Lt. Commander Quart will lead the other search."

"Aye, Captain. Rowell out."

The search of the freighter also produced nothing but dead bodies, but most of the bodies were Tsgardi. After an exhaustive search, Captain Hoyt felt that he was in a position to report their findings with reasonable certainty. Communication time from the attack site to Stewart was just ninety minutes, so Stewart would receive the news quickly.

Jenetta returned to the Ops Center upon receiving notification of a second message from the *Calgary*.

"To Stewart Base Operations Center, from Captain Charles Hoyt of the GSC Destroyer *Calgary*.

"Numerous members of the *Lisbon* crew are dead, and many hundreds are missing, including Admiral Vroman. We found the body of the admiral's aide, killed when a section of hull ruptured. Some crewmen could have been sucked out when the hull breached, but not hundreds, and a quick sweep of space around us hasn't produced more than a dozen bodies. I would venture to guess that the crewmen who survived the attack are prisoners of whoever is responsible. Although the freighter's log records the crew as being mostly Terran, my teams have reported finding only dead Tsgardi bodies in the ship. I'm appending a partial copy of the *Lisbon's* video log to this message. It covers the time of the attack."

Captain Hoyt of the *Calgary*, message complete."

"Record a message to be sent to the *Calgary*," Jenetta said to the chief petty officer manning the com console.

"Go ahead whenever you're ready, Admiral."

"To Captain Hoyt of the GSC *Calgary*, from Admiral Carver, Stewart Space Command Base."

"Captain, after completing a thorough sweep of the area for bodies, return to Stewart with the *Lisbon* and *Galadvia* in tow. If your space tugs can't handle the two ships because of their condition, the *Sydney*, *Athens*, and *Miami* will be joining you in the next few days. Each has at least two space tugs aboard.

"Admiral Carver, Stewart Space Command Base, message complete. Play the video log for me, chief."

The chief petty officer tapped a few contact points on his console, and the view from the *Lisbon* as it had approached the freighter appeared on the screen.

Suddenly, the ends of several cargo containers flew off, as if from the detonation of exploding bolts. Torpedoes then erupted from the containers and flew towards the *Lisbon*. Within seconds, the torpedoes had found their marks. Explosions rocked the ship. Another round of torpedoes flew from the freighter before the first return fire, but once the gunners on board the *Lisbon* had gotten started, they'd filled space between the ships with torpedoes and deadly laser pulses. The fight had been intense for perhaps several minutes, but a freighter was no match for a GSC destroyer, even if it had scored the first hits. If the freighter had first targeted the body of the ship instead of the Temporal Field Generator and Sub-Light engines, they might have had a chance, however slight.

The scene then changed to the larboard side of the *Lisbon* where several warships had approached while the *Lisbon* was engaging the freighter. The warships opened up with their laser weapons and pummeled the damaged destroyer repeatedly as they maneuvered quickly around the two disabled ships. The outcome of the fight had never been in question once the three warships arrived.

Jenetta watched the short battle in grim silence. Unable to move under its own power after the initial barrage, the *Lisbon* had been a sitting target. Although its defeat was never in question, the *Lisbon* had scored some respectable hits on the warships before its weapons were silenced.

At the end of the log replay, Jenetta left the Station Control Center and walked immediately to her office. She had another message to send, but this one was private. As she entered the outer office, she said to her aide, "No interruptions for ten minutes, Lori."

"Aye, Admiral."

Jenetta tapped the record button on her com unit as she sat down at her desk.

"To Admiral Richard Moore, Admiral of the Fleet, Space Command Supreme Headquarters, Earth. Priority One message from Admiral Jenetta Carver.

"Sir, I have bad news to relay. The destroyer *Lisbon*, with Admiral Vroman on board, has been attacked. The admiral is missing, as are hundreds of crewmembers. The *Lisbon* was the victim of a phony distress signal put out by a freighter that fired on our ship when it arrived to assist her. The destroyer *Calgary* has now arrived at the scene, just five light-years from Stewart, and found the severely damaged *Lisbon* and the freighter calling itself the *Galadvia*. The original crew of the freighter is missing. Search teams only found the bodies of Tsgardi aboard the ship.

"I've viewed the *Lisbon's* video logs and observed that she would have won the engagement but for the arrival of several warships. Sir, those warships were of Milori design. I don't know if Milori warriors manned the ships or if Raiders have acquired Milori ships, but their appearance was most disturbing. I shall keep you apprised of any new developments.

"Jenetta Carver, Rear Admiral, Upper Half, Commander of Stewart Space Command Base, message complete."

Considering the immense distance between Stewart and the Hudeerac Home World, a response to Jenetta's message came surprisingly quickly. Just fifty-one days after Jenetta had transmitted her message and hours after viewing the video log of the *Lisbon*, an encrypted message simply marked Vertap appeared in Jenetta's message queue. Attempting to play it, she encountered encryption garble, so she recorded her retinal image and touched the ring she still wore on her left hand to the media tray spindle. Instantly, the message cleared, and the image of Minister Aloyandro appeared.

"Good day, Admiral. My Sovereign is most pleased that you've agreed to the sharing of information. Our operative within the Milori palace had already informed us of the retreat and has given us other information that I will now relate. During their evacuation of your territory, the Milori fleet detached thirty of their best warships and sent them to positions of concealment within your Frontier Zone. They are to remain there and await further orders. The Milori felt that you wouldn't notice a few missing ships traveling independently to different destinations and the Raider organization helped them avoid your patrols. I can confirm your suspicions that the Milori have no intention of living up to the terms of the treaty they've signed with you. They are bristling over the subterfuge you employed at your last encounter with them. They will attack again, as soon as they feel their ship strength is adequate. They have tasked their spies with the chore of learning everything they can about your new weapons. You should be very wary.

"Minister Vertap Aloyandro. End of message."

That the Milori would be back as soon as they could assemble sufficient warships came as no surprise, but the information about the thirty ships hidden in the Frontier Zone made her sit up a little straighter. Arriving in the wake of the attack on the *Lisbon*, Jenetta didn't doubt the accuracy of the message. It now appeared that Milori had been manning the warships in the attack on the *Lisbon*, unless the Raiders had become emboldened by the presence of the invaders. But Jenetta had never heard of instances where the Milori sold their warships, just as Space Command never sold *its* warships. Prior to the Milori invasion, decommissioned GSC vessels were cut up into unusable pieces before being sold for scrap, but only after having remained mothballed for at least twelve years. Since the invasion, a refit program was underway to prepare all previously mothballed ships for rear area patrol duties.

"As you were," Jenetta said, as she strode into the conference room with Lt. Commander Ashraf close on her heels. The captains of the only five warships in port, the senior officers from the Intelligence Section, and the most senior officer from each of the other sections on the station had started to rise, but now settled back into their chairs. "As you've all no doubt heard by now, the *Lisbon* was attacked by a freighter faking a distress call. Commander, play the video log," Jenetta said to her aide. The large monitor in the conference room displayed the battle as recorded by the *Lisbon*. Everyone watched intently as the attacking forces overwhelmed the ship.

"I can't believe the *Lisbon* moved to within a few kilometers of the freighter without checking it out first," Captain Jason Fowler of the GSC Destroyer *Bogotá* said as the vid log ended.

"In the rear areas they haven't had to worry about such treachery from freighters asking for assistance because the Raiders have been rocked back on their heels during the past decade," Jenetta said. "Captain Lindahl has never been out this far before and it's clear that he didn't exercise proper precautions. Let this be a lesson to everyone here to never let down your guard." Jenetta knew Lindahl would face a court-martial if he survived. If he wasn't found guilty of dereliction of duty, he would be found guilty of ineptitude for failing to follow proper procedure when approaching an unknown ship. If not imprisoned or discharged from the service, he would probably be reduced in rank and spend the remainder of his career dirt-side, or perhaps in an administrative position on a minor space station in the rear areas. There was no doubt whatsoever that he would never command a warship again.

"Even if he *had* exercised the proper precautions, they would have been overwhelmed," Captain Lofgren of the Intelligence section said. "They couldn't have stood against the armed freighter and three *warships*."

"But they could have fled if the freighter hadn't been able to knock out their temporal generator and Sub-Light engines so easily." Jenetta sighed. "We're not here to discuss the actions of the *Lisbon's* captain or crew. There will be plenty of time for the assessment of crew actions later. We have problems that are more pressing. As you saw, the three warships are clearly of Milori design. I assume that none of our captured ships are missing, are they Commander Jacoby?" Jenetta asked her chief engineer.

"No ma'am. Definitely not."

"I thought not. A few hours ago, I received a message from a source I can't divulge at this time, the purpose of which was to inform me that during the Milori exodus, thirty ships broke off and sped to positions of concealment within our inner border. They traveled independently so as not to attract attention. With assistance from the Raiders, they were able to avoid our patrols."

"That was a short-lived treaty," Lofgren said.

"Yes," Jenetta said. "In prior centuries I believe the expression would be that the ink hadn't even dried on the treaty before the Milori were breaking it."

"If this is an advance guard, why have they chosen to reveal themselves before the main fleet gets here?" Lofgren asked. "Shouldn't they have remained hidden until just before the rest of the invasion fleet arrives?"

"Even more puzzling is their choice of targets," Captain Laramie Cossa of the GSC Destroyer *Kabul* said. "Why would they have chosen to assault a GSC destroyer just five light-years from this base? They could have attacked a ship much further away where the risk was much lower."

"I think I know the answer to that," Jenetta said. "Admiral Vroman was aboard that ship. The Tsgardi deliberately targeted the engines, to their own detriment, so they must have been under orders not to harm the Admiral. Perhaps they expected Captain Lindahl to simply surrender once he knew he couldn't escape. If so, they don't understand Space Command personnel. The *Lisbon* responded to the torpedo attack with everything they had and made it clear that they wouldn't simply capitulate."

"Assuming that Admiral Vroman is still alive," Captain Barbara DeWitt of the Weapons Research section said, "what can we expect? A ransom attempt?"

"I don't think so," Lofgren said. "Everyone knows we don't ransom Space Command personnel because it would turn every officer and enlisted person into a kidnap target. They must be after information. As the incoming base commander, Admiral Vroman has had access to secure data about this base and its weapon systems, and in his year and a half aboard the *Lisbon*, he must have reviewed every report ever submitted to SHQ by Admiral Carver. The Milori would have no better candidate from which to learn about Stewart, except possibly Admiral Carver herself."

"We'd better immediately change all access codes and passwords that were established for Admiral Vroman," Jenetta said.

"Already taken care of, Admiral," Captain Wavala said, "along with the access codes and passwords of everyone else aboard the *Lisbon*. I saw to that the minute I learned the *Lisbon* was under attack and wasn't responding to hails."

"The patrol routes of our ships should also be changed," Lofgren said.

"Also done," Jenetta said. "I've notified all ships on patrol to pull back to within twenty light-years of the base and vary their patrols from established routes. I don't want them too far away if this is the opening volley in a second Milori invasion."

"We can't adequately patrol our sectors if we're limited to twenty light-years, Admiral," Captain Cyndee Pasqua of the GSC Destroyer *Chicago* said.

"It can't be helped," Jenetta said. "For the Milori to expose their presence here must mean that an invasion by a large force can't be very far off."

"What if that's exactly what they want us to believe?" Lofgren asked.

"They expose their presence and we pull back behind the castle walls and raise the drawbridge?" Jenetta asked.

"Something like that," Lofgren said. "Admiral, I think we've skipped an important question. If the Tsgardi were after Admiral Vroman, how did they know he was aboard? I'm sure his trip here wasn't publicized, and even if people knew he was coming, how would they know what ship he was on?"

"That's a good question, Captain, and one that I don't have an answer for right now, other than to say we've always known the Raiders have an incredible intelligence network. We know they've turned Space Command crewmen, NCOs, and even officers in the past. The investigation following the theft of the two battleships from the Mars facility proved that. We also know they have ships stationed throughout Galactic Alliance space reporting on the movement of both Space Command vessels and commercial ships. We've sent out spotters of our own, but we need to stem the flow of information to the Raiders."

"How about picking up some of those *watchers*?" Lofgren asked.

"You're talking about the Raider spotters?"

"Yes, ma'am. Perhaps they can be arrested on charges of conspiracy or something similar."

Jenetta nodded and said thoughtfully, "Even if they don't provide us with any useful information, we'll at least be able to move around without having our every position reported to the enemy, and it will take some time for the Raiders to replace them. Good suggestion, Captain. I'll issue an order to search for any ships stopped in space or planetary orbit. If their navigation logs show they spend a lot of time sitting in one place without valid reason, we'll bring them here for incarceration on a charge of conspiracy or whatever other charge is applicable. Sedition is a possibility, as are treason and spying since the Raiders have now shown themselves to be in league with an invading nation. I'll leave that up to you, Captain Donovan," Jenetta said to the head of the JAG office."

"Yes ma'am," he said in acknowledgement.

"We still haven't addressed the problem of finding the thirty ships the Milori have sent into our space," Jenetta said. "Any suggestions?"

"It'll be like finding a needle in a haystack," Captain Pasqua said, "an infinitely large haystack."

"I think finding the needle would be easier," Jenetta said. "At least you'd know it wasn't moving around under its own power in an effort to avoid detection."

"What if we use the seized ships of the watchers for our own purpose?" Lofgren suggested. "After we arrest the crews, we place our own people aboard and have *them* report every ship they spot, but they'll be reporting to us instead of the Raiders. Even if we don't know whom they're seeing, we'll at least have a record of every ship and its course. We might be able to spot a trend."

"Okay, good idea," Jenetta said. "I'll order that. Any other ideas?"

"Admiral, even if we spot the Milori ships, we won't be able to apprehend them," Commander Jacoby said. "The ships shown on the *Lisbon's* vid log are the newest design being built by the Milori. The specs we found in the captured ships list their top speed as Light-450. Even the *Prometheus* and *Chiron* won't be able to overtake them, or even stay up with them."

"What's the speed of the ships we captured?"

"Of the ships that have been repaired and converted for our use, three are capable of Light-450, and the others are capable of Light-412."

"So we have at least three ships that can keep up with them if they flee?"

"Yes, we can keep up with them if any of those ships happen to make contact with the Milori, but the retrofitted Milori ships aren't even being used because they haven't been sufficiently staffed."

"I'll see that they're adequately staffed and provisioned within a week. I want them ready to go out at that time. What's the situation with armament on the ships, Commander?"

"The laser arrays and torpedo-launching systems have been checked and repaired where necessary, and we have sufficient torpedoes for the present because we were able to salvage the inventories from all captured ships. Space Command Weapon Arsenals have received the torpedo specs and begun production, but it will be a year or more before they can possibly re-supply us out here. Space Command torpedoes can't be substituted because they're radically different in both dimensions and targeting systems."

"How many Milori torpedoes do we have?"

"Each repaired ship has a normal load of one hundred sixty in its armaments holds and there are roughly ten thousand more here in the base armory. The captured Milori warships were all carrying hundreds of extra torpedoes in their holds, probably because they couldn't rely on supply ships keeping up with them during their invasion. But rather than trusting any that showed the slightest bit of damage, I had their detonators and warheads removed before they were taken to a secure area of the scrap yard."

"Please see that each retrofitted ship receives one hundred additional torpedoes. Since they represent some of our fastest ships, they have a greater likelihood of meeting the enemy in combat. The Milori will know they can't outrun them, so they may choose to turn and fight. Does anyone have any other suggestions?"

When no one spoke up, Jenetta said, "Okay, keep your people ready for action. Things may heat up very quickly."

Two weeks following the attack, Jenetta received the following message from Admiral Moore at Supreme Headquarters:

"The Admiralty Board is duly concerned over this critical development. We weren't expecting the Milori to violate the terms of the treaty quite so soon. You should spare no effort in finding Admiral Vroman and effecting his rescue. You will remain in command of Stewart until you recover him or until a replacement flag officer arrives.

"Reassigned ships should soon begin to arrive in ever increasing numbers until the full complement is in place, so you'll be in a much better position to repel an invading force this time. You have our full faith and confidence, Admiral."

"Richard E. Moore, Admiral of the Fleet, Supreme Headquarters, Earth, message complete."

* * *

Jenetta's prediction of possible increased Milori activity turned out to be completely inaccurate. Following the attack on the *Lisbon*, the sectors around Stewart immediately resumed their formerly tranquil status. Not a single sighting of Milori ships occurred in the months following the attack.

With the arrival of more and more Space Command ships and no sightings of Milori ships, Jenetta made the decision to extend the patrol area to fifty light-years out from Stewart. Thus far, eleven small spotter ships had been seized and their crews taken into custody. In each case, the engines and communications equipment were in good working condition and the small crew couldn't provide a reasonable excuse for why it was sitting in the same place along normal shipping lanes for months at a time. A replacement crew of several Space Command crewmen took their place onboard each ship with orders to report all ship passages.

* * *

Eighty-three days following the attack on the *Lisbon*, Milori guards took Admiral Vroman from the brig and escorted him to the shuttle bay of the Milori cruiser

Rowlidph, where they prodded him to board a shuttle. He moved into the small ship and took a seat, then stared venomously at the guards while senior officers from the *Lisbon* slowly took the remaining seats. The guards stepped off the ship after ensuring that all seats were occupied. Within minutes, the small vessel was sealed and it moved out of the shuttle bay. Simultaneously, a message began to play over the announcement system.

"Attention, Space Command personnel. You are being shuttled down to the fourth planet in a system identified on your charts as Siena. The planet has a breathable atmosphere, with a gravity that's 1.13 times that of Earth. The landing site, presently in what you would describe as springtime, offers a temperate climate with all the necessities of Terran life. If you make no resistance to this resettlement, the last delivery to the surface will be cargo containers with basic tools, food for thirty days, scientific equipment that can analyze water and food to ensure it's safe for consumption, and medical supplies. If anyone attempts escape, we'll put down the rebellion with extreme prejudice and won't send down the cargo containers. We are piloting this shuttle remotely so you cannot overpower a cockpit crew and assume the controls. Should you attempt to take control, the shuttle will most likely plummet into the atmosphere and burn up. We are maintaining a targeting lock on the ship, so if you somehow override our control, we will simply open fire."

The Space Command officers, whose first thoughts had been of attempts to storm the cockpit now that the guards were gone, settled back into their seats. No one doubted that the Milori would shoot the craft down without a second's hesitation. And if the Milori were marooning them in a primitive environment, they would need the promised equipment and supplies.

As the shuttle settled onto the planet's surface, the hatch opened. The Space Command officers waited until Admiral Vroman rose from his seat and walked to the door before moving into the aisle to follow in order by rank. The scene that greeted them was of a primeval world, unblemished by civilizations or intelligent life, where giant trees stretched upwards, as if reaching for the system's single sun. The dense undergrowth showed no sign of ever having been trampled underfoot. Flying creatures, probably stirred by the noise and appearance of the shuttle, circled overhead. Even at this midday hour, two of the planet's four moons were very visible in the sky, although obscured somewhat by the bright light of the sun as it diffused in the atmosphere.

The Milori had chosen to land their prisoners in a large clearing atop a rocky knoll. The LZ offered a panoramic view of a sizeable green valley, surrounded by barely scalable mountains with snow-capped peaks. Narrow passes at two places appeared to limit entry and egress. Water flowed from the mountains in a dozen places, forming a river that ran the length of the valley.

Admiral Vroman led the way down the landing ramp and away from the ship, which resealed and lifted off as soon as the officers were clear. He turned and watched the shuttle climb into the atmosphere before addressing the group.

"I don't know whether we're better off here or in the Milori ship, but I'm looking forward to having a decent meal as soon as we learn what's available on this planet; Milori food is barely fit for human consumption. I'm going to assume from the way they worded the announcement that our crew will be following us down. The most important task we have before us now is maintaining order and discipline. We're alive, and we'll be getting off this planet as soon as we can get word to Space Command, but we may be here for a while. I'm sure Admiral Carver is already scouring the deca-sector for us. I don't know where this Siena system is in relation to Stewart, but we know that it's less than ninety days away from the base, if I calculated the days correctly."

"Sir," Captain Lindahl said, "I believe it's located well inside the Frontier Zone."

"That would make sense, and we could be as far as eighty light-years inside the Zone. There has to be less SC patrol activity and less civilian traffic here, so the Milori would believe there's less chance of our being found. Very well, from this day forward we shall refer to this planet as Siena, and we have three top priorities. We need protection from the elements, protection from potentially hostile indigenous life forms, and good sources of food and water. Eat and drink nothing until we've checked the source for toxicity.

"Captain, you're responsible for arming our people. We'll start with rocks, advance to clubs, and then to slings, spears, and archery components. I'm sure the Milori won't be giving us any laser weapons, but eventually we'll want to manufacture rudimentary firearms. Commander Fannon, you'll assemble search teams to locate water and food sources. I'll take charge of providing protection from the elements, so I'm initially assigning all engineers to my group. We'll need to discover what talents, interests, and skills our crewmembers have outside their normal shipboard duties. For example, are any of our people knowledgeable in agronomy, zoology, entomology, paleontology, ancient weapons, carpentry, hunting, blacksmithing, etc.? I'm sure you get the idea. We have a major advantage over our Stone Age ancestors; we have intelligence and the knowledge of what our species has accomplished on Earth. Once you know what is possible, it's only a matter of figuring out ways to make it happen."

A noise from overheard drew everyone's attention and they watched as another shuttle descended, touched down, and disgorged its cargo of *Lisbon* crewmembers.

"Okay," Admiral Vroman said to the senior officers, "you know what we need to do initially. Let's get started organizing our people."

The overnight temperature at the encampment dropped to about twelve degrees Celsius, but the stranded *Lisbon* crewmembers had been able to ignite campfires for warmth. Five hundred forty-six had survived the attack on the *Lisbon*, owing mainly to the Milori's desire to take Admiral Vroman alive, and were now on the planet's surface. They accomplished much on the first day. One group had followed the river to the place where it disappeared down into a narrow, impassable gorge, while others examined the two passes, one of which they designated as the North Pass, leaving the other to become the South Pass by default. Weeks later, some of the crew would argue in favor of changing the name to the East Pass because of its distance from the southern end of the valley where the river disappeared. Although only a quarter of the way from the North Pass, people had been using the name long enough for it to stick. They had established the pole designations based on the travel of the sun overhead rather than planetary magnetic alignment.

After determining that the river water was potable, the engineers under Admiral Vroman's direction established a base camp on a flat area near the river's edge where a wide stream flowed briskly down from the mountain peak. The teams responsible for food foraging had meanwhile brought back numerous varieties of berries, tubers, and vegetation for testing. They would use the food supplies left by the Milori as sparingly as possible while safe alternatives were available, with remaining stocks saved as emergency rations. The hunters sighted a number of small animals, but they remained too elusive for capture. They also found large cloven-hoofed tracks in soft dirt, but so far there was no sign of the animals that had made them. The hunters speculated that the shuttle arrivals and departures might have sent the larger animals running to the far reaches of the valley.

The second day on the surface was devoted to laying out the permanent camp and beginning construction of shelters. If the climate was like that of the temperate regions on Earth, they could expect both hotter and colder days ahead. The tools provided by the Milori included half a dozen water saws and power-nailers. Both were powered with cells that quickly recharged by solar energy. The saws fired a concentrated stream of water under such incredibly high pressure that it could cut wood, stone, or metal. Actually, it just wore its way through anything within two meters of the jet. It was equally useful for felling trees or making board lumber, but it would have been so much easier if the Milori had simply left them portable shelters. A solar power collection unit that would recharge their energy cells was included with the equipment, as well as a few dozen solar-powered camp lights that they placed at work and gathering points, such as the food preparation area and along the main street of the camp.

Obviously, the Milori expected the *Lisbon* crew to be on the planet for some time, but Admiral Vroman had other ideas. He detailed one of the engineers to find a way to transmit a distress call, even if the call was limited to old RF frequencies.

"But Admiral," the engineer had replied after receiving the assignment, "RF communications can only travel at the speed of light. It'll take ninety years for the signal to reach Stewart."

"Have a little faith, Chief. I remember reading that Admiral Carver ordered transmission of a repeating RF message when the Tsgardi besieged her on Mawcett. Her hope was that a ship in space would pick up the RF signal, then retransmit it to Higgins Space Command Base on the IDS band. With luck, that same tactic could work for us."

"And did it work for Admiral Carver, sir?"

"Uh, no, but only because it proved unnecessary. I'll be happy to accept rescue by a Space Command ship or even a private enterprise ship before the signal is intercepted, but let's get a signal out anyway."

"Aye, Admiral. I'll do my best to make a transmitter of some sort. May I cannibalize some the Milori equipment for parts?"

"Better check with me before rendering anything unusable."

"Aye, sir.

* * *

A month after being marooned on the planet, the *Lisbon* survivors had established a camp that would see them through the immediate days ahead. They'd felled trees for simple post and beam buildings that would serve as shelters, and the camp was taking on the look of small village. The water-saws were invaluable for producing the framing beams, and then the board lumber to be used for clapboard siding. The roofs would be thatch over a bed of rough planks, and the floors would be dirt, but plans called for wooden floors once all shelters had been sealed against the elements. Scrap lumber was stacked in piles to be used for firewood once it dried out.

Knowing they would quickly exhaust nearby wild food sources, they had cleared a ten-hectare section of forestland referred to simply as *the farm*. They had succeeded in germinating most of the berry plants and tubers found in the valley and were already harvesting edible, fast-growing leafy green vegetables in the thick, rich black dirt that carpeted the former forest floor. Efforts to clear another hundred hectares were underway.

The fishermen, operating without nets, hooks, or fishing gear, had only had limited success in the river, but they were persistent in their efforts to learn about the aquamarine life. While trying to construct a simple wood and stone trap along the river's edge, one crewman had almost been lost to a plant at the water's edge that wrapped itself around any creature venturing too near and then began to crush the unwary victim. The crewman's screams brought the other fishermen running and they were able to save him before he suffered any serious damage to his legs. Afterwards, they discovered the decomposing bodies of small animals at the base of the plant. One of the agronomists theorized that after crushing its victim the plant pulled the remains into the wet soil at its base so the decaying body fertilized the roots. They quickly eradicated the plant along the shoreline for hundreds of meters from the camp, and so began the first serious efforts to alter the ecosystem for human habitation.

The hunters at last succeeded in trapping two of the cloven-hoofed animals, and an experiment was under way to domesticate them. They named the four-legged creatures 'gelks' because they had thick, curved horns like those found on Terran mountain goats and were as large as elks. They had so far proven to be unmanageable, but fortunately they didn't have the ability to jump very high, no doubt due to their large size and the seeming lack of predators in the valley. A two-meter-high fence was adequate to contain them. The goal was to tame them and train them to pull a plow, but right now the biggest chore was keeping their voracious appetites sated. The production of additional fertilizer for the farm helped make the project worthwhile.

The hunters had also been providing wild fowl for the table, but they hadn't been able to trap any alive yet. Admiral Vroman kept after them to bring back some specimens for domestication efforts, especially any that were prolific egg layers. A good omelet would be a very welcome addition to the menu.

Craftsmen had succeeded in fashioning a pottery kiln and were producing terracotta earthenware for everyday use, as well as pipes for water and waste movement. They were developing an irrigation system for the cleared land and making wooden farm implements. So far, they didn't have the ability to mine and refine metal ore, but several amateur geologists and mineralogists were working on it.

Not all was perfect however. Clothes were beginning to show wear and they hadn't had any success yet in finding plants like cotton or flax with which to make cloth. Insects were a problem and they hadn't yet found a repellant for a species of biting flies that left nasty welts on the skin. A specimen of every new creature found was brought to the camp for study by the doctors. Most of the reptile-like creatures were non-venomous, although repulsive in appearance, but one was extremely venomous. They destroyed it at every opportunity. The doctors were working on developing anti-venom. Eventually, one of the creatures would succeed in biting someone.

Chapter Six
~ April 6th, 2279 ~

Jenetta stood at her SimWindow, staring at the operations in the port and thinking about the latest news from her captains. There had been no sightings of any Milori vessel or the missing crew of the *Lisbon*, and in the five months since the attack, the sectors around Stewart had remained calm. A message from her aide interrupted her reverie.

"Admiral, Trader Vyx is here in the outer office. He's asking to see you."

"Send him in, Lori."

As the door opened and Vyx entered, Jenetta turned from the window and said, "Welcome back, Trader. Was your trip to Koppreco successful?"

Jenetta's two large cats rose to their feet and sniffed towards Vyx. Recognizing his scent, they relaxed again.

"Exceptionally so, Admiral. By the time we reached the planet, we had nearly a thousand of the noisy little fur balls in our hold. It took the buyer a few extra days to come up with the additional credits, but he was delighted with the delivery."

Jenetta sat down at her desk as Trader Vyx plopped, uninvited, into one of the overstuffed chairs that faced her. Although only a Lt. Commander in the Intelligence section, he usually maintained his undercover persona at all times and rarely bowed to military protocol.

"I've heard that the government of Koppreco is finally considering lifting the ban on Aluvian mamots," Jenetta said. "They've finally realized they can't stop the smuggling and hope to at least control the health of the creatures brought in."

"Although our mamots were all certified virus-free by the quarantine station on Aluvia before they were brought on board the *Scorpion*, I'm sure other smugglers haven't been as careful. Anyway, my reputation as a smuggler and generally disreputable person is secure and I'm available for any undercover assignments you have. I was surprised to find you still in command of the base. I thought you were leaving."

"I was, and fully expected to be gone by now, but my replacement, Admiral Vroman, was aboard the *Lisbon*."

"I heard that a Space Command destroyer was attacked by Raiders. Is that the one?"

"Yes. They were responding to a distress call. The Raiders attacked when the *Lisbon* stopped to offer assistance. It turned out that Tsgardi had hijacked the freighter and issued the phony call for help. As the *Lisbon* was fighting the Tsgardi, three Milori warships jumped them. We released a statement that the Tsgardi were in the employ of Raiders, but they may have been working directly for the Milori. We lost a lot of people and hundreds more are missing and presumed prisoners of the Milori."

"Milori, huh? I thought we'd seen the last of them for a while. I hadn't heard they were involved."

"That part of the attack has been kept secret. We don't want the sectors to erupt in panic. We've only briefed key government officials on Galactic Alliance member planets. Since the one attack, there hasn't been any further sign of the Milori."

"Want me to put out feelers?"

"Yes. I have reliable information that thirty of the newest Milori ships left the fleet after the Milori headed for home. Their orders were to secret themselves inside our inner border and wait for additional orders."

"How do you know all this, Admiral?"

"I'm sorry, Trader, but that's need-to-know information. Our problem now is twofold. One, we don't know where the thirty Milori ships are hiding, and two, we don't know when or where the main fleet is scheduled to begin their invasion. I'm hoping you can glean some information from your sources."

"You feel sure they intend to invade again?"

"There's little doubt about that; there can be no other deduction from the facts. They're simply awaiting reinforcements and marshalling their forces in preparation for the next attack. Following the attack on the *Lisbon*, I recalled all Space Command warships and restricted them from patrolling further than twenty light-years from Stewart, but as reinforcements began to arrive, I expanded that to fifty light-years, and I recently amended it again to allow full coverage inside our inner border and one hundred light-years into the Frontier. The number of ships patrolling in the Frontier Zone is triple the number we have inside the 'regulated space' border in the hope that one will spot the Milori fleet in sufficient time for us to amass our forces. We've also impounded dozens of small Raider spotter ships and replaced the crews with our people, setting up a spotter network of our own."

"It sounds like you have all the bases covered. Do you have any clever little surprises waiting for the Milori? Your bluff with the freighters was priceless," Vyx said, chuckling.

"I'm afraid clever maneuvers won't get the job done next time; only brute force will turn the Milori back. And this time we'll have to take the fight all the way to their home world. The emperor must understand that he won't be given a third opportunity to mount an invasion against us."

"Milor is eleven hundred light-years from here. They'll have years to prepare a defense once they receive word that their forces have been defeated— if they are defeated."

Jenetta was quiet for a few seconds. "Victory will be ours. I'm sure of it. And if we must travel to Milor and defeat their home guard to seal that victory, we shall."

Trader Vyx stared at Jenetta with respect. "If anyone can, Admiral, it's you. My team and I will leave for Scruscotto immediately and learn what we can."

"Thank you, Trader. Expend whatever funds are necessary for the procurement of useful information. I'll see that your account is adequate."

"No need, Admiral. I have ample credits coming from the Koppreco contract, and I received an additional five hundred thousand credits beyond the original amount, thanks to the highly active mating habits of Aluvian mamots when on their own planet. I think every female in the original batch was pregnant when we took her aboard. We can buy a lot of information with a million credits."

"Very well, Trader, but I'm sure your supplies are low after seven months of travel. You'll receive top priority down at the warehouses."

"Thank you, Admiral. I'll be in touch as soon as I learn anything." Vyx stood, turned, and left without further word.

After notifying the Supply officer to provide whatever basic supplies Trader Vyx requested, Jenetta prepared a fresh mug of coffee and returned to her contemplations.

*　*　*

Exalted Lord Space Marshall Berquyth entered the private office of Emperor Maxxiloth and stood in front of the enormous, embellished desk.

"My Lord, we've received word from Supreme Lord Space Marshall Dwillaak that all assigned ships have joined up with his forces outside the Galactic Alliance Buffer Zone."

"Berquyth! I've told you that I don't recognize that area as belonging to the Galactic Alliance!" the emperor bellowed.

"Yes, my Lord," Berquyth said calmly. "I was using the term simply as a reference because we have no other formal designation for it."

"Call it 'a point one-hundred-light-years from the former outer border of the Galactic Alliance.'"

"Yes, my Lord," Berquyth replied, trying to conceal his increasing frustration towards Maxxiloth's tirades over inconsequential issues. "I shall refer to it that way from now on. Shall we commence phase two of the plan?"

"What about Space Command's invisible bombs?"

"We've learned that the bombs are not invisible. That was merely propaganda spread by Admiral Carver's staff. They use a standard torpedo casing covered in some sort of energy-dampening material for delivery, but they are detectable."

"And there are no other surprises?"

"We feel confident that Carver used every trick she had available because she was so vastly outnumbered. We know now that our forces are capable of destroying their ships as easily as we destroyed the fleets of the Hudeerac. The attack on the *Lisbon* proved that. Our interrogation of the Admiral being sent to replace Carver yielded little we didn't already know."

"You're sure you got everything out of him?"

"Absolutely, my Lord, We milked him like a farmer milks his herd of Verliqs. He probably doesn't even know he talked so freely."

"What about this new material, Dakinium, we've heard about?"

"It does exist, and it is as impervious to laser fire as we were informed, but the first ship covered with it had massive problems during its space trials and was returned to their Mars shipbuilding facility many annuals ago. It makes sense that if the material were acceptable for a ship's skin, they would have it in general use by now. They must fear using it, so we're not concerned that it poses any threat to our plans. Once we control GA space, we'll take over their research and make it work for us."

"Very well, Berquyth. Send the order to begin Phase Two. The fleets will proceed into Galactic Alliance space with all possible speed."

* * *

Admiral Thaddeus Vroman awakened from a fitful night of tossing and turning. He sat up on the edge of the coarse bed in his darkened shelter and let his head hang tiredly. The eighteen-hour days were taking their toll on the octogenarian, and he felt completely exhausted. But he had to go on while not showing any sign of fatigue in front of his people. He had expected to be sitting out the rest of his active service years in reasonable comfort on Stewart and later possibly at Supreme Headquarters on Earth, not trying to get a decent night's sleep on a straw-filled mattress. Field operations were for the young, or possibly someone like Admiral Carver, who still had the looks and apparent vitality of a twenty-one year old despite being forty-three. *Forty-three*, he thought, *and already an upper for several years.* He hadn't gotten his second star until he was seventy-six. It was an old story in the military; promotions went first to those who distinguished themselves in combat— and lived to tell about it. No one could deny that Carver had seen more than her share of action and consistently come out on top. Despite her documented successes in battle, ridiculous rumors abounded in the rear echelons about her merely being the darling of the Admiralty Board. Perhaps most irritating to many senior rear area officers was that she was entirely deserving of every honor bestowed upon her because it was far easier to hate someone who had risen through the ranks as the result of nepotism or favoritism.

Although never tested in battle himself, Vroman didn't hold any jealousy or animosity towards Admiral Carver. And he wasn't ashamed to admit he was damned glad she was still the base commander of Stewart. He was convinced that if rescue were to come, it would mainly happen through her efforts.

Struggling to his feet, he winced in pain as his stiff and aching muscles strongly protested being worked again so soon, but the distressed facial expression would be the last sign of weakness he would exhibit throughout the rest of the long day. Almost no amount of pain would be enough to contort his features in front of his people as he spent the day supervising activities in the wilderness base. He was very satisfied with their progress so far and very proud of them. They were well motivated because their lives depended on how they met the challenges before them, but they had also maintained a strict sense of military order, conduct, and professionalism.

Opening a door that hung suspended on thick strips of leather made from the hides of gelks slaughtered for meat, he stared out at the sun as it slowly peeked above the horizon. This was a beautiful planet, and if this small valley was representative of the rest of it, it was not unlike Earth before mankind began to bury its surface beneath layers of people, cities, and concrete highways. Under other circumstances, people might consider this planet a paradise. The air, without a molecule of unnatural pollution in it except for an occasional wisp of smoke from cooking fires, was always crisp and wonderful in the early morning hours. The doctor was concerned about some microorganisms he'd found in the gelks, but so far they hadn't appeared to infect any human hosts. Space Command personnel were regularly inoculated against all known virus and bacterium, but the doctor worried that the hard work and poor diet might affect their immune systems.

The camp was already alive with activity when Admiral Vroman stepped from his quarters and walked towards the mess building. Officers and NCOs each had a dining area separate from the large dining room used by crewmen, but there were no mess attendants here, so everyone went through the same food line before carrying his or her food to the appropriate dining area. It would have been awkward for all three groups to eat in the same dining hall because they would be unable to talk freely.

Today's breakfast fare included local fruits, spicy broiled gelk meat patties, boiled vegetables, and unleavened gritty-tasting bread made from a sort of wild emmer found in the valley. It was virtually the same every day, and Admiral Vroman would have paid a month's salary for a three-egg omelet with side orders of hash browns, pork sausages, and buttermilk biscuits. *In time*, he kept telling himself. The variety of food was slowly improving as food foragers roamed further afield and returned with new items for testing, and the cooks experimented with new recipes, spices, and food preparation methods. They were desperately seeking a proper leavening for use as a baker's yeast.

The heavy work schedule and general lack of time for meetings required that the officers deliver their status reports each morning during breakfast. One by one, each officer would pause his or her eating to give their report. Following the reports, anyone could comment on them or bring up new subjects for discussion. Breakfasts in the officer's private room often lasted long after the other rooms had cleared and the cooks had begun cleaning up so they could begin preparing for lunch. Without the array of automated food preparation machinery available in a shipboard galley or base mess hall, preparation for every meal took many hours. The cooks actually completed much of the evening meal preparation work during mid-morning so they could be off for a few hours in the afternoon to make up for the hours they worked before breakfast.

Admiral Vroman was consulting with Lt. Pyers, the farm manager, as they surveyed the newly planted fields of emmer when the wind carried the first sounds of alarm to them. Shouting in the forest just beyond the land cleared for the farm turned quickly to yelling and then to panicked screams. Admiral Vroman and Lt. Pyers hurried towards the sounds but stopped in their tracks as a large creature emerged from the distant tree line. Quickly reversing their course, they raced to retrieve weapons back at the camp. In the minutes it took to reach the stockpile of spears near the corral, the creature had stomped halfway across the farm as crewmen stood off throwing rocks.

As large as the largest elephant on Earth, and with a mouth full of dagger-like teeth, a ferocious creature resembling a giant lizard was making a plodding beeline on powerful rear legs towards the corral containing the gelks. The gelks, having spotted the oncoming creature, were in a panic. They began throwing themselves violently against the rails in an effort to break free. Although they didn't have the ability to jump, there was no doubt that they could easily outrun the hulking monster looking at them as its next meal if they could only break out of their confinement.

Rocks thrown by *Lisbon* crewman were bouncing off the creature's hide without effect or even distracting it from its single-minded goal. On Admiral Vroman's orders, crewmen near the corral began sticking upraised spears into the soft dirt at a forty-five degree angle towards the approaching beast. As it drew closer, they moved out of its path and began throwing the remaining spears with all their might. Most glanced off, but a few penetrated the thick hide and, for the first time, the creature seemed to acknowledge the puny creatures that populated the area. Fortunately, it didn't slow its gait towards the corral.

Reaching the area where the spears had been jammed into the soil, the creature rampaged through, pieces of snapped spear shafts flying in all directions. But some spears had already done their work, sinking deep into the creature's less-armored chest and underbelly. It reached the corral, but collapsed against it, cracking one of the upright posts. Its legs thrashed wildly for a minute as it lay on its side, and then it was still, the heaving chest having sucked its last air.

As it became almost a certainty that the creature was dead, crewmen moved in closer for a look, and tension drained from their faces. The entire incident had lasted less than five minutes, but it had seemed much longer, and some would later say it seemed to occur in slow motion.

"Is everyone okay?" Admiral Vroman asked loudly.

"A few of our people were injured when the creature bulldozed through us," one of the hunter/crewmen said. "I don't know how serious the injuries are, sir."

"Let's get them to the medical shelter immediately. Are there any more of these things out there?"

"We only saw the one," the hunter responded, "but there have to be more where it came from, sir. Fortunately, it didn't appear to be very intelligent and only seemed interested in getting to the gelks. It must have picked up their scent while it was still in the forest."

"I suppose we're lucky it didn't decide to dine on any of our crewmen as appetizers. The species hasn't developed a taste for our flesh yet, but we can't count on that protecting us for long. When there aren't any gelks around, they might decide to see how we taste. Judging from the rows of sharp teeth in its jaws and the way that it moved towards the gelks, it's undoubtedly a carnivore. As soon as our crewmen are looked after, we have to start preparing a defensive perimeter against attack by these things." Under his breath, Admiral Vroman said, "I knew things were going too well here."

With much effort, crewmen dragged the six-meter-long creature to the center of the camp for study. Life slowly returned to normal and engineers began making repairs to the corral and farm fencing. The gelks had quieted down as soon as the monster was dead but used the limits of their corral to remain as far away from it as possible.

"It appears to be reptilian," Lt. Croff, the crewman with the greatest knowledge of paleontology said as he examined the creature. "Or at least what we would define as reptilian. The closest Terran creature that I'm familiar with might be the dinosaur Alioramus Remotus, an early member of the Asian

Tyrannosauridae family in Earth's distant past, although this one is about a meter longer than those were reputed to be. Ours disappeared on Earth by the end of the Cretaceous period, about 66 million years ago."

"A dinosaur?" Admiral Vroman said.

"Well, this planet's equivalent. We can't assume this world or any other is on an equal evolutionary path with Earth. The gelks are obviously familiar with this species, or they wouldn't have been so panicked when it moved towards them."

"Which indicates that there may be many more of these things out there?"

"Or even worse creatures, posing greater dangers. We haven't even explored a miniscule part of this world yet. I just hope we don't encounter any of this guy's bigger relatives. I doubt we could have brought down a Tyrannosaurus Rex with the ease that we felled this small fellow."

"Small?"

"In dinosaur terms, six meters and one ton is small. Tyrannosaurus Rex could be up to twelve and a half meters long, stand six meters high, and weigh up to seven tons. Fortunately, the really large dinosaurs were herbivores on Earth; I hope that's the case here."

"What else do you think we can expect?"

"Impossible to say, sir. This isn't Earth and we can't apply our knowledge of Earth's history to what we might find here. We haven't seen any indication that this world is in anything like our own Cretaceous period. This may be the only creature of its type on this planet, just as alligators, crocodiles, a few snake species, and Komodo dragons are the only very large reptile species to have survived on Earth. But I'm confident that where you find one of these creatures, obviously well fed and healthy, you'll find a lot more. That's simple logic."

"I agree." Speculatively, Admiral Vroman added, "Do you think this thing is edible?"

"I don't see why not. But its flesh should be tested before any of it is eaten."

"Okay, let's get this thing skinned and butchered," Admiral Vroman said to the hunters who were standing around the beast. "Maybe it'll taste better than the gelk we've been eating."

Chapter Seven
~ May 5th, 2279 ~

The *Scorpion*, with Vyx at the helm, approached the planet Scruscotto slowly. A busy mining planet with no approach or departure control was not the place to be lax, and Vyx's senses were at full alert. He had nearly wound up as a bow ornament on a large freighter here once, and that near miss had used up all the good luck he ever expected to have when negotiating heavy traffic at Scruscotto.

He'd planned the arrival time so they'd be landing at Weislik during the slowest traffic time of the day. Although it was the planet's largest colony, third-shift miners would be mid-shift, and most of the residents would be asleep. Planetary arrivals and departures occurred around the clock, but just prior to dawn at any colony was the slowest time for takeoffs and landings at the local spaceports.

After setting the ship down on the assigned pad, Vyx sat in the pilot's seat and relaxed. Brenda Cardiz sat in the co-pilot chair and silently watched Vyx. She had been with him long enough to know not to bother him until he moved. Not that he would have lashed out or anything, he just wouldn't respond to questions until the tension of landing at an uncontrolled colony had fully dissipated. He and the rest of his team, consisting of Cardiz, Nelligen, Byers, and Earlich, would start work after grabbing a few hours' rest.

When he was once again unwound, Vyx walked to the spaceport office and paid the pad rent for a full week. Even at this hour, the office held a collection of colony denizens whose job it was to note all arrivals and departures for various information brokers. Vyx, already well known among this group in the colony, returned the nods of several who knew him as a smuggler and illegal weapons trader. After completing all the necessary paperwork, he returned to his ship.

By mid-afternoon, the five agents were well rested and ready to begin their day. Splitting up into their usual two teams, they set off to learn every bit of information about the Milori that was floating around this colony. They had discussed the mission at length during the month-long voyage and all knew their assignments and assigned territories.

Vyx and Byers headed directly to the tavern that had more or less become their defacto headquarters when on Scruscotto. If anyone had pertinent information to sell and heard that they were buying, they'd come looking for them there. The first shift at the mine had just gotten off work, so business at the tavern was starting to pick up. Their usual table was unoccupied, so they settled in and ordered a couple of ales. Over the next few hours, half a dozen acquaintances visited them and welcomed them back after their year-and-a-half absence, but no one had any information about Milori operating in the area. Vyx and Byers knew it would take time for the word to spread that they were willing to pay for information about Milori sightings. If they were patient, the information might come to them.

Remaining at the tavern through the supper hour, and even ordering a meal there instead of going to one of the restaurants that served better fare, Vyx and Byers were finally rewarded with a visit from the individual they'd most hoped to meet tonight. Before their greasy meal had even begun repeating on them, Ker Blasperra approached the table. Displaying the usual toothy grin of his species, the tall, gaunt, Hominidae-like Wolkerron with yellow skin and large black eyes said, "Trader, welcome back to Scruscotto. You also Mr. Byers. Might I sit down?"

"Of course, Ker," Vyx said. "We've been waiting for you."

"Naturally, Trader," he said, after sitting down. "As soon as I'd learned of your arrival, I notified my banker to process your payment. Here is your draft." He pushed an envelope across the table.

Vyx opened the envelope and looked in. The sole content was a certified bank draft for five hundred thousand credits.

"Thank you, Ker. It's been a pleasure doing business with you."

"Likewise, Trader. The client was most pleased with your delivery and the excellent health of the delivered mamots. I understand that he has already moved the entire consignment. Unfortunately, the government is making noises about legalizing the import of mamots, so interest in smuggling the furry little creatures has dropped off considerably. No one wants to get stuck with a large consignment of the animals if they become legal to import because the selling price would drop precipitously to a fraction of its current high."

"I understand, Ker. I already have something else in the works anyway."

"Anything I might assist you with?"

"Perhaps. I'm looking for Milori again."

"Milori? I understood that Space Command sent them packing back to their own empire."

"They didn't go, at least not completely. I've learned that a number of ships have remained hidden in this sector and the surrounding sectors."

"I admit I have heard a few rumors, but I dismissed it as bad information."

"I would be willing to pay handsomely for information about their whereabouts that proves reliable."

"Handsomely?" Ker Blasperra asked, suddenly becoming very interested. "How handsomely?"

"If the information proves accurate, I'll pay a thousand credits for the first report about any location."

"That *is* a very handsome sum for such a trivial bit of information. One might wonder why you'd be willing to pay so well for information such as that. One might think you were in the employ of Space Command, especially after you hired so many freighters to participate in Admiral Carver's plan to deceive the Milori into withdrawing from the Frontier Zone a couple of years ago."

"Space Command pays very well for information and assistance. Knowing what they want and who will pay is the trick to doing business with them or anyone else. I can verify that Space Command credits spend every bit as well as any

I've ever earned through smuggling, but I've never informed on a fellow smuggler."

"If you do get a reputation as being a Space Command informant, life could become very precarious around here. The Raiders frequent many of these colonies."

"I have no particular love for Space Command, and I'm as careful with what I tell them, or do for them, as I am with all my other business dealings. But I have no regrets when it concerns keeping the Milori out of Galactic Alliance space. This is *our* backyard and I don't like the Empire thinking we'll stand for their taking over. I'm sure I don't have to tell you how unhealthy it would suddenly become in our business if this was to become Milori territory. The Milori have no use for humans, or human-like species, to begin with and wouldn't hesitate to kill any of us in the blink of an eye."

"Quite so, Trader, quite so."

"At least Space Command demands definite proof of illegal activity before arresting you. And arrest doesn't mean automatic and immediate execution, as it does with the Milori."

"I see your point, Trader. Forgive my earlier remarks; I would also very much dislike seeing this become Milori territory. I'll check with my contacts and see if I can learn anything about a Milori presence in these sectors."

"Okay, Ker. Remember, the fee is only payable for the *first* report of any verifiable location, so timing is key."

"I'll remember. Good evening, Trader. Mr. Byers."

Vyx and his team remained at Weislik for a full week before moving on to one of the other major mining colonies on the planet. Vyx rented a shuttle and paid three more weeks pad rent at the Space Port instead of moving his small transport. They'd transmitted all reports of Milori sightings to Stewart within hours of receiving them, relying on Space Command to determine the veracity of the informants. Vyx paid out fifty credits for each report with the promise that the rest would be paid, but only when and if the information proved accurate. Most of the informants would have sold out their mother for a thousand credits, so selling information about Milori didn't create any misplaced twinges of conscience.

* * *

"We have eighteen different reports regarding hidden locations of Milori ships in our sectors," Jenetta said to the eighteen ship captains assembled around the table in the large conference room. Except for Jenetta and the captains, only her aide, Lt. Commander Lori Ashraf, and Captain Benjamin Lofgren, the head of Intelligence at Stewart, were present for the meeting. "Because of the sensitivity of this information, I've kept it a close secret until the nearest eighteen ships could arrive back here. We've known since the Milori attacked the *Lisbon* that they still have ships in Galactic Alliance space, but we haven't released that information except to certain high-ranking individuals. We've since learned that thirty of their newest and fastest ships broke away from the retreating fleet and traveled independently to places of concealment within our borders. We've had months to round up all the Raider spotters we could find and replace them with our own people, and we're now ready to take on any Milori ships we can locate."

"Who's provided these reports, Admiral?" Captain Cyndee Pasqua of the GSC Destroyer *Chicago* asked.

"Our intelligence operatives have secured the leads from miners, traders, smugglers, and other assorted space— travelers. We've purchased the information, so the reliability is questionable, but it's the best we have. If the Milori spot us while we're setting up this operation, I expect they'll attempt to notify the other ships, which will then immediately travel to alternate secret locations. This is both good and bad—bad because we might miss them, but good because there's a chance the ones we don't know about will also attempt to move and they may be spotted by the people we've placed in the former Raider spotter ships. The Milori ships will be easy to identify because of their speed. Ships moving beyond Light-262 can only be ours, Raider ships, or Milori ships."

"When will the attacks commence, Admiral?" Captain William Payton of the GSC Battleship *Thor* asked.

80

"Just as soon as we can get everyone in place. I've sent the ships unable to get here in time for this meeting directly to rendezvous points without explanation. To avoid the slightest chance of having this information leak, I didn't include it in the orders to the ship's captains. You'll leave here today and travel to the RPs where you'll personally brief the other captains of your battle group. You should brief no one else, except your first officers, before then. The most senior captain in each group will lead the attack in a simultaneous operation with all other attack groups. Using space tugs because of their small DeTect signature, we'll first place IDS jamming satellites at maximum distance around the perimeter to prevent the Milori from contacting other ships. We'll then position electronic barrier equipment in the hope that we can shut down their Light Drive engines if they try to escape. As soon as you activate the equipment, you'll move in, using coded RF communications for coordination. If the Milori ships are where we expect them to be, they'll probably attempt to build an envelope as soon as they detect your presence. If they haven't deactivated their ACS, it will shut down their FTL drive and cancel their envelope. They'll have to rebuild it again. That will give us at least four minutes to disable their temporal envelope generator. At the very least, we should have a window of at least two minutes from the point where they detect our presence. We have to move in fast and strike them hard. With at least three warships at each location, the odds should be on our side this time, if the Milori ships are alone."

The captains around the table were silent as they digested the plan. Jenetta waited for a couple of minutes before saying, "I'll assume from your silence that no one objects or wishes to suggest an alternate plan, so let's cover the specifics."

Over the next ten minutes, she gave each Captain the reported coordinates of the Milori ship that he or she would be attempting to capture or destroy. She specified where the group would wait until the space tugs placed the electronic barrier equipment and the simple code phrase that would include the time the operation was set to begin. She wouldn't establish and transmit the attack time until all ships had arrived at their RPs and communicated that fact to Stewart. When she was done, she asked if there were any questions.

"Just one," Captain Simon Pope of the *Geneva* said. "What happens if we're spotted by the enemy? Do we give chase?"

"Yes. You probably won't be able to catch them, but you should try. I'm sure they'll expect you to give chase and we don't want to disappoint them just yet. Break off after you lose contact. Anything else?"

Jenetta waited for ten seconds and then said, "Okay, let's send them to hell if they won't surrender."

All eighteen ships left Stewart SCB within two hours of the meeting's conclusion. There had been a sense of eager anticipation and perhaps a little nervousness in the air as they left the conference room. Supply crewmen had given the ships requiring provisions top priority during the meeting and they were ready for departure by the time their captains returned. Jenetta stood at the SimWindow in her office and watched them move out of the port, all the time wishing she were going with them. She hated sending people out to face danger while she remained safe back at the base. She knew that some of those aboard the fifty-eight ships participating in this effort might not be returning. She would have committed a larger part of the forces available to her, but the other ships had been too far away and the information too time sensitive, so the others were allowed to continue their regular patrol routes while the selected ships prepared to engage the enemy.

There was little to do now except wait. Some of the ships wouldn't reach their RPs for up to twenty days, and then it would take another day to reach the deployment point once Jenetta gave the order to proceed.

* * *

"I don't like it," Admiral Hubera said gruffly to the other members of the Admiralty Board. "I don't like it one bit. Pulling over fifty ships off patrol is the same sort of irresponsible behavior that she exhibited when she counter-manded orders and sent the battleship *Thor* off looking for three missing agents, thereby putting the entire base in jeopardy when the Raiders attacked Stewart."

"There was no way she could have foreseen that attack, and the lives of three brave individuals were in danger," Admiral Platt said. "Besides which, this is totally different, Donald. We can't just ignore thirty enemy warships secreted inside our inner border."

"We have no proof that there are thirty ships. We're being asked to accept that a government, with whom we have no formal diplomatic relations, made such a claim in an alleged report from a source who will only communicate with Admiral Carver. For all we know, the individual sending the information is in the employ of the Milori. They may just want us out chasing fictitious ships so they can attack our bases while they're relatively unprotected."

"Donald," Admiral Hillaire said, "we've seen the video log from the *Lisbon*. Those were definitely Milori warships attacking our destroyer, not fictitious ships."

"We saw three ships, Arnold, only three. What if that's all there are in our space?"

"Then our bases are in little danger," Admiral Bradlee said, "and sending these ships out to look for the Milori risks little. But what if the reports are true? Can we afford to sit back and do nothing, allowing the enemy to take up positions in our territory?"

"Admiral Carver is doing the right thing, in my opinion," Admiral Plimley said. "She's only allocated half her forces to this operation, while allowing the other half to continue their patrols. It's better to fight these enemy ships now, singly or in small groups, than after they've assembled for a full assault."

"I've told Admiral Carver she has my full faith and confidence," Admiral Moore said. "I meant it when I said it and I see no reason to change. She's out there taking the fight to the enemy and doing a damn fine job of it under very trying conditions. She's proven herself to be a very competent and effective leader, and she deserves our full support."

"She should be out looking for Admiral Vroman and the crew of the *Lisbon*," Admiral Hubera said.

"I'm sure every ship in her command has orders to watch for any sign of the Admiral and our missing crew," Admiral Burke said. "I'm also willing to bet that Admiral Carver is hoping to learn something from any Milora she might capture in this operation. What more can she be doing, Donald?"

Admiral Hubera simply leaned back in his chair and muttered something unintelligible under his breath before saying clearly, "You all have too much confidence in this child. You mark my words; her reckless behavior in spreading her forces all over our Frontier sectors will be responsible for the greatest loss of life Space Command has ever experienced."

* * *

Despite the fact that they had seen no dinosaurs since the one attack, the crewmembers of the *Lisbon* couldn't seem to stop looking over their shoulders. The hunters had found numerous recent tracks outside the pass leading into the valley, but it was impossible to tell if they were from the Alioramus that had found its way in or from others.

They had built huge, palisade barricades with double rows of sharpened logs positioned upwards for defense. The first row rose forty-five degrees from horizontal, with the second row set to about seventy degrees. Placed where the pass emptied into the valley, they would hopefully prevent any creature larger than a gelk from passing. Any Alioramus trying to get through would impale itself, as had happened with the first creature, but the thickness of the shafts of the logs guaranteed they would never break with any creature weighing less than five tons. Guards patrolled each pass into the valley around the clock and crude horns had been fashioned for use as a warning system.

The meat of the first dinosaur had proven far too oily to eat, but an engineer discovered he could extract the oil if he ground up the flesh and pressed it. The extract burned cleanly, with just the slightest hint of a smell. When a cook added a ground-up, aromatic herb he'd found in the nearby forest, the smell became pleasantly fragrant and made the oil ideal to fuel lamps. Gelk bladders full of the oil were stored for later use, and the bones made good weapons and tools once the remaining flesh had been stripped clean. The hide was extremely tough, so it became outer protective clothing for the hunters whose clothes had taken a real beating as they passed through the heavy brush and undergrowth in the forest.

Efforts to domesticate the gelks had shown some progress, and the animals now remained calm when the handlers entered the corral, even accepting food directly, but it might be a long time before they would be tame enough for training to pull a plow. Based on the progress to date, Admiral Vroman decided they should begin breeding the animals, so the hunters set out to capture more alive. One of the crewmen responsible for working with the gelks suggested they train them to provide transportation, just as horses and camels had once been used on Earth. A saddle and bridle was fashioned, and, in an adjoining corral, the bronco busting commenced in earnest.

Few of the *Lisbon* crew had ever ridden a horse, but several had grown up in the western portions of North America or the central plains areas of South America where recreational horseback riding was still a part of normal life. It took fifteen minutes to get a bridle on the gelk and another hour to get it saddled, but it was finally ready for the experiment. Within seconds, the gelk ejected the first hardy souls who attempted a ride. But then Chief Petty Officer Josh Cody of Oklahoma got an opportunity to try. Chief Cody had once bragged he was a direct descendant of the famous buffalo hunter and showman, William 'Buffalo Bill' Cody, but the claim had met with some skepticism by crewmates. The female gelk, named Crusher because she had almost crushed a crewman to death against the side of the corral soon after her capture, eyed Cody warily as handlers held her steady in the center of the corral so he could mount. When released, Crusher started to spin and buck immediately. The three handlers ran for the corral walls, climbing to the top rail to get well out of the way.

The gelk twisted, turned, and bucked with all her strength, but Cody hung on as if glued to the saddle. Slowly, as the animal tired, the jerking movements became less violent and then just stopped, the gelk remaining perfectly still in the center of the corral except for its heaving chest. A cheer went up among the crewmen watching the historic event, but the gelk hadn't given up just yet and it suddenly exploded in a new round of twisting and bucking. It attempted to dislodge the rider for several more minutes but finally realized the futility of the action and surrendered it's free will to that of the rider. Cody tugged gently on the bridle while lightly kicking the animal in its haunches until the gelk got the idea and started moving around the corral. Rather than dismounting immediately, Cody stayed in the saddle until the animal understood what he wanted, and by the end of ten minutes, the gelk was loping around the corral with Cody grinning proudly at the amazed spectators.

The three handlers jumped down to hold the animal as Cody reined her in, but Cody waved them away and dismounted without problem. The animal was panting hard after the run around the corral, but it seemed to have suddenly lost its uneasiness around the handlers. She sensed the rider wasn't going to injure her as long as she cooperated, and that feeling now extended to the handlers.

The handlers immediately saddled and bridled the other gelk and potential broncobusters tried their hand at duplicating Cody's feat. The gelk tossed each off within a minute. Cody, after an hour's rest, mounted the gelk, a male named Thrasher, and showed the animal who was master. Thrasher was gently loping around the corral, as Crusher had, within ten minutes of Cody climbing into the saddle. With both gelks now saddle broken, it was expected that with a bit of training they could be used to round up other gelks, both inside and outside the valley. The breeding effort would still go forth to improve upon desirable traits and breed out those less desirable in future generations. Admiral Vroman realized he was admitting to himself that they might be on the planet for many years, but it was necessary to think that way if they were to survive. If they just sat around waiting for rescue, they would surely perish.

A week later, the two gelks provided riders with a first lope around the camp. The hunters had already managed to trap another female and bring it back alive, but it would be a couple of weeks before anyone attempted to break it. Once the new gelk became familiar with the corral and began to trust the handlers, Cody would again exhibit his bronco-busting expertise. The presence of the two original gelks would help considerably as they now stood perfectly at ease when around the handlers.

That same afternoon, the camp celebrated the completion of a mill powered by the stream that ran alongside the camp. They'd now be able to grind their flour easily instead of using the difficult process of hand grinding every ounce. It would be a tremendous time and energy saver, not to mention providing a finer flour that didn't taste the least bit gritty. Perhaps one day they'd be able to use the stream's abundant power for manufacturing cloth and other processes. Water diverted from the stream already irrigated the fields and provided running water in the mess hall and lavatory facilities.

The discovery a few days later of a plant, the leaves of which had flax-like properties, was another cause for celebration. At last they'd have new garments to replace the tattered remnants of clothing everyone had been wearing since arriving on Siena, although it would be weeks before they would manage to spin the fibers into yarn. And they still needed to construct a loom for producing cloth from the yarn.

It was less than an hour since sundown and most of the crewmen were still in the mess shelter enjoying their evening meal and their respite from the day's work when the emergency horn at the South Pass sounded. The building cleared quickly as everyone ran for weapons. The pattern of the signal indicated the danger was extreme, and everyone assumed that another dinosaur was at the barricade. As they ran to the South Pass and the defense of the settlement, they brought their heaviest spears and arrows.

Admiral Vroman, being the oldest member in the camp, was the last to arrive at the South Pass. The sight that greeted him in the flickering light from half a dozen raging bonfires made his stomach churn and his blood run cold. It wasn't another dinosaur threatening the safety of the camp; it was an entire *herd* of dinosaurs.

Chapter Eight
~ June 3rd, 2279 ~

Several dinosaurs, larger than the one that had previously attacked the base, hung impaled on the deadly, sharpened logs of the double-palisade barricade when Admiral Vroman arrived. Others were trying to climb over their still-twitching bodies to enter the valley. The weight of the latter dinosaurs pushed the first ones further down on the poles, impaling the dinosaurs climbing on their backs. Smaller, perhaps younger, dinosaurs had made it between the poles, and crewmembers were jabbing at them with spears to drive them back while the dinosaurs snapped at them with deadly jaws and spun to use the whip-like power of their tails. Several of the smaller dinosaurs had already fallen, but not before imposing a deadly toll on *Lisbon* crewmembers. Wounded fighters were carried away from the melee by their fellows, while reinforcements filled the vacated positions. Everyone knew they couldn't allow a single dinosaur to get past. One crewmember with a laser pistol could have beaten back the attack by themselves, but clubs, bows, arrows, and spears were all they had for this fight.

The fight raged on for more than half an hour. After running out of spears, the fighters retrieved as many as possible from the bodies of fallen creatures, and Admiral Vroman yelled orders that no more be thrown. The fighters used them only to jab at the dinosaurs still trying to enter the valley. The archers, out of arrows, threw rocks.

The intelligence of the dinosaurs wasn't equal to their ferocity, and they continued their assault on the barricade despite the heavy losses the herd was suffering. Just when it seemed that they would breach the barricade, they retreated. Many carried severe wounds, spears, or arrows as reminders of their effort. The crew of the *Lisbon* would have celebrated, but far too many of their number were down. In case this was merely a retreat to regroup, Admiral Vroman ordered half his force to hurry out beyond the barricade and retrieve as many spears and arrows as possible. Large dinosaurs still hung on the poles, thrashing and kicking in a futile attempt to dislodge themselves, and Admiral Vroman ordered the rest of the standing force to finish them off. Standing beyond the reach of snapping jaws and teeth, flailing legs, and whipping tails, the crewmen sunk their spears into the creatures repeatedly until the dinosaurs stopped moving.

The next step was going to be more difficult. They had to remove the dinosaur bodies so the posts would again function as a barricade. They tried pushing them up and off with poles, but it was useless without block and tackle. In the end, the task fell to the hunters who climbed atop the bodies and hacked the dinosaurs to pieces with stone axes until the remains fell from the post under its own weight. They then dragged the pieces of carcass between the barricades so the dinosaurs could neither use the mass to climb on, nor draw the dinosaurs back to feast on the remains if they were cannibalistic.

Severely injured crewmembers were carried back to the camp, while the walking wounded were bandaged and allowed to remain at the pass. Wood for new bonfires was stacked in preparation for when the dinosaur herd returned.

At first light, the carnage at the pass presented a sickening reminder of the previous night's battle. The only positive thing was that the remaining herd of dinosaurs hadn't returned during the night. Blood was pooled in places around the barricade where the ground was too saturated to accept more. Thankfully, most of it was dinosaur blood. Admiral Vroman decided that after cleaning the area, half the force should go get some sleep. Two-wheeled carts brought from the camp were loaded with dinosaur carcasses and hauled back to the butchering area.

After six hours' sleep, the rested crewmen relieved the people at the pass. There hadn't been any sign of the dinosaur herd survivors. The crewmembers who had remained at the pass had used torches to burn the blood and tiny pieces of flesh from the impaling posts, then sharpened the tips again. Rather than having the relief crew simply standing around the pass, Captain Lindahl gave permission to begin the butchering work on the carcasses. Clouds of flies, attracted by the blood, were already becoming a serious nuisance. As had been done with the earlier Alioramus, they ground the flesh, then pressed and filtered it to extract the oil for lamps. They wound up with so much oil that they didn't have enough gelk bladders to hold it all, so they borrowed all the earthenware pots and jugs they could find. They stretched intestine across the top and secured it with tendons.

As often happens, valuable information was discovered by pure chance. One of the butchers, covered in dinosaur blood, walked down to the river to wash it off instead of using the washbasins. As he stood in the shallows rinsing himself off, fish began to collect around him, nibbling at his blood-soaked clothes. He quickly backed out of the water but wisely called to one of the fishermen, who tried a piece of dino flesh as bait. Each time a fisherman dropped a bent-nail hook into the water with a tiny piece of dino flesh, fish swarmed the line, each trying to be the first to swallow the bait. Such serendipitous occurrences could make a tremendous difference in the lives of those wise enough to recognize them when they occurred.

"It's been three days," Admiral Vroman said during the breakfast staff meeting. "It doesn't appear they're coming back. We were lucky they broke off their attack when they did; they were almost among us."

Lt. Croff stopped eating and said, "Actually, I'm surprised they attacked at all at that hour. I doubt they could have sustained an attack much longer."

"What do you mean?"

"Based on what I've observed, I placed the beasts in a reptilian category. On Earth, reptiles rely on the sun to warm their body, unlike warm-blooded animals. When the sun goes down, they slow down. They might have been extremely anxious to get past the barricade before their body temperature dropped too far. They probably found a place in the pass to spend the night not far from the barricade."

"Then the logical conclusion is that they would have returned in the morning for another assault."

"Yes, logically, but we haven't studied them, so their behavior is totally unknown. Perhaps the loss of so many alpha leaders in their herd caused confusion and they're still trying to determine who to follow."

"Why did they fight so hard trying to get in here in the first place?" Admiral Vroman asked.

"They might be migrating in advance of colder weather. Perhaps this valley has been part of their migration path for centuries, or even millennia."

"And the first one that came into the valley? Do you think it was a scout of sorts?"

"I doubt it. We can't attribute that kind of intelligence to these creatures. Perhaps it was just one that was separated from the herd and continued on while the others laid up somewhere for several days to eat and rest. It's fortunate it happened because it prompted us to build the barricades at each pass into the valley."

"Yes, and even with the barricades we barely kept them at bay. We'll have to improve our fortifications and it's time we stepped up our efforts to build a forge. We can't rely on stone axes and stone-tipped spears and arrows any longer. We need steel for spears, swords, axes, plows, and a multitude of other things."

"We still have several crates of nails left," Lt. Pyers said. We could melt them down and use them for other purposes until we can set up a smelting operation."

"But then we'd expend ten times the effort making nails again later and it's doubtful that we could make them to the tolerances required for use in the nailers. No, let's concentrate on working from raw materials. Our geologist, Lt. Rimes, has found iron ore sand in a dry riverbed near the cliff wall on the other side of the valley. Our first step is to cut a road through the forest, then set up a smelter operation to remove the slag and create the iron blooms. There's plenty of firewood nearby to make charcoal for the smelting process. We'll set up the foundry over here where we can use the stream to provide power for a bellows and trip hammer. We're about to move out of the Stone Age and into the Iron Age."

"We're skipping the Bronze Age, Admiral?" Captain Lindahl said jokingly.

"If anyone can find deposits of copper and tin nearby, I'd love to add bronze to our available materials list." Smiling, he added, "I'd love to get some razor blades and be clean shaven again."

After breakfast, the Admiral visited the shelter temporarily turned into a hospital ward. He already knew sixteen crewmen had died of wounds received while fighting the dinosaurs.

"How are they doctor?" he asked of the chief medical officer.

"We have no plasma on hand, but we've been able to get enough donors to fill our blood supply needs with whole blood. The medical supplies left by the Milori have been barely adequate to halt infection, but we're getting by. Several will be laid up for months, and many are permanently disfigured unless rescue comes. In a properly equipped medical bay with a good supply of surgical nano-bots, we'd have everyone on their feet in thirty days."

"I understand. Space Command will find us eventually. I'm sure Admiral Carver is turning over her entire command area searching for us. Make them as comfortable as you can."

A burial ceremony for the deceased crewmembers was held a couple of days later because there was no way to preserve the bodies, and they were beginning to decompose quickly. The entire camp attended, except for guards at the two passes.

* * *

Vyx stood staring in disbelief at his ship, the *Scorpion*, or rather what was left of it. Several frame sections of the fuselage were missing, and what remained was charred and melted beyond recognition. You couldn't actually call it a ship anymore. It was just a few hundred tons of worthless scrap metal now.

"Quite a fireworks show," the spaceport administrator said. "Damn good thing we have reinforced blast walls between pads or it could have taken out a dozen other ships."

"You say they were Tsgardi?"

"Yep, all nine bodies. Don't know how many others there might have been; we only found nine. Even at that, we're sort of guessing. I suppose I should say that we found enough *parts* for nine bodies."

"Any idea why they were messing with my ship?"

"No. I thought you might know. Tsgardis don't usually get involved in vandalism or petty theft."

"Perhaps they were trying to steal my ship. That's hardly petty theft."

"Even Tsgardi should know that most ships here have theft-prevention devices, although they don't usually blow with the force we saw from yours."

"Tsgardis aren't known for their intelligence, but this reaches new heights in stupidity."

"How do you want to handle the damage?"

"Just have it towed to the nearest scrap yard; it's worthless to me."

"No, I meant the damages to other ships."

"Didn't you just say the blast walls protected them?"

"It protected them from the blast but not the debris that came raining back down."

"How much are we talking about?"

The administrator looked at the invoice on his electronic pad. "A hundred twenty-seven thousand credits."

Vyx looked the administrator sharply. "What?"

"A hundred..."

"I heard the amount," Vyx said loudly, interrupting the administrator. "I just didn't believe my ears."

"Four other ships were damaged, one quite extensively. They've been working on it for four days trying to make it space-worthy again. That's where the largest share of the credits will go. They estimate it will be another two weeks before the work is completed."

"Which ship?"

"The one on that pad," the administrator said, pointing. "It's called the *Whirm*. The owner is a trader from Eulosi. Our adjusters checked the damage. They agree it was the result of debris raining back down from your ship after the explosion, so the expenses are justified. Ten thousand of the credits will be used to repair and repaint the blast walls, rip up the destroyed plasticrete pad, and pour a new one."

"Okay," Vyx said, sighing. "I authorize you to charge my account for that amount." He held up his hand and pressed his thumb onto the ID circle of the administrator's electronic pad.

"Very good, Trader. Uh, what will you do now? I know of a couple of good ships that are available. I could direct you for a small finder's fee."

"Thanks, but I don't want to even think about it tonight. I'll let you know."

"Yes, sir. I'm at your service any time."

The administrator turned and left the landing pad, leaving Vyx to stare at the remains of his ship. After a few minutes, Vyx became aware that someone else was standing next to him.

"It's a shame," Brenda said. "Who could have done such a thing?"

"I did."

"What? You did this? Why?"

"The ship was rigged with explosives in case anyone tried to break in, remember?"

"Yes, but I thought you meant a small explosion designed to kill the intruder."

"I guess I used more explosives than necessary. The intent was both to make the ship incapable of take-off and destroy the cargo hold in case it contained weapons."

"You certainly accomplished that, but who was trying to break in?"

"The port administrator said they found enough body parts for nine Tsgardis. If they were all standing close to the ship, I suppose it could have been as many as two dozen."

"But why?"

"It might have been Recozzi's family. Recozzi is a criminal I arrested about nine years ago. Seven years ago, I killed his brother on Gollasko when he attacked me. They've sworn a blood feud against me, and the family's had enough time now to get here from their home planet."

"The whole family would come looking for you?"

"At least the male members; that's the way it is with the Tsgardi. It makes no difference that Recozzi was guilty of a crime and that a Galactic Alliance court sentenced him to his punishment. The family blames me as the arresting officer and also blames me for killing Recozzi's brother when he attempted to kill me in cold blood."

"Will this be the end of it?"

"I don't know how many came or were killed. It's certainly going to slow them down, but they'll no doubt blame me for their new losses. Their home world is a thousand light-years from here, so that makes their roundtrip travel time six to eight years."

"It's a shame," Brenda said, again looking at what remained of the *Scorpion*. "I'm going to miss that little ship. Especially the cozy spot you prepared for us in the hold."

Vyx smiled as he turned to look at her. "Next ship we'll make a better love nest."

Brenda returned the smile and took his hand. "How about a nice warm shower at the hotel? I'm feeling a little dirty after seeing this mess. We'll have a meal sent up to the room and not come out until noon tomorrow."

"You're on." He took one last sad look at his former ship, sighed, then left the pad with Brenda. Since their first job together, they'd been exploring their mutual feelings and interests. Byers, Nelligen, and Kathryn, who'd been standing nearby, followed, but would have to get their own rooms at the hotel.

"What now?" Nels asked during lunch the next day.

"We get another ship," Vyx answered after chewing the food in his mouth and swallowing.

"Do we have enough credits?" Byers asked.

"Not for anything as large as the *Scorpion*, but we can get a ship. We'll still have about eight hundred thousand credits left after setting aside enough to pay the informants who provided leads to the Milori and paying for the damages to the *Whirm*."

"What about Carver?" Brenda asked.

Vyx looked at her. "You mean get a ship from Stewart?"

"Why not? You've done it before."

"Hmmm, that's a possibility, if they have anything that might be suitable. The last time we were there, the pickings were slim. The Admiral had sent all the small ships out to function as spotter ships."

"Then take something bigger."

"If we get too big we can't land. We'd have to leave the ship in orbit and take a shuttle down to the surface."

"What's wrong with that?" she asked.

"For one thing, it leaves your ship undefended, unless someone stays aboard."

"Doesn't that make it less susceptible to tampering than a ship on the ground would be? Just rig an anti-tampering charge as you did on the *Scorpion*. I think people will take your warning seriously now," she said, smiling.

He smiled back. "You're probably right. I doubt if anyone will try getting into any ship of mine for quite awhile. That doesn't really apply to the Tsgardi, of course. They never learn their lessons. But that still leaves the other problem: a large ship is harder to conceal and a bigger target. In the past, I've simply landed on a moon or planet to hide from my enemies, but I couldn't have done that in a large ship. When I borrowed the *Maid of Mephad* from Admiral Carver to move the shipment of illegal weapons for Shev Rivemwilth, we had to leave it in orbit and shuttle the ordnance up to it for loading. Like Rivemwilth said, it was like a huge sign proclaiming 'Secret Base Located Here.'"

"Yes, I can see that being a problem," Brenda said. "Well then, we'll just have to a find a ship that can land."

"That leaves us back where we started. I suppose before we consider leaving Scruscotto, I should check out what's available here. The spaceport administrator said he knew of some available ships; let's check them out this afternoon. You never know, we might find someone who's desperate enough to sell their ship for a song."

* * *

"We're approaching the deployment point, Captain," the helmsman of the *Thor* said.

"All ahead slow. Stop when we reach the coordinates. Tactical, where are the *Berlin* and *Atlanta*?"

"Just off our stern, larboard and starboard, Captain. Both ships are slowing also."

"Com, notify the shuttle bay that the tugs responsible for placing the IDS band-jamming satellites and the electronic barricade equipment should commence operations as soon as we drop our envelope. Notify the *Berlin* and *Atlanta* as well, using a narrow laser beam."

"Aye, Captain," the com operator said. A few seconds later, he added, "Messages sent and receipt acknowledged, Captain."

Captain Payton relaxed in his bridge chair to await the conclusion of the first stage.

Several hours later, the com operator said, "The *Berlin* and *Atlanta* report their space tugs have returned. They're ready for stage two, Captain."

Payton looked down at the small monitor mounted on the left arm of his chair. The chronometer showed that it was not yet time for the coordinated attack to begin. It was imperative that all eighteen task groups move in on their targets at the same time.

Some eighty minutes later, Payton looked at the tactical officer and nodded. The *Thor's* tugs had returned over an hour earlier. The nod to the tactical officer was a signal to activate the jamming satellites and electronic barricade equipment. "Com, advise the *Berlin* and *Atlanta* that we're commencing the attack following the established battle plan. Helm, engage."

The helmsmen entered the commands and the enormous battleship surged forward. They were ten billion kilometers from the reported location of the Milori ship, well outside the range of even the most sensitive scanners, but at Light-275 they would close the distance to the target in a few minutes.

Jenetta sat in the Combat Information Center at Stewart anxiously waiting for the first reports from her captains sent to find the hidden Milori warships. Several days ago, she had established the time for the coordinated action to commence once all ships reported they'd reached their initial rendezvous locations five trillion kilometers from the reported positions of their Milori targets. By now, they had sprung their traps and Stewart should begin to receive reports any time. No doubt, some would be reporting that no enemy ships were at the locations provided by the informants, but with any luck they'd bag at least a couple.

Jenetta was on her fourth mug of coffee when the first report came in. The captain of the *Calgary*, Captain Charles Hoyt, reported finding no Milori at the target location. That didn't bother Jenetta, but over the next several hours they received three more messages from task groups who also hadn't encountered any Milori ships at the reported location. Jenetta began to wonder if they had a leak in the command structure, and the Milori had learned that a surprise attack was set to begin.

Fourteen hours passed before Stewart received the first report of contact with the enemy. The *Thor* and its two companion ships had encountered a Milori ship exactly where it was supposed to be. They had set their electronic gear before moving in and the plan had worked as scripted. The Milori had tried to run but couldn't engage their FTL Drive. Before they could deactivate their ACS and build a new envelope, gunners aboard the *Thor* had destroyed their temporal generator. After that it had become a simple shoot-out, with all ships firing for all they were worth. The Milori ship, almost as outnumbered as the *Lisbon* had been, had taken a real pounding from the Space Command ships, while the SC ships escaped without major damage. The new Phalanx weapon system prevented any torpedoes from getting through and damage was limited to laser hits. In a more evenly matched fight, torpedoes might have breached the defense, but the battle was over so quickly that it hadn't been much of a test for the new weapon system. No one had been anxious to give the new system any more of a test than was necessary and had dispatched the Milori ship as quickly as possible. The video log from the *Thor* was included in the transmission.

After that, report after report was of a quick battle with successful results. Jenetta realized all the earlier messages had been reports of no contact because the other operations had been too busy fighting and then mopping up to file immediate reports.

Unfortunately, a few torpedoes had gotten through in a couple of the encounters, and there had been Space Command fatalities. But overall, the operation was a resounding success. Only one Milori ship had managed to make its way out of the trap laid for it. Its course setting on a second FTL escape attempt was fortuitously established through a gap in the electronic cage grid. The large cruiser successfully engaged its Light Drive but not before suffering multiple torpedo strikes and sustaining considerable laser damage. In fact, its escape had come as a complete surprise to the captains of the three Space Command ships because they had thought it disabled by that point. It had ceased firing torpedoes, and the laser fire had decreased by over seventy-five percent.

Aside from the good news that Space Command had captured or destroyed fourteen ships, two at one location, was the news that spotter ships had detected eleven unidentified ships traveling at speeds in excess of Light-375. They plotted the courses and other spotter ships watched for them to the extent possible. Several Space Command ships, not part of the operation because there hadn't been any reported sightings in their patrol areas, had identified Milori ships deserting their hiding places and given pursuit, but the faster Milori vessels quickly outdistanced the Space Command vessels.

It took several days for all the reports to come in, and Jenetta was exhausted from spending long hours in the CIC. She looked forward to spending a night in her own bed, because she'd been sleeping on a cot in a room near the CIC since the first reports arrived. The ships were still cleaning up the battle sites, collecting prisoners who hadn't killed themselves to avoid surrendering, collecting bodies blown out into space, tending to the injured on both sides, and making emergency repairs to the Space Command vessels. One of the SC ships in each task group, likely the one with the worst damage, would tow the enemy ship back to Stewart where intelligence groups would take over. Experts would examine any intact computer records and begin the interrogation of the Milori prisoners.

Jenetta prepared and sent a report to the Admiralty Board once the actions were over and the captain of each ship involved in an action had forwarded his initial reports and vid records. Over the next few days, she would again review each of the videos carefully. As commanding officer at Stewart SCB, responsibility for rating the performance of each captain and ship under her command fell to her. However, her immediate interest was in getting to bed as quickly as possible. She had one last task to perform before heading for her quarters, and that was to stop at her office and send a message to the Hudeeracs. She touched the special data ring on her left hand to the spindle in the media drawer to load the proper encryption algorithm.

"To Vertap Aloyandro, Minister of Intelligence for the Hudeerac Order, from Admiral Jenetta Alicia Carver, Base Commander of Stewart Space Command Base.

"Minister, in a series of coordinated raids upon suspected locations of Milori warships, we've been able to capture or destroy fourteen vessels. A fifteenth escaped our grasp, but we damaged it sufficiently for us to remove it from consideration as a serious threat. I believe that either it has retreated to a place where the crew can transfer to another ship, or they might be quitting Galactic Alliance space entirely.

"I trust this news will be greeted as warmly by your people as it has been by mine. We'll continue our efforts to find and destroy the other Milori ships that have entered our space and are by no means complacent about the larger threat we anticipate.

"Admiral Jenetta Carver, Stewart Space Command."

She closed the media drawer, stretched, yawned, and left for her date with her bed.

* * *

"Well, Donald, what do you say now?" Admiral Hillaire asked of Admiral Hubera after the Admiralty Board had reviewed Jenetta's latest report. "Admiral Carver destroyed fourtccn Milori warships without losing any of our own. And we only lost thirty-one crewmembers in the entire operation, while capturing or killing almost twenty thousand Milora."

"I say she was damned lucky after leaving her patrol routes uncovered to engage in this dubious operation. We need the ships out there watching for the invasion fleet, not a few rogue Milori ships. The warships involved will now have to travel back to Stewart for repairs."

"Although she didn't elaborate in this report," Admiral Platt said, "It appears that most of the ships only suffered minimal damage. They'll make their repairs quickly, at the site of the battles, and return to their patrol duties. Only the more seriously damaged ships will have to return to Stewart and remain there for a short time. And we did forever remove the threat represented by fifteen of the empire's newest, fastest, and most dangerous ships. That's half the group that left the fleet during its journey out of our space."

"Half of a group that Donald didn't believe existed," Admiral Hillaire said. He was deriving great pleasure from teasing Donald, although his features remained completely impassive.

"All right, I admit there were at least fifteen Milori ships in our territory," Admiral Hubera said. "But fifteen ships hardly pose the threat you espouse. Admiral Carver has a hundred warships in her command."

"Even one Milori ship is a violation of the treaty, Donald," Admiral Bradlee said. "If they were not planning an attack, they wouldn't have taken the reckless action of secreting these ships inside our borders. By finding and destroying half this group, Admiral Carver has no doubt upset the plans of the Milori Empire. I'm not saying they won't attack now, only that the loss of so many ships will surely affect their plans. I'm extremely pleased by this operation and we've once more been shown that the confidence we've placed in Admiral Carver is justified."

"As far as posing a threat, Donald," Admiral Hillaire said, "let me remind you it was just three Milori ships that attacked the *Lisbon* and killed or captured Admiral Vroman and the entire crew. Just how many ships does it take to pose a threat in your opinion?"

"I haven't said they don't pose a danger. I'm only saying I don't like Admiral Carver setting aside her other responsibilities to chase after a few enemy ships. The real threat will come from the enemy fleet when it arrives."

"The enemy fleet is the real threat, as Donald says," Admiral Moore said, "but the ships that have been secreted in our territory pose a very real danger as well. If our ships move into the Frontier Zone to meet the enemy fleet while there is a substantial enemy presence inside the inner border, we'll be leaving ourselves open to an attack from the rear. By destroying an important part of this enemy fleet, Admiral Carver has significantly strengthened our position. I'm going to send her my congratulations on a job well done. What else do we have for discussion today?"

* * *

Admiral Moore's aide told Admiral Hubera to go right in as soon as he arrived in Moore's outer office later that morning.

"Come in, Donald," Moore said when the door opened. "Coffee?"

"No thanks, Rich. I've had my three cups already this morning. I'll be running for the head every twenty minutes if I drink anymore before lunch time."

Moore smiled pleasantly and then got right down to business. "Donald, I'm concerned by this increasingly hostile attitude you're exhibiting towards Admiral Carver. With each of her successes, you seem to become more antipathetic to her. I want Board members to speak their minds, but I believe your personal attitude towards Admiral Carver is affecting your judgment."

Hubera turned his head and looked over at the beverage synthesizer. "I think I'll have that coffee after all." He rose and walked to the equipment, where he ordered a steaming cup of Colombian with five percent chicory and a spoonful of sweetener. Returning with his coffee to his seat facing Moore, he said, "I don't like her, Rich; I admit that. I think she's risen too high, too quickly. She's only thirty-three years old for god's sake, when you discount her stasis time, and she looks twenty."

"Her appearance isn't her fault, Donald. She's not using medical techniques to look younger; in fact, I understand she has long believed it to be a great handicap, fearing people won't take her seriously because of her perceived age. And as for her age, since when has it been criteria for promotion? We promote on merit and Admiral Carver has consistently displayed abilities and judgment far beyond her years, justifying her rank and position."

"She's had much too much success too quickly. I'm sure she's become over-confident in her abilities. She's heading for a major fall, Rich, and I don't want half of Space Command to go down with her. Over the past several years, we've incrementally placed the fate of the entire Galactic Alliance in her hands. We've made ourselves dependent upon this child's ability to stop the Milori invasion fleets."

"Granted she's half our age, Donald, but she's hardly a child. Answer this question for me. Whom would you really prefer to see as base commander of Stewart right now? Do you think someone never tested in battle, such as Admiral Vroman, would do a better job than Admiral Carver simply because of his age and administrative experience? Would you have supported his replacing Admiral Carver if we knew the Milori were already commencing another invasion, or would you have insisted that Admiral Carver remain on as base commander to meet the new enemy threat? You don't have to answer me right now. All I ask is that you be honest with yourself."

Chapter Nine
~ July 8th, 2279 ~

Exalted Lord Space Marshall Berquyth entered the emperor's study quietly and walked silently to the desk where the emperor was reading.

"What is it, Berquyth?" the emperor asked, his voice suggesting displeasure at being disturbed.

The tone of voice intimidated Berquyth and made him dread the chore ahead even more. "My Lord, I— have word from our ships secreted inside the Alliance's inner border."

The emperor stopped reading and looked at his minister with impatience. "Out with it, Berquyth. What is it?"

"The Alliance has apparently captured fourteen of the thirty ships," he said quickly, as if conveying the information rapidly would somehow make it more palatable.

The emperor jumped up from his chair. "What? How? How could they?"

"We don't know, my Lord. All we know for sure is that fourteen ships aren't responding to hails. One ship, the *Xiouthet*, reported an attack by three Space Command vessels that left it with crippling injuries. It managed to evade capture, but the captain reports that they're returning home. The ship is no longer able to fight or even mount an effective defense because of battle damage. The report states that Space Command had jammed IDS band communications, but once they got far enough away, they were able to send a warning message to all other ships."

"And what of the other ships?"

"Upon receiving the warning from the *Xiouthet* and failing to make contact with many of the others, Lord Space Marshall Pwinnuth immediately ordered all ships to leave their primary locations and move to their alternate locations. Several ships were pursued by Space Command warships, leaving Pwinnuth to conclude the ships had been moving into position to attack the other half of the task force. The attacking ships must have been part of two different fleets. If their commanders had coordinated the operations a bit better, they might have gotten all our ships. They must have felt that no one would be able to get a message off."

The emperor paced angrily around the room while Berquyth stood still, nervously waiting for the usual tirade.

"How, Berquyth? How did they locate our ships? Most haven't moved since arriving at their hidden locations." The calm and reasoned remarks of the emperor caught Berquyth completely off guard.

"Uh, we don't know yet, my Lord. Usually, their news services break stories like this immediately, but so far we've seen nothing. Carver must be keeping a very tight lid on the news."

"Carver again. I'm getting so tired of hearing that name. Perhaps I should have let Vroman replace her, after all."

"But then she would have been too far away for you to get her head, my Lord."

"Yes, but I have to wonder if it's worth it. I may have erred when I ordered that we contrive a way to keep her at Stewart after her tour of duty was up."

Berquyth was speechless. He had never heard his emperor admit to having made a mistake and he didn't know how to respond. He couldn't possibly agree with the emperor that he had made a mistake and one simply didn't argue with the emperor either. He was relieved when Emperor Maxxiloth broke the silence.

"How does this affect our operation?"

"Minimally. We'll simply have to reduce the scope of the diversionary operations we'd planned, unless we send only one ship to each location."

"No, that's not acceptable. We must have at least two ships for each attack."

"Then we'll have to prioritize the list and reassign ships to just the top seven targets."

"See to it."

"Yes, my Lord."

Berquyth turned and hurried out while the emperor walked slowly around the room, speaking to the mounted heads hung high on the walls around him. "Carver's head will yet grace these walls, my old enemies. She will have a place of honor among you, for she is proving to be worth any two of you."

* * *

Trader Vyx emptied the mug and ordered another ale. His dinner of real Terran beef and potatoes had left him thirsty, and this would be his third. The five undercover agents were sitting in the tavern Vyx and Byers used as their unofficial headquarters while on Scruscotto. Before Vyx's third drink arrived, Ker Blasperra approached the table and asked if he might sit down.

"Sure, Ker, take a load off."

The tall, gaunt alien pulled a chair out and sat down. "I was sorry to hear about the loss of your ship, Trader, but I suppose it's better that you happened to be away."

"Perhaps. Do you have any information about the Tsgardi who are responsible? They owe me a ship."

"Alas, I have little information. I only know that the ship on which I believe they arrived left the planet a few hours after your ship was— lost. I heard that only two Tsgardis, one limping very badly, reentered the ship before it left."

"Do you know how many disembarked from the ship originally?"

"My information is that twenty-one left the ship just after it landed."

"It sounds like it was a bad day for the Recozzi tribe."

"Recozzi?"

"I'm guessing it was Recozzi clan members on a blood feud who attempted to board my ship. I had to kill a Recozzi on Gollasko a while back."

"Yes, I heard about that. Shev Rivemwilth was very fortunate to have lived through the attack."

"Yeah, Recozzi left quite a hole in one of his hearts."

"What will you do now, Trader, without a ship?"

"I'll find another ship and get back down to business, of course."

"I'm pleased to hear that. I have several lucrative deals available, but I'm afraid they're time sensitive."

"I understand, Ker. I've traveled all over this planet and looked at everything available here, but nothing suits my particular needs."

"Then you'll be leaving Scruscotto?"

"I've already booked passage to Stewart. If I don't find anything there, I'll travel on to Urgucet. I know a used ship dealer who can usually find something special if he doesn't have it himself."

"Surely you can't steal another ship from Stewart?"

"Steal? No, the early days of confusion at the base have passed, but they might be interested in liquidating some of the old ships they've commandeered during interdiction activity. I understand they're building quite a collection."

"Yes, the Raiders are getting desperate for people in this sector. Aside from the seizure of ships carrying stolen goods or illegal contraband, Space Command has been arresting their spotters, charging them with sedition, and confiscating their ships."

"I can see where losing all their spotters would put quite a crimp in the Raider operations."

"If you get a ship, I can place you with the Raiders immediately. They paid quite well before Carver started impounding ships, but now they're paying triple for spotters."

"Getting many takers?"

"None. Everyone is afraid of losing their ship and being sent to a prison colony just for reporting ship movements."

"I can understand that. However, I'm no more interested now than the last time you asked. If I risk going to prison, it will be for something that holds the opportunity for substantial rewards."

"Very well, Trader." Ker Blasperra stood up. "When you've acquired another ship, I'll be happy to find an acceptable deal for you. Will you be leaving soon?"

"Tonight is our last night on Scruscotto. This has been a sort of 'last decent meal' party before we face the reality of suffering with freighter food for a month."

"I wish you well, and limited digestive problems. Until we meet again."

Vyx grinned. "Ditto, Ker."

* * *

The three-ship taskforce led by Captain Payton of the GSC Battleship *Thor* had attacked the Milori location closest to Stewart, so it was logical that it would be the first to arrive back at the base following its confrontation. Stewart's ship maintenance crews were alerted while the ships were still several hours away and they were waiting at the shipyard area as the ships entered the asteroid base. Repair crews and bots deployed as yard tugs moved the GSC ships into the enclosed docks. The tugs had earlier removed three former Milori ships from the enclosed docks and re-anchored them against the cavern wall where they would remain until all SC ship repairs were completed.

The tugs also moved the Milori ship brought back by the three-ship task force to the far wall and tethered it there. Once teams recorded identifying information about the dead Milori, the bodies would be disposed of. Following previous hostilities, the Milori had stated they had no interest in recovering bodies of deceased crewmembers. Graves registration had interred the bodies in shipping containers of the type carried by freight haulers and ejected the containers towards a nearby sun.

The captain and first officer of each returning ship would report to Admiral Carver's office for a debriefing session where Jenetta and Captain Lofgren of Intelligence would discuss the entire mission from arrival at the deployment point to completion of the cleanup. Each ship's captain had already complied with the standing order to submit a report and ship's logs directly to SHQ within twenty-four hours following the completion of the action.

All severely damaged ships involved in the operation returned to Stewart over the course of the month following the *Thor's* return. Engineers had quickly repaired most and returned them to service. They had patched every hole in the hulls, with entire plates replaced if deemed necessary. The ships struck by torpedoes required much more extensive repairs, but all would return to service within three more months. The least severely damaged ships had performed their own repairs at the battle site and continued on their patrols. Jenetta arranged for a memorial ceremony in the convention center for those crewmembers killed in action. She knew it might only be one of many as the date for the Milori invasion grew closer.

* * *

Siena had seen few *real* celebrations by the crew of the *Lisbon*, but the first blooms of iron produced by the new smelting process screamed for a party. The first production of iron was no less important to the *Lisbon* crew stranded on a hostile planet than it must have been to humankind on Earth, perhaps more so because bronze, copper, and tin had already been available on Earth before iron-making had begun . With the advent of iron and steel production on Siena, their lives would improve measurably. Wood, bone, and stone implements wore out much too quickly and didn't have the strength to complete many of the tasks required. Wooden axles on the carts added too much weight because they had to be many times thicker than a steel axle would be. Stone axes, stone spearheads, and bone knives broke or wore out quickly and needed replacement often.

On this occasion, Admiral Vroman was actually the driving force behind the party. He knew they needed the relaxation that a real party would offer after the stress they had endured for months. He'd even consented to the production of a fermented liquid similar to ale weeks earlier, although individual allotments at the party would be limited. Starting at dinnertime, the party was open to everyone in the camp except those individuals who had guard duty at the two passes. Non-drinkers would relieve them a couple of hours before midnight so they might enjoy the festivities as well. Using basic musical instruments fashioned since the camp had come into existence, amateur musicians would provide something akin to music during the festivities. Flutes were plentiful, in addition to a few stringed instruments made from dinosaur tendons and drums covered in stretched gelk or dinosaur skin.

The party was a huge success. Admiral Vroman's fear that an emergency would interrupt it was groundless. He decided he was just becoming paranoid because every time things had started to look up, something happened to dampen spirits.

The weather was changing. Everyone noticed that the days were becoming cooler and the temperature dipped significantly once the sun set. This was a sure sign it was almost time for the harvest to begin. The peaks of the mountains surrounding the valley had never completely lost their snowcaps, and now the white area was expanding noticeably. Lt. Rimes, the camp's geologist, believed that temperatures would drop into the freezing range overnight during the coming months but that little or no snow would fall in the valley. They had constructed a special building to function as a cold storage warehouse. Water from the cold stream flowing down from the mountain behind the camp ran through terracotta piping laid in the floor and walls. They expected a bumper crop of the tubers and vegetables they had planted and cultivated during the growing season. Following the harvest, the cold storage building should help preserve freshness levels.

In case the hunters couldn't provide enough fresh meat in the months ahead, they had jerked great quantities of gelk meat. They had increased the camp's gelk herd from the original two animals to sixteen. All had been broken for riding and/or drawing wagons, and it would upset the crew to kill any for food, but they would if necessary for survival. Since breaking the first two for riding, rounding up gelks had become almost an easy chore. They only killed new animals for food at present. They had built a special corral on the other side of the river for animals rounded up for food, but the number they kept was limited by the amount of vegetation that could be gathered for feed. If they were able to domesticate the gelk sufficiently for pulling a plow by the new planting season, they would plant feed hay in a couple of enormous fields recently cleared.

At the breakfast meeting the day after the party, Admiral Vroman asked if everyone felt good. The smiles around the table were sufficient proof of that.

"Good, because it's time to start a new project. We must reinforce the North pass against the time when the dinosaurs begin their spring migration south. I propose we build a stone wall, much like the castle walls of medieval Europe. It will have a door that we can open or lower, but the dinosaurs should see nothing but an impenetrable barrier when they try to come through the valley. I don't want to have to fight them off twice each year. I want them to find a new migration path."

"A stone wall, sir?" Lt. Pyers said. "That will take huge blocks of stone and we don't have cutting instruments or the means to transport the blocks."

"We have *some* tools and we'll have more soon. The water saws will cut stone, and, although it takes significantly longer than cutting wood, they do a good job. They were invaluable for making the grinding stones for the mill. In addition, the new forge will soon begin making iron sledge-hammers, wedges, drills, and chisels as part of our first products. We'll need to begin planning the wall immediately and excavating for a foundation. As far as transporting the blocks, we have wagons and gelks. Lt. Rimes has found an excellent grade of granite for the wall and we need only cut a road for the carts."

"How high of a wall are you proposing, sir?" Lt. Commander McCloud, the base's architect, asked.

"Ten meters minimum, since we've already seen dinosaurs that long, but preferably fifteen."

"But they were only six meters high when they were standing on their hind legs," Lt. Pyers said.

"That's why I said ten meters was the minimal acceptable height. At the south gate, we saw them climb on the backs of other dinosaurs to breach the barriers, and we don't know if there are even larger creatures out there. I'd like to see the wall's foundation designed to support a wall of thirty meters, but we need only raise it to fifteen unless we find a need to extend it higher."

"Thirty meters will require a considerable foundation," Lt. Commander McCloud said. "And we'll need to manufacture some sort of bonding material such as cement."

"I know where a deposit of limestone is located," Lt. Rimes said. "We could make a form of cement using crushed limestone and clay. It's going to be a bit of work crushing the limestone, but we can do it using the forge's trip hammer and the mill's grinding stone."

"I never said it was going to be easy," Admiral Vroman said, "but I feel it's necessary to guarantee the safety of everyone in the camp. We lost sixteen people to the last attack. I don't want to lose another crew member in that way. There're only two passageways into this valley and this is the one we must address first. Come spring we'll start work on the South Pass wall so it will be ready before their fall migration."

"We can do it, sir," Captain Lindahl said.

* * *

"Trader Vyx is here, Admiral," Jenetta heard from her com unit as she worked at her desk. "He requests a few minutes of your time."

"Send him in, Lori," Jenetta said to the com unit.

As Vyx entered the room, Jenetta stood to greet him. "Welcome back, Trader. It's good to see you again. It gives me an opportunity to personally thank you for the leads you provided."

"I haven't seen anything on the news services except coverage of a memorial ceremony. Did we find many Milori ships?"

"I've managed to suppress any mention of it with a promise to the news services that they'll get a firsthand opportunity to witness a story a hundred times better in the not-too-distant future. They're contacting everyone they've ever met on the base trying to learn what I'm alluding to, but so far they haven't found out or released anything about the attacks. I couldn't possibly keep them from reporting on the memorial ceremony, but they only reported it as resulting from a run-in with unidentified hostile forces. As to finding the Milori ships, the operation was extremely successful. We located fifteen of their best warships and only one managed to escape capture. From what I saw on the videos, that ship won't be participating in any battles for quite awhile. It's amazing that it was even able to get away."

"Fifteen? Half the force left behind? That's wonderful, Admiral. I guess it was worth losing my ship."

"Your ship? What happened?" Jenetta asked, concern obvious in her voice because she thought the agents might have had their covers blown. "Was anybody hurt?"

"No, no injuries. Not to my team anyway. We were away, trying to pick up more information in the other colonies on Scruscotto, when a group of Tsgardis tried to enter my ship. They found enough body parts for nine, but information I've received since leads me to believe that quite a few more died. They must have been carrying a bomb intended for placement aboard my ship and it detonated when they triggered my trap. The damage from the explosion was considerably greater than what could have occurred from the explosive charges I had rigged. Nevertheless, I let people believe it was entirely from my charges. I doubt anyone will tamper with a ship of mine in the near future."

"Tsgardi? Do you suspect they were working for the Raiders? Has your cover been blown?"

"I'm speculating they were Recozzi's relatives out to settle the blood feud. Nineteen of them won't have to worry about it anymore."

"I'm glad. Not that the Recozzi tribe is after you, but that you weren't injured and that your cover appears to be intact."

"I'm sure that many people on Scruscotto believe me to be providing information to Space Command, but only as an informant rather than an agent. To anyone who asks, I openly admit I despise the Milori so much that I would happily provide information on their movements in our space for free, so I'm happy to accept a few credits for doing it. Most people I meet share that sentiment and know I've never informed on their smuggling activities."

"It's a narrow line you walk."

"All part of the job. And speaking of the job, I need a ship to continue mine. I thought you might fix me up with something from the stuff you've confiscated."

"Sure, we've got plenty—so many that we don't know what to do with them all. The base is filled with them and we have a secure farm in orbit that contains another large group. Take your pick."

"I need one as large as possible but still able to land on a planet or moon. The *Scorpion* was ideal."

"I'm not sure how many tiny ships we have available, but I'll ask Commander Jacoby to speak with you. If we don't have anything small enough, take a bigger one off my hands and trade down to whatever you need. Are you staying in the station?"

"Yes, as soon as we book rooms."

"The housing officer will find first class accommodations for your team. Please extend my gratitude to the others for the excellent work you've all done."

"I will, Admiral."

Commander Derrick Jacoby was one of the very few people on the base who knew Vyx was an officer in Space Command and an undercover agent, so with him as a guide, Trader Vyx began a thorough scrutiny of every confiscated ship at Stewart. Space Command was converting the former Milori warships for their own use, but Vyx looked at everything else. When nothing inside the base proved adequate, they moved to the confiscated ships in the 'farms.' Maintaining a similar orbit in the system, although ten thousand kilometers closer to the sun to keep the traffic lanes to Stewart free of obstructions, the farms were guarded twenty-four/seven by security forces. Most of the farms held cargo containers awaiting pickup by freighters bound for other points, but the base used one farm exclusively for impounded ships. The number of ships astounded Vyx as the shuttle approached and received clearance from security. Derrick flew the shuttle very slowly between the rows of ships so Vyx could get a good look.

"I had no idea you had so many," Vyx remarked.

"Stewart has more territory to cover and more GSC ships on patrol duty than any other base in Galactic Alliance space. During the past year, the Admiral has really stepped up interdiction activities in the Frontier Zone. Many criminals still think the Zone is wide open and lawless like it used to be, but that isn't the case in our sectors. There's never been any legal reason why Space Command couldn't enforce the law in the Zone; we simply didn't have the resources, so we only answered distress calls, concentrating our search-and-seizure activities in what we generally call 'regulated' space. Admiral Carver has certainly changed that, actually stopping far more ships in the Zone for inspections than inside the inner border. Either the criminals are getting the word, or most of them have been locked up because we're seeing a markedly lower amount of illegal cargo smuggling."

"I remember every criminal on Gollasko leaving for the new border when the Frontier Zone was pushed out a hundred parsecs. They thought they'd be safe if they could make it into the new Zone."

"That was B.A.C."

"Bac?"

"Before Admiral Carver."

"You sound like her biggest fan."

"Perhaps not the biggest, but definitely a major fan. Just one of millions, I suspect, and not just because I owe my promotion to her. I've met a couple of other admirals during my time in the service, neither of which had their flag at the time I first met them, but she's nothing like *them.* They were mostly bluster and brass. She's more like a fellow officer than an apotheosis of Space Command regulations, but she does enforce the book."

Vyx chuckled.

"I wouldn't expect *you* to understand or share my opinion," Jacoby said. "You'd have to be around her and work in her command on a regular basis to understand what I mean."

"Quite the contrary, Commander. I understand *exactly* what you mean and I agree completely. It's just that it's so unusual for so many people to share a common opinion about a commanding officer. A good opinion, I should have said."

"Oh, I'm not saying that everybody likes her," Jacoby said. "I have a few Academy friends with whom I communicate regularly who simply can't understand my total devotion to a commanding officer, but *they've* never served under Admiral Carver. The fan club seems to be mostly limited to just the officers, NCOs, and crewmen who have served in her commands. I guess knowing that she's saved your arse more than once helps a bit."

"Were you in the first fight with the Milori?"

"No, but this station would have been in their sights next if the Admiral hadn't stopped them cold. I *was* aboard the station when the Raiders arrived to take it back. The Admiral turned what looked like certain doom into an incredible victory. Since then, no officer I know has ever questioned any order from her, even in private conversations among close friends. If she told me that I could get into a shuttle and drive it straight through the heart of a sun without even getting a mild tan, I'd believe her because I know how much she cares about her people. She does her level best to live up to that Ice Queen reputation, but I've seen the look in her eyes when operations are underway. If she could, she'd be out facing the enemy all by herself instead of sending other people to face them. Every life is dear to her. She'll do what she has to do and order people into dangerous situations where their chance of survival is negligible, but she won't risk their lives unnecessarily. That's the kind of officer you want as a CO."

Vyx nodded. "Yes, I know her concern is genuine. She risked her career to search for me and two of my associates a few years back when an arms merchant left us trapped in an underground complex. I'll always go the extra kilometer for a commanding officer who values the lives of their people above career advancement." Scrutinizing a small ship they were passing, Vyx said, "I hope we can find something here. I need to get back to work. Time is too important right now for me to take a trip to Urgucet to get a new ship."

"Urgucet?"

"Yeah, I know a used ship dealer there who can always find what you're looking for, but it could take me away from here for as long as two years."

"I think the Milori will be here long before then. You'll miss all the excitement. Some officers are already taking bets about the tactics the Admiral will employ against the Milori this time."

"There's a very old saying that goes, 'Fool me once, shame on you, fool me twice, shame on me.'"

Derrick chuckled. "What the hell does *that* mean?"

"People aren't as easy to fool the second time around. The Milori know we led them into a trap at our first encounter, and that we conned them into retreating in disgrace at the second. They won't allow us to trap them that way again, nor will they fall for any subtle tricks at our next meeting. It's going to be a toe-to-toe slugfest with warships against an enemy that's just as powerful as we think we are. I'm sure Admiral Carver's present efforts are an attempt to whittle down the numbers that will be opposing us. The recent attacks took out fifteen of the enemy's best. Too bad we couldn't have gotten them all."

"Admiral Carver will find us an edge. She's at her very best when the odds against us are the heaviest."

"I hope she can, or there's going to be a memorial service that will make the one after the last invasion battle pale by comparison." Pointing to a ship, Vyx asked, "What's that?"

"That's a one-hundred-eighty-three-meter transport made on Uthlarigasset for the Raiders. It was just recently brought in by the battleship *Chiron*."

"Big ship."

"Yeah. Half the size of a GSC Light Destroyer. Almost three times the size of your last ship."

"Can she land on a planet?"

"No reason why not. She has retractable landing gear, but she's somewhat big for spaceports. Most landing pads are designed for ships no larger than a hundred meters."

"Uh-huh. What kind of condition is she in?"

"I haven't had time to completely survey her yet, but I did a preliminary check and she looked good."

"Is she available?"

Commander Jacoby punched a few numbers into the computer in front of him. "I'm sure she is. We found two hundred eighty tons of mining equipment stolen from a warehouse on Kethewit in her holds. Her crew is going to wind up being put away for a whole bunch of years."

"Was it damaged in the seizure?"

"No, her crew knew it was a choice between surrendering peacefully and spending some time on a penal colony or dying horribly in the vacuum of space. They didn't have a chance of outrunning the *Chiron*, so they surrendered."

"What's its top speed?"

"Don't know for sure. I'd guess about Light-262 because the ship is only three years old and the Uthlaro have been making Light-262 ships for that long. The Raiders would probably want as much speed as possible, although they still couldn't have outrun the Light-375 speed of the *Chiron*."

"Light-262? That's perfect. The *Scorpion's* best speed was only Light-187. Most of Space Command's old destroyers can barely make Light-262. What kind of weaponry does it have?"

"Twelve laser arrays and six torpedo tubes in the bow."

"No stern tubes?"

"No, such small ships never have stern tubes. Your old ship was the only one I ever saw rigged that way."

"It was a custom install. They saved my life at least once because my foe wasn't expecting it. Can we rig something up in this ship?"

"It would be tough from what I know of its construction, but we might be able to mount tubes externally and conceal them with a cowling to make them look like maneuvering engine nacelles."

"Would I have a way to reload them without landing?"

"Sure. We could construct an automatic reloading assembly that would appear to be a support strut. It would function like a conveyor, extending forward to where it would enter the ship. But if it jammed or was damaged, you'd have to stop to make repairs."

"Could the cowling be made from tritanium?"

"Sure."

"Good. That will help protect it from most damage."

"Are you saying you want this ship?"

"No, not yet, but it's a good candidate. Let's look over the rest."

After finding two other possible ships and taking a tour in all three, Vyx decided on the first one, mainly because of its speed capability but also because of its young age. Commander Jacoby issued orders to have it brought into the base and put at an empty airlock at the far end of the habitat.

"I have to finish up work on the ships that suffered damage in the recent attacks, but we'll be able to get to your ship in a few weeks."

"Okay, Derrick, thanks. We'll just hang out in the station until you can get to her."

"I'll send over the specs on the ship and whatever information I can find that pertains to her. I'm sure you'll want to familiarize yourself with her. I'll arrange for access in case you want to get inside at any time."

"That would be great. We could start cleaning her up and preparing her for our use."

"How do you want her registered?"

"I'll name her the *Scorpion*. My old ship was completely destroyed so there won't be any conflict with the previous registered name."

"You've got it. This ship is now the *Scorpion*."

Chapter Ten
~ September 2nd, 2279 ~

Six weeks into construction, the North Pass wall was beginning to take definite shape. The floor of the pass where the wall was to be erected had been excavated down to bedrock and a four-meter-wide foundation of steel-reinforced concrete had been poured. Stonecutters had delivered the first of the two-to-three ton granite blocks to the site, and the masons would place them as soon as the concrete foundation had set sufficiently. There would actually be two stone block walls built, with steel-reinforced concrete poured between them to make one very thick wall that should stand up to any pounding the largest dinosaurs could give it. The smelter, forge, and mill were working overtime to produce the cement and steel reinforcing rods.

Those not involved in the construction of the wall were harvesting food crops. Although the nights were getting progressively colder, they were still above freezing. The cold storage shelter was bulging with winter supplies and starvation wasn't a concern, although the variety of food was going to be a problem. It appeared that most meals would consist chiefly of gelk meat, potato-like tubers, and bread. Most fresh vegetables would soon be scarce and everyone was getting their fill before they were gone. The supply was adequate, but long-term storage was a problem without the ability to flash-freeze. After learning of something the fish would bite on, the fishermen had laid in a large supply of dinosaur flesh in the cold storage shed. Twice a week the entire camp enjoyed a fresh fish fillet dinner and there was no reason to suspect that fish wouldn't be available all winter. Things didn't look too bad, although everyone longed for rescue.

A few weeks later, work on the wall had slowed considerably. The first few rows of stone blocks were in position, but it had become increasingly difficult to raise the new blocks up to the top of the wall. A jib crane made of wood had cracked as they tried to move a large block into place, very nearly crushing one of the masons. Only his quick reflexes had saved his life. A steel crane would do the job properly, but that was a bit beyond their present capabilities. In the end, Lt. Commander McCloud designed a ramp system like that theoretically used to construct the ancient pyramids on Earth, and as the wall grew, so did the ramp. Constructed from a mixture of crushed limestone and stone chips from the granite quarry area, it easily supported the enormous stone blocks as they were rolled up to the new height of the wall using logs as rollers and a block-and-tackle assembly to pull them up the slope.

* * *

Among the many messages waiting for Jenetta when she arrived at her office in the morning was one marked 'Vertap.' She immediately bent over to provide a retinal scan and touched the ring on her left hand to the spindle in the media tray so it could decrypt the message.

"Hello, Admiral," the image of Vertap Aloyandro, the Minister of Intelligence for the Hudeerac Order, said. "I congratulate you on your outstanding success against the hidden Milori ships. To have located so many is a tribute to your intelligence services. It would behoove you to search out and destroy as many of the remaining ships as possible before the arrival of the invasion force.

"We have information that four Milori fleets entered your Buffer Zone on 4323-korei-293 on our calendar. On your calendar that would be the 14th of April 2279. We estimate they will arrive at Stewart on or about your 11th of May 2280. The coordinates of the point where they entered your territory are known only to the commander of the armada in order to keep them secret.

"Their target is Stewart. They will arrive in many dozens of small clusters after following different paths through your space to avoid giving you the opportunity to entrap them as you did their Third Fleet. They know Stewart is the key to security in your sectors of space and will not leave it intact as they advance. We believe four hundred ten ships will make the assault. They have left only one fleet behind to protect their Empire, but as much as we would like to open a second front against them, one hundred ships is still too large a force for us to attack. We wish we could be of more help, but our inside contact was uncovered after passing this information to us and I may not be able to offer such detailed information for some time.

"Good luck, Admiral. We wish you success against the Milori invasion force.

"Minister Vertap Aloyandro. End of message."

Jenetta sent a quick reply thanking the minister and then leaned back in her chair. She had a date now, if not a planned course for the Milori fleet, but the Space Command fleet assigned to her would still be outnumbered four to one.

"That's not as bad as last time," she reminded herself aloud, "when we were outnumbered seventeen to one, but then we had the element of surprise on our side."

Leaving her chair, she prepared a mug of coffee to help her think about the message. There was always the possibility that the message was deliberately designed to mislead. After all, the Hudeerac's spy had been caught. She knew that meant someone had probably given their life to procure and transmit the information, but it could also mean the Milori intelligence services had intercepted the message and altered it before passing it along as disinformation. Still, she couldn't argue that Stewart would be the most likely target. While Space Command still held it, it would be as a dagger pointed at the backs of invaders who bypassed it to attack the planets of the Galactic Alliance.

Jenetta made her decision and immediately prepared a message to her captains. She sat up straight, looked directly into the lens of the vid camera in the com console, and tapped the record button.

"Priority One Stage-One message to the captains of all warships under my command, from Admiral Jenetta Carver, Stewart Base Commander.

"Captain, the contents and purpose of this message should be shared with no one except your first officer.

"It's imperative that you return to Stewart no later than the 30th of April, 2280. An arrival on or before April 15 would be preferable.

"Contact Stewart for additional instructions before approaching closer than one light-year.

"Jenetta Alicia Carver, Rear Admiral, Upper Half, Base Commander of Stewart Space Command Base, message complete."

Jenetta sent the message and then went to stand at the SimWindow and stare out at the port while she thought. The development of a battle plan would never be out of her thoughts for very long over the next nine months.

* * *

At a hastily convened meeting of the Admiralty Board on a Sunday morning a week later, Admiral Moore greeted the other admirals.

"I assume everyone has viewed the secure message forwarded to you overnight?"

"I was at a conference on Supply Logistics and didn't have a secure com unit available to me until I arrived back here this morning," Admiral Ahmed said. "I haven't viewed it yet."

"Let's play it then," Admiral Moore said, nodding to his aide.

The head-and-shoulders image of Admiral Carver appeared on the giant screen and she began speaking. "I've received information from my contact in the Hudeerac Order that over four hundred Milori warships will attack Stewart from different approach paths on or about May 11th of this coming year. I have ordered all warships to return to Stewart no later than April 30th, specifying that a slightly earlier arrival date is desirable. I believe the Hudeerac message to be accurate and I am preparing my forces based on that assessment. I'll leave it to the Board to figure a way of alerting other commands about the invasion date. Base commanders should not take any overt action that will serve to alert either the Raiders or the Milori that we know of the planned attack. It would be best if the arriving Milori believe they have surprised us.

"Although I believe the information to be accurate, I don't expect further help from SHQ. The ships under my command will meet the enemy when they arrive. Other ships are too far away to arrive in time.

"Jenetta Alicia Carver, Rear Admiral, Upper Half, Base Commander of Stewart Space Command Base, message complete."

Admiral Moore looked around the conference table. Only the other admirals and their chief aides had been summoned to this meeting. Even the clerks, normally present at meetings where top-secret matters were discussed, had been excluded. "Although we've expected an attack," he said, "seven months seems barely enough time to marshal our forces and complete preparations for this invasion."

"Are we going to just accept this date as accurate?" Admiral Hubera asked.

"Donald," Admiral Moore said reproachfully.

"Now wait a minute, Richard. I'm not criticizing Admiral Carver. I'm questioning the report from the Hudeeracs. Are we going to trust this information from them? Are we going to scramble all our forces and turn our part of the quadrant upside down because they report the Milori are coming?"

"We already knew the Milori were coming, Donald," Admiral Hillaire said. "We just didn't know when. This gives us a date to plan around."

"And what happens if they don't come on the 11th of May?"

"Then we wait until they do come. Can you predict a better date? At least this one makes sense when coupled with the distances involved and all our other information."

"On the assumption that the date is correct," Admiral Moore said, "is there anything we can do to further support Admiral Carver? She'll be outnumbered four to one."

"As she acknowledged, additional ships can't possibly reach her in time," Admiral Platt said, "even if we had additional forces to send."

"There are *two* ships we could send," Admiral Plimley said, "ships that are currently being tested at the Mars Shipbuilding facility."

"At Mars?" Admiral Burke said. "They couldn't possibly reach her in time."

"I'm talking about the two scout-destroyers that are sheathed in Dakinium."

"But I understood those ships were still in experimental status," Admiral Platt said.

"Technically they are. We haven't been able to overcome all the problems associated with speeds in excess of Light-487 or completely verify the hypothesized mechanics."

"We can't send ships that might break down in the middle of a fight," Admiral Bradlee said. "The crews would be left defenseless."

"We have devised a way of using the ships safely," Admiral Plimley said. "Light-9790 only became possible because the Dakinium hull plating begins to resonate as the light speed increases. In physics, as you know, resonance refers to an excited state of a stable particle causing a sharp maximum in the probability of absorption of electromagnetic radiation. Once the speed of the ship exceeds Light-487, the resonance in the hull is responsible for causing the formation of a second temporal envelope around the first. Think of it like an echo. The problem occurs when a second temporal envelope actually begins to take shape around an existing envelope. Like a sound and its echo, the envelopes are out of sync. This causes an electrical charge to build in the Dakinium hull that reverse-flows through the main ground, overloading most circuits. We haven't yet been able to find a way of isolating the spike without the occurrence of damage while still permitting the creation of a second envelope around a formed envelope. But, if we eliminate the sync problem, Light-9790 speed is achievable."

"You've managed a stable Light-9790?" Admiral Hubera asked.

"Yes. We've experimented with a lockout device that blocks any speed above Light-487 and found everything to be fine. A special override, one that allows the helmsman to enable Light-9790 while disabling all other FTL speeds, eliminates the power spike problem that crippled the *Colorado* when Admiral Carver was testing it. We've found a method of instantly creating the resonance in the hull that allows both temporal envelopes to develop simultaneously. Creating them simultaneously means that both are in accord while also out of phase. Being out of phase keeps them from simply merging."

"So you're saying if the ship engages Light-9790 from outside a temporal field, such as from a dead stop, there's no problem?" Admiral Moore asked.

"Exactly. The ship can even be moving at any sub-light speed. As long as it's not accelerating from any FTL speed, the process is stable because we create the two temporal envelopes at the same moment. Given enough time, we're sure we'll find a solution to the original problem. But under the circumstances, i.e. the seriousness of the situation confronting us, I think we should authorize the use of the ships despite their limitations."

"Can the helm console be set so there's absolutely *no* chance of the temporal envelope problem occurring?" Admiral Bradlee asked.

"Yes, as long as no one disassembles the console with the intent of overriding it."

"Given the higher speed, can the crew identify potential obstacles in time to avoid them?" Admiral Woo asked.

"It's not really necessary, Lon."

"Not necessary? What do you mean?"

"Admiral Carver reported that the drive of the *Colorado* was shut down automatically by the ACS, but they were never able to identify what the sensor net might have seen. Her chief engineer on board, Commander William Cameron, hypothesized that they had flown through the object without impacting it."

"What? How could that be possible?" Admiral Platt asked.

"Our finest minds have been grappling with just that question since we learned about the possible occurrence. Commander Cameron is a very gifted officer who ought to be heading up a research section, but he prefers to remain a ship's engineer. His theory that the double envelope effect moves the ship out of phase in dimensional space has been the subject of much study. Our scientists constructed a wall of easily breakable plastic components in space and we drove the ship through it. Nothing happened."

"Nothing?"

"Nothing. It was as if the ship never arrived at the wall, but telemetry data confirmed it did, and that it flew through it. So we were emboldened to try with something more solid. We constructed a wall of titanium plating and tried again. This time, we remotely piloted the ship because of possible danger. Again, the ship passed through the wall without impacting it."

"Through titanium?"

Yes. For our final test, we flew the ship through Leda."

"Leda? The Jupiter moon?"

"Yes. Leda is sixteen kilometers in diameter. The Colorado emerged from the back side of the moon as though it wasn't even there."

"Amazing," Admiral Platt said. "How come you haven't mentioned this before?"

"We wanted to be sure, and have verifiable evidence, before we said anything lest people think we were certifiably mad. We had trouble even believing it ourselves. The test at Leda took place just yesterday. You can see why knowing about obstacles ahead is unimportant; however, the Colorado will still have to be wary of other ships using the double envelope system. We don't yet know what will happen if they cross paths while traveling at Light-9790. Much more research is required."

"And these ships are ready to go now?" Admiral Moore asked.

"Not immediately, but they can be made ready within five to six months and still make it to Stewart before the Milori."

"Has the Dakinium been tested against a nuclear torpedo strike?" Admiral Woo asked.

"Yes, thoroughly. We estimate the damage to the ship would be less than ten percent that of an equivalent force on a three-layer tritanium-sheathed hull, such as on our newer battleships. While the ship certainly isn't indestructible, it's as close to that as we can make it at this time. We have plans to add the new automated anti-torpedo weapons system developed at Stewart, and that should add another measure of safety."

"Then I agree with the proposal to send the two scout-destroyers to Admiral Carver as soon as they're ready," Admiral Woo said. "They may add just the extra bit of firepower that can help repel the Milori."

"Does anyone disagree?" Admiral Moore asked. "Very well," he said after a few seconds when no one spoke up. "Loretta," he said, addressing Admiral Plimley "please see that the ships are made ready and sent to Admiral Carver in time for her to employ them against the Milori."

"Can we use this new technology on our other ships, Loretta?" Admiral Bradlee asked.

"Yes, if we completely strip off their outer hull and replace it with Dakinium. It's the new material that allows the formation of the second envelope. Although we've tried to simulate creation of the resonance in every other material used for hull plating during the past century, we've had no success."

"So there's no chance that an enemy can duplicate the speed capability as a result of a close inspection of one of the ships."

"None. Moreover, we're reasonably certain they can't reverse-engineer the Dakinium material simply by getting a sample piece. We were only able to produce it because we had the benefit of the research files in the computer core that Admiral Carver found in the underground facility on Dakistee. The files put us on the right track, but they were incomplete, so our best chemists and metallurgical engineers conducted thousands of experiments in their effort to reproduce the almost indestructible material we found on Dakistee. It was pure chance we developed a material with the unique properties it has. Since then we've continued to experiment, hoping to improve the durability of the hull material, and we've come up with similar compounds that offer even better protection against attack, but none resonate like the Dakinium. Even a sample piece of the original Mawcett material doesn't create the necessary resonance."

* * *

Vertap Aloyandro knocked and then entered the royal chambers. He walked quickly to the small group of Hudeerac noblemen who sat in sumptuous sofas and chairs, comfortably facing a roaring blaze in the ornate fireplace.

"Vertap," one of the group members said, "I understand you've received a reply from Space Command?"

"Yes, my Lord. Admiral Carver thanked me for the intelligence data."

"Did she pass on any new information?"

"No, my Lord, nothing new since she reported the success of her attacks on the Milori ships that were hidden in GA space."

"That's all, Vertap."

Vertap bowed, turned, and left the chambers.

The nobleman who had spoken to Vertap said, "Okay, we've prepared her for the attack. That's all we can do."

"Why are we even bothering with these Terrans?" one of the others asked. "They're so far away that they can never be good allies."

"Don't underestimate the value of an alliance, regardless of the distance. We want them to be as prepared as possible for the attack by the Milori because it will enable them to cause more damage to the Milori fleet. Once the Milori have been sufficiently weakened, we'll strike and take back our territory."

"The Milori won't go easily."

"That's why we're pouring all available resources into shipbuilding. We'll be so strong that they won't be able to stand against us after they do battle with the Galactic Alliance."

"But their shipbuilding capacity is incredible. If Maxxiloth remains on the throne, it'll only be a matter of time before he rebuilds his fleet and counterattacks us."

"The Galactic Alliance knows they can't simply spank the Milori and send them home this time. If they defeat the invasion force, they'll have to go to Milor and dictate the terms of a new treaty directly to the emperor. He'll have put all his resources into producing new ships to replace those destroyed, but it won't be enough if the Galactic Alliance somehow manages to destroy his invading fleets. He can't replace five hundred ships in two annuals. Space Command will then destroy all his new ships, leaving him defenseless. As soon as Space Command leaves, we'll step in and finish him off, all without sacrificing any of our people. Space Command will have done most of the fighting and dying for us, and we'll have retribution for our slaughtered Hudeerac countrymen. We'll also have the Milori Empire and a fleet capable of defending our new territory against the Tsgardis, Gondusans, and Uthlaro."

"What about the Galactic Alliance? What if they decide to annex the Milori Empire, including our former territory, instead of just leaving?"

"They've just expanded their territory beyond what they're capable of managing and they only want to be left in peace. Maxxiloth was a fool to attack them. And by the time they arrive in this part of space, we'll be strong enough to convince them to leave our new empire should they be foolish enough to consider staying around after they've eliminated the Milori threat for us."

* * *

Stewart's engineers did a great job of fabricating and attaching four torpedo tubes and reloading assemblies to the exterior stern of the *Scorpion* and then camouflaging them to appear to be part of the propulsion systems. Without close inspection, no one would ever guess they weren't what they appeared until they were on the receiving end of the torpedoes. The five undercover agents had spent their time getting the inside cleaned up, provisioned, and adapted for their personal use. Unlike the old ship, this one had a bridge large enough to seat six individuals and the holds were many times larger. The crew quarters were also a vast improvement over the old ship, and Vyx and Brenda would finally have a private place where they could engage in whatever suited them without any of the others happening by. Vyx was extremely pleased with the new ship; now all they needed was an assignment.

* * *

Waiting was something military people were familiar with but that few enjoyed, and Jenetta was no exception. There was little more that could be done to prepare for the Milori this far in advance, but the base was always in a state of active readiness anyway. Once she had recalled all ships and sent a few special messages, she could do little except think about the coming tide of enemy warships. She had long ago turned over most of the day-to-day management duties to her officers, and she didn't go out of her way looking for political contact with the various governments in her sectors or with the ambassadorial staff posted on Stewart. Most of her day was consumed with reading reports or writing them, and in between she thought about the Milori and what she would do when they arrived.

She always looked forward to returning to her quarters each night because there would invariably be several personal messages waiting for her. Before she did anything else, she would sit down and view them, then begin composing responses in her head. It was a wonderful way to get her troubles off her mind, if only for a short time.

On this evening, she had messages waiting from her mom, her sisters Christa and Eliza, and her brother Richie. Since Christa and Eliza were aboard ships that were part of her command, she was able to exchange messages with them most evenings while they were away from port. Richie, six years older than Jenetta, was aboard the *San Francisco* on patrol duty in the sectors adjoining Stewart's. In the new message, he announced that he had received his promotion to Commander. He also said he would be remaining aboard the *San Francisco* but now as First Officer. Jenetta was glad his promotion had finally come through. It seemed reasonable to assume her brothers had some mild embarrassment or held some resentment toward Jenetta's meteoric climb through the ranks, although they professed none. Billy, upon being appointed as interim captain to the *Mentuhotep* following the first battle with the Milori, had confessed he had taken some

132

ribbing from his shipmates for serving in his kid sister's command. He had since been promoted officially to Captain and given permanent command of the GSC destroyer *Seoul* when its former captain moved up to a frigate. Jenetta sent a message to Richie congratulating him on his promotion before responding next to her mom's message and then to Christa's and Eliza's.

After sending her messages, she knelt on the floor to groom her cats. The hundred-sixty-pound Jumakas purred and rubbed against her as she pulled the wire brush through their short, dense fur. Although fully grown, they always loved rolling around on the floor with Jenetta after a grooming and never extended their claws or nipped at her, no matter how rough the play got.

* * *

When the North Pass wall on Siena reached ten meters in height, two giant wooden doors, each fifteen centimeters thick and eight meters high by three meters wide, were hung on thick steel hinges made at the new forge. At ten meters, no one felt completely safe yet, but they were at least as safe as they would have been with the barricade and probably much more so. With the ability to close and bar the doors, the barricade of sharpened poles was dismantled and transported to the South Pass, then re-erected there as a secondary line of defense. Any dinosaur that managed to jump over the first barricade would now impale itself on the second.

The wall of stone blocks, although incomplete, provided great peace of mind and everyone was breathing a little easier. Two massive wooden bars could be turned to lock the door when it was closed, and it was doubtful the dinosaurs would find any give if they pushed against it. Thick steel straps ran across the rear surface and heavy timber support posts could be propped between the door and concrete foundation to reinforce the doors further when closed.

Admiral Vroman continued to push for the additional five meters before it became too cold to work on the wall. When completed, the wall would resemble parts of the Great Wall of China. A three-meter-wide walkway on top would allow a solid platform from which the sentries could watch the pass and from which defenders could mass to repel the expected visitors. A counter-balanced drawbridge, which could be closed by one person in seconds, was also planned, even though the doors were so well balanced that one person could close and lock them given sufficient time.

The forge had made a world of difference, as everyone had known it would. The blacksmiths were kept so busy throughout the day with people pestering them for various items that Admiral Vroman finally had to step in and require that all blacksmith requests go through him. Steel knives, axes, and steel-tipped spears had replaced the stone versions, and iron hinges and door closures had replaced the leather versions on all buildings and shelters. Now that steel bands were available, coopers were able to make wooden barrels and the farmers were drawing up plans for new plows to be ready for planting season. The new plows would be far cry from the thick, pointed sticks originally used to open furrows.

"You're exhausted," Doctor O'Hara said. "If you don't slow down and get some rest, I'm going to relieve you of duty. I've been telling you for months to stop working so hard, and now I mean it."

"Just a few more weeks, Doc," Admiral Vroman said. "The wall is almost done and then I'll take some time off to rest."

"That's exactly what you said at harvest time, exactly what you said when the forge was being built, and exactly what you said when you directed the cutting of trees across the river so the cleared area spelled out a message which could be read from orbit. If you don't stop now, you won't be around to say it during the next project. You're trying to run around like a sixty-year-old, but you're not a sixty-year-old. If you don't immediately schedule some time off and get some rest, I'll relieve you of duty. As the chief medical officer, I have that power, Admiral."

Admiral Vroman scowled. He knew the doctor was right. He knew his health was declining because he was pushing himself too hard. However, he had to keep pushing to get his people through this difficult time, but he also couldn't afford to have the doctor relieve him of duty. "All right, doctor, I'll slow down."

"No, you'll stop for one week. Then you can return to duty for two hours a day if I approve. It's up to you, Admiral. Get plenty of rest and you'll be upgraded a little at a time until you're back to an eight-hour day, but there will be no more eighteen-hour days."

"Yes, doctor. I'll go tell Captain Lindahl," he said as he started to get off the examination table.

"No, I'll have Captain Lindahl sent to you. You'll stay in your cabin for the next week, except for lavatory use. I'll have your meals brought there and you will do no work. No meetings, no planning sessions, nothing for one week."

Admiral Vroman sighed loudly. "Very well, you're the doctor. Am I permitted to sit outside my shelter for a few minutes each day?"

"Just for a few minutes at a time, while the sun is up. The weather is getting cold and I don't want you to get a chill in your condition. Your body is not strong enough to fight off influenza, and our medications are limited."

"Very well, Doctor."

"Come," Admiral Vroman said in response to a knock on the door.

Captain Lindahl opened the door and stepped into the shelter, pushing the door closed behind him. Admiral Vroman was sitting on the edge of his bed, his head hanging wearily. Lindahl had watched the Admiral drive himself tirelessly for months and always marveled at the strength of the octogenarian. As he moved closer to the bed, he said, "You wanted to see me, sir?"

"Yes, Captain. The doctor has ordered me to get some bed rest. You'll have to take over my duties and select someone to assume yours."

"Aye, Admiral. For a couple of days?"

"No, I'm going to be stuck in here for at least a week, and the doctor says I can only slowly resume my activities after that. Better figure on performing most of my duties for as much as a month."

"Aye, Admiral. Get your rest and don't worry about a thing. You've got us running pretty smoothly, and we'll carry on until you're better."

"Good. That's all, Captain."

"There is one thing I've wanted to discuss with you, sir, but I've been holding off until the North Pass wall was completed. Since we're quickly nearing that point, I guess now is a suitable time."

"Go on, Captain."

"It appears we're likely to be here for a while. I believe we should send out some small expeditions to explore the surrounding territory. We could use additional food items since our diets have become pretty static."

"I'd like to approve such trips, but we know that great dangers exist outside our valley. We're not yet prepared to face dinosaurs without walls or barricades."

"But the dinos have moved north until spring. We have months before they return."

"We don't know that for sure."

"No, sir, but everything points that way. If we wait until spring, the dinos will be back and we'll definitely be stuck inside the valley again. We have the gelks for transportation and we can move pretty fast if we have to."

"If we had decent weapons I'd consent in a minute, but without weapons the explorers would be almost defenseless. Spears, knives, and bows aren't substitutes for a laser pistol. We still have much to do in the valley. For example, we need an entire road system so we can travel to any part of our valley and back in one day."

"Unless we leave the valley, we may never have any better weapons. We've made a few flintlock rifles, but we don't have any gunpowder. We produce charcoal for the smelter and the forge, and we can make potassium nitrate easily enough from excreta and rotting vegetable matter, but we need sulfur, the final ingredient, and we haven't found any in this valley. We also need lead for bullets, another item we haven't found in this valley. We have to get out and explore, sir."

Admiral Vroman knew they'd eventually have to send expeditionary teams out of the valley. Now, before the dinosaurs returned and before it got too cold—if it was going to get colder—might be the best time. "Okay, Captain. No more than two teams of five crewmen should be sent out initially."

"Aye, sir," Captain Lindahl said, smiling. "Commander Fannon will lead a team of foragers looking for new food sources and plants we can transplant to the farm, and Lieutenant Rimes can lead a team searching for the minerals and ores."

Admiral Vroman smiled weakly, trying to cover a sickening feeling of impending tragedy. No one knew what dangers existed on this planet, but the presence of dinosaurs was a good indication that the environment outside the valley was extremely hostile. Anything able to survive had to either be pretty fast or pretty damn nasty itself, so the dinosaurs probably weren't the only danger.

* * *

"Commander Jacoby to see you, Admiral," Jenetta heard as she sat at her desk reading a report.

"Send him in, Lori," she spoke back at the com unit.

A few seconds later, Jacoby entered her office and stopped in front of her desk. Her two cats sniffed the air and then relaxed as they recognized his scent.

"Have a seat, Derrick."

"Yes, ma'am," he said as he sat, selecting the chair that faced Jenetta from her left side.

"Almost two years ago you estimated we could have sixty of the former Milori ships ready for service in three years. According to your reports, you've completed thirty-eight so far. How many more do you think we could have completed by April of this coming year?"

"April? Is there a particular reason for that date?"

"Yes, there is. What I'm about to tell you is top secret and you mustn't repeat it. Understand?"

"Yes, ma'am."

"Our intelligence information indicates that the Milori will attack this station before the middle of May. We must be ready to defend ourselves with every ship available by the end of April."

"Wow."

"Now, understanding the reason for my question, how many of the former Milori ships will be ready?"

"All sixty that I promised if I can delay unnecessary work."

"Define unnecessary work."

"All work which is not related to the performance of our spacecraft. For example, clearing waste disposal chutes in quarters where people have tried to jam objects too large for the chute instead of taking it to a large central chute in one of the corridors. The only one affected would be the one who caused the problem by improper use and they'll just have to take *all* their waste to a central chute until we find the time, manpower, and bots to clear theirs."

Jenetta grinned and chuckled. "Permission granted to delay such work."

"Okay, Admiral, we'll have the sixty ships ready by April. Perhaps a couple extra because we have the fourteen that were just brought in. A few are repairable."

"Excellent, Derrick."

"Uh, that figure includes the three ships that have already gone out on patrol.

"I understand. Thank you, Derrick. Dismissed."

"Aye, Admiral."

Jenetta had time to have a cup of coffee before her next appointment arrived. This time it was Commander Hammonton, the base's personnel officer.

"I know most ships are back to full strength now," Jenetta said, "thanks to the replacement crewmen who have arrived over the past year, and I need to put together some crews for ships that will be entering service for the first time. You're aware that Space Command Headquarters has promised the personnel to staff the new ships, but we can't wait for them to arrive. We must start putting the crews together now."

"How large should the crews be?"

"At least large enough to handle a destroyer in a fight. We'll need a full bridge complement, full gunnery complement, and about half the usual engineering complement. We can skip the fighter jocks and shuttle pilots, along with flight operations. We'll need a few cooks, a couple of doctors, half a dozen nurses, and whatever other support personnel are required for a basic crew complement of about two hundred."

"How many crews are you putting together, Admiral?"

"Sixty."

"Sixty?" Commander Hammonton croaked. "That's twelve thousand personnel."

"Yes, but I don't need them all immediately. I'd like to get them as soon as possible so they can begin training on the new ships, but I can wait until January for the entire group."

"But Admiral, most of these people would have to come from the personnel already assigned to ships on patrol."

"About three quarters of the ships in this command will be reporting back here before January. You can pull all the crews we need from them, Commander, and then refill key positions in the decimated crews from the remaining quarter when they arrive. I expect all ships in this command to be in port no later than May 1st."

"Is something big coming down, Admiral?"

"Yes, the biggest, but keep that under your hat. I have thirty-five new ships ready to go right now, and as soon as you can get me some crews they'll begin training in their operation."

"The former Milori vessels?"

"Yes, we're going to need them very soon and the crews must be proficient."

"I see," Commander Hammonton said, nodding. "I'll get working on this immediately, Admiral."

"Make everyone understand this is a temporary re-assignment. Once the new personnel arrive from Space Command and they're trained, the reassigned people can return to their former posts, if they wish to."

"Aye, Admiral."

"Thank you, Leslie. Dismissed."

* * *

Trader Vyx took a circuitous route to Admiral Carver's office to ensure no one was tailing him. When he was satisfied, he calmly entered the outer office. As Admiral Carver had become more and more disassociated from the station's day-to-day business, her contact with anyone other than Space Command personnel or the representatives of planets in her sectors had decreased substantially, so there was no one waiting to see her. Commander Ashraf announced his presence and he was invited to enter the Admiral's office almost immediately.

"Good morning, Admiral," he said. "I received your message. Do you have something for us?"

"Good morning, Trader. Coffee or tea?"

"Coffee sounds good."

"Help yourself and then have a seat."

Jenetta finished the report she had been reading while Vyx prepared his coffee and took a seat in one of the overstuffed chairs facing her desk. She looked up when she was done.

"What can we do to help, Admiral?" Vyx asked.

"I have a little project in mind for your team that should keep you busy for several months. Is your new ship ready and provisioned?"

Vyx nodded. "We can leave within an hour."

"Good. I'd like you to leave for Scruscotto today."

"We're ready, Admiral. Just tell me what you need."

Over the next ten minutes, Jenetta outlined her plan as Vyx listened intently, nodding occasionally.

Chapter Eleven
~ September 25th, 2279 ~

Commander Fannon led the two expeditionary groups out the North Pass gate and through the narrow mountainous pass. Each member of the expedition anxiously scanned the steep cliff walls that seemed to stretch endlessly towards the sky, alert for any sign of danger. Several kilometers later, they emerged on a ridge above a flat, heavily forested expanse. A magnificent snow-capped mountain range was visible in the far distance. Not knowing what they'd encounter, they hadn't been able to make specific plans for the two teams, so he and Lt. Rimes sat on their gelk mounts and quickly decided the direction each group would take. The foragers would turn west and travel down to the forest below, while the geologists would turn east and stay on the ridge that ran along the mountains. Each team consisted of an officer, three crewmembers who had knowledge useful to the expedition, and a Marine guard who would protect their rear and flanks. Both teams were carrying sufficient food and water for two weeks on pack animals. They intended to stay out for as long as possible, although they had standing orders from Admiral Vroman to return immediately if they encountered dinosaurs. The Admiral had insisted that each team take one of the power-nailers, an ample supply of nails, and two extra power packs. That, plus steel-tipped spears, steel knives, and crossbows with steel-tipped arrows, constituted their full array of weapons.

After a few more minutes of idle speculation about the vast panoramic scene before them, the two teams split up to begin their independent investigations. They'd made no plans to meet again before traveling back into the valley because they'd be without a means of communication once they'd lost sight of one another and wouldn't be able to coordinate their travels.

Commander Fannon's group picked its way slowly down the slope, all the time watching for signs of danger. They didn't need to remind one another that this was an alien and hostile world with potentially deadly threats at every step and turn. Fannon, the fully loaded power-nailer hanging by a lanyard around his neck, held his crossbow at the ready as he scanned both the trail ahead and the ground in front of his gelk, looking for signs of danger and animal tracks. As they moved into the forest, the dense overhead canopy of tree branches and leaves cut the light considerably, but it was still early on a cloudless day and they had adequate daylight for their work.

Most of the trees and plants were similar to those found in their valley, but they began to spot new species as well. Since this was an expedition to find new plants for food, medicine, and other practical applications, they stopped and cautiously took samples whenever they spotted something unique. Fannon made indications on a crudely drawn map of where they found each sample as they continued their trek. Small animals scampered through the forest undergrowth and swung or darted through the trees, but the foragers didn't bother with them as long as the animals appeared not to pose a threat. Most were similar to the small animals found in the valley. They also began to see dinosaur tracks, but the tracks were not fresh. The edges of the footprints were indistinct, and they could discern the tracks of other creatures inside many of the dinosaur footprints.

*　*　*

Lieutenant Rimes' team rode along the ridge examining the rock and mineral structures from the back of their gelks until they saw something interesting. Each time they stopped, they took a small sample and made a notation on a hand-drawn map. Just a few hours into the trip, Lt. Rimes knew they'd have weeks of work examining and identifying everything that had captured their interest.

As the ridge slowly disappeared into the rock face of the mountain, it was necessary to work their way down the slope to where the edge of the forest met the descending wall of grey rock. They continued to stay close to the mountain as they moved farther and farther away from the narrow pass that led into their valley.

* * *

The foragers made their first encampment in a large clearing they happened upon several hours before sunset. Having come across few such clearings, Commander Fannon decided to stop there for the night rather than risk an encampment in the dense woods. After setting up their camp, they had plenty of time to investigate the surrounding vegetation and examine the ground for unusual tracks. Their saddlebags were beginning to fill up, and they had to make sure any new samples were in fact unique before adding them to those already gathered.

As night fell, they started their campfire, the consensus being that a fire would keep away the smaller creatures and perhaps even make larger ones more wary. So far, they hadn't seen any sign of dinosaurs; the largest creatures had been wild gelks. After watering the gelks, they constructed a simple corral of sorts around a good grazing area using ropes and wooden branches. The hobbled mounts could easily push their way out if they tried, but the hobbles would keep them from moving very far away. A sentry, armed with a crossbow and the power-nailer, would remain awake, waking his replacement after two hours. The power-nailer wasn't very accurate beyond five or six meters, but when testing it on the carcass of a dead dinosaur on the day after the herd attack, they had found that from six meters away the nails would penetrate up to half a meter if they didn't strike bone.

To judge the time for guard duty, they'd brought along a simple wooden timepiece constructed by one of the *Lisbon's* engineers. It wasn't accurate enough for telling time, but it provided a consistent measurement. It would serve well as a timer. Dinner consisted of pre-cooked fish warmed over the fire, boiled tubers, and bread. They wouldn't eat anything newly discovered until the doctors back in the valley had checked it. They had enough pre-cooked fresh food for a week and then they'd be eating jerked gelk because they didn't have a means of preserving fresh food any longer than that while traveling.

143

As soon as the sun had set, the temperature dropped dramatically, but gelk hide blankets kept them warm and comfortable, even without the heat from the fire. It was difficult falling asleep that first night outside the valley, but weariness eventually won out over apprehension and sleep cocooned each of them until it was their turn to stand guard.

On the fourth day outside the valley, the foragers encountered a wide, slow-moving river. Fannon was about to attempt a crossing when Chief Petty Officer Paula Corinth noticed a skeleton beneath the water a couple of feet from the shore. A closer investigation showed it to be the skeleton of a dinosaur. Commander Fannon used a tree branch to dislodge a bone, working it along the bottom until he got it ashore.

"It looks like a young Alioramus didn't make it across."

Examining the bone after the Commander was done, Chief Corinth said, "Sir, it looks like something's been chewing on this. The bone isn't smooth; it has tiny cuts all over it."

"Let me see it again, Chief," Fannon said, this time giving it a very close look. "You're right. It looks like it was stripped clean by something with very sharp teeth."

"Do you suppose it was something that waded in to eat, or something that swam to the shore to dine? For that matter, if the dinosaur was okay before he went into the water, what if he didn't drown?"

Fannon looked intently at the young chief petty officer, then at the river. "Uh, I think we'll postpone our crossing until we know. I'd hate to be attacked in the middle of that river by creatures just waiting for something edible to jump in. Let's follow the shoreline north for a ways. Everyone, keep your eyes open for anything unusual in the river, but don't ignore the forest."

Still following the river hours later, they rounded a bend and surprised a large herd of grazing gelks. Some of the animals stood their ground and stared at the approaching gelks with the strange things on their backs, but others panicked and fled in different directions. One young gelk ran into the river but stopped as if suddenly aware that in its fear it had erred. It was too late! Something pulled the animal's feet out from under it and it disappeared beneath violently churning water. A stain of red foam and bubbles continued to spread quickly across the surface minutes later as the water returned to its tranquil appearance in all other respects.

Fannon looked at his team, all of whom had witnessed the spectacle, and said, "I guess we'd better not enter the water under any circumstances."

"What *was* that, sir?" Chief Corinth asked.

"I didn't see anything, Chief, except the gelk. We don't even know if it was one creature in the water or many. However, we do know that we probably wouldn't stand any better chance than that gelk if we go in. Even if a dino comes along, I'm not going into the water."

"Aye, sir. I'll take my chances on land as well."

As they broke camp on the seventh day, Fannon made the decision to begin the trip home, but they would follow a different route back. Swinging south from their encampment, they descended into a misty valley containing trees still bearing ripe fruit. The temperature continued to climb with each passing kilometer until they at last reached the floor of the basin and encountered a series of hot springs. They had already removed their heavy winter clothing, and sweat dripped from every pore. The bubbling water looked some-what inviting after a week of not bathing, but they knew the temperature of the water would melt the flesh from their bones within minutes. The rotten-egg smell coming from somewhere nearby did little to make them wish for a way to cool the water to human tolerances.

"Be extra vigilant," Fannon said. "The high temperature here might mean that all the dinos didn't migrate north for the winter. Let's collect some samples of the fruit and vegetation down here and get out."

After adding samples to the ones already stored on their pack animals, they remounted and continued their journey, eventually beginning the climb up a steep slope.

At the summit, they paused for ten minutes to rest the gelks and then started following a game trail that led southeast towards the mountains surrounding their valley. They hadn't traveled more than a few kilometers when, abruptly, a snarling creature leapt into their path from the forest undergrowth. The gelks panicked and tried to run away from the ferocious beast that looked like a cross between a bear and an enormous lion, but their riders tugged on the reins and kept them facing the animal.

Fannon needed both hands to steady his mount as the four-hundred-pound creature stood on the trail snarling, growling, and staring at the group. The brute would normally have attacked immediately but was confused, either by the strange things atop the gelks or the fact that they weren't running away. Its hesitation was its undoing.

Having lost his crossbow when his mount initially panicked, Fannon grabbed the power-nailer hanging from the lanyard around his neck and tried to take aim at the ferocious animal from five meters away while also controlling his mount. He emptied the construction tool in rapid fire and at least half the fifty nails found their mark. The brute fell onto the trail, mortally wounded, and not understanding what had hit it.

Upon seeing the monstrosity fall, the gelks calmed a little, but it took all the strength of the riders to keep them from bolting, even with the creature down. Fannon dropped the nailer and sat atop his mount, holding the reins tightly with both hands until the animal stopped moving. With that, the other gelks stopped moving as well, relying on the member of their species closest to the danger to establish the degree of alarm they should feel.

Fannon used the period of calm to reload the power-nailer from a nail cartridge case on his belt. The power cell wasn't even ten percent drained, so he didn't bother swapping that with a fresh cell. When his mount had calmed sufficiently, he dismounted, keeping a tight grip on the reins. The others dismounted as well.

Passing the reins to Chief Corinth, Fannon stepped closer to the fallen creature. Little blood was in evidence, probably

146

because the nails made comparatively small entrance holes, but it was obvious the brute was breathing its last. It tried to move but was unable to do so because each movement caused more internal damage and pain. Fannon retrieved his crossbow and put a steel-tipped arrow into the animal's head, causing it to jerk once more from a muscle spasm before slumping in death.

"That is one ugly critter," Fannon heard Specialist Jason Carmoody remark from behind him. "I did a lot of hunting back home in Montana as a kid, but I never ran across anything like that."

"You ain't in Kansas anymore, Dorothy," Specialist Delores Trent quipped.

"Yeah, I'm beginning to realize that," Carmoody shot back.

"Who wants the honor of skinning this thing?" Fannon asked.

No one spoke up quickly and Carmoody asked, "You want to eat it? It has fifty nails in it. That'd be worse than eating a pheasant full of buck shot."

"No, we don't eat anything that hasn't been proven safe. But I think we should take the head and pelt back to the camp, along with a small sample of flesh for testing."

"Okay, Commander, I'll do it," Carmoody said.

"I'll help," Trent said, "just so we can get moving quicker. Where there's one of them things, there might be more."

While the others stood guard, the two members of the foraging team made quick work of the creature, leaving the skinned carcass on the side of the trail where other creatures would no doubt avail themselves of a free meal. Loading the pelt and head aboard a pack gelk proved more difficult than killing the creature. The gelk didn't want the trophies anywhere near it, and it took Fannon, Carmoody, and Trent, working together, to get the head and hide tied onto the pack animal.

In late afternoon on the thirteenth day, the foraging expedition entered the pass that lead to Castle Vroman, as the valley had come to be known since the stonework had begun on the wall. Each member of the expedition was anxiously looking forward to the relative safety that would soon be theirs once again. As they emerged from the pass and the wall came into view, Specialist Jason Carmoody couldn't resist letting out a loud "Wahoo."

The sentry on the wall blew a signal on the horn to alert the camp of the expedition's approach and then hurried to help open the gates. A hero's welcome awaited the team when they reached the buildings area.

"Thank God you're all safe," Admiral Vroman said.

"Has the other team returned?" Commander Fannon asked.

"Yes, yesterday afternoon. We lost Marine Corporal Rogers to a creature that had a head like a bear and a body like a lion. The creature was seriously wounded but got away after killing Rogers."

"We encountered one of those creatures also, but we were able to drop it before it harmed anyone. It couldn't be the same one because it wasn't wounded. We brought back the head and pelt, but it's starting to decompose after six days of traveling, even in this cold weather."

"I'd like to see it, but why don't you relax and unwind first. I'll have someone build a fire in the lavatory fireplace so you can all take a hot shower."

"That would be great, Admiral. A hot shower and clean clothes is about all I've thought about since I woke up this morning. A hot, fresh meal would be almost as good; we've been eating jerked gelk for a week."

"We never saw what it was," Commander Fannon said later during dinner, as he gestured with his hands. "It just sucked the gelk down in a meter of water and nothing appeared above the surface again. We didn't dare enter the river after that."

"Could it have been one of those plants that wrap around the victim?" Lieutenant Pyers asked.

"I don't think so, because it happened too fast. The plants we have in our river are quick, but nothing like this. It was more like a crocodile attack, or maybe piranha."

"We were quite lucky in the choice of landing site the Milori made," Admiral Vroman said. "I'm certain it was just pure dumb luck they selected a valley that wasn't infested with dinosaurs, those bear-lion creatures, or unseen monsters in the water. If they had dropped us off in the forest outside this valley, the indigenous wildlife might have killed most of us by now. We never could have withstood a dinosaur attack in the open."

"The loss of the Marine corporal shows us we're still in constant danger," Commander Fannon said. "We need better weapons, and future expeditions should be made in larger numbers."

"My team located a large rich deposit of galena," Lieutenant Rimes stated proudly.

"Galena?" Commander Fannon said. "What's that?"

"It's a mineral that contains lead. For each metric ton of ore smelted, we should get between eighty and ninety kilograms of lead and several kilograms of silver."

"Each *ton* of ore?"

"Well— yes. Lead rarely occurs naturally in a concentrated form. It has to be smelted from various ores."

"I see," Commander Fannon said. "I have something for you." Reaching into his pocket, he pulled out a small gelk skin pouch and tossed it to Lt. Rimes, who caught it and opened it, realizing what it was from the smell before he even looked into the pouch.

"Sulfur! Where did you find it?"

"In that misty valley I mentioned. There's an open pit of it there and it doesn't have to be smelted or anything. We just have to take a wagon and load it up with chunks of sulfur."

"Is there volcanic activity there?"

"No, just hot springs and geysers. That's what we believe is responsible for the mist that hangs over the whole valley."

"That explains it," Lt. Rimes said. "The superheated water from the geysers must be melting concentrations of either monoclinic or rhombic sulfur, then spraying it out where it collects in pools, re-solidifying as it cools and the water evaporates. This is fantastic. We'll be able to manufacture the gunpowder now, not to mention sulfuric acid and many other sulfuric byproducts that will make our lives easier."

"You said the misty valley is six days away on gelkback?" Captain Lindahl asked.

"Yes, but we stopped for plant samples all along the way, so you could probably make it in half that time. It will probably take several weeks each way with a wagon since there aren't any roads."

"How about if we take extra gelks as pack animals and just fill up sacks or barrels with the sulfur?" Lieutenant Rimes asked.

"That would work. We could make the round trip in a week if we used pack animals. How far is it to the galena?"

"We'd definitely have to use wagons for the ore. I'd say about two weeks to get there because we'll have to cut a rough road, a couple of more weeks to dig the ore and fill the wagons, and then two weeks to get back with full loads."

"Six weeks for a first load? How far on gelkback?"

"About two days if you're not stopping for samples."

"Then we could potentially send a group on ahead to mark the path of the new road and start mining the ore so they'd have the load ready by the time the wagons arrived. They could all return together in four weeks."

"The wagons would need extra protection going to the site," Admiral Vroman said, "in case they meet one of those bear-lion things, or something else. They wouldn't be able to run from the danger."

"Yes sir, but afterwards we'll have real firearms, so it'll be worth the effort. The dinos will get a real surprise if they attack us again."

The first expedition for sulfur left a few days later. Commander Fannon led a group of ten members, six of whom were Space Marines. Knowing the danger posed by the creatures, now referred to as bearlons, kept the party as wary as the earlier, smaller party had been. Commander Fannon always kept his crossbow at the ready, with the power-nailer hanging from the lanyard as before. Marine Lieutenant

Mercurio guarded the rear flank, likewise armed with a crossbow and power-nailer.

At night, two sentries guarded the sleeping expedition members in two-hour shifts. Although the gelks were a little uneasy at times, the team detected no sign of bearlons on their way to Misty Valley. They did spot large herds of wild gelks along the way.

Arriving at the sulfur deposit, the crew immediately began to break up the deposits and fill canvas sacks brought for this purpose. The sacks, made from fabric produced at the camp, were stitched closed using coarse thread and thick steel needles after they'd filled them with about twenty-five kilograms of sulfur each. Commander Fannon was anxious to get the sulfur and return to the valley, so he kept pushing the group to work harder. Less than five hours after arriving at the sulfur deposit, the six pack gelks were loaded and ready to start the return trip. Commander Fannon didn't want to spend the night in the Misty Valley, although he couldn't have explained why. Perhaps it was because they hadn't seen any animals in there, or perhaps it was the unpleasant smell. Having to smell the sulfur all the way back to Castle Vroman would be bad enough.

Back at the valley, workers were making potassium nitrate using gelk excreta and rotting vegetation from compost heaps placed in specially prepared hotbeds situated well away from the camp buildings. Once the potassium nitrate, also known as saltpeter, was ready, they would mix it with carbon and sulfur, soak it in urine, and allow it to dry thoroughly. The caked residue would be broken up and granulized to produce gunpowder. A special belowground shelter had been prepared to function as the armory. In the event of an accident, the main camp was in no danger.

The sulfur mining expedition returned without incident, bearing their cargo of almost seven hundred kilograms of sulfur. They encountered no bearlons, leaving Commander Fannon to wonder how many of the creatures lived outside the valley and how far they roamed in pursuit of food. The number of gelks observed outside the valley was prodigious, so predators shouldn't have to roam far for a meal, but territory size probably depended upon their social structure.

The geologists were anxious to begin their second expedition but decided they should delay the mining operation until the first batches of gunpowder tested success-fully. Extracting the ore would be far easier if they could utilize the new explosive. They would make holes using their new steel drills and pack them with gunpowder. Long fuses would then ignite the powder. It wouldn't have the punch of dynamite, but it would have to suffice until they could develop the more powerful explosive. Already the engineers were working to produce glycerol and nitric acid. When combined with the new sulfuric acid, it would produce nitroglycerine. When further mixed with silica, they would have the paste known as dynamite. A blasting cap made from a wooden plug filled with gunpowder would be all that was required to detonate the charges.

For their trip, they prepared a number of small charges of gunpowder tightly rolled in dried leaves that had the consistency of paper. They could toss them like fireworks as a defense against possible predators. The concussive force wouldn't be adequate to disable the animals, but the noise might be enough to frighten them away or perhaps distract them long enough for a team member to kill them.

Lieutenant Rimes led the first part of the expeditionary force consisting of himself and four Space Marines. For this expedition, strong arms and backs were more useful than geological skills. They would make for the galena deposit with all haste and begin mining operations.

The second group left a few hours later, led by Lt. Commander McCloud, who would plot the best course for the rough road they would cut. Chief Petty Officer Demetta, a member of the original mineral expedition, would point the way to the mine. While they wanted to reach the mine as quickly as possible, establishing an easy wagon route was critical, and they took great care to ensure the gelks could traverse the new route with a ton or more of ore in the wagon.

The value of the ore to the camp meant they would continue to use the new road until the dinos returned from the north, so the extra time spent now would save time over the coming months.

It took the road-building group three weeks to reach the mine, a full week longer than originally estimated by Lieutenant Rimes, but it wasn't their fault. The track followed by the original expedition just wasn't suitable as a wagon road capable of supporting wagons laden with ore. The ground was either too marshy in places or the incline too great for the gelks to pull the heavy load. Lt. Commander McCloud would have preferred to find a route that could be utilized year round; however, no one really expected to be outside the valley once the dinos migrated south again so it was really only important that the ground be firm enough to use for transporting ore until spring.

To establish the road, trees had to be cut down, boulders moved or blasted, gullies filled, and streams forded. Even a rough, barely-traversable road was a major job without modern equipment and Captain Lindahl had only sent thirty crewmembers with the two wagon drivers. Most had worked at clearing farmland all summer and then on constructing the North Pass wall, so they were in excellent physical condition for the heavy work. Since there weren't enough gelks for everyone, they'd have to walk back to the camp when the four wagons returned with their loads.

The wagon crew began to hear muffled explosions two days before they reached the mine. They hoped the explosions were charges placed inside the mine to dislodge ore rather than charges fired to frighten away predators. There were never fewer than two guards on duty near the wagons, at the head of the column and at the rear, while the roadwork progressed, and the road crew workers were never far away from their own weapons.

Reaching the mine was cause for celebration by the road-building crew. Although facing a difficult journey back to the camp with the ore, they could relax and enjoy a full day off to rest before they started loading the wagons. The mining group had been busy, and an enormous pile of ore sat outside the mine. The miners had brought two wheelbarrows on their pack animals and it made the job much easier, although they longed for an ore trolley.

"Any problems?" Lt. Rimes asked Lt. Commander McCloud when the two groups met up.

"No attacks, but lots of problems. I never realized that blazing a simple wagon trail could be so difficult. What I wouldn't give for a couple of laser pistols and several freight loaders. We'd have been here two weeks ago."

"Yeah, I know what you mean. In five minutes, a boring rig could have produced the same amount of ore it took us three weeks to extract. It's amazing when you think this was how it was always done as recently as four hundred years ago on Earth."

"Yeah. Any sign of bearlons?"

"Nope, none at all. Someone's always on guard duty, though. We established a position on the rock face." He turned and glanced up at a spot ten meters above the mine entrance. "Chief Halsey is on duty right now and we change every couple of hours." Looking at the lead wagon, Lt. Rimes said, "I see you brought dinner."

"Yeah. We didn't want to risk the smell of cooking meat before we got here, so we ate jerked gelk once the fresh food ran out, but I couldn't resist dropping this fellow when he stepped out in front of us a couple of hours back. I'm looking forward to a nice rare steak tonight."

"Sounds good. My people could use some fresh meat as well. We just finished the last of a gelk we killed about a week ago. The meat was becoming pretty dried out, so we cooked the rest of it last night in a stew. I thought we'd be back to eating jerked gelk tonight."

After their day of rest, the road crew turned their efforts to loading up the wagons with the mined ore. Once the wagons were filled to capacity, the entire group worked to mine enough ore for another load, piling it up outside the mine. The wagons could return to get it without the miners having to come along next time. Just a week after the wagons had arrived at the mine, the entire group started back.

The fully loaded wagons left deep ruts in the new road, and the wagons got stuck a couple of times, but the route chosen by Lt. Commander McCloud proved to be adequate for the job once the crew put their shoulders to the wheel—literally.

Lt. Rimes later estimated that they returned to Castle Vroman with almost five tons of ore. With luck, they'd be able to smelt over two hundred kilograms of lead from each trip.

The success of efforts to bring back sulfur and galena prompted Admiral Vroman and his officers to plan additional expeditions. They would have to complete their ore retrieval operations, as well as any other expeditions, before the weather turned nice and the dinos returned, but a newly developing situation with the gelks threatened to delay their efforts. It seemed that all the females had suddenly started putting on substantial weight. The doctor confirmed the females were pregnant, and Lieutenant Croff, the camp's paleontologist, explained his theory.

"It makes perfect sense for the gelk population to have evolved with this common time for their gestation period. They seem to be the main food source for the carnivores in this region, and during the warm months they must be able to elude the Alioramus, Bearlons, and other predators. They'll probably drop their offspring before the return migration, giving their babies a little time to mature so they have a good chance of being able to outrun the dinos."

Being restricted to using only male gelks meant the expedition schedule would have to be trimmed down and trips would have to begin immediately to complete as many as possible before the dinos returned. Besides, as soon as the weather began to warm, it would be time to begin planting on the farm. Admiral Vroman had already started work on the wall for the South Pass. Stonecutters were cutting blocks of granite in preparation for construction and laborers were preparing the building site in the pass by excavating dirt for the poured foundation.

Chapter Twelve
~ November 15th, 2279 ~

The *Scorpion* hung seemingly motionless over Scruscotto, locked into an orbital track that varied slightly with each pass. There was always the danger of collision in the uncontrolled space around the mining planet, but that mostly occurred between ships attempting to move into or out of a standard orbit. The *Scorpion* had been circling the planet for weeks, clandestinely studying the movement of ships to and from the surface. The busy mining planet had an incredible amount of traffic, with outgoing ore shipments responsible for most shipping, but incoming freight operations ran a respectable second. It took enormous quantities of supplies to sustain the hundreds of thousands of miners and support personnel on the surface of a planet that neither grew crops of its own nor raised any animals for food. The situation was unlikely to change anytime soon since a miner could earn several times what a farmer or rancher could make.

After weeks of documenting ship movements, the team of intelligence agents was no closer to an answer than they had been when they arrived. They held a meeting in the mess hall after their evening meal.

"This is getting us nowhere," Vyx said. "We'll have to go down to the planet and intensify our search."

"It'll take us months, maybe years, to find their location," Byers said, "if they're even here. We could be conducting a search for something that doesn't exist."

"Admiral Carver is pretty sure it exists down there, and I've learned to trust her instincts. She wasn't just trying to get rid of us."

"What if they've moved their base?"

"That would be inconsistent with the way they operate. They normally only move on when they're threatened; so far as we know, no one has gone after them here."

"The planet is so big," Kathryn said. "Where do we even start?"

"Where we always start on Scruscotto— in Weislik, the largest town on the planet."

"They're not going to be obvious," Nelligen said, "or we would have heard about them already. They'll have a lot of Terrans providing a front for their operations."

"Yes, that's true. The front will almost definitely be a mining operation, one shipping a considerable amount of ore. Their operation will be mainly below the surface to hide its size from observers."

"Then how can we find it?" Brenda asked.

"We have to find an operation that receives a lot more food and supplies than the apparent number of working miners would consume."

"We've been watching ships for weeks without spotting anything unusual," Byers said.

"They must be bringing in their supplies loaded in ore containers, then filling the containers with ore to ship out. That's why we haven't seen any unusual freighter activity."

"So how are we supposed to find their operation?" Kathryn asked. "We can't stop all the space tugs bringing ore containers down to the surface to search them for supplies."

"We'll have to do it the old-fashioned way. We hang around listening to conversations in restaurants and taverns until we hear something suspicious. Eventually we'll hear somebody complain of having to unload freight from ore containers or complain about something else relevant. Then we tail them."

"I repeat my earlier statement," Byers said, "It'll take us months, maybe years, to find their location."

"Got something better to do?" Nelligen asked.

"I'd rather be at Stewart, getting ready to greet the invasion force. We'll need every ship we have when the Milori arrive there."

"Admiral Carver will recall us in time," Vyx said, "if she feels we can be useful. Right now, she wants us working on this assignment. If we find our quarry quickly enough, we can be back in plenty of time for you to die gloriously for the Galactic Alliance."

"Uh, well— I wasn't exactly planning on dying," Byers said. "I was thinking more along the lines of helping some Milori *invaders* die gloriously for their emperor."

The *Scorpion* settled lightly onto a pad at the outer edge of the Weislik Space Port where enough space was available to accommodate the largest ships likely to land. As usual, Vyx stressed out over landing at a busy, uncontrolled space-port, but there was a smile on his face as the tension drained slowly from his body. This was his first landing in his new ship and she had handled like a dream. Her size meant that other ships found her easier to spot and were more fearful of a collision than they would have been with the old *Scorpion*. They would exercise more caution. In addition, on the run from Stewart, Vyx had clocked her top speed at Light-300. She'd never win a race against any of SC's big ships, but she'd walk away from any Light Destroyer or Destroyer currently in service. She was just as powerful and responsive as he could have wished. For the first time he began to feel that the Tsgardi had done him a favor by destroying his old ship.

There were only a couple of other ships in this remote section of the spaceport. Most captains of ships over a hundred meters preferred to have the vessel remain in orbit and use their space tugs or shuttles to commute to the surface unless they needed to land for loading or unloading.

Vyx called for a spaceport visitor carrier to take him to the office, and the driverless vehicle arrived in a few minutes. Once inside the building, Vyx walked slowly to the counter, nodding to the seated regulars. Paying a month's rent in advance, he was about to leave when the spaceport administrator approached.

"Welcome back, Trader. I see you've acquired a new ship. She's a real beaut."

"Thanks. I think she'll serve my needs."

"A hundred eighty meters is quite a bit larger than your old ship. She was about a seventy-meter job, wasn't she?"

"All the better for your operation, Administrator. The rent is twice as high."

"It's necessary, Trader," the administrator said defensively. "The pad is three times as large, requires four times the materials for construction of the blast walls, and we provide visitor carrier service to that section of the port."

"I wasn't complaining, Administrator, just making idle conversation."

The administrator smiled and nodded. "You're always welcome here at Weislik Space Port, Trader. I just hope Tsgardi don't show up to attack your new ship."

"If they do, it sure as hell won't be the same batch as last time."

"That's for sure. No one ever came to claim the body parts we found, so the body depot disposed of them in their cremation furnace."

"That's too bad. If someone had come to claim them, I might have been able to find out what they were after."

"As you said at the time, they were probably just looking for a ship to steal. The *Whirm* completed its repairs and left for Eulosi about a month ago. The captain certainly didn't blame you for the damages to his ship, and he appreciated your taking care of the repair bill so quickly."

"I'm glad his repairs weren't major. Losing one ship was bad enough."

Having lost a ship to intruders who never even gained access, Vyx had redesigned the security system on the new vessel. Any attempt to enter the new *Scorpion* would first set off alarms, while automatically phoning security at the spaceport administration building. No charges would detonate unless intruders actually gained access to the interior, and then only in the area breached. Small, antipersonnel charges, sufficient to kill any intruders but not large enough to destroy that part of the ship, should be enough to stop them without depriving Vyx of his new vessel.

Moving into town after securing the ship, the group of agents divided into two teams to cover the north and south parts of Weislik. Vyx and Byers took the south part of town, knowing from experience that it was the rougher of the two. That part of the colony was inhabited mostly by miners because all ore shipments left from the South Spaceport and each mining company maintained facilities there. Nelligen and the two women would cover the north side, working as a single team, as in the past.

Collecting important information while not appearing to be collecting information was a practiced art, and all of the agents had spent years refining their techniques since their training by Space Command. Brenda and Kathleen were still quite young and had benefited greatly from their close working association with Nelligen, Byers, and Vyx.

* * *

After a week in Weislik, the agents had picked up a lot of information about illegal activities but nothing pertaining to their current mission. Vyx and Byers had spent most of their evenings sitting in the tavern they had established as their defacto headquarters over the years, drinking their ales and listening to the conversations around them. A thick veil of smoke always hung in the dim light of the room while the odor of stale ale, mixed with the greasy smells of cooking food coming from the kitchen, assailed the nostrils of patrons. Although they appeared to be solely occupied with their drinking and totally oblivious to the patrons around them, Vyx and Byers were keenly aware of every person in the room. When Ker Blasperra entered and approached their table, Vyx finally looked up.

"Good evening, gentlemen. Might I be allowed to join you?"

"Sure, Ker," Vyx said nonchalantly, pushing a chair lightly away from the table with his foot. "Have a seat."

"Congratulations, Trader," Blasperra said after pulling the chair the rest of the way out and sitting down, "your new ship is quite an improvement over the last."

"I can carry twenty times the cargo, if that's what you mean, but I still sort of miss the old ship. We had a lot of years together."

"Yes, I was referring to the cargo capacity. I was surprised to hear you had returned so quickly. I thought it might be years before you were seen in this area again."

"I lucked out. Stewart is absolutely awash with confiscated ships, and I was able to convince them to sell me one at a decent price."

"If you're available, I'm sure I can find you a very lucrative deal. I have a couple that might be ideally suited for a smuggler with your exceptional talents."

"Perhaps in a month, Ker. Right now, my associates and I are taking it easy. We've worked our tails off getting the new *Scorpion* in shape and we're just looking to relax for a bit. I'll let you know when we're ready to start working again."

"Very well, Trader. Is there anything I can assist you with in the meantime?"

"Nope, not right now. I'm on vacation."

"I see. I thought you might be seeking something since you've spent so much time in the south part of town."

Ker Blasperra didn't miss much. His small network of information collectors reported on anything out of the ordinary. Vyx was well known on the colony, especially since the destruction of the first *Scorpion*, and his movements were always noteworthy.

"Just taking advantage of our time off to renew old friendships and make new ones," Vyx said. "I had a few debts to pay also. Speaking of which..."

Vyx withdrew an envelope from an inside pocket of his jacket and passed it to Ker Blasperra, who opened it and looked at the contents before sliding it into his own pocket.

"The information was verified then?" Blasperra asked.

"It was confirmed as accurate."

"If there's ever any additional information you need, I hope you shall call on me."

"Thanks, Ker. Right now we just want to relax and enjoy the fruits of our labors."

"I'll leave you gentlemen to your drinking then. Have a pleasant evening."

"And you, Ker," Vyx said as the Wolkerron stood and left.

Sitting on the floor of her living room, Jenetta leaned back against the sofa and stroked the fur of her pet Jumaka, Cayla, who was lying by her side. Tayna, her other pet Jumaka, was being similarly stroked by her sister Christa, who was lying on the thick, rich carpet several meters away. Eliza entered from the galley carrying three large bowls of chocolate ice cream and handed one to each of her sisters before taking a seat on the floor against a chair.

"Jenetta, how many ships are in port, or nearby?" Christa asked.

"Warships?"

"Yes."

"Twenty-four."

"Isn't that a little bit— unusual?"

Jenetta hesitated for a second before answering. She knew where the questions were leading, but there was a limit to what she could tell her sisters at this time. They were, after all, only lieutenants, not senior officers privy to top-secret information related to tactical operations. Still, there was no way Jenetta could hide the fact that an unusually large number of ships were in port.

"Yes, it is."

"So something is up then?"

"Always."

"You know what I mean," Christa said irritably. "Something big is coming."

"We're engaged in a lot of shipboard reassignments to staff the newly commissioned ships. It's necessary that all the ships assigned to Stewart actually come into port so we can shift personnel to the new vessels and begin the training."

"Yes, we know, but why are the ships still in port after dropping off their reassigned crewmembers? Aren't they needed out on patrol?"

"I'm sorry, but there are some things I can't tell you until it's time for all personnel at your level to hear the news."

"That has to mean the news is really big. Does it concern the Milori?"

Jenetta was saved from further interrogation when the com unit buzzed. She leaned over to the coffee table and lifted the cover, which illuminated to show a head-and-shoulders image of Captain Wavala.

"Yes, Captain?" Jenetta said.

"Admiral, we have the final incoming traffic regarding Operation Clean Sweep. I thought you might wish to view the reports right away."

"Quite right, Captain. I'll come down to the CIC immediately. Carver, out."

Jenetta pushed the top down on the com unit and stood up. "I'll be back as soon as I can."

"Operation Clean Sweep?" Eliza said. "What's that?"

"That's something that I *can* tell you about, but I don't have time right this minute. If you're still here when I get back, I'll tell you all about it."

"I'll be here," Christa said.

"So will I," Eliza said.

"See you in a while then," Jenetta said, turning and walking quickly to the door. As the door closed behind her, her two sisters exchanged glances and began speculating about the purpose of Operation Clean Sweep.

Jenetta found Christa and Eliza still waiting for her when she returned to her quarters some three hours later. "Still here?" she asked, smiling.

"You knew we would be," Christa said lightly. "Now tell us all about Operation Clean Sweep."

Jenetta sat down on the sofa and stretched. "This past June we conducted an operation to find and destroy a number of Milori ships that were operating in Galactic Alliance space. We successfully located fifteen and destroyed fourteen of them. One managed to escape, but we're sure we damaged it so badly it no longer represents a threat to us. It was damaged beyond self-repair and must still be headed back to the Milori Empire."

"We know all about that," Eliza said. "Everyone does."

"Yes, but what only a few people knew is that there were more Milori ships. The ship that managed to escape our net alerted the other ships and we believe they took off for alternate places of concealment operating on the belief that their original hiding places had been compromised. Our spotter network identified and tracked eleven of them. We knew they'd be extra vigilant for any sign of SC ships, so we backed off and let them calm down for a few months. Then last month I ordered thirty-seven warships that were on patrol routes close to the projected locations of the remaining Milori ships to move to positions from which we'd launch Operation Clean Sweep. I gave the order to commence the operation five days ago, and for the past several days I've been monitoring reports from our ships that participated. The last task group to report in is the one furthest away, and we just received their report tonight. We outnumbered the Milori ships by three or four to one at each location and I'm happy to say that all eleven Milori ships have been destroyed, while our forces only suffered minimal ship damage and the loss of just sixteen crewmembers from a torpedo that got through."

"Wow," Eliza said.

"Twenty-six fully staffed ships lost to the Milori," Christa said, shaking her head. "For what, a few thousand parsecs of space in a universe that's vast beyond comprehension. It's so senseless."

"Christa, you know it's not just the parsecs of space," Jenetta said. "It's the freedom to live our lives in the manner we wish. The Milori Empire enslaves worlds and dictates how everyone should live or die according to the whims of one tyrannical ruler."

"What makes his crews fight so hard?" Eliza pondered. "What makes them so loyal?"

"You know why; it's all they've ever known. From the day they're born, they're indoctrinated with the goal of sacrificing everything, including their lives, for the glory of their ruler. We're more selfish. We feel that each individual has the right to life, liberty, and the pursuit of happiness. We band together to protect our rights, while they band together to serve an emperor who's only goal is more supreme power over more subjects."

"Well, there're several thousand fewer cogs in the emperor's machine now," Christa said.

"I'd say about eleven thousand fewer cogs, according to the reports," Jenetta said. "Hey, what happened to my ice cream?"

Christa and I shared it rather than letting it go to waste," Eliza said, getting up. "I'll get you another bowl."

* * *

After two more weeks of watching and listening in Weislik without success, the Space Command agents loaded up the *Scorpion's* two shuttles and set out to visit every mining town on the planet. As Byers had said, it could take months, possibly years, but that was the nature of this work. The two teams headed to different colonies but would remain in communication daily. Each would always know the location of the other. In the event that one failed to check in, the other team would immediately travel to the last reported position of the missing team. Vyx and Byers would handle the southern hemisphere of the planet while Nelligen, Brenda, and Kathryn would take the other.

* * *

"I'm afraid the report's accurate, my Lord," Exalted Lord Space Marshall Berquyth said. "We're unable to contact eleven of the remaining ships in Galactic Alliance space."

Emperor Maxxiloth smashed a gripper claw down onto the desk. "How, Berquyth, how? How have they been locating our ships?"

"We don't know, my Lord. We thought we had stopped our leaks when we found the spy. It's unfortunate that he was able to take his own life before we had a chance to question him and learn to whom he reported."

"But only a few senior officers knew the locations of those ships, and I'm sure none of them is a traitor. It has to be one of the clerks on their staffs."

"Not necessarily, my Lord."

"What do you mean? Who else knew?"

"The Raiders, my Lord. They advised us on both the original placement of the ships and the alternate locations so that we might avoid Space Command notice. They knew where every ship was located."

"Yes, you're right. Advise the four remaining ships to move to new locations not known to the Raiders. Is everything else proceeding according to the established timetable?"

"Yes, my Lord, all is on schedule. But without our hidden ships we won't be able to attack most of the targets planned for the diversionary operations."

"Don't worry, Berquyth. I have a special target in mind for the diversion."

* * *

Some eleven weeks later, Vyx and Byers entered yet another small mining town in the planet's southern hemisphere, if the motley collection of buildings could be called a town. Situated on a flat plateau over a hundred kilometers from its nearest neighbor, the community of NeTrediar was spectacularly nondescript. Almost completely devoid of vegetation, the hot, arid region was as inhospitable as any area the agents had ever visited. Most of the structures, pitted from years of sandstorms and bleached from the unrelenting intensity of the sun, belonged to the mining company, but there were privately owned buildings as well. Numerous bars catered to a population with heavy thirsts, half a dozen restaurants offered better food than the mining company did, and there were a few hotels where modest rooms with clean sheets could be rented by the hour.

The mine was located on the west side of town, and, although not unheard of, it was a bit unusual to see the entire area fenced and heavily guarded, considering it was in such a remote area. Refused landing permission at the mine's spaceport, Vyx had set the small shuttle down in an open area on the east side of town. He and Byers had let their beards grow out in recent weeks, and while wearing the same type of coveralls preferred by the miners, they managed to exude the same scruffy look displayed by most tavern denizens as they relaxed and sipped ale in one of the many bars. When the first shift ended, the tavern filled quickly. Miners in filthy coveralls lined the bar and occupied every other available seat.

The agents sat listening to the boisterous conversations going on all around them as the miners unwound after an arduous shift, but they learned little of importance as conversations centered mostly on sports, difficult mining tasks, and a plethora of personal problems.

As the crowd began to thin around dinnertime, Vyx and Byers finished their drinks and stood to leave, their plan being to check the fare at one of the restaurants. A bewhiskered miner stepped directly in front of Vyx, looked him in the eye, and exclaimed, "I'll be damned. How are you, Vyx?"

Vyx looked at a dirt-encrusted face covered with a month's worth of beard and replied, "Meader?"

"Damn right," he said, smiling as he extended a hand caked with dirt and grease. "How have you been? It's been a while since we met up on Bajurrsko. Looking for work?"

Vyx shook the proffered hand. "Buy you an ale?"

"I never refuse to have an ale with an old friend. Let's sit."

Byers and Vyx sat back down in their chairs while Meader motioned to the waitress for three ales. Grabbing a vacant chair from another table, he sat down with the two agents.

"You looking for a job?" Meader asked again.

"No, information."

"About Milori? I can't help you this time. I haven't seen any of those ugly cusses since Bajurrsko."

Vyx looked at him and spun the cover story that the five agents had concocted to mask their true assignment before splitting up to head in different directions. "No, this time we're on the trail of a Povarian Orb."

"Povarian Orb? I've heard of them, but never seen one. Is it true they have magical healing powers?"

Vyx shrugged. "Don't know. All I know is I have a buyer looking to recover one and I've followed the trail to Scruscotto. It was sold to a miner headed this way by a gambler who was down on his luck and desperate for a stake."

"What's his name?"

"I don't know. The gambler couldn't remember because he was pretty well soused when he sold the Orb."

"Good luck then. There must be a hundred thousand miners on this planet."

"At least. We've been searching for weeks without a lead. But someone has to know something, and we'll find them. If you pick up any information, I'll pay you a hundred credits when I verify it. If we locate the Orb using your info, I'll cut you in on the deal."

"Really? How much?"

"Oh, say ten percent of a hundred thousand credits if you actually find the owner of the Orb."

Meader's eyes glazed over for a few seconds. "Ten thousand credits? It'd almost be worth quitting this job and joining the search."

"Don't be too hasty. We've been looking for months without getting a single lead. We must have visited a hundred mining towns already."

"Yeah, you're right. It's tempting, but I'd better stay where I am. At least I have a steady paycheck and the money is good— real good."

"What are you mining here?"

"Palladium and platinum ores."

"Ah, I knew it must be something valuable, considering the heavy security."

"You can't see a tenth of it. Anyone trying to get onto mine property without authorization is going to disappear faster than a fart in a windstorm. Even the miners are restricted to where they can go on the company's grounds. I haven't been in the spaceport section since the day I arrived, and I'm only allowed in shafts one and four. Do you know they even have Phased Array Lasers hidden in four buildings here in town? And I'm talking about major arrays, like you'd find on a Space Command battleship or used for planetary defense. They could probably knock down anything in orbit around the planet."

"Inside buildings? What good is that?"

"The buildings are just false fronts to disguise the weapons. If anyone was to attack, the company can roll back the roofs and raise the arrays so they can fire at ships overhead from each corner of the town. I can tell you no one is going try robbing this mine and live to talk about it."

"I guess not."

Meader hoisted his glass and drained it. "Well, that's enough for me, my friends. I have a date later with a cute little waitress from Marie's, so I have to get cleaned up. Maybe I'll see you fellas around town tonight. I'll ask around about the Orb and see if I can come up with anything. Later, guys."

"Later," Vyx and Byers mumbled. Both were deep in thought about the unusual defensive measures employed by the mine operators. While true that the mine was a little remote and the planet wasn't exactly a model of law and order, laser arrays suitable for a battleship fell well outside the norm for protection, unless destroying something that was in orbit was really the intent. Significantly smaller arrays would be more maneuverable and still be more than adequate to repel any attack from sub-orbital craft.

Meader had risen, but before he moved away from the table Vyx asked quickly, "What's the best restaurant in town?"

"Depends on what you're looking for. The best chow can be found at Buster's Place just down the street, but if you're looking for a restaurant with a view, head over to Marie's. She has the best-looking waitresses this side of Weislik. The food's not very good, but that's hardly noticeable while you're enjoying the eye candy."

Meader turned and walked away, headed towards the tavern exit.

"Think this is it?" Byers asked quietly.

"Maybe," Vyx responded. "Let's be extra sharp from now on." Raising his voice slightly, he said, "Buster's?"

Byers nodded and said, "Buster's."

The place wasn't much to look at and the waitresses might never be able to land a job at Marie's, but the food at Buster's was excellent and plentiful. After paying their bill, Vyx and Byers left the restaurant and walked to a tavern a block away.

It was almost a carbon copy of the place where they'd been drinking earlier, and the same filth-covered miners sat at tables or stood around drinking their dinners. They weren't the same people of course, but while covered in dirt and wearing the same kind of dirty coveralls, it was difficult to distinguish differences. Not all patrons were covered from head to toe in dirt. A few, dressed like miners, were fairly clean. Vyx assumed they were part of the third shift, fortifying themselves in advance for hours underground without benefit of inebriating liquids.

Vyx and Byers remained in the bar for only a couple of hours before deciding to move on. The conversations they'd overheard hadn't revealed anything they hadn't already known. They needed to find out where the security types and middle-management types relaxed because that group would be more likely to discuss topics of interest to the two agents.

As they stepped out the front door, they almost bumped into three men striding down the sidewalk as if they owned it. Jumping back quickly to avoid a collision, they watched as the three men continued on, hardly taking notice of the scruffy-looking pair that had almost blocked their path.

Vyx followed their travel with his eyes but didn't say anything until the trio was out of hearing range.

"Did you see him?"

Byers nodded. "You think it was really him?"

"Pretty sure. He looked like the pictures I've seen and fits the physical description. Too bad they weren't talking. I would have liked to hear his voice. Let's follow them and see if we can get within hearing range."

The two agents turned in the direction of the trio and slowly closed the distance between them to less than two meters. Following the three men closely but not so close that it became apparent they were following them, Vyx and Byers were disappointed to never hear a word uttered amongst the trio. The agents stepped into the doorway of the last tavern on the street and watched as the three men continued on towards the mine property.

"It was him," Vyx said. "I'm almost positive even if I didn't get a chance to hear his voice."

"What now?" Byers asked. "Do we hang around and watch?"

"Let's head back to the shuttle and alert the others so they can join us here. Then we'll try to find a way to get inside the grounds."

"You're kidding."

"No, we have to verify that this is his base and not just a visit to a mining operation."

Chapter Thirteen
~ February 18th, 2280 ~

The crew chief assigned Vyx to the third shift, as was standard policy with new hires. Because of the strict exercise regime he followed, months of virtual inactivity in space hadn't left him soft, so as he stood in line to enter the mining compound he appeared to be exactly what he professed to be— a deep-shaft miner. He mused to himself that he had once been destined to become a miner in a slave colony after being betrayed by an arms dealer, and here he was voluntarily choosing to descend into the bowels of the planet and toil in a dirty, menial job that prized brawn over brain. At least here he would be free each day after completing his shift.

Holding up his new ID for the guard to check, he passed through the security gate and followed the other miners to the shaft entrance. The foreman pulled Vyx aside and told him to wait with him until the shift was ready to descend, while the other miners, mostly men, separated into their normal work groups. As the first group entered the car, the foreman brought Vyx to a group with a missing man and introduced him to the group leader. The group waited their turn and then climbed into the car for the half-kilometer descent.

Although machines and bots performed all the actual digging and tunneling, the miners had to constantly monitor their performance and occasionally struggle to free drilling equipment that had become stuck or jammed. The group leader took Vyx to a previously opened ore vein and showed him what to look for and how to operate the machinery. He watched as Vyx started work, then left after being satisfied he was sufficiently proficient to handle it alone. Vyx didn't mind the dust, dirt, dark, din, and danger half as much as the full-face respirator mask he had to wear. Although absolutely necessary, he hated the tight fit and discomfort. His beard made it that much more uncomfortable because he needed a reasonably tight seal. He considered shaving it right after his shift ended, then changed his mind because it was a necessary part of his disguise.

After three days, Vyx knew the routine in the mine and his co-workers had accepted him into their fraternity. All miners lived in a large dormitory on the plant grounds, with each miner allocated two and a half cubic meters of space. The cubicles, a little larger than a coffin at two and a half meters long by one meter wide by one meter high, were stacked five high and radiated out on either side of long corridors on several floors in the dorm. Once inside his or her soundproofed cubicle, a miner could sleep undisturbed in air conditioned, noiseless comfort at any time of the day or night. The closeness of the walls in the sleeping cubicles didn't bother people used to working underground. Vyx had opted to reside in the company-provided housing to infuse himself further into the mining society instead of staying aboard his shuttle. He joined his mining co-workers for several hours of drinking after the shift ended each day before returning to his cubicle to get some sleep.

After rising, Vyx used every excuse imaginable to visit the different areas of the compound. His ID badge limited him to areas requiring only the lowest security clearance, but being on the inside allowed him to gain knowledge that he would use later.

On the fourth day, Vyx returned to the shuttle. The other team had arrived and parked alongside. Vyx found all four agents inside the second shuttle.

"God, you look terrible," Brenda said as he entered the small ship.

"Then my look matches the way I feel. This beard is starting to drive me wild. The damn thing itches like crazy."

"Have you checked it for lice?" Byers said. "Mine's not that uncomfortable."

"You don't have to wear a respirator mask seven hours a day."

"Yeah, that could have something to do with it."

"What's going on?" Nelligen asked. "Have you learned if this is what we've been searching for?"

"Not yet. So far, I can only descend in shafts one and four. I have to find a way to get into two or three. I *have* noticed that workers exiting two and three are never dirty and many of them aren't even wearing mining gear. The suits never come down one or four."

"That should be enough by itself," Kathryn said. "What else could it be except a base?"

"It could be just a few dozen workers in an underground ore processing operation. Ore buckets bring the ore up to a processing level about fifty meters below the surface and load it onto a conveyor that passes through a horizontal shaft. I don't know how much they refine the final output from the mines, so the heavy security could simply exist because of the value of the platinum and palladium."

"Can you get onto the conveyer?"

"Yeah," he said, grinning. "But I'm not going to. First, there are security cameras all over the place on that level and they'd definitely notice someone climbing onto the conveyor or trying to ride it through the shaft. And two, what if it just feeds everything into a rock crushing machine on the other side without any way to get off."

"Ouch!" Byers said.

"You ain't kidding," Nelligen said in agreement.

"After the processing is complete, the waste is fed to a conveyor that runs it out to the edge of the plateau and drops it into the canyon. They can run this mine for a hundred years and never worry about filling that canyon. There's no way of getting in that way unless the conveyor stops, and there's no way of predicting when the thing will break down or be taken down for maintenance."

"So how do you get in then?" Kathryn asked.

"All I can think of is to get an ID that will get me past the security check. We— meaning you guys— will find someone who is close to me in appearance, height, and weight, and get him back here on some pretext or other."

"Hi, Pretext," Kathryn said to Brenda.

"Hi, Other," Brenda said back to her, smiling.

"Whatever works," Vyx said. "Grab him just after the second shift starts so we know he won't be missed for at least eight hours. Make sure you don't grab any supervisors or leaders everyone would know. A nice, low-level laborer would be nice. Then I come here, change clothes with him, try to make myself look like him, and see if I can get into the ore-processing area without getting my head blown off."

"What if they require handprint or retinal scan?" Byers asked.

"If they require that, it's after you get down below, because they only require a proper ID badge to get onto the shaft car. I'll try to get back out if they require physical identification. If you don't hear from me within six hours of going in, get out of here and back to Stewart."

"We're not going to just leave you here!" Brenda said vehemently.

"You don't have a choice. If they catch me, they're going to start looking around for accomplices and whoever's ID I have. You can't save me, so just save yourself. That's an order. Got it?"

Vyx looked around, not taking his eyes off each of the agents until they nodded or conveyed their understanding verbally.

Vyx rose before the end of the first shift the next day and walked to where the shuttles were parked. Both were locked, so he opened the one he and Byers had arrived in and sat down to relax while he waited. He didn't have to wait long.

Brenda and Kathryn, dressed in clothes that barely covered their delectable anatomical attributes, appeared less than thirty minutes after the first shift ended. A mine employee wearing the tan coveralls of ore-processing personnel accompanied each. Vyx watched on the shuttle's monitors as Brenda unlocked the second shuttle and the group disappeared inside. Vyx gave them a few minutes, then walked to the vehicle and opened the hatch. As he stepped inside, he saw both men lying on the deck, sleeping off the

176

effects of the sedative administered as soon as they were inside and the hatch was closed.

"Why the second one? He doesn't look anything like me."

"The first one wouldn't go without his friend and he was too close in appearance to pass up. With that beard covering his face, he looks like he could be your brother."

"He is a good match," Vyx said, nodding. "It's getting dark already and they'll probably never realize I'm not him; they're usually more concerned with scanning the badges for proper security clearance."

Byers and Nelligen showed up a few minutes later.

"No one followed you," Byers said. "We're clear."

While Nelligen stripped the coveralls off the one that was closest to Vyx's size, Brenda went to work trimming Vyx's beard and hair to match the ID picture. A little dye made Vyx's hair color a better match, and a sweater wrapped around his middle under the tan coveralls gave him a paunch matching that of the sleeping worker. The last step was to put on the dark blue overalls he wore as a miner.

"Why the extra coveralls?" Kathryn asked.

"They check much more closely when you're trying to get into the compound, so I'll go in as myself. Then I'll take off the outer coveralls and see if I can get into Shaft Two with the other ID. Give me six hours from now. Either way, we're lifting off at midnight, so get the ships ready. We'll dump these two sleeping beauties outside without their clothes just before we leave. They'll think they had a wild night when they wake up and may not even report the incident, having no recollection of events." Smiling, he added, "Maybe they'll even lie to each other about the wonderful time they had."

Vyx made it into the compound without raising any suspicions, as he knew he would. Although his hair was now darker than it was in his picture, the guard at the gate either never noticed or didn't say anything because the facial features were an exact match.

Lights on poles illuminated the areas around the mineshaft entrances, but there were plenty of dark shadows near the outbuildings. Stepping behind a maintenance shed for a minute to cast off his outer skin, he jammed the blue coveralls into a waste barrel. He then patted at the hidden sweater to smooth it before re-emerging to walk toward the Shaft Two entrance.

As he passed the booth, the guard held up his hand and said, "Your badge indicates shift one. Why are you going down now?"

"I left my medication down there. If I don't get it, I'm going to have a pounding headache and won't be able to sleep all night. I'll only be ten minutes."

The guard scowled. "Okay, go ahead. But get it and get back out. You know the company doesn't like employees loitering around inside the plant."

"I'll be out before you know it."

Vyx stepped into the shaft car, pulling the gate closed as the guard started it down. Initially moving downward at thirty degrees, the angle quickly steepened to forty-five, but the car adjusted to keep the occupant compartment perfectly level. As the car arrived at the bottom of the shaft, Vyx stepped out into a corridor that led in only one direction. The sounds of powerful machinery in full operation cascaded towards him. He eventually emerged onto an enclosed, elevated walkway that circled an enormous cavern filled with ore processing equipment. Separated from the equipment and much of the noise by a wall of glass, he had an unobstructed view of the process. Vyx saw nothing to make him believe it was anything other than an ore processing plant. At first glance, the equipment far below seemed to be unattended. However, upon closer scrutiny, he observed a number of small control rooms situated at points around the cavern where operators were busy monitoring various pieces of equipment or observing processes.

Walking with purpose so as not to draw attention, Vyx completed a counter-clockwise half circle of the cavern without spotting anything unusual. He was on his way back, trying to come up with an excuse for descending into Shaft Three, when a set of doors he had assumed to be an elevator when he passed them earlier, opened immediately ahead of him on the wall to his left. A technician in a white lab coat drove out on an 'oh-gee' standup scooter and turned left, moving away from Vyx without seeing him. Noticing that the doorway opened into a passageway that required a handprint for entry, Vyx stepped in quickly as they started to close.

The corridor extended a hundred meters before branching and he paused momentarily before following the branch to the left. Walking for what seemed like a half-kilometer brought him to another enormous cavern, this one filled with cargo containers. Workers in red coveralls were busy performing warehouse operations with cargo loaders. He was confused until he spotted an enormous freight elevator capable of lifting a cargo container to the planet's surface.

"It must come up inside one of the hangers at the spaceport," he muttered to himself.

Retracing his steps back to where the corridor split, he took the other branch, again walking almost half a kilometer before reaching the end. He found himself in a labyrinth of corridors with no idea which way to go and no idea if it was even worthwhile to proceed. He had already determined that there was far more to this underground complex than anyone above could imagine, but his curiosity got the better of him and he began following the corridor to his left. He walked past dozens of doorways, most requiring either a handprint or retinal scan for entry. Their only identification was a number.

Deciding that he was wasting his time, he retraced his steps back to the corridor, intending to leave the underground complex. However, as he reached the corridor, a security guard exited on a scooter. Vyx tried to appear nonchalant, and stepped aside to allow the scooter to pass, but the guard positioned the scooter to confront him.

"What are you doing in this area?" the guard asked in an authoritative and challenging voice. "Tans aren't permitted in here."

Remembering one of the numbers on a door, he replied, "I was told to report to room C9516, but no one answered when I knocked."

Looking at his ID badge, the guard said, "This isn't even your shift."

"I know. I was in the dorm when I was given a message to report here."

"Where's your escort?"

"I was sent down alone."

The guard was reaching for his stun baton when Vyx hit him in the face with all the force he could muster. The blow stunned the guard and he fell backward off the floating scooter. Vyx was on him immediately, pummeling him with blows. The guard never had a chance after being dizzied by the first blow and sank into unconsciousness, his face bloody and bruised. Vyx lifted him up and, using the guard's hand for the handprint scanner, opened the nearest door.

After dropping the guard unceremoniously to the floor of the storage room, Vyx took his stun baton. He verified that it was on the highest setting and touched it against the guard's head to ensure he'd have hours before the guard awoke. He dropped the baton next to the sleeping guard, then straightened his clothes, left the room, and climbed onto the guard's scooter.

The oh-gee vehicle got Vyx back to the Shaft Two tunnel in minutes and he wasted no time getting into the car and signaling the guard to bring him up.

"That was a hell of a lot longer than ten minutes," the guard complained.

"You know how it is. One of the new operators was having a problem with the slag scraper and he asked me to help. It took a while to get it straightened out. I just gave the company an hour of free labor, so I'm sure they aren't going to complain."

"They better not or I'll find you and take it out of your hide. Now get out of here, fast."

"Sure thing, pal. I'm gone."

Years of practice had given Vyx the ability to appear totally calm on the surface and he strolled casually towards the compound's exit, whistling as he walked, as if he hadn't a care in the world. No one who saw him would ever guess that ten minutes ago he had fought with a guard in what was probably a life-or-death situation.

Badges weren't checked when workers were leaving the compound, so Vyx just walked nonchalantly past the guard booth and into town. Twenty minutes later, he was at the shuttles.

"How did it go?" Brenda asked anxiously as Vyx stripped off the tan coveralls.

"There's a hell of a lot more going on down there than ore processing. Let's get out of here and we can talk later. I had a fight with a guard and I want to be long gone before he's missed or found."

They moved the bodies of the two sleeping workers out of the shuttle and were lifting off in minutes. The other agents had performed the preflight of the two small ships while he was gone and Nelligen was already in the pilot's chair of the second craft just waiting for the word to leave. Vyx didn't even take time to get dressed; he just hopped into the pilot's seat in his underwear and started the liftoff sequence after the hatch was sealed.

When they arrived back at Weislik, hours later, Vyx pulled on a pair of pants and a shirt before calling for a spaceport visitor carrier to take him to the office. The driver-less vehicle arrived in a few minutes and while Vyx was settling the bill for pad rent, Nelligen and Brenda stowed the small shuttles aboard the *Scorpion*. When he returned, the *Scorpion* was ready to go because Byers and Kathryn had completed the preflight of the freighter. Vyx sat in the pilot's chair and started the sequence to lift-off, breathing a sigh of relief that there hadn't been any pursuit.

Achieving a position in orbit was as nerve-wracking as always when leaving Scruscotto. Vyx breathed a double sigh of relief as they left the planet behind. A few billion kilometers out, he set the auto controls and headed for the bathroom in the quarters that he shared with Brenda. As the last of the beard fell from his face, he felt like a new man, and he stepped into the shower to further wipe away the memory of the weeks spent in the filthy disguise of a miner. Brenda slipped into the shower as he rinsed off soap. There wasn't any sense wasting an entire shower on just one body.

Chapter Fourteen
~ February 24th, 2280 ~

The horn on the North Pass wall sounded around noon while most of the camp was just sitting down to lunch. There was no mistaking the message; it was the alarm for extreme danger. The mess hall emptied quickly and everyone grabbed at weapons stacked neatly outside the building before heading for the North Pass. According to plan, some raced to saddle gelks, while others quickly hitched gelks to wagons, but the majority of the camp simply took off on foot. The mounted riders would naturally be the first to arrive, with half a dozen wagons containing the best marksmen and fighters not far behind. These crewmembers formed the first line of defense and would already be manning the wall when the rest of the camp arrived after sprinting the more than three-kilometer distance. Only the guards at the South Pass would remain at their posts, alert for an attack at the rear.

Those first to arrive on the wall got a frightening view of several large dinosaurs stopped in the pass just twenty meters from the wall. They were apparently perplexed and sniffed at the strange object before bellowing, either to convey a warning to the object blocking their path or to convey a message to the others behind them. The sudden appearance of numerous small animals on top of the strange object seemed to embolden the dinosaurs, and they advanced cautiously. As they did, the narrow pass behind them began to fill with more dinosaurs.

Captain Lindahl had been in the first group to arrive and he ordered the newly arriving riflemen to hold their fire as the dinosaurs approached. When the first Alioramus reached a point just ten meters from the wall, Lindahl told everyone with flintlock rifles to open fire. They directed the first volley solely at the three lead dinosaurs. Lead projectiles immediately opened gaping wounds in heads and necks.

About the size of large marbles, the heavy lead bullets were capable of shattering bone and pulverizing flesh at this distance. Although the rifle barrels were smoothbore because they didn't yet have the ability to cut the internal spiral grooves known as rifling, accuracy at fifty meters was excellent. The length of the barrels and standardization of bullet size and powder charges were no doubt responsible for the high degree of accuracy achieved by the practiced riflemen.

Two of the dinosaurs dropped almost immediately. The third trumpeted loudly for half a minute before succumbing to its wounds and falling to the ground. Its legs continued to thrash for at least another fifteen seconds. The herd halted its forward progress as a thick cloud of black powder smoke was sucked up and away by the updrafts in the pass. This was without doubt the first time the herd had ever experienced the roar of firearms, and the still-reverberating noise had been deafening within the narrow pass. The dinosaurs began to bellow as if in defiant response to the invisible force that had dropped three of their leaders.

While half of the fighting force on the wall dropped back to reload their weapons, the other picked up waiting crossbows and took aim at the herd. As the dinosaurs again began to advance, Lindahl gave the order to fire and a volley of arrows sailed silently forth. Where the bullets had dropped the dinosaurs, the arrows just seemed to make them angry. It was with distinct relief that Lindahl was able to order the riflemen with freshly loaded rifles back to the forefront while the others fell back to reload rifles for a second volley. The dinosaur herd was beginning to climb over the carcasses of the first three reptiles when Lindahl gave the order to fire. Again, the lead dinosaurs fell, but the herd didn't halt this time as they pressed forward towards the wall.

After the last expedition had returned in March, they closed, locked, and braced the door with all of the timber supports constructed for that purpose. Lt. Commander McCloud had estimated the door could withstand a hundred thousand pounds of force and, although the dinosaurs caused the wall and door to vibrate slightly as they threw their weight against it, everything held. The greater threat was that the wall would be scaled by dinosaurs climbing on the backs of fallen herd members, but McCloud had foreseen that possibility and, during construction, directed the embedding of two-inch thick steel rods with sharpened points into the wall a meter apart and two meters from the top. Angled downward at a hundred twenty degrees and projecting two meters from the stone blocks, the spear-like rods would slow any attempt to breech the walls.

By the time the first of the crew coming on foot reached the wall, dinosaurs standing on the bodies of fallen comrades were snapping at the defenders on the wall. Lindahl was trying to get rifles reloaded for another volley while half the defenders used spears to jab at the heads of the dinosaurs. The still-out-of-breath reinforcements were able to fire their weapons almost point blank into the faces of the dinosaurs, coating the wall and clothes of the defenders with splattered blood and pieces of flesh and bone, but for each dinosaur that fell, another took its place immediately. By now, dinosaur bodies were stacked against the wall in a mountain of flesh, but the undamaged creatures didn't even seem to notice they were standing on the bodies of family members as they fought to overcome the defenders and enter the valley.

It was only through strength of numbers and the use of firearms that the defenders were eventually able to drive the dinosaurs back. The bulk of the camp was now at the wall, although less than half could fit on the top walkway, and firearms sounded almost continuously. The dinosaurs must have finally realized they weren't going to get through and the herd turned to abandon the effort, leaving many seriously wounded and bellowing members behind. Many of the dinosaurs retracing their path through the pass had serious wounds that would eventually lead to their deaths over the following weeks if they were unable to catch food. None of the defenders on the wall would mourn their passing.

The dinosaurs had come very close to breeching the wall, a fact not lost upon the defenders, but unlike the previous encounter, not a single crewmember had been lost or even injured, except for a few cases of severe powder burns common in situations of close fighting with flintlock weapons.

With the immediate threat gone, the sentry on duty blew the all-clear signal on the horn, mostly for the benefit of the guards at the South Pass who would be anxious to know the situation. Although limited to eight-hour days, Admiral Vroman was now back to work. He looked out over the parapet at the dead and dying dinosaurs, shook his head, then turned to the fighters.

"Good job, Captain," he said to Lindahl. Raising his voice he said, "Well done, everyone."

"Admiral," Lindahl said, "should we begin mopping up?"

"Let's ask our paleontologist and dinosaur expert. Lieutenant Croff, what do you think? Will they attack again?"

"My first impression is not, sir, but I'm sure you realize they fought more ferociously today than they did at the South Pass. Part of that is probably because it's midday and the sun is shining directly down into the pass. Remember, as cold-blooded creatures, they need the sun to help warm their bodies."

"But will they attack again, Lieutenant?"

"They didn't attack a second time last fall, so I would guess they won't, but it's just a guess. I'm sorry, sir, but I can't be any more specific than that."

"But last fall it was already after dark."

"Yes sir, I'm sure that was a factor, as was the fact that we had probably killed all the alpha leaders in the initial attack. The latter holds true for today."

Vroman turned again to look out over the parapet. They couldn't just leave the dinosaur carcasses outside the wall to rot. Besides providing a platform for future dinosaur attacks, they would start to stink, draw flies and scavengers, and represented a waste of resources. A winter of shorter daylight hours had depleted the camp's lamp oil supplies; the carcasses would allow them to refill all storage bladders.

"Captain, start mopping up. Kill the wounded dinosaurs and drag all the carcasses inside the wall. Reseal the door as quickly as possible."

"Aye, Admiral," Lindahl said and immediately began issuing orders.

It required a great deal of effort to remove the support posts that helped seal the doors because of all the dead weight pressing against them, but it was finally accomplished. Using ropes attached to gelks, they dragged the carcasses inside the wall one by one. The gelks didn't need much encouragement to pull because they were extremely anxious to get away from the dinosaurs. The difficult part was getting them to come back to drag another.

It was almost dinnertime when they dragged the last carcass inside the gate, then closed and sealed the enormous doors. The cooks had been excused earlier, so as soon as the bracing supports were reinstalled, everyone except the sentries headed back to the camp to eat. After their meal, workers would attack the wagons piled high with dinosaur flesh they had brought back to the camp. The oil extraction process would then begin in earnest while available crewmembers would return to the pass to continue skinning and carving up the other dead creatures.

The camp was still talking about the dinosaur attack the following morning. It would probably continue to dominate the conversation because it would take days to process all the carcasses and clean up the mess.

At breakfast Vroman said, "I'm sure we can all see the importance of completing the South Pass wall as quickly as possible. Last year the dinosaurs had already passed through the valley before we arrived so, we didn't encounter them until they started their return migration. But now we've interfered with that migration twice and there's no telling what consequences that will have. From what we know of the topography of this region, it's possible to reach the South Pass from the North Pass without traveling through our valley, but it will probably take several weeks."

"Are you suggesting that the dinosaurs will attempt to outflank us, sir?" Lindahl asked.

"Not at all. I don't credit them with that kind of intelligence, but they may accidentally enter the South Pass while searching for a new migration path to their summer grounds. We must push the construction along as quickly as possible. We can't count on the wooden barricades to contain them if they come through the pass at noon."

"We've made a hell of a dent in their herd size, sir," Commander Fannon said. "At some point they're going to learn not to attack us."

"It seems that if they were going to learn a lesson about taking on mankind they would have learned that lesson last fall."

"Not necessarily, sir," Croff said. "Last fall they faced a barrier of sharpened logs, but this time it was a stone wall. Their simple minds might not have connected the two situations as being related."

Vroman nodded. "Perhaps, Lieutenant. I still feel we need to complete the South Pass wall as soon as possible. Does anyone feel it would be wasted effort because the dinosaurs might fear attacking the wooden barriers again?"

When no one spoke up, Vroman said, "Okay, the construction of the wall in the South Pass gets top priority, except for the planting of crops. As we've previously discussed, there will be no more expeditions outside the valley until after the dinosaurs move North in the fall."

* * *

Jenetta stood at the SimWindow in her office, sipping from her coffee mug while watching the activity in the port. Using the window's controls, she zoomed to different parts of the cavern and checked on the progress of various projects. Engineers were completing repairs to the ships involved in Operation Clean Sweep, while others continued to work on captured ships, making them ready for action against their former Milori owners. They had moved the recently captured Milori ships too badly damaged to repair quickly, into a secure area outside the asteroid to await final disposition. They were available for parts should the engineers need them.

Jenetta was increasingly aware of the extra burden of a command preparing for war. The expected arrival date of the Milori invasion fleet was still more than two months away, but time was slipping away faster and faster. Ships returning from patrol duties were being provisioned, rearmed, and checked for battle-worthiness before being sent back out to wait in one of the half dozen staging areas located in remote regions a few hundred billion kilometers from the base. Well away from any normal traffic routes, the areas had been carefully selected as most unlikely to be in the path of Milori ships headed for Stewart, yet the Space Command ships would be just minutes away when needed. On Jenetta's orders, any private vessels unfortunate enough to happen across one of the staging areas would be detained incommunicado until after the engagement. Each of the areas had previously been carefully swept for hidden Milori or Raider ships or observation equipment.

By April 30th, everything should be ready for the conflict. The details of her plan played over and over in Jenetta's head as she examined the minutest details, even to rehearsing what she would say to the Milori commander when he arrived and demanded her surrender, as she knew he would because the asteroid would be sealed. He would want to avoid using his precious torpedo resources, knowing they would be needed later to combat Space Command forces. Jenetta took another sip from her coffee mug and returned to her desk in time to hear her aide announce a visitor.

"Admiral, Trader Vyx is requesting a few minutes of your time."

"Send him in, Lori."

"Aye, Admiral."

A few seconds later, the office door opened and the familiar figure entered.

"Welcome back, Trader. How's your new ship performing?"

"Thank you, Admiral. The new *Scorpion* is wonderful. I really appreciate having a sixty-percent improvement in speed and the larger space, although I occasionally miss the intimacy of my old, smaller ship."

"I understand. It's like losing an old friend."

"Yes," he said, smiling. "What is it about us humans that allows us to form personal relationships with inanimate objects?"

"I suppose it's our need to love and be loved. When we feel most lonely, we channel those feelings to objects around us, especially those objects we associate with fond memories. How did you make out on Scruscotto? You've returned a lot sooner than I expected."

"Your hunch was right, Admiral. I found him."

"You're sure?"

"As sure as I could be without getting his fingerprints and a retinal image. After spotting him, we hung around until every member of my team had seen him and agreed. My team recorded as much as they could. Here's the data."

Jenetta took the data ring he was holding out and touched it to the spindle in her media tray while Vyx walked to the synthesizer and prepared a beverage. When he returned to the desk and sat down, Jenetta was engrossed in watching the video footage.

"It's him, Trader!" she said when the video had ended. "Well done! I didn't expect you to find him so quickly. What about the base?"

"It's located in, or rather under, a town named NeTrediar in the southern hemisphere. The residents there just refer to it as Nee. They have a legitimate mining operation as a front. Penetration of the base is difficult. I took a job as a miner and it got me inside the compound, but much of the company property is restricted even to the miners who have been with the company for some time. However, we were able to determine that there's a great deal more cargo container traffic than could reasonably be expected as necessary for operations, so I penetrated the underground using a stolen ID badge. Admiral, there's a vast underground complex down there with a staff that's apparently never permitted to go topside. I found one cavern that's over fifty meters below the surface and at least two kilometers long. It was filled with shipping containers. I'm guessing the floor of one of the hangers at the mine's spaceport is used as an elevator. Another enormous underground cavern is segmented into a labyrinth of rooms. I have no idea how many or what they're used for because I was confronted by a security guard and had to get out of there in a hurry."

While he talked, the computer had recorded his report, printing it out on Jenetta's com screen. Jenetta suddenly smiled as she looked at the screen.

"NeTrediar," Jenetta said. "That fits right in with Mikel Arneu's ego and ironic sense of humor."

"How so, Admiral?"

"It's 'Raider Ten' spelled backwards."

Vyx stared at Jenetta for a second. "I'll be damned. I never realized that."

"Decryption was a favorite mental exercise of mine at one time." Sighing, she said, "I'd love to launch an attack on the mine immediately, but with the pending arrival of the Milori I can't afford to divert any of our forces. I just hope Arneu will remain on Scruscotto until we can go after him."

"When you do decide to take him down, exercise care. A normally reliable informant has told me he has four battleship-sized phased array lasers hidden in buildings within the town. When needed, the roofs will roll back and the arrays will be able to knock out anything in orbit. I wasn't able to confirm that personally, but I wouldn't dismiss it out of hand."

"Thank you, Trader; I'll keep it in mind. As I said, I didn't expect you to find him so quickly. Excellent work. Extend my appreciation and gratitude to your team."

"Will do, Admiral." He paused and then added, "Uh, my people would like to know what role they can play in the upcoming— event?"

Jenetta looked at him for a few seconds before saying, "Your contributions to the safety and security of this base have been of immense value and I understand your desire to take an active role in the upcoming fight, but this is a little out of your area of expertise. Your ship, while armed, would not be suitable for the expected engagement, and you haven't functioned as officers aboard regular military vessels since your academy days. My other officers and crews have been training together for this engagement for months."

"I understand, Admiral," Vyx said, somberly.

"However, we could always use another spotter vessel. We don't have half enough to cover all the approaches to

Stewart. And every minute of warning time will be invaluable."

Vyx brightened. "We'll be happy to serve in whatever capacity we can, Admiral."

"Okay, Commander. Get your ship provisioned and you'll be given an assignment area, operations designation, and the proper encryption codes for reporting to the CIC."

Standing up, he saluted as he replied, "Aye, Admiral. Thank you."

As an undercover agent, Vyx was exempted from normal military protocol, even behind closed doors, and this was just the second time in many years he had felt inclined to salute a superior officer. The recipient of the other salute had also been Admiral Jenetta Carver.

Returning his salute, Jenetta said, "Thank you, Commander. Carry on."

As the office door closed behind Vyx, Jenetta turned her attention to Vyx's report. "Computer," she said, "display a bas-relief image of Scruscotto, highlighting the town of NeTrediar in blinking red." A holographic sphere appeared, suspended in front of her just above her desk. The sphere, showing all the major population areas, rotated slowly as Jenetta studied the planet.

"Okay, Mikel," Jenetta said aloud in the empty room. "I know where you are now and I'm going to pay you a visit real soon. Please just stay there until after we deal with the Milori."

* * *

"This stinks," Byers said as he cooked breakfast in the *Scorpion's* galley for the team.

"I hope you're talking about your feet and not about the breakfast ingredients," Nelligen quipped.

"I'm talking about our being stuck out here recording blips on a screen while everyone else is preparing to defend the Galactic Alliance against the single greatest threat that's ever faced any of us."

"They also serve who only stand and wait," Vyx said.

"Huh?" Byers said quizzically.

"Isn't that from a sonnet by Milton?" Brenda asked.

Vyx nodded. "He was reflecting that he still had a place in God's universe despite his disability. He went blind in about 1654. My adaptation is that we have an important part in this upcoming engagement despite how it may appear on the surface. Our intelligence indicates that Stewart is the target, and every minute of warning they receive as the invasion fleet approaches will help them be better prepared. We will therefore stay here recording blips on a screen until we're reassigned or we know Stewart has been captured or destroyed."

"Destroyed?" Kathryn asked.

"It's always a possibility. The admiral believes the Milori are coming with an overwhelming force of ships. That makes sense. After what our forces did to the first fleet that arrived last time, they'll probably send everything they have. Moreover, they have to know we suckered them last time, so they won't fall for such tricks this time. They might just stay out of range and pummel the station with torpedoes. How much damage they do will depend on how powerful those torpedoes are and how many get through. However, the admiral has really fortified the base since she captured it from the Raiders. We aren't trying to conceal its identity, so she's mounted every gun possible on the outside surface. For Space Command's part, they've assigned almost a hundred ships to the Admiral's command, and she's added another sixty from the ships taken in her last two battles. That still leaves us outnumbered three to one, facing a fight with ships every bit as capable as ours and a military every bit as dedicated to their task, but I'd put my money on the Admiral. I'm reasonably sure she has something up her sleeve that will put the enemy at a great disadvantage."

"Disadvantage?" Nelligen said incredulously. "With a three-to-one ship superiority?"

"She faced down two hundred Milori ships in the last engagement with just a dozen SC ships."

"But she fooled the Milori into believing she had hundreds of warships at her command."

"Yeah," Vyx said, chuckling, "kind of makes you wonder what she'll pull this time."

"But didn't you just say tricks won't work this time?" Kathryn asked.

"Not exactly. What I said was *such* tricks as she used last time won't work. I meant that the Milori won't again believe she has a larger force than their intelligence has told them. It's how she uses her forces this time that will make the difference. I've never played chess with the Admiral, but I suspect she'd wipe the board with me."

"I don't understand," Kathryn said. "We know we're greatly outnumbered by equally powerful military forces, we know the Milori won't throw their ships away by attacking the base as the Raiders did, we believe the Milori won't fall for any tricks about phantom forces, and yet you have this unshakable confidence in Admiral Carver to defeat the Milori through chicanery?"

"I prefer to call it battle tactics. Throughout the history of combat, the most successful strategists have been those who were most brilliant at the art of deception. We know our ships are assembling in staging areas well away from the station. The Milori will probably think the ships are still all out on patrol. The admiral might be counting on being able to draw off part of the invasion force to corral them in an electronic cage where they can be destroyed."

"The old 'divide and conquer' ploy?" Nelligen said.

"Why not? All she'd have to do is allow a couple of warships to approach Stewart, fire a spread of torpedoes, and then appear to run away. With four fleets of warships at his disposal, the Milori commander would probably decide to send a couple of dozen ships in pursuit. He knows he's eventually going to have to fight every warship we have."

"Why not just have all our ships attack the Milori fleet once they surround the station like she did when the Raiders tried to recapture Stewart?" Byers asked.

"She could, and that's a standard tactic taught at the academies. While the enemy has their attention focused elsewhere, hit them on their flank with everything you've got, and when the smoke clears there will be a lot less enemy to hit back. But when the smoke clears, the enemy is going to come at you with a vengeance, and if the enemy had

193

overwhelming superiority to begin with, it's a pretty good bet there'll still be a superior force to be dealt with."

"But at least you've whittled their numbers down a lot," Nelligen said. "It will give our forces a much better chance."

"True," Vyx said, "and that may be her plan, but I'd wager her strategy is a lot more sophisticated than that. She told me she expects the Milori to travel in small groups this time so we can't cage them in an encircling minefield. Perhaps she intends to intercept some of those groups before they even get to the station and destroy them before they can link up with the main body."

"Now that makes *real* sense," Byers said. "We can catch them in situations where *we'd* have the superiority."

"But in order to do that," Vyx said with a hint of a smile, "the base will need as many spotters out here as possible to report the routes of the various groups in time to establish ambushes."

Byers' jaw dropped momentarily. "I take back what I said before about this job." A bit red-faced, he added, "The food is ready. Let's eat."

Chapter Fifteen
~ March 28th, 2280 ~

Using the SimWindow in her office, Jenetta watched the newly arriving ships enter the cavernous port and moor at their assigned docking piers before she rushed down to the docking level. She hurried aboard one of the ships, barely taking time to complete the formality of asking for permission to board. She had to maneuver her way through corridors filled with boxes and equipment as she made her way to the bridge.

"Admiral on the bridge," a young ensign shouted out as she entered. Everyone immediately came to attention.

"As you were," she said. Walking to the lieutenant commander standing next to the command chair, she said, "Commander Gallagher?"

"Yes ma'am, Admiral," The sandy-haired officer said. "Welcome aboard the *Colorado*."

"Thank you. Welcome to Stewart Space Command Base. It's wonderful to see this little ship again. How was your trip?"

"Fast, ma'am, incredibly fast. The entire trip took just twenty-one days instead of the eighteen to twenty-two months it would take most other Space Command ships to make the same trip. I'm glad the trip was so short. It's been pretty crowded aboard ship with all the extra ordnance and personnel. We've got supplies and non-crew personnel tucked into every spare cubic centimeter of space on this ship."

"Any problem with the shipboard functions? Communications, power, navigation?"

"None whatsoever, Admiral. This ship must be the most studied and tested ship ever produced at the Mars facility, at least since its initial trials when you discovered its incredible capability."

"And the *Yangtze* was able to keep up with you?"

"We traveled abeam one another for the entire trip. The ships were in constant telemetric communication."

"Very good, Commander. These two little ships are more welcome than the newest battleships would be."

"Really, ma'am?"

"You'll understand soon enough. Have you received your new orders?"

"Yes ma'am. We had originally been directed to dock with the *Prometheus* and the *Chiron* using the special docking collar each has for this class of scout-destroyer ships."

"For the immediate future these ships will be operating as independent vessels. They'll join their battleship hosts at a later date."

"Aye, Admiral."

"The base housing officer will be aboard shortly with billeting orders for non-crew personnel, and the warehouse officer will begin cargo operations to clear your decks of supplies intended for the base. You and your crew will remain aboard for the present. The base personnel office will begin issuing new assignments very soon."

"Oh, I assumed we were being assigned to the *Prometheus*."

"As you'll come to learn, we're very short-handed out here. We find ourselves in the unique position of having many more warships than we have crews to man them. Until Space Command can fill the majority of our empty slots, we're staffing ships through temporary reassignments. I don't know which ship you'll be assigned to, but once everything settles down in a few months you'll be permitted to request transfer to your original posting, or you may wish to remain where you are."

"Aye, Admiral. I'm ready to go wherever I'm needed."

Jenetta nodded once. "Welcome to Stewart, Commander. Carry on."

* * *

"Captain Gavin is here, Admiral," Jenetta read on her com unit when it buzzed. "He'd like a few minutes of your time if you're free."

"Send him in, Lori," Jenetta said.

Jenetta stood and came out from behind her desk as the Captain of the *Prometheus* entered the office. "Larry, welcome back."

"Thank you, Jen. It's good to be back." Changing his tone to one of concern he said, "What's going on here? Why were we directed to station the ship a few billion kilometers from the base? And my engines hadn't even cooled down before shuttles started arriving to take more than a third of my crew off the ship for reassignment elsewhere."

"It's necessary. I've recalled all ships not scheduled to return before the middle of April. The *Prometheus* was assigned to just one of six staging areas."

"Staging for what?"

"Grab a cup of coffee and have a seat. I'll tell you what I can."

After preparing a mug of coffee at the beverage synthesizer and taking a seat in one of the overstuffed chairs facing Jenetta's desk, he asked again, "Staging for what?"

Jenetta had returned to her seat behind the desk and taken a sip of coffee from her mug. "Repelling an invasion. The Milori are returning, in force. My information is that they're coming at us with over four hundred ships this time, less the twenty-six we found hiding and engaged."

Gavin just looked at her for a few seconds, then scratched his cheek lightly. "Four hundred? It's going to be quite a party. Any idea when?"

"Our best guess is on or about May 12th. We've received two reports of passing Milori ships from spotters on the fringe of our network. They're traveling in small groups this time rather than one large fleet. I'm sure the intent is to avoid being corralled, but, interestingly, it makes them easier to spot because they're so spread out."

"How many ships will we have to put up against them?"

"One hundred sixty-three, if everyone gets back in time. More than a third of those are ships we captured in battle. That's why we needed so many of your people. We began stripping crews from other ships months ago so the people assigned to the newly commissioned ships would have plenty of time to train and become proficient in their operation. With each returning ship, we're reestablishing decimated crews where we had to make drastic reassignments. When we're done, most ships will be operating at about sixty percent of normal crew strength, but that should be enough for the battle."

"Just barely. What's our plan?"

"Our intelligence is that the Milori will come directly to Stewart and encircle the asteroid. We'll seal it up when we know they're close and try to ride it out. If they're sloppy and get too close, we'll show them we're not defenseless. I've beefed up the number of gun emplacements on the surface again and greatly reinforced the doors against possible ramming. I'll remain on the station to talk with the fleet commander and try to 'mess with his head.' If I can't convince him to abandon his plan and return peacefully to Milor, then we'll have to engage. When I give you the word, the ships in your battle group will move in fast and strike. With any luck, the Milori will be so pre-occupied with my 'head game' strategy that you'll have a slight initial advantage. We'll transmit the CIC live action video to all our ships via an encrypted signal, so you'll know what's going on at all times."

"Then we just slug it out?"

"Until the very last Milori ship is destroyed, or we are."

"Any chance of more reinforcements arriving?"

"Nope, we're on our own. If we can't destroy the Milori, then we must inflict as much damage as we can. If we don't stop them here, this part of Galactic Alliance space could be lost to us. We'll be pushed back to the pre-expansion border."

"I'm not too crazy about the odds. We learned during the last fight that the Milori ships are almost as powerful as ours. Our taskforce of fifteen ships was barely able to defeat the two dozen damaged Milori ships that escaped the cage."

"I'm not crazy about the odds either, but we have to play the cards we're dealt."

The two officers stared at one another without speaking until Gavin said, "When my shuttle was approaching, I saw a couple of ships that resembled the *Colorado* at the docking piers."

"Yes, the *Colorado* arrived yesterday, along with the *Yangtze*, the scout-destroyer for the *Chiron*."

"I assume they'll play a part in this engagement?"

"Of course. I'll be using all of our available assets. By the end of April there won't be a single warship left in port, except for the five normally remaining for the protection of the base. Rather than coming here to re-provision the *Prometheus*, send your list to the Supply Officer. We'll send your supplies out to you by transport. Most station personnel and all private citizens are totally unaware of the ship concentrations in the staging areas, and I haven't allowed shore leave to make sure it remains a secret. I don't want Milori spies to know we're aware of the pending invasion any sooner than necessary. The warships that are currently in port will leave on different days so they don't appear to constitute a taskforce, and the last five warships will leave when we know the Milori are only about a day away."

"You think it's still a secret?"

"I'm sure of it."

"How can you be so definite?"

"Simple," she said, smiling. "Not a single newsie has been to my office to ask about it."

Gavin grinned. "Newsies! I'm thankfully not burdened with them. Has Space Command made contingency plans to handle the Milori if they get past us?"

"They haven't told me of their plans, but I asked them to notify the commanders of the other sectors discretely so word of our preparations doesn't get back to the Milori. I'm sure the Milori plan on attacking one of the bases on our flanks next and they realize they'll have lost the element of surprise, but Stewart has to be the larger threat to them, considering their past defeats, and they'll want to take us on while their fleet is at full strength. Revenge against me is also a consideration."

"I agree, especially after the way you made them look like complete fools last time. Any word on Admiral Vroman and the crew of the *Lisbon*?"

"None. For all we know, the Milori have sent them back to Milor."

"I really hate to say this, and I know how it sounds, but I'm not completely displeased that Admiral Vroman never made it here. I feel much better about our chances with you preparing the reception for the Milori."

"Thanks, Larry, but I'm sure Admiral Vroman is a good base commander or the Admiralty Board would never have assigned him to a forward base."

"I've met him several times and I know he's a great organizer, but I'm not so sure about his abilities to handle a situation like the one we face now. He would probably never consider engaging in 'head games' or subterfuge to confuse an enemy in battle. He's more of a 'damn the torpedoes and full speed ahead' type officer, and that's not good when you're facing an enemy that has vastly superior numbers."

"I thought by now I'd have my own ship. If Admiral Vroman hadn't been abducted, I'd probably be almost to Higgins Space Station."

"I don't think so."

"Why not?"

"As soon as the Milori threat was known, the Admiralty Board would have had your ship turn around and return to Stewart. They couldn't afford to have their most battle-experienced flag officer sitting behind the lines with a major invasion coming."

"But Admiral Vroman would already have been installed as the base commander."

"I'd be willing to bet that the Admiralty Board would have found a way to put you in command, even if it meant giving you a third star."

"Oh my god, don't even suggest such a thing," Jenetta said, laughing. "I've got two too many now."

Gavin smiled and said, "It might have been the only way to put command back into your hands without insulting Admiral Vroman. If they had simply taken responsibility away from him, it would have been like a slap to the face of an excellent officer. It would still have been something of an affront to see you promoted to Vice-Admiral just so you could assume command, but not nearly as bad as being replaced by someone of equal rank and much less seniority."

"You've always been a hundred percent accurate when predicting such events before, so I won't disagree with you. I guess I should be thankful I never turned over Stewart to Admiral Vroman. I was looking forward to it though. It's hard to believe it's been more than a year since the *Lisbon* incident."

"You don't look a day older."

Jenetta smiled again. "No, I don't. You'd think I'd have a few gray hairs after serving as base commander for more than six years, but my modified DNA prevents that from happening. Oh, by the way, I know where Mikel Arneu is holed up! And I do mean holed."

"I'm surprised you don't have him in custody already if you know where he's been hiding."

"I would, except I can't spare the resources right now to pick him up. But as soon as this thing is over, if we survive, I'm going to get that bastard, put him in a detention cell, and toss away the key."

"How did you find him?"

"During my years as base commander, I've had ships check out every asteroid within twenty light-years of Stewart. I knew Arneu was close because a message he sent to me congratulating me on my promotion to captain was too timely to have come from very far away. But for all of our searching, we couldn't locate any hollow asteroids nearby. Then one day it occurred to me he might be hiding in the open this time. Scruscotto is close enough for the message to have reached me when it did, and the planetary traffic is heavy enough to conceal Raider traffic. Not having a real planetary government, it would be possible for the Raiders to conduct business without any regulatory agencies to worry about. So I sent a team of intelligence people to investigate and they managed to locate the Raider Ten base. It's underground to hide its size and has a working mine fronting for its real activities of theft and smuggling."

"Congratulations."

"We haven't got him yet, but we will. When I think of confronting him, I almost have trouble staying focused on the threat from the Milori, but the more imminent problem always pulls me back."

"As it should. How's the rest of the family?"

"Very good, thanks. Billy, Christa, and Eliza are here, of course, and we see each other often. I hear from Mom, Dad, Richie, Jimmy, Andy, and my two sisters-in-law almost every week. Mom keeps asking when I'm coming home for a visit." Jenetta paused to sigh. "I tell her soon, but I'm beginning to think that's a lie. Even after this fight, I'll still have to wait one or two years for another flag officer to be assigned to Stewart and travel here. But enough about my problems. How are you doing? How's the *Prometheus*?"

"Still the best ship in the fleet. At least until they christen the three new battleships in a couple of months. I understand they're pushing hard to complete them. Too bad they won't be ready in time to greet the Milori."

"Yes, they should be something. But I bet they can't compare to the *Prometheus*. You know I've been in love with him since I first since saw him?"

"They say the new ships, the *Themis*, the *Boreas*, and the *Hyperion* are incorporating engine changes that will let them run circles around us."

"There's more to a ship than just speed."

"All three new ships are *Prometheus* class, so other than the speed enhancements there's little difference. I was inform- ed that the *Prometheus*, the *Chiron*, and the other three *Prometheus*-class battleships will be recalled to the Mars facility sometime in the next two years to receive the same engine upgrades. They just want to wait until all the bugs are worked out. I also hear they've started laying the skeletons for the next generation of battleships. I was offered one if I wanted it. I said yes."

"You'd really leave the *Prometheus*?"

"I love the *Prometheus*— but I also loved the three ships I captained before it. Time moves on and so must we. We've talked about someday visiting distant galaxies, but that won't be possible if we mire ourselves in the present or the past. We must keep pushing the envelope of technology and design if we're to open new frontiers for mankind and the Galactic

Alliance. Right now, the *Prometheus* and its sister ships are the biggest and baddest battleships in the fleet, but that will change with the next generation of ships. The *Prometheus'* design is already fifteen years old, and the small *Colorado* now holds the record for speed. It's only a matter of time before that speed is incorporated into all new ships and possibly adapted to older ships. Things change and we have to change with them."

"I guess you're right, but I'll always have a special place in my heart for the *Prometheus*."

"I have extremely fond memories of my first real command, and I wouldn't trade those days for anything, but I also look forward to new ships and new adventures."

"You're right. Sentimentality has its place."

"If I were you, I'd ask Admiral Moore if I could have one of the new battleships that are being built now. You're one of the senior admirals in Space Command at present and *the* single most important officer in our defense of Galactic Alliance space."

Jenetta looked at him without speaking for a few seconds. "I've never asked for any favors."

"Maybe it's about time you did. Lord knows they owe you a few. You've done everything they've asked of you and far more. It's about time they reciprocate a little. It can't hurt to ask, and it might make having to remain on Stewart for a few more years more tolerable. Try to pin him down to a commitment. Don't threaten him with resigning, but if he hesitates, ask him why not. Ask him why you can't finally be given a ship."

"I've always intensely disliked the idea of playing politics for personal gain. It seems so dishonest and against the principles of the oath we've sworn."

"We swore to protect and defend to the best of our ability. Asking for a little consideration in ship posting assignments doesn't violate that, especially when the one making the request is as deserving as you are."

"I appreciate that, Larry. I'll have to think on it."

"I once read an article about selling, written by a top salesman. He said the reason most inexperienced salespeople fail to close a sale is that they don't ask the buyer to complete the sale at the end of the pitch. The successful salesperson wraps up his spiel and then says something like, 'Do we have a deal?' It's time you asked Supreme Headquarters if you have a deal. If you don't speak up, they might just continue shifting you around from place to place wherever they have a serious problem that must be resolved, without any regard to your feelings or wishes."

Jenetta took a sip from her coffee mug. "They haven't exactly been using me for a doormat. I've been given a great deal of latitude to handle my commands as I judged fit."

"They know that you play by the rulebook, that you're smart, honest, brave, and worthy of their trust, but that doesn't mean they won't continue to use you in ways that give you little personal happiness."

"I don't remember anything in the oath about being promised happiness. Shouldn't we just be satisfied that we're being allowed to serve?"

"The oath neither promises happiness nor precludes it. Any crewmember aboard my ship can request a transfer to another command where they might be happier. Shouldn't we, as commanding officers, have the same rights as a cook's assistant?"

Jenetta smiled at the example. "Yes, we should."

"Then compose a message to Admiral Moore and tell him you'd like to be given command of one of the new battleships that have just begun construction at the Mars shipbuilding facility. He knows it will be more than five or six years before any of them are ready for space trials, and that will give them time to get one more boring posting out of you before they lose you to a shipboard command. And make sure he commits."

"Thanks, Larry. I'm glad you stopped by today. You've given me the first laughs I've had in this office in a long time, and I appreciate the advice you've given me."

"My pleasure, Jen. You've done so much for Space Command and the Galactic Alliance that you deserve a little happiness. And I know that nothing would make you happier than having command of a battleship. You know I'll support you in any way I can, and I'm sure Admiral Holt will do everything he can also. Now I guess I'd better get back to the *Prometheus* and see about organizing my remaining crew into a fighting force. The weapons simulators will be getting quite a workout over the next five or six weeks."

* * *

"Is everyone in agreement?" Admiral Moore asked, looking around the table at the Admiralty Board members. After each had nodded, he said, "Good. Admiral Shindu will assume full command of the base as soon as he can wrap up his present duties and travel there. It should take him about a year to a year and a half to reach Retting SCB. Admiral Edwards will return to headquarters for his final months before retirement. The next item of business concerns Admiral Carver." Turning to a clerk, he nodded. A head-and-shoulders image of Admiral Jenetta Carver appeared on the wall monitor and all heads turned to watch the message.

"Admirals, preparations to meet the Milori threat are nearing completion. Most ships have returned to base and taken up position in their designated staging areas fifty billion kilometers from Stewart. The areas were carefully selected for their isolation and it's unlikely that any private or commercial ships will be traveling in their vicinity. All warships under my command will wait until they receive the appropriate signal from me and then attack the Milori ships surrounding the base. Although vastly outnumbered, I promise we'll acquit ourselves with honor, and, should we fail to defeat the Milori, we'll at least reduce their numbers dramatically. I expect any remaining Milori forces would pose little threat to the overall safety and stability of the Galactic Alliance.

"Jenetta A. Carver, Rear Admiral, Upper Half, Commander of Stewart Space Command Base, message complete."

"She sounds pretty confident they'll essentially stop the invasion at Stewart," Admiral Burke said.

"She's overconfident," Admiral Hubera said gruffly. "Always has been. I've said that all along. We must accept that the Milori will destroy Stewart and be prepared to engage them at their next target. Admirals Martucci and Rhinefield must begin assembling their forces now."

"They are, Donald," Admiral Platt said, "but as Admiral Carver requested, they're doing it subtly, without actually conveying the reasons for the revised patrol routes to their captains. Once the Milori attack Stewart, the entire Galactic Alliance will learn about the invasion and we can prepare openly, but for now the enemy must believe we are unaware of their plan to attack."

"Stewart is hundreds of light-years from its nearest neighbor, so there will be plenty of time for the other forces to prepare, Donald," Admiral Hillaire said.

"Admiral Carver's forces are outnumbered three to one," Admiral Plimley said, "by a force whose ships are comparable to our own. Hull integrity on our battleships might be a little better, but that margin of difference can't make up for the disparity in numbers. I feel certain Stewart will fall. And knowing that our people will fight to the last, I fear that the entire force is lost to us."

"I feel so helpless," Admiral Woo said. "I want to do something to help Admiral Carver battle this enemy, but I can't think of a thing we haven't already done. The rest is up to her and her captains. The fate of the Alliance is in her hands."

"Her very capable hands," Admiral Moore said.

"Of course, Richard," Admiral Woo said. "That's what I meant."

"A few hours after we received that message, I received another one addressed to me," Admiral Moore said. "Since the subject is one that should come before the Board, I'd like to play it now." He nodded to his clerk.

Again, the image of Jenetta filled the wall screen.

"Admiral Moore, for most of my life I've desired nothing more than to be posted aboard a military ship in space. The thought of senior command was never uppermost in my mind, and while I naturally wish to make as great a contribution to Space Command as possible, I desire to make my contribution aboard a ship. I have served the Galactic Alliance faithfully and, I believe, well during my years in uniform and

206

have performed every job assigned to me to the best of my ability. I believe the time has come for me to ask when I will be allowed to return to a ship. The responsibilities you've entrusted to me in recent years make me believe you have confidence in my abilities and judgment, and with that in mind, I request that I be named as captain to one of the new class of battleships currently beginning construction at the Mars shipbuilding facility. I expect the years between now and their completion will be sufficient to accomplish whatever administrative job you had intended for me when Admiral Vroman was sent to relieve me at Stewart. Thank you for your consideration. I await your response.

"Jenetta Alicia Carver, Rear Admiral, Upper Half, Commander of Stewart Space Command Base, message complete."

"I guess she saw through my little ploy to have Admiral Holt break the news of her reassignment," Admiral Moore said, smiling.

"She's extremely intelligent, Richard," Admiral Platt said, "and I'm confident it didn't take much for her to realize she wasn't getting a ship."

"Should we even be discussing this now?" Admiral Hubera asked. "I mean, she probably won't even be alive in a few weeks."

"All the more reason to discuss it, if we really intend to give her one of the ships," Admiral Ahmed said. "If she is to die, let her die happy."

"We can't promise her a ship unless we really mean it," Admiral Bradlee said. "Should she miraculously survive the Milori attack, she'll be expecting us to keep our promise."

"If I could, I'd make her present rank permanent, thereby preventing her from ever getting a ship," Admiral Moore said. "Not because she isn't capable, but because she's too capable. I hate the idea of seeing her returned in rank to a Captain because of her value as an administrator, tactician, and leader. There are so many places where we could better use her talents, but we have to face the fact that this is what she wants."

"I think she *deserves* to be a ship's captain," Admiral Hubera said.

"Anything but a flag officer, eh Donald," Admiral Hillaire said. "You can't wait to see her lose her stars."

Admiral Hubera scowled.

"All in favor of posting Admiral Carver as the commanding officer of one of the new battleships?" Admiral Moore said, then looked to each of the admirals at the table. "Agreed. One of the new ships will be hers *if* she can be freed from whatever duties she's currently assigned when the ship is ready to be launched."

* * *

Jenetta sat at her desk a week later, contemplating the message from Admiral Moore. Although delighted that he promised her one of the new battleships, she was concerned over the condition that it would only happen if she could be freed from whatever job she held when the ship was ready to be launched. Under conditions such as those while commanding Stewart, she would have lost the ship before she even got it because of the kidnapping of Admiral Vroman. For that matter, if she had been traveling to Mars and been turned back as Captain Gavin suggested, she would have lost it when news of the Milori invasion became known. She shuddered to think they might actually have given her another star so she could reassume control of the forces at Stewart without Admiral Vroman losing face. That would have been the death knell on her chances of ever becoming a ship's captain because the promotion would have had to be permanent. The worst part is that she knew she wouldn't have refused acceptance of the star if it were the only way she could participate in repelling the invasion. Duty still came first, above all else.

208

Chapter Sixteen
~ April 15th, 2280 ~

Fresh vegetables highlighted the noon meal at the camp. Lieutenant Pyers, the farm manager, had had his hands full trying to get the vegetables close to ripened maturity before they were picked. As it was, they should have had a few more days in the sun, but he knew everyone was salivating just thinking about them. The camp had been living on gelk meat, fish, tubers, and bread throughout the winter, and they desperately needed the luscious green and yellow vegetables. Pyers suspected that the hunters were gorging themselves on wild vegetables they found during their hunting trips because Commander Fannon was eating very little at evening meals, a highly unusual situation with someone as active as he was.

Initially, each crewmember was limited in the portion size they were permitted, but that would change in a couple of weeks as the farm output increased dramatically. The doctor was perhaps the happiest person in the camp, not because he longed for the taste of fresh vegetables more than anyone else, but because he had lately started to worry about hypo-vitaminosis outbreaks among the vitamin-deficient crew. The vegetables would improve their well-being tremendously. The mood in the mess hall was noticeably lighter this day, with far more laughter and grinning than was normal. After lunch, many rubbed or patted their stomachs as they left the mess hall very sated.

The camp had made great progress during the months since the attack by dinosaurs at the North Pass. Before the dinosaurs had been turned away last year and been forced to find a new trail North, it was hoped they wouldn't even try to use the old trail this year. Come fall, the camp would again be on high alert until they were certain the dinosaurs had already migrated north, but having completed the wall at the South Pass, they now felt very secure. Numerous excursions outside the valley were already planned for the winter months, and Lieutenant Rimes had prepared a long list of ores and minerals for which the explorers would search. Each find had improved the living conditions tremendously, but there was a long way to go. Number one on the list was to find a source of copper, with tin being number two, and bauxite being third. Bauxite, when processed, can yield up to twenty percent of its weight in aluminum ingots. Of course, there were still problems to be resolved with refining the aluminum, number one being the amount of power needed for the electrolytic process.

The engineers were presently completing a new two-lane bridge over the river to replace the crude single lane bridge constructed during the first few months in the valley. Since it had originally been necessary to wade across the river, they had chosen the shallowest part when selecting a crossing point, and the road on the other side was found at this spot. The new bridge would rest on piers constructed from stone blocks like those used to construct the walls in the two passes, with the superstructure being made from hard woods found in the forest.

Except for small patches of trees scattered about, the rows of trees used to prevent soil erosion, and the trees lining the roads, the entire forest on the east side of the river had now been cleared for farming. An aggressive program of removing stumps using teams of gelks had been underway for months. Although the east side of the river comprised only a very small portion of the valley as a whole, the cleared land was considerable. It ran six kilometers from the North Pass to the gorge where the river disappeared in a series of quickly descending rapids.

Another project underway was construction of a new cold storage warehouse. The old warehouse had proven to be much too small, and it couldn't lower the temperature to desired levels since it relied on simple convection. An arrangement of terracotta pipes funneled cold water from the mountain stream through the building. The new warehouse would also use the stream for cooling, but additional refrigeration would come from a compressor under development by the engineers.

Admiral Vroman moved from project to project, discussing the progress with each of the supervisors before moving on. His health had improved and the doctor had even stopped requiring daily checkups. He was standing on the new bridge over the river, discussing the surface covering, when Lt. Commander McCloud suddenly pointed to the sky and said, "Look, sir!"

Vroman and Lindahl immediately turned and looked skyward. A blazing object was streaking across the sky. They watched as it passed directly overhead and continued moving away.

"Is it a rescue ship?" McCloud asked.

"Impossible to say for sure," Lindahl said, "but I'd have to say no. It was definitely something entering the atmosphere, but it could have been a small meteor or just a piece of space junk caught in the gravity of this planet. A ship under control would have slowed its entry enough to reduce friction to a minimum."

"I agree," Vroman said. "No ship's captain would ever subject his vessel to that kind of heat stress and possible damage if he was still in control. It must have been a tiny meteorite or something."

It was the first time in months anyone had even mentioned possible rescue, but the subject was dropped almost immediately. The crew had accepted that their internment might be a very long one and were working hard to make this planet into their home. The engineers were even working on developing a Stirling Engine that would run on a form of Ethanol made from the farm produce. A few donkey engines and farm tractors would increase productivity tremendously.

* * *

Exalted Lord Space Marshall Berquyth entered the office of Emperor Maxxiloth after knocking and receiving an invitation to come in. The emperor was lying on a sofa with his eyes closed, but he was fully awake. "What is it, Berquyth?"

"My Lord," he said in the usual soft voice used when speaking to his monarch, "we've received a message from Supreme Lord Space Marshall Dwillaak. He reports that the invasion force is on schedule and will reach Stewart on the projected date. He asks that we immediately relay any new instructions that would contravene those of the plan. If nothing has changed, he requests that we send the attack code as soon as possible because of the transmission distance."

"Send the attack code. The changes will not affect Dwillaak's operation. Send the other prepared message to the four ships that will create our diversion. They must commence their attack fifteen solars before the attack on Stewart is set to begin."

"Very good, my Lord. Is there anything else?"

"I've been lying here thinking about the attack. Our spies report that operations at Stewart are normal. There's been no flurry of activity to suggest they know about the invasion. Carver is observed daily, walking through the concourse without a care on her face. It appears our arrival will be a complete surprise. There are fewer than a dozen warships in the port, and half of those are loading supplies in preparation for their patrol activities. This is going to be so easy that it wasn't necessary to send those extra two hundred ships. When I close my eyes, I can already see Carver's mounted head decorating my wall. I think I'll place it over the door facing my desk so I can relish our victory every time I look up."

"Yes, my Lord."

"Things are going so well it's beginning to feel almost anti-climatic already. I hope the meager forces at Stewart are able to put up at least token resistance. The next engagement will be more difficult because we'll have lost the element of surprise, but after we wipe out Stewart so easily, their morale is sure to have suffered, and they won't have the number of ships that Stewart has. Where do you suppose the ships on patrol in Stewart's sectors will head?"

"I would say that they'll immediately head for one of the two bases on Stewart's flanks, so the next battle may be more difficult than originally projected. We expected a much greater concentration of ships at Stewart, believing that our invasion forces would be spotted in time for them to gather for its defense."

"Yes, I suppose you're right. It's good that we did send all the ships we could spare."

"Yes, my Lord. It's better to have too many than too few. Is there anything else, my Lord?"

"No, that's all, Berquyth. Send the messages."

"Yes, my Lord."

* * *

"What do we know?" Mikel Arneu asked rhetorically of the four security people assembled in the conference room, his anger somewhat under control but obvious by his demeanor. "We know that a miner calling himself Jason Brown took a job in the mine and worked here for only a very short time before breeching our security and making it from the processing facility into the base. He accomplished this by having two attractive female confederates lure a couple of fools back to a shuttle where they were drugged and had their IDs stolen. Brown looked enough like one of the fools that he was able to pass visual inspection by a guard. This intruder then passed from the processing plant into the base through an access tunnel that's supposed to be secure and for which the drugged technician didn't even have an access card, so someone else must have allowed him into the tunnel. Then we lose track of him until a guard found him in the lab complex and demanded an explanation. He overpowered the guard and made his way out of the base through the processing plant, up the shaft, and out of the compound. The questions are, who let him into the access tunnel, what was he after, what did he do while he was in here, and where did he go afterwards? Anyone wish to offer any ideas?" he asked angrily.

"We've deduced it wasn't necessary for anyone to actually let him into the access tunnel," Captain Whittle of the Guard Force said. "The doors remain open for seven seconds after someone passes, so he may have just waited until someone exited and stepped through."

"Why do you suspect it happened when someone exited?"

"Because someone would have noticed him following them into the tunnel. Traffic is very light and the tunnel is quite long. His tan coveralls would have alerted them to his unauthorized entry."

"Okay. How do we prevent it from happening again?"

"We've adjusted the time from seven seconds to two seconds. The person opening the door has to move quickly to get through before the doors start to close and is still near the door when it closes. We also require a valid ID now to exit the tunnel. He'd be stuck in the tunnel until someone opened the doors the next time."

"Okay. What was he after?"

"There's nothing of any real value in the section where he was found, so maybe he was just exploring, hoping to find where the refined platinum and palladium is stored."

"Simple theft?"

"It's the most likely reason."

"Or maybe he was a spy, searching for information about the base?"

"We can't be sure until we find him and question him, sir."

"Which brings us to the next question: where is he and where are his confederates?"

"We've searched every city and town on the planet," Sergeant Sadar said, "without success. We must have interviewed ten thousand miners but no one knows any Jason Brown, nor could anyone identify him from his picture. He's disappeared completely."

"Since he had two shuttles, it's reasonable to assume he had a ship," Arneu said. "Has anyone checked to see if there were any ship departures in the twenty-four hours after the break-in?"

"Checked with whom, sir? Planetary arrivals and departures aren't recorded anywhere, and since he had shuttles, he might have had a ship in orbit."

"So what you're telling me is that someone can just break in here any time and we can't stop them?"

"The only way to stop them is to control the workforce better," Captain Whittle said. "We should stop hiring outsiders and use only our own people inside the compound."

"Impossible. Mining is such a miserable job that our people don't want to do it. Would you?"

"Uh, no sir. Perhaps we should close off the access tunnel between the processing facility and the base. We make everyone go to the surface and pass an examination each time to access each area. And we can put everyone going into Shaft Two or Three through a more extensive screening process, such as handprint or retinal scanning."

"If we close off the access tunnel we'll have to take our refined ore to the surface and bring it back down again for shipment. That's too much effort. Instead, lets restrict tunnel use to just ore shipments. All personnel traveling between those points will have to go up and then down. It will make things more difficult, but do it. And I don't want anyone allowed into Shaft Three unless the guard is one hundred percent sure of their identity. Tell your guards that I'll have the ears of anyone who passes another unauthorized intruder through. And I mean that literally."

"Yes, sir," Captain Whittle said. He had no doubt Arneu meant what he said.

"All right, get out of here," Arneu said.

The guard officers were more than happy to vacate the room. They knew just how dangerous Arneu could be when he was in this kind of mood.

Arneu sat at the table after they had left, thinking about the break-in. He hadn't had a good night's sleep in the many weeks since it had occurred. "What was he after?" he said aloud in the empty room.

* * *

Vertap Aloyandro knocked lightly and then entered the royal chambers. Walking to where the king was working at his desk, he said, "You sent for me, your majesty?"

"Yes, Vertap. I haven't read anything in your reports regarding the situation with the Galactic Alliance. Brief me please."

"Our agents report that all is quiet at Stewart. Admiral Carver is conducting business as usual and is seemingly unconcerned that the Milori will be arriving soon. Only a handful of ships are in the port and one would think that Space Command is completely oblivious to the imminent arrival of the invasion force. It's most peculiar."

"Yet you have considerable confidence in this Terran?"

"Oh yes, your majesty, I do. She has demonstrated her abilities time and again. I would not like to launch an attack against her. She's brilliant and unpredictable, and her tactics are unlike any I've studied. Just when you think you have her beaten, she does something so fantastic and incredible that you swear she's a conjurer. Upon later examination, the tactic seems logical, almost simplistic, but not at the time she sets it in motion. You later find yourself shaking your head and wondering how you could have failed to think of it yourself. By keeping her enemies constantly off-balance, she gains an incredible advantage."

"Then you believe the Galactic Alliance will prevail?"

"Even if Admiral Carver does not personally survive against the overwhelming superiority of the Milori invasion fleet, I believe the Galactic Alliance will prevail. I don't know how, but she will destroy enough of the Milori fleet to tip the balance in their favor."

"Then you feel we should send our forces out?"

"That's not up to me, but if it were I would say no. At the very least, we know the remaining Milori forces are very spread out, so this appears to be the best time to re-take our territory. But if the Milori are successful, they could come after us with renewed vengeance when their fight with the Galactic Alliance is over. It could be argued it's prudent to wait until our forces are stronger. If we don't swat at the giant, perhaps he'll leave us alone for a little longer."

"But each year we wait, the Milori produce more ships. We can't possibly keep up with their war production and we can't continue to hide the number of ships we're accumulating."

"It's a difficult decision, Sire."

"Yes, Vertap. When will the attack on Stewart begin?"

"We expect the Milori to arrive at Stewart in about fifteen Earth days. That's a little over two weeks of their time."

"Thank you, Vertap. That will be all."

"It was my pleasure, sire."

* * *

Brenda snuggled in the crook of Vyx's arm and twisted her head to see what he was reading. He wrapped his arm around her and turned his head to plant a long, slow kiss on her lips.

"Ummm," she said when he pulled away. "Now this is the kind of duty I enjoy. And to think we're doing it all for the Galactic Alliance."

"Well, maybe not all," he responded. "I'm doing a little of it for myself."

She giggled, then pinched his side gently.

"Ouch!"

"Oh stop it. That didn't hurt."

"Yes it…"

His sentence was cut off by an alarm from the automatic sensors. In a second, they were both on their feet and racing for the bridge. The proximity sensors were flashing wildly.

"What is it?" she asked excitedly, as he stared at the monitor.

"It's a group of ships. They'll pass about a hundred-thousand kilometers off our larboard side. They're heading towards Stewart."

"Milori?"

"It appears so. They're traveling at Light-375 so they're not freighters, and we know they're not Space Command."

"Can they see us?"

"No. We're not under power, in their path, or actively scanning."

"We'd better send a message to Stewart immediately and advise them that we've spotted the fleet."

"In a few minutes after they've passed us by. We don't want to alert them that they've been spotted."

"What's going on?" Byers asked from the doorway of the bridge.

"A fleet of Milori ships is passing," Brenda said.

"Have we told Stewart?"

"Not yet," Vyx said. "We'll wait until the ships have passed us so they don't know they've been spotted. Even at Light-375, we're two weeks from Stewart. And it isn't a fleet, it's only eight ships."

"Eight? That's all?"

"The admiral said she expected the Milori to travel in small groups this time to hide their numbers. It looks like she was right again."

Vyx waited five minutes before sending the encrypted report to Stewart. By then Nelligen and Kathryn had joined the three already on the bridge. "Well, the excitement's over. We've done our duty. We can return to whatever we were doing before the alarms sounded."

"Aren't we going to follow them to Stewart?" Byers asked.

"Follow them?" Vyx said. "They're traveling at Light-375. The best we can do is Light-300. The battle will be over long before we could get there."

"We're not doing any good out here," Nelligen said. "Not now that the Milori fleet has passed us."

Vyx looked at the anxious faces. "Oh, all right. We might as well. Perhaps we'll be able to help with *something*."

Chapter Seventeen
~ April 27th, 2280 ~

Jenetta was having dinner alone in her dining room when she received the call from Captain Wavala, the officer in charge of the Communications and Computing section at Stewart, who was on duty in the CIC. Not having a com unit at the table, she received the message on her CT.

Pressing her SC ring, she said, "This is Admiral Carver."

"Admiral, I'm sorry to disturb you during dinner, but we've just received a message from Scruscotto. Four Milori ships have begun attacking the planet. They've destroyed a number of ships in orbit and are bombing mining colonies in the southern hemisphere."

"Immediately recall all personnel to their ships using the base's PA system. Issue orders to the ships in port to get underway within two hours. Destination Scruscotto."

"But Admiral, the only ships in port are the five warships remaining here for the protection of the base."

"I'm aware of that, Captain."

"But Admiral, shouldn't you send some ships from the staging areas instead?"

"No, Captain. Carry out your orders, please."

"Yes ma'am. Will do, Admiral."

"Carver, out."

Jenetta picked up her fork and continued her meal. A few seconds later an announcement came over the little-used public address system. "Attention. All Space Command personnel assigned to warships in port should immediately report to their ships and prepare for deployment. I repeat, all Space Command personnel assigned to warships in port should immediately report to their ships and prepare for deployment." Jenetta knew the same message was being heard throughout the station, especially in the concourse area where speakers were located liberally throughout the restaurants, retail stores, and walkways. Additionally, every room in the housing section had at least one speaker.

In one hour, any personnel who had not reported aboard their ship would be summoned again, using their CT if they were an officer or their ID if they were a NCO or crewman.

Within two hours, the five warships were backing away from their docking piers and leaving the port. Reporters had begun besieging Jenetta's office with calls, so she had scheduled a press conference for later in the evening. She waited until twenty minutes after the last ship had exited the port and then walked to the CIC.

"Captain Wavala, please send an encrypted message to the captains of all five ships that just left the port. Tell them to execute special order 86-3."

"86-3 ma'am?"

"That's correct, Captain."

"Uh, if you don't mind my asking, what is 86-3?"

"It's a recall. But they will not return here. They will proceed to their designated staging area."

Captain Wavala grinned. "Yes, ma'am."

After Wavala issued the recall, Jenetta left to prepare for her press conference.

Jenetta stepped up to the rostrum after a quick introduction by the station's public relations officer. Reporters and news people representing newspapers and media stations around the Galactic Alliance packed the small hall. Stewart, standing at the gateway to the center of the galaxy and being a key element in the defense of the Alliance, had become a magnet for every news service.

"Good evening and thank you for coming. I've called this press conference to announce that tonight, four Milori ships attacked the mining planet Scruscotto located just inside the Frontier Zone. I have no information yet regarding casualties or damage, other than there are reports that ships in orbit have been destroyed and towns on the surface in the southern hemisphere have come under direct assault.

"Since we only have two ships on patrol routes which would enable them to respond within thirty days, I've dispatched the five ships we had in port. Scruscotto is twenty light-years from here, so I'm afraid the attackers will have time to do all the damage they intend before our ships reach the planet, but we will engage the Milori ships whenever and wherever encountered. Questions?"

Nearly every reporter in the crowd raised their hand, and Jenetta spent the next hour answering questions. She limited questions to topics regarding the Milori because the reporters tried to direct the questioning away to other topics of special interest after Jenetta had covered the issue of the Milori attack on Scruscotto thoroughly.

Analyzing the reports received from spotters allowed Jenetta's staff to estimate almost to the minute when the Milori would first arrive at the station. Several days before their arrival she gave orders to bring most of the confiscated ships in from the farms and tether them in the now almost empty port. Stewart, being a transportation hub, had a large number of shipping containers in various farms awaiting pickup by freight companies. They used confiscated freighters to haul containers away, and the ships in transit would be a half light-year from Stewart by the time the Milori arrived. Although the preceding actions might have escaped the attention of the news media, Jenetta's announcement to all freighter captains advising them to get their vessels away from Stewart would not. Newsies again besieged her office with calls about the evacuation. The station's public relations officer held a special press conference and read a prepared statement about a possible threat from the Milori. It was the usual rhetoric about reports suggesting a few Milori ships had been observed heading towards Stewart and that the Station's command was taking the reports seriously given the verified attacks on Scruscotto.

The lower half of the station, off limits to unescorted, non-military personnel, was already in war mode. The CIC had established encrypted video links to each of the ships in the staging areas, both so the ships would be in constant contact and so the officers on the bridge would be able to observe everything that occurred in the CIC. Likewise, the Center could see the bridge of every ship and talk with the captain, although only the bridges of the battle group leaders were displayed constantly.

In the hours before the expected attack, 'pool' reporters were escorted to a special room not far from the CIC. Most had been roused from their beds and received no briefing of any kind. They were just assigned seats and told to watch the two monitors at the front of the room. One showed the image that was displaying on the large monitor in the CIC, while the other would show any open broadcasts originating *from* the CIC.

Jenetta had done her best to appear calm as the hours and minutes ticked down towards the Milori arrival, but a nervous stomach prevented her from eating a decent meal at dinner. Expected at just after two a.m., the Milori didn't disappoint, the first ships arriving at precisely 0208. Jenetta and her senior staff had assembled in the CIC at midnight to begin the interminable wait for the confrontation.

Sitting ramrod straight in her chair, Jenetta waited for the Milori commander to make the first contact. The holographic map of the area around the station showed the arrival of the first Milori ships. They took up positions twenty-five thousand kilometers away, creating a ring of warships much like the rings around Saturn. As each new group arrived over the next few minutes, its ships joined the growing circle, filling in wherever gaps existed.

"Admiral, we're being hailed by the Milori commander," the com chief said at 0212.

"Order all ships in the staging areas to move to their designated RP five-billion kilometers from the station. Then put the Milori commander on the big screen, Lieutenant, and open the outgoing broadcast line."

"Aye, ma'am."

A second later, the large monitor at the front of the room filled with the visage of Supreme Lord Space Marshall Dwillaak. A smaller screen showed the image of Jenetta being broadcast over the open channel.

"Admiral, I order you to open your doors and surrender your station immediately or be destroyed."

"Ahh, Space Marshall Dwillaak, isn't it?"

"Supreme Lord Space Marshall Dwillaak."

"Is that a promotion? Wasn't it just Space Marshall the last time? Congratulations Supreme Space Lord Marshall," Jenetta said with a perfectly straight face. She was well aware of Dwillaak's rank and title.

"It's *Supreme Lord Space Marshall* Dwillaak, and no, my rank has not changed," he said with obvious irritation.

"Oh, sorry. I hadn't expected to ever see you again."

"I've come to erase the dishonor of our last encounter."

"By dishonoring your word to leave and never return? Really, Dwillaak, committing one dishonor to erase another is no way to clear your record."

Dwillaak sputtered. "You lied to me about those ships. They weren't warships at all."

"I never lied to you about those ships, and I never said they were warships. I only referred to them as ships. I'm sure you have video records, so you can check for yourself. I was fully prepared to engage your fleet with just my twelve warships. If you jumped to the erroneous conclusion on your own that the others were warships, I can't be held responsible."

Dwillaak forced himself to calm down. He had expected Carver to be beside herself with worry once his armada circled the station. But she appeared as unruffled as when she had dictated the terms of surrender at their last encounter. He wondered if she could possibly believe she had a chance of surviving this new confrontation. The emperor had charged Dwillaak with the task of bringing back her head, and he looked forward to personally separating it from her shoulders. He felt supremely powerful in this situation, so he could afford to be a little patient. "Very clever, Admiral, but I won't be jumping to conclusions this time. I know you have no ships inside the port. You foolishly sent them off to protect Scruscotto."

"Oh, that's because we don't need them here anymore."

Dwillaak flinched, unsure if he had heard correctly. "What?"

"I said we don't need them here anymore. We have our new Madness Ray to protect the station if our laser arrays aren't adequate."

"Madness Ray? What foolishness is this? Another attempt to have me surrender without a fight?"

"Not at all, Marshall Lord Supreme Dwillaak. It's an incredible new weapon devised by our Space Command Weapons Research people for defending the station from attack. We're very proud of it. Granted, we haven't perfected it yet, but it's worked incredibly well against twenty-five to thirty percent of the subjects we've used in the tests. A few species have shown remarkable resistance to it, but most exhibit early signs of violent psychosis within minutes, and many have succumbed to *complete* insanity. The intense aggression they've exhibited has been horrendous."

"I don't believe you. You have no such weapon, just as you didn't have a large fleet of warships at our last encounter."

Jenetta shrugged her shoulders. "I really didn't expect you to believe me, but I had to give you one last chance to leave before we turn your brains to mush. Once we begin hostilities, all bets are off and it will be a fight to the finish."

"My sentiments exactly, which is why I offer you one chance to surrender the station."

"Then I guess we've reached an impasse, for I will never surrender."

"Nor will I."

"Too bad." Turning towards a CPO at the com station, she said loudly, "Engage the Madness Ray."

The chief depressed a button on her console and a fluctuating, piercing, high-pitched whine filled Dwillaak's bridge and every Milori ship that was watching the open broadcast.

"And this very annoying sound is supposed to drive us mad?" Dwillaak asked with obvious amusement.

"Not just mad, Supreme Marshall Lord Space Dwillaak. It causes you to lose control and begin lashing out violently at anyone and everyone. As I said, it isn't a hundred percent successful yet, but it's effective enough. We haven't pin-

224

pointed the problem, but we believe it's owed to refractive resonance of the hull."

Dwillaak sat in the command chair on his bridge and smiled, unwilling to rise to the bait Jenetta had cast out by scrambling his title for a third time. "More foolishness. Your ploy isn't working, Admiral. Now, before I order my ships to attack, I offer you one final chance to surrender."

Suddenly, the image of Dwillaak's bridge shook violently and several Milora crewmembers behind him sprawled onto the deck.

"What was that?" Dwillaak screamed at his tactical officer.

"We were hit by a torpedo from one of our own ships. Several of our ships have broken formation and are beginning to attack the others." After a few seconds he added, "Now there are dozens attacking. They're beginning to circle the base, firing on our own ships."

Dwillaak screamed into his com microphone, "All ships break off your attack and hold positions. Do not listen to the lying Space Command Admiral. Stop firing immediately and halt your ship. Do not fire on your fellow warriors." Looking at Jenetta, he said, "What kind of trickery is this, you witch?"

"I warned you, Marshall Lord Dwillaak Supreme," Jenetta said smugly, "but you chose to ignore my warnings and forced my hand. Since we don't have sufficient forces to fight you, I must get your forces to destroy each other. In the interest of self-preservation, I suggest you order all your ships to fire on the other ships around them."

Dwillaak glared at Jenetta. "You hope to have me destroy my own ships? No, Admiral, I'm not going to play your game. My warriors are too well trained to keep this up for long. I'll stop them all by myself." As Dwillaak's ship shook violently for a second time, he screamed into his mike, "Stop firing, I said. You are being tricked by the Space Command witch. I order all Milori vessels to stop firing immediately and hold their positions. Do not fire your torpedoes or laser weapons at any Milori ships under any circumstances. Do you hear me? Do not fire on any Milori vessels."

Suddenly, Dwillaak's ship shook violently for a third time and then shook again a second later as a fourth torpedo found its mark. Dwillaak's image disappeared from the monitor.

"The transmission was lost at the source, ma'am," the com chief said. The large monitor began showing a view from the port entrance of the area outside the asteroid. Explosions and laser pulses could be seen in the distance where Milori ships continued circling as they fired on other Milori ships.

"Close the open broadcast."

"It's closed, ma'am."

"Do you have Dwillaak's last order not to fire?"

"Yes, Admiral."

"Broadcast it continuously, audio only, every thirty seconds."

"Aye, Admiral."

Jenetta sat back in her chair and watched the holographic map. Dozens of Milori ships were circling the base now, firing with abandon at any Milori ships they passed. Nuclear explosions blinked like enormous fireflies everywhere as torpedoes found their targets. The space around the asteroid was alive with a light show of laser pulses.

Jenetta slowly and very deliberately took a sip from her coffee mug. It appeared as if she hadn't a care in the world other than that she might be scalded by the hot coffee. The officers around her watched in nervous but quiet desperation. On the bridges of the Space Command warships in the battle groups, the captains, officers, and crew watched the images of the battle forwarded from the CIC and waited anxiously for Jenetta to indicate they could join the melee. Some marveled at Jenetta's amazingly calm posture and referred to her by her 'Ice Queen' nickname.

The one-sided destruction raged for perhaps fifteen minutes. The ring of stationary Milori vessels began to take on the appearance of a huge vessel graveyard as the circling Milori ships continued to fire an unchallenged storm of torpedoes and laser pulses that opened huge sections of the ships to space. Ships bleeding life-giving atmosphere were everywhere.

When the destruction of the Milori ships was almost complete, Jenetta said, "All Space Command battle groups move in and mop up this Milori detritus."

The circling Milori ships immediately broke off their attack and moved out of the holographic image. The first of the battle groups arrived a few minutes later. As planned, the Space Command ships began circling and firing in a similar fashion on any Milori ship that fired a weapon. The Milori, for their part, liberated from the restriction that they hold their fire, released their frustration by using every weapon still functional. But the destruction rained down upon them by their own had reduced their capability to almost insignificant levels. Nevertheless, the fire drew an immediate return from Space Command vessels and the space around the asteroid once again filled with torpedoes and laser pulses.

The battle seemed to rage forever, but in reality it lasted less than thirty minutes from the time the first Milori ship was struck by a torpedo or laser blast. When space around the station was again clear of weapons fire, the Milori ships had been reduced to lifeless, twisted hulks. The Space Command ships, while mainly targeting those ships returning fire, had poured laser fire into practically everything that might represent a threat, further guaranteeing that no more fire would come from the ship once the fight had ended.

Satisfied the Milori ships posed no further threat, Jenetta said, "All ships break off your attack and secure your vessels."

"What about the Milori that escaped, Admiral?" Captain Donovan, the head of the JAG office asked from just behind her left shoulder. "Aren't we going to pursue them?"

"No Milori ships got away, Captain. Captain Wavala, compile damage assessment lists and begin the clean up. I have a message to send from my office and I'll return when I'm through. Carry on."

"Aye, Admiral."

Jenetta calmly stood and left the Command Center, with her aide, Lt. Commander Ashraf following. Captain Donovan waited until the door had closed behind them before turning to Captain DeWitt, the head of the Weapons Research section.

"What did she mean 'no Milori ships got away?' I saw them leave with my own eyes."

"Michael, there's no such weapon as a Madness Ray. We simply emitted a low-power, high-pitched noise on all IDS bands. Research showed us that the Milori were extra-sensitive to sounds in that precise range. The hair that covers their body actually begins to vibrate ever so slightly and that makes their skin tingle. The sound was picked up and heard on any ships with open com channels. Since all ships had to remain in constant communication, the sound was acoustical-ly prevalent on all the bridges of the Milori ships. Our own ships filtered the sound frequency, and the Milori could have done that as well if they'd had enough time to solve the problem. Did you notice that when our Space Command battle groups moved in there were only a hundred and one SC ships circling the station?"

"No, of course not. Who could count circling ships during an engagement?"

"Don't feel bad. Dwillaak never noticed that his invasion fleet had increased by sixty-two ships."

"Sixty-two? You mean that the Milori ships attacking the others were ours?"

"Yes," she said, smiling, "they were the M-designate ships Admiral Carver captured in previous battles with the Milori. They disconnected their Space Command signature transponders before their arrival, so they had to get out of the way before our task groups reached the station. They arrived here in small clusters, like the Milori vessels, and took up positions around the asteroid, interspersing themselves in the ring of genuine Milori ships."

"So the Milori never fired at them because they thought they were fellow ships that had fallen under the spell of the Madness Ray?"

"Yes, it's just another of Admiral Carver's incredibly innovative battle tactics. And it worked as well as the Admiral outlined it. She figured Dwillaak would eventually order the other ships to destroy the circling ships purely out of self-defense, so she planted the idea in his head that she wanted him to destroy those ships. She knew he would resist any such suggestion by her. She had given orders that his ship, once identified, be especially targeted. After he was taken out, the repeating message held the others at bay while they were destroyed, or nearly destroyed. The Milori are trained to obey their commanders at all costs, even to their deaths."

Captain Donovan began to laugh, slowly at first, then more and more heartily. The release of tension became infectious and the normally somber crew in the CIC broke into laughter, clapping, and hugging.

When the merriment had subsided, Captain Donovan said to Captain DeWitt, "I actually sat down last night and updated my Last Will and Testament. I guess I temporarily forgot just who our base commander is."

Jenetta sat in her office and tried to calm down. Although appearing icily calm on the outside while in the CIC, her stomach had been churning and was only now starting to settle. The adrenaline rush was over and her hands were shaking slightly, so she wrapped them tightly around a mug of coffee. She wanted to wait until she was perfectly composed before recording the message, so she used the time to call up and review the latest damage assessments. By the time all ships had reported in with their preliminary information, she was prepared to send her message.

Sitting up ramrod straight and straightening her tunic, she tapped the record button on her com unit.

"Message to Admiral Moore and the Members of the Admiralty Board, Space Command Supreme Headquarters, Earth.

"Ladies and Gentlemen, the Milori invasion force arrived at Stewart at 0208 on this date, immediately encircling the station and demanding my surrender. I naturally refused and the battle commenced. Lasting just twenty-nine minutes, the battle is now over and I'm pleased to announce that we have destroyed the entire Milori force of three hundred eighty-eight. We lost no ships, but I regret that we did lose twenty-one crewmembers and have eighty-six injured. We suffered two torpedo strikes and hundreds of laser hits. The station itself never came under attack and so suffered no damage. All ships but two are fully space-worthy. Repairs to the destroyers *Lima* and *Atlanta* should be completed within thirty days. Copies of all video logs of the engagement will be forwarded within twenty-four hours for assessment by evaluation teams.

"Jenetta Alicia Carver, Rear Admiral, Upper Half, Base Commander of Stewart Space Command Base, message complete."

Jenetta tapped the send button and sat back in her chair to finish her coffee, then rose and walked back to the CIC. As she entered the Center, she was greeted by loud applause. She smiled and sat in the commander's chair as the clapping died down and everyone got back to work. The brief departure from military protocol was acceptable.

"Any update on the damage assessments?" she asked.

"Negative, Admiral. All ships have begun making emergency repairs."

"Should we open the port doors, Admiral?" The port operations officer asked.

"Not yet. Let's wait until we're sure the Milori ships near the doors are definitely out of commission. I don't want to risk having any stray torpedoes entering the port from a ship that's playing possum."

"Aye, Admiral, but perhaps we can tow the Milori ships near the entrance to the rear of the asteroid for now so port operations can begin."

"Very well. Com, contact the M-designate ships to learn if they've reengaged their Space Command signature. If they have, have them return to assist with the cleanup."

"Aye, Admiral."

Several minutes later, the com chief said, "All M-designate group leaders report their ships have reengaged their Space Command signature transponder equipment. They're returning to the base to assist."

"Very good. Tell them to dispatch their space tugs and begin hauling the Milori ships near the port entrance to an area well away from the base. Have them coordinate with

Port Control to establish a farm somewhere that will contain the wrecked ships."

"Aye, Admiral."

After that, there wasn't much to do except watch the cleanup efforts. Once the area facing the port entrance was clear, Jenetta ordered that the enormous doors on the asteroid be opened. The port's space tugs began returning the confiscated ships to the farms where they'd been stored before. The freighters that had taken the containers away were ordered to return to the station and restore the cargo farms that had been emptied. It would probably take a couple of days just to get the farms properly re-established.

Remaining in the CIC for several more hours, Jenetta finally lowered the status from 'War Active' to 'Standby' and left for her quarters to get some sleep. She would have to conduct a press conference sometime during the day, and she didn't want to be falling asleep on the rostrum.

Rising in mid-afternoon, Jenetta showered, fed her hungry pets, and headed directly to her office. Her aide, Lieutenant Commander Ashraf, again congratulated her on a stunning victory and then briefed her on the current situation. The station, never having been attacked, was operating normally, although traffic was light on the concourse. Ships were still making emergency repairs. The two struck by torpedoes were secured in enclosed shipyard docks so repair efforts could begin. The station's engineers and the ships' own engineers would not have to wear bulky EVA suits while working on the hull repairs. The Milori ships had all been moved to a farm area, and the crews of the rechristened M-designate ships were going through them one by one looking for Milori survivors. So far, with almost half the ships checked, they had found just a hundred eighty-four Milori still alive.

The freighters with the containers from the farms hadn't made it back to the station area yet but should all be back within another twenty-four hours. Eight commercial ships at the station when the evacuation was announced had returned already.

"The news media organizations have been calling all day," Lt. Commander Ashraf said. "They want private interviews."

"No private interviews yet. Perhaps in a week I'll consider it."

"They're pretty angry about being kept in the dark on most of this until the last second. Private interviews might help a little."

Jenetta smiled. "You know me, Lori. I'm not really concerned if they're a little put out. The safety and security of the station and our crews comes first. How could I trust them to keep such a secret as our Madness Ray? We know there are spies and informants on the station, just as there are in any society. The media people will just have to wait. They each received edited video copies of the main battle action between our regular SC warships and the Milori ships, along with a copy of the holographic image file after the M-designate ships were away, right? The explosions and violence viewable on the vid copies will have to quench their thirst for my blood at the moment."

"Yes, ma'am."

Jenetta walked into her office and prepared a mug of coffee before sitting down and facing the dozens of messages in her queue. Most were normal business stuff, but some concerned the invasion. She skipped the day-to-day business and concentrated first on the others, mostly requests by various sections for authorization to use special resources to return the station to normal.

After dinner, Jenetta walked to the conference hall where the press conference was to be held. Her senior officers were there, and she talked with them briefly before stepping up onto the rostrum.

"Good evening. I have a brief statement and then I'll be happy to take your questions.

"At 0208 this morning, a fleet of three hundred eighty-eight Milori warships arrived at Stewart and encircled the base. I don't yet have numbers on how many were destroyers, frigates, cruisers, and battleships, but I'm assuming an average mix. The fleet commander, Supreme Lord Space Marshall Dwillaak, demanded my immediate surrender of the station. I naturally refused and the battle ensued. Lasting just twenty-nine minutes, all Milori vessels were destroyed in the engagement. We're presently searching the vessels for survivors and have so far found two hundred sixty-two. The station suffered no damage and we're working to restore normal operations outside. I believe that very few station inhabitants were even aware a major confrontation was occurring, so disruption inside has been minimal.

"That's the end of my prepared statement. I'll take questions now. Let's limit it to one question each for now."

Jenetta pointed to one of the correspondents.

After standing and identifying himself, the newsie asked, "How many Space Command vessels were lost, how many damaged, and what's the casualty count?"

"We lost no vessels, although the destroyers *Lima* and *Atlanta* were each struck by a single torpedo. Both will be fully operational in a few weeks. Ninety-nine other ships were mildly damaged by laser pulse hits, but very few lost atmosphere in any sections and they will all be repaired within a few days. As to casualties, we lost twenty-one brave crewmembers and have eighty-six injured. Most of the injuries are not life threatening. Next?"

The public affairs officer chose the next newsie. After identifying herself and her media organization, she asked, "How many Milori warriors were killed?"

"I have no precise information on that at this time, but I expect the number will top out at around three quarters of a million. That number is based on the average staffing levels of their ships involved in deep space operations. Next?"

Another reporter asked, "How do you account for such a huge disparity in the number of dead between Space Command and the Milori?"

"I'll leave that for others to speculate upon. My job is to protect the people of the Galactic Alliance from an empire that would enslave them while minimizing injuries and loss of life aboard our ships. I do that to the best of my ability. Next?"

"It's been suggested that you have some new, special weapon that no one will talk about," a correspondent said when pointed to by the PA officer. "Can you verify that?"

"I can neither confirm nor deny information about our weapons arsenal. Our Weapons Research and Development people do an incredible job in keeping us prepared for all contingencies. Their contributions are often unappreciated or underappreciated, but they are a very important part of the effort to protect you all from forces that would do you harm and control your lives. Next?"

"But don't you control our lives?" the same newsie asked.

"No, we exercise a certain amount of control over events in order to protect your freedoms. I don't make the laws; your elected representatives make them. I simply administer those laws and my actions are subject to constant review, as are those of my officers and crews. Next?"

"How long have you known the Milori were approaching with an invasion fleet?" another reporter asked.

"Space Command has known for some time that the Milori would not honor the terms of the treaty we signed after the last engagement. Emperor Maxxiloth is notorious throughout the quadrant for being completely without honor. That's why we won't bother to ask him to sign another treaty. A state of war has existed from the moment the Milori entered our Buffer Zone, the one-hundred-light-year-wide area of space outside our Frontier Zone. We have destroyed the Milori armada sent by the emperor, but the war isn't over. We shall not let down our guard again until Maxxiloth's power to threaten his neighbors has been ended. Next?"

"Does that mean you'll take the fight to him?"

"I know of no other way to end his aggression, do you? Next?"

"Isn't Milor over a thousand light-years away? It will take years to get there."

"Yes, that's correct. Milor is about eleven hundred light-years from Stewart, but that won't deter us from doing what we have to do. If we must take on Maxxiloth's forces in his own front yard, so be it. Next?"

"We can't understand how you were able to defeat his armada with so little damage to your own ships. Aren't their ships as powerful as ours?"

"In many ways they are. Like all commanding officers in wartime, I simply use our enemy's weaknesses against them. Next?"

"How can we hope to take the war to Milor? The crews would have to be away for a decade, operating in enemy territory without a supply line."

"We have to do what we have to do. We'll find a way. Next?"

"If the Milori lost almost four hundred ships this time and more than a hundred ships last time, how many more do you believe them to have?"

"I estimate that they could have anywhere from one hundred to two hundred left at present. I don't think the number is higher than that or he would have sent them as part of this invasion force, but it's possible. In any event, Maxxiloth hasn't left us a choice. If we don't carry the fight to him, he'll only come at us again when he's rebuilt his forces. Next?"

"Do you have any special weapons that you plan to use against his remaining forces?"

"We'll use whatever we need to use. You don't swat a housefly with a sledgehammer, and you don't use a flyswatter on a Marovian lizard. Next?"

"When do you expect to leave for Milor?"

"I didn't say I was leaving, only that Space Command must take the fight to Milor if we're to have a hope of ending this conflict. I have a job to do here and I couldn't leave unless I was relieved. Next?"

"Why did the Milori attack Scruscotto?"

"I believe it was a diversion intended to pull forces away from here. Next?"

"How many ships did you send?"

"None. Although we would normally have rushed to defend the planet, we already knew about the Milori invasion fleet and had to keep all our forces here. By the time our ships could have arrived at Scruscotto, the Milori would have been long gone, leaving us nothing to do. Next?"

"But why did you scramble the ships you had in port?"

"To make it appear that we were leaving ourselves completely defenseless. Milori spies would report that all ships had left, while our protection group simply joined the others in staging areas. Next?"

"You think there are Milori spies on the station?"

Jenetta gave the supposedly savvy reporter a withering look. "No, I don't *think* it. Next?"

Jenetta's response to the question about spies brought a chuckle from the press corps.

The press conference continued like that for an hour. Jenetta answered all questions honestly, but not necessarily fully, using evasive techniques to avoid answering questions that might impair future operations. The press conference seemed to satisfy the news media. When Jenetta announced the press conference was at an end and stepped down from the rostrum, the assembled press corps stood and applauded her. She hoped it was from a sense of appreciation for her job as a military commander and not simply because she had ended the long press conference.

Chapter Eighteen
~ May 18th, 2280 ~

"This emergency meeting of the Admiralty Board will come to order," Admiral Moore said as he banged the gavel lightly. "We've received a priority-one message from Admiral Carver. It's quite short and I've viewed it already. My aide will play it for you now."

He nodded to his aide, who was sitting at the computer interface console. The large wall monitor lit up with an image of Admiral Carver as she began to speak.

"Did she say she destroyed almost four hundred Milori warships and lost *no* ships of her own?" Admiral Hubera asked incredulously as soon as the brief message was over.

"Let's play that again, because it's so unbelievable," Admiral Moore said, nodding to his aide.

When the message ended again, Admiral Hubera said, "I don't believe it. She *can't* have destroyed that many Milori ships without suffering the loss of even a single ship. It's impossible. How could she have done that?"

"Are you suggesting the report is false, Donald?" Admiral Plimley asked. "For what purpose?"

"I don't know," he responded. "Perhaps it was made under duress to placate us and get us to drop our guard. It's absolutely impossible for her to have done what she claims."

"Before I came here," Admiral Moore said, "we performed an audio test on the message. While there was a slight increase in stress levels, certainly to be expected after a major engagement, there was no indication that Admiral Carver was under duress. The experts say it's genuine and I can't believe that Admiral Carver would report the situation inaccurately."

"But how could she *possibly* have done what she claims with so few losses?" Admiral Hubera asked.

"Perhaps it was that vaunted overconfidence you keep ranting about, Donald," Admiral Hillaire said, smirking. "I only wish that I had such overconfidence."

Admiral Hubera scowled and muttered something unintelligible.

"Then if we believe this message, the threat from the Milori is over?" Admiral Woo asked.

"For now, at least," Admiral Platt said.

"What about Admiral Vroman?" Admiral Bradlee asked.

"He may be lost to us," Admiral Moore said. "If Admiral Carver knew where he was, she'd have rescued him already. We know she was looking forward to coming home for a visit, but she can't leave Stewart until her relief arrives."

"She definitely deserves a long rest after the things she's done for us out there," Admiral Burke said. "We should bring her back here to be honored. The long trip will give her a good rest and a chance to see her family. And she also deserves some formal recognition."

"Another Medal of Honor?" Admiral Hubera said facetiously.

"Perhaps, Donald, perhaps," Admiral Burke said. "Does anyone second Admiral Hubera's recommendation?"

Immediately, everyone around the table raised their hand.

"It's unanimous," Admiral Moore said. "We'll adopt Admiral Hubera's recommendation."

"Wait a minute. I didn't recommend that she get a second MOH."

"It sounded that way. Are you saying now she doesn't deserve the medal for what she's accomplished by destroying the entire Milori invasion fleet without losing a single ship?"

All faces turned towards Admiral Hubera. He looked around the table and thought about the repercussions of being the only dissenting member of the board. If word leaked out that he opposed presentation of a medal to the individual soon to be hailed around the Galactic Alliance as the greatest heroine in Space Command history, his own reputation would suffer greatly. He meekly raised his hand. "I'm happy to make the nomination."

"Good," Admiral Moore said. "Admiral Carver promised to send the video logs within twenty-four hours, so we'll meet again this time tomorrow to watch the log from the CIC and whatever other logs you wish to view. I'm taking the rest of the afternoon off to play a round of golf, and then I'm going to have a few drinks and get my first good night's sleep in months. Meeting dismissed."

* * *

When Vyx and his team of agents arrived at the station, they couldn't believe their eyes. They had approached cautiously, but followed instructions when the station's Approach Control vectored them directly in. There wasn't a sign of visible damage, except for the bots and engineers that were climbing over almost two-thirds of the hundred-sixty-some-odd Space Command warships in orbit outside the asteroid, welding small plates in place. Not a single ship seemed to be damaged seriously.

"What happened?" Byers asked. "Didn't they show up yet? Did the Admiral get them to turn around and head for home again?"

"I don't think they'll be going home," Vyx said, adjusting the main viewer to enhance the image of the farm where the destroyed Milori ships had been towed.

"Holy God!" Nelligen said. "Is that the invasion fleet?"

"Can't be none other," Vyx said. "There weren't four hundred destroyed Milori warships over there when we left."

"But how?" Kathryn asked. "They had us outnumbered three to one. And our fleet looks barely scratched."

"The admiral— is— a magician," Brenda said. "A wizard, a conjurer, a sorceress. I can't *wait* to hear how she pulled this one off."

Port Control directed the *Scorpion* to wait while hazmat and biotox teams inspected her. She was permitted inside only when they had finished. The port looked almost deserted with all the confiscated ships moved back to the farms.

"There's the first real sign of damage," Vyx said, pointing to the closed doors on two of the three shipyard docks.

"But it must be only two ships," Byers said.

"Minor or not, I bet we lost people," Kathryn said.

"Not like I was expecting," Nelligen said.

"Nor I," Byers agreed. "I expected to find scenes of destruction and death on an unprecedented scale. I'm glad I was wrong."

"Let's dock at our assigned pier and maybe we can learn what happened," Vyx said.

* * *

Virtually every representative on the Galactic Alliance Council, and every senior member of the government, was present in the gallery of the Admiralty Board meeting hall. With the room filled to capacity, lesser officials were forced to stand along the walls wherever a vacant spot could be found.

"Ladies and Gentlemen," Admiral Moore said, "as you know, we've only just received the raw vid footage from the Stewart CIC during the past hour and we haven't had a chance to preview it prior to this meeting. Admiral Carver has also forwarded vid logs from each of the ships involved in the operation, and although it will take weeks for the complete computer simulation to be assembled, we should at least be able to learn how Admiral Carver achieved her spectacular victory over the Milori. I remind everyone not to discuss what you see here today until it's been declassified."

Admiral Moore nodded to his aide and the large, full-wall monitor showed an image of the CIC minutes before the Milori arrived. Holographic projectors mounted in the ceiling of the meeting hall created images over the heads of the attendees at half a dozen places around the room, duplicating the holo maps that Space Command officers in the CIC would have seen during the battle.

Everyone in the large meeting hall watched the monitors or holograms closely, straining to hear every possible sound. The Space Command officers picked up the audio signal on their implanted CTs and the gallery visitors used portable headphone receivers handed to them as they entered.

Not a sound could be heard from people in the meeting hall as the Milori encircled the station, nor while Jenetta talked with the Milori commander, but muttering and general confusion was rampant in the hall when they witnessed the

Milori ships begin to attack their fellow warriors because no one had heard anything about a Madness Ray. A cheer went up when the SC battle groups arrived to finish the Milori in response to Jenetta's summons.

After the battle was over, Jenetta calmly stood and left the room to send her messages, but the vid log continued to show the situation in the CIC and everyone was able to hear the conversation between Captain DeWitt and Captain Donovan. As had been the case with Captain Donovan, everyone in the room immediately understood the battle tactics used by Admiral Carver.

The entire gallery stood up as if on cue and began applauding. Although Jenetta was many hundreds of light-years away, she received a standing ovation that lasted for at least five minutes. Even the admirals at the large table, and their aides, stood and applauded.

"Ladies and Gentlemen," Admiral Moore said when the applause finally subsided, "you've been granted viewing access to this vid log by virtue of your position with the Galactic Alliance Council, Space Command, or the Space Marine Corps. I remind you again *not* to discuss this viewing with anyone until it's been declassified. Each of *you* knows there is no Madness Ray, but the enemy does not, and we may wish to employ Admiral Carver's brilliant tactic again. This was but one battle. We are still at war with the Milori and they must *not* yet learn how we defeated them. The copies distributed to the press only contain the main battle action between our regular Space Command vessels and the Milori ships. Thank you for attending today."

The admirals waited until the gallery had been cleared before they began their regular meeting.

"Does anyone wish to view the vid log again?" Admiral Moore asked.

Several members nodded, so the admiral's aide replayed the thirty-five minute log.

When it had ended again, Admiral Hillaire said, "Astounding. I never would have thought to pull something like that. I was as taken in by the ploy as the Milori commander."

"As was I," Admiral Plimley admitted, "and I would have known if there was research going on with a Madness Ray. Since hearing from Admiral Carver yesterday, I racked my brain trying to fathom how she could have defeated the invasion force while suffering virtually no losses. I couldn't conceive of a single scenario that would lead to such an outstanding accomplishment. It's almost hard to believe that a few months ago we were discussing whether she would even survive the attack."

"You're all getting carried away *again*," Admiral Hubera said loudly. "It was a simple ruse. The Milori commander was an *idiot* to fall for such an asinine tactic. Carver has been lucky again, plain and simple."

"It's only a *simple* ruse once you've seen it used, Donald," Admiral Bradlee said. "What would your strategy have been for meeting and defeating the Milori?"

All eyes turned to Admiral Hubera.

"I haven't developed a strategy because I'm not the base commander of Stewart."

"Well, give it a try now," Admiral Bradlee persisted. "You've studied all of history's most famous battles and tactics. How would you have greeted the Milori at Stewart?"

"Well, uh, I would have cleared the area of ships and cargo, bringing as much inside as possible."

"Yes, as Admiral Carver did. And then?"

"Uh, I would have secreted my forces away from the base, but close enough to call them in when needed."

"As Admiral Carver did. And then?"

"Uh, I, um— look, what is this supposed to prove? The battle is over, and anything I offer would be pure speculation."

"Every time we discuss Admiral Carver, you denigrate her actions and accomplishments," Admiral Bradlee said. "Her battle tactics are clever, innovative, and usually result in outstanding results with minimal losses on our part, yet you continually attribute them to mere luck. I was attempting to show you it's anything but luck. She's nothing less than brilliant. As Loretta alluded to, how many of us in this room could have conceived a plan that would have resulted in our

242

not losing a single ship during the recent engagement against three hundred eighty-eight powerful enemy warships? How many of us thought we would even control Stewart after the conflict? I seem to recall that less than two months ago you implored us to have Admirals Martucci and Rhinefield immediately assemble their forces in anticipation of attacks on their sectors."

"Suppose the Milori commander hadn't fallen for her ruse?" Admiral Hubera shot back. "Suppose he had realized that our ships had infiltrated his ranks? Where would we be then?"

"If Dwillaak realized that Carver's M-Designate ships had infiltrated his ranks from the very beginning, he might have immediately attacked them, in which case I'm sure Admiral Carver would have called in the battle groups and we'd have been forced to slug it out. We'd be no worse off than whatever attack scenario you might have come up with, Donald. And if Dwillaak became aware of the subterfuge immediately after the M-Designate ships began their attack, at least we would have gotten in the first licks before the Milori could respond. Our other ships were ready and standing by to attack as soon as Admiral Carver gave the word. But— I wouldn't be a bit surprised to learn that she had a second ace up her sleeve, one that we haven't seen because she didn't need to pull it out, this time."

"What other sort of trickery could she possibly have pulled?" Admiral Hubera said angrily.

"As I said," Admiral Bradlee replied, "I don't know what the other ace might be. I do know I didn't see the two scout/destroyers arrive with the other SC ships. Considering that they're invulnerable to laser weapons, I expected them to play a major role in the battle. We know they arrived at Stewart in plenty of time to participate. If I had to speculate, I'd say they were her second ace. I don't know how she intended to use them, and we may never know, unless one day we have an opportunity to discuss the battle with her, but I'd bet my retirement pension she had a backup plan other than just calling in the battle groups."

"After viewing the log, does anyone wish to withdraw their support of Admiral Hubera's nomination that Admiral Carver be awarded a second Medal of Honor?" Admiral Moore asked. No one raised their hand as all eyes looked at Admiral Hubera. "I thought not, but I felt I should ask. If anything, the log reinforces our nomination. Judging from the reaction of the gallery, I suspect the medal award nomination won't meet with any resistance in the Galactic Alliance Council."

* * *

A week later, ships were again being deployed on patrol routes. Everything had returned to normal on the station, except that the newsies were still hounding Jenetta for private interviews. During her daily walk on the concourse, her two pets kept the annoying reporters well away. A memorial service had been held for the lost crewmembers, whose number had increased by one due to the death of one of the critically injured. The rest were all expected to make a full recovery, and only a couple remained in intensive care.

Work on the two damaged ships, the *Lima* and the *Atlanta*, was progressing quickly, thanks to the availability of so many engineers, and they expected to have the hulls repaired and pressure-tested within the week.

Jenetta received congratulations from Space Command Headquarters and word that she was to be honored with another Medal of Honor. She would gladly have traded it for a ship now instead of receiving one in five to seven years, but she felt honored by the award. Her mail queue was always bulging as congratulations flooded in from all over the Galactic Alliance. She had to prepare a standard response for most of the senders, but as in the past, family and special friends, dignitaries, and certain others received a personal message.

As always, her favorite time of the day was when she arrived back in her quarters each evening and found vidMail from home or from one of her siblings waiting in her personal mailbox. Billy, Christa, and Eliza had toasted her privately in several evening dinner parties in her dining room, and tonight she had messages waiting from Hugh and her mother. Hugh's had arrived first so she decided to play that first. She tapped the play button and sat down to watch.

"Hi, babe. You are so awesome. We've all seen the vid images of the battle, but you have the entire senior staff of the *Bonn*, and probably every other ship outside your command, trying to figure out how you did it. I wish I could have been there.

"I guess the threat from the Milori is over for the present. Are you going to be relieved of command now so we can finally get together? It seems like years since I've seen you. Wait a minute," he said, smiling, "it has been years since I've seen you. It's a darned good thing your picture is on every news broadcast and on every newspaper or magazine in the galaxy or I might forget what you look like. Of course, the picture on my nightstand helps keep the memory fresh. I have to clean it every day though because it keeps getting smudged when I kiss it before going to sleep each night, and I'd much rather have the genuine article to kiss.

"I've been saving my leave time so we can get together for shore leave on Higgins when you come home. Has Supreme Headquarters given you any kind of date for when you might be relieved? Probably not or you would have told me, but I keep hoping. They can't keep you out there forever, can they?

"Time to go. I love you and can't wait to see you again. I hope it's soon. All my love." Hugh kissed his forefinger and pressed it to the vid lens in the com unit.

"Commander Hugh Michaels, First Officer of the *Bonn*, message complete."

Hugh's messages never failed to bring a smile to Jenetta's face, and she played it again before replying.

"Hi, sweetheart. I look at your picture and think of you each night before I fall asleep also. I miss you and I wish with all my heart that I could be there to tell you in person what I'm feeling. Eventually they'll have to let me come back for a visit, if only for the medal ceremony, and I promise you we'll get together. Right now it's impossible to get away. A front line commander can't just leave her post for two years to visit home.

"The imminent Milori threat is over, but as long as Maxxiloth sits on his throne we'll be at risk. He didn't learn his lesson the first time and I've no delusions that he's learned it this time. He's hurting right now, but as soon as he's strong enough he'll come at us again. The only way to stop him is for us to invade his territory and hurt him so bad that he'll never want any part of us again. That may be difficult because he has no regard for his people, so we'll have to threaten his *personal* safety. Someone will have to take this war to his home planet and attack his palace.

"I haven't heard anything from Supreme Headquarters about them sending a replacement flag officer to assume command, so I guess I'm stuck here for at least another year. I suppose things could be worse. I could be stuck at Supreme Headquarters in some dull administrative job. At least out here I get to face a small challenge once in awhile." Jenetta grinned.

"I love you and I'm looking forward to that shore leave on Higgins." Jenetta kissed her finger and pressed it to the vid lens on the com unit. "See you just as soon as I can."

"Jenetta Alicia Carver, Rear Admiral, Upper Half, Commander of Stewart Space Command Base, message complete."

Jenetta sat and thought about Hugh and the month they'd had together when he'd been to Stewart while working for the freight-hauling company. Her mood changed from one of happiness to one of sadness as she thought about the length of time since they'd been together. To avoid sinking into depression, she played the message from her Mom.

"Hi, honey. Gosh, I'm so very proud of you. Your name is on everyone's lips again and your face is on every news show. They're talking about how you defeated an enormous invasion force from that alien empire intent on enslaving all of us. And I've heard that you're to be given another Medal of Honor for your actions. Will they be sending you home for the award? I hope so. It's been so long since I've been able to hug you, or your sisters or brothers.

"Can you tell me how you defeated the Milori, or is it a secret? I'll understand if you can't talk about it, but everyone

246

on the base keeps asking me, as if I've got special military clearance that their spouses, parents, or children don't. Anyway, as much as I miss you, I'm glad you're out there protecting us. Sometimes I feel so useless here. Daddy and all of you kids are out there watching over us and I just stay here on Earth, safe and secure while you're all risking your lives.

"I played bridge with Dorothy Nelson the other day and learned that her daughter, Beverly, is in your command. She's on board the *Lima*, but she wasn't hurt when a torpedo struck her ship. And Linda Reilly has a son in your command. I think he's on the cruiser *Plantaganet*. Sometimes it seems that half the people on this base have a relative or close friend in your command. They all tell me how proud the family members and friends are to serve under you and how confident they are that you'll do your best to keep them safe. From what little I know about the recent battle, I know they're right. I can't imagine how you managed to stop three-quarters of a million invaders while losing fewer than two dozen of our people.

"My time is almost up so I have to go. I'll be watching for your messages. I love you, honey. Be safe and take care of yourself.

"Annette Carver, Officer Housing, Potomac SC base. End of message."

Jenetta smiled and watched the message again before recording her reply. She wished she were close enough to have a real conversation.

"Message to Annette Carver, Officer Housing, Potomac SC base, from Admiral Jenetta Carver.

"Hi, Momma. I wish I could tell you I'll be on my way home soon, but I can't, and I doubt that I'll be home before this war is over. I don't like it any more than you, but I'm needed out here and I can't leave until my job is done. The award of the medal will have to wait for a while.

"The Admiralty Board has promised me a ship after my next tour of duty is complete. I'll be getting one of the new battleships they've just started constructing at the Mars facility. If I don't manage to get home before then, I'll at least have to travel home when my ship is ready."

"The tactics I used to defeat the enemy forces are classified and I can't talk about them yet or I would be happy to tell you all about it. Perhaps when I finally get home I can explain it all. All I can say right now is that I do everything I can, and everything I have to, to protect my people and all the people of the Galactic Alliance. I'm not proud of the fact that I've been responsible for the deaths of more than a million Milori in recent years, but I'm very proud that I've helped keep our people free. Unfortunately, I'll probably be responsible for the deaths of many more Milori before this terrible war is over, but I can't let that sway me from my duty. We didn't ask for this war and did nothing to provoke the Milori, but we have no choice other than to respond when attacked. It's an immutable fact of war that you must be just as brutal as the enemy is if you're ever to see an end to a conflict. We extended an olive branch once and you see the results. I pray that God will forgive me for what I've done—and will have to do again.

"I love you, Momma, and I wish I could be there with you now, but we'll have to be content that our family is safe, and the enemy has been stopped, at least for the present.

"Jenetta Alicia Carver, Rear Admiral, Upper Half, Commander of Stewart Space Command Base, message complete."

* * *

Exalted Lord Space Marshall Berquyth entered the ostentatiously decorated private office of Emperor Maxxiloth quietly and approached the desk of his monarch. He had dreaded this task for hours. Messengers who bore bad tidings had all too often been carried out of this room while attendants tried to staunch the flow of blood. However, no one else would do it and he couldn't delay any longer.

"What is it, Berquyth?"

"We've picked up a news broadcast that might explain why we've received no word from our invasion fleet, my Lord."

"Really, what does it say? Has Dwillaak destroyed Stewart?"

"I've had it sent to your com unit. You can play it like a message."

"Good. Let's take a look." He used one of his tentacles to start the playback, then stared at the machine as Jenetta's press conference played. Watching in stunned silence until the conference was over and the reporter had added his comments, Maxxiloth suddenly erupted and threw the com unit through a nearby window. Berquyth thought he was next.

"How, Berquyth, how? How could Carver destroy our entire force and not lose a single ship? She's a devil, that one. It must be black magic."

"We don't know any of the details, my Lord, although there has been some talk overheard on the station about a Madness Ray, but no one knows how it works."

"A Madness Ray! I knew it must be something like that. We must get the plans to it before she arrives here. How soon can we expect to see her enter our space?"

"Their newer battleships are said to be capable of Light-412, so we have at least two annuals before she could enter our innermost territory."

"How many ships will we be able to throw against her?"

"If we continue to put all available resources into ship production, we should be able to gather as many as three hundred for our defense, although almost a third of those will be the oldest ships we have. Their speed is limited to Light-262 and their plating isn't as heavy as the newer ships."

"Three hundred," Maxxiloth said thoughtfully. "And she just destroyed four hundred without losing a single ship of her own." Imploringly, Maxxiloth said, "What have I done, Berquyth? I've antagonized a peaceful neighbor whose technology is clearly superior to ours and turned their wrath against us. Should we sue for peace?"

Berquyth was aghast, but tried not to let it show. He had seen many sides of his emperor, but this was a new one. He wondered if the news of defeat might have driven him insane. "Judging from the press conference, I don't think that would work anymore. We did just violate the last peace treaty signed in the name of the empire. She was pretty specific about ending our ability to wage war."

"Yes, she was." Maxxiloth's mood turned angry again. "So be it! If that's what she wants, that's what she'll get. I'll fight her to the very last warrior on this planet."

Berquyth nodded and backed away, slowly working his way towards the door to the corridor as Maxxiloth paced around the room, ranting.

* * *

Captain Lofgren entered Jenetta's office and took a seat after being invited. "We've completed a survey of NeTrediar, Admiral."

"And?"

"There's no sign of Arneu, but that's not surprising since half the underground complex was crushed when the roof caved in. There could be hundreds of bodies interred down there."

"And the town?"

"Totally destroyed, probably during the first pass. We found those guns you mentioned, but I don't know if they even had time to get the roofs rolled back. The Milori hit them with everything they had."

"No one left alive?"

"No one that we found, although survivors would have had weeks to clear out before we got there. Somebody dug a grave for the people killed on the surface, a mass grave. I'm sure it wasn't the Milori."

Jenetta nodded. "How many other towns were hit?"

"None. The Milori hit a few ships in orbit that had torpedo capability, then went straight to NeTrediar. When they were done, they left, probably speeding off to meet up with the invasion force headed to Stewart."

"Okay, thanks. It was worth the effort. I wish we'd had time to get there before the invasion."

"If Arneu's alive, he'll pop up again."

"Yes, I'm sure you're right."

* * *

"Come in, Vertap," the King said from his cozy chair near the fireplace. "We just heard the news that Carver defeated the invasion force."

A group of powerful noblemen sat in chairs around the hearth, drinking assorted beverages and listening to the conversation.

"That would be severely understating the situation, my Lord. She utterly *crushed* the entire invasion force while losing not a single ship of her own."

"Not one?" the king said, his jaw dropping.

"Not one. Two ships received minor damage and are being repaired. They'll be fully space-worthy in a matter of days, if repairs have not already been completed."

"How did she do it, Vertap?"

"We're not sure, my Lord, but it's safe to say she's a formidable foe. If she can't finesse a victory, she'll win by outright brute force. Our operatives say there's little left of the Milori ships. They were so utterly destroyed that some are mere shells, while others are in pieces. Reports say almost seven hundred fifty thousand Milori died in the battle. Carver lost twenty-two."

"Twenty-two thousand?"

"No, my Lord. Twenty-two crewmembers."

The king was silent for a few seconds. "Interesting. Thank you, Vertap. That will be all."

"Yes, my Lord."

Vertap bowed, took several steps backward, then turned and left the room. As the door clicked shut, one of the noblemen said, "We may have underestimated this Carver in our plans. If she could destroy the Milori with such ease, imagine what she could do to us. We must tread carefully in our dealings with her."

"I'd say we backed the right side," another said. "The Galactic Alliance is bound to be grateful for our help."

"I hope so. And I hope we've been correct in our assessment of the Alliance. We don't want to simply substitute one powerful master for another."

"I'm sure we took the only logical path. The Galactic Alliance has no interest in our space. Once Carver has destroyed Maxxiloth, they'll pack up and head home, leaving us free to take over the Empire. And all with us not having to break a sweat."

"I don't know. You never know what Carver is going to do."

"Oh, have another rum and go back to sleep, Nedweth."

* * *

"Admiral, Captain Lofgren would like a few minutes of your time," Jenetta read when the com unit buzzed.

"Send him in, Lori."

A few seconds later, the head of the Intelligence section on Stewart entered her office.

"Hi, Ben, grab a beverage and have a seat."

"Thank you, Admiral. I'm fine," he said as he sat without having visited the beverage synthesizer.

"What can I do for you?"

"As you know, we've been interrogating the Milori prisoners. Most claim to know nothing and I'm inclined to believe them if they come from the lower ranks. We're using the technique of telling them they'll rot in our jails until they die if we find they've lied. It's worked with a few. We've put together a token file of interesting facts. This morning, I was re-interviewing one I had spoken with a week ago and he told me something of great interest. I had isolated him after the last interview because I felt he was holding back. Anyway, today he told me he knows what happened to the crew of the *Lisbon*. He said he'll tell me if I promise to release him and let him return home."

"And?"

"I wish to know how you want to proceed."

Jenetta thought about it for a minute. "Agree to it. If his information is accurate, we'll let him go. I had intended to let them all go anyway."

"You're going to let them go before the war is over?"

"Yes, I had thought to give them an old, slow, unarmed transport from our confiscated ship farm and send them on their way with enough food for ten and enough stasis beds for the rest. I figure they should make it home in about ten or eleven years."

"Unless they call home and get help."

"We'll disable their IDS communications but leave them with RF. They'll be able to communicate with anyone who challenges them but not send for help. I expect this war to be over long before they get home."

"Sounds like a good idea, Admiral," he said, smiling.

"So promise them they'll be released and sent home once they talk and the information is confirmed but not before."

"Aye, Admiral," he said, standing up.

"And Ben?"

"Yes, Admiral?"

"See if you can discover the locations of any other Raider bases. There must have been some sort of a falling out between the Milori and the Raiders for them to have attacked Raider Ten. Perhaps they'll be willing to speak about it."

"Okay, Admiral."

Jenetta leaned back in her chair and stared vacantly at the ceiling after Captain Lofgren left. The Milora's information could significantly affect her personal situation. If she could find Admiral Vroman and bring him back here, she could be relieved as base commander and then be free to handle whatever other job they had for her. She'd have more time to complete the chore and so be available when the new battleships were ready to be launched. If the thought of rescuing a Space Command crew and senior admiral was not enough to make her smile, this thought was.

Two days later Captain Lofgren returned with new information.

"He says he was a member of the crew on board the Milori cruiser *Rowlidph*. They dropped off the admiral and crew on a planet in the Siena system. It's about sixty light-years inside the Frontier Zone."

"Computer," Jenetta said, "show me a holographic map of the Siena system."

Instantly, an image appeared above Jenetta's desk. It showed a sun surrounded by twelve planets.

"Computer, how many planets are capable of supporting human life without special breathing apparatus?"

"The fourth planet from the sun is suitable for human habitation, and the inner moon of the fifth planet has a barely breathable atmosphere."

"Computer, tell me about the fourth planet."

The computer began reeling off facts and figures, but when it said the presence of creatures like those of prehistoric Earth had been reported, Jenetta stopped the computer.

"Computer, you mean like dinosaurs?"

"Affirmative, according to a survey report filed by a mining company."

"Computer, tell me about the moon of the fifth planet."

"Little information is on file, except that the temperature drops below zero Celsius each night."

"The prisoner said the planet was tropical to temperate," Captain Lofgren said.

"Good God," Jenetta said. "They left them defenseless on a planet with dinosaurs. I hope there's someone left to rescue. The prisoner understands the deal is contingent upon us finding the crew?"

"I made that abundantly clear."

"Okay, Ben, good job. I'm going to arrange for a rescue mission right away. Thanks."

"My pleasure, Admiral. I hope you find them."

"If we do, it's through your efforts, Ben."

Three days later the *Colorado*, with Jenetta aboard, and the *Yangtze* entered orbit around a planet in the Siena system and began mapping the surface. The captain of the *Yangtze* called Jenetta just an hour after starting their sweep.

"Do you have something, Frank?"

"Aye, Admiral. We've found a valley in the eastern quadrant. I'm sending you the coordinates. There's a sign carved out of the forest that says 'GSC *Lisbon*,' and we can see humans moving around."

"Is there room for a shuttle to land?"

"There's enough room for a hundred shuttles."

"Okay, I'll take a party down and investigate. Stand by. If it's our people, I'll call for all our shuttles to come down and pick up the survivors."

"Aye, Admiral. *Yangtze* out."

The noise overhead drew the attention of everyone in the camp. They watched in slack-jawed amazement as a GSC shuttle slowly settled onto one of the fields near the camp. Admiral Vroman blinked twice, rubbed his eyes, and blinked several times again before rushing towards the shuttle's landing position.

As the hatch opened, a Space Marine Major carrying a stun pistol stepped out. He glanced around before turning to say something to someone behind him. Then another person emerged, followed by two Space Marine Sergeants. Admiral Vroman would have recognized her anywhere, even without the two stars on each shoulder.

She slowly scanned the assembled group, who seemed to be holding their breath while trying to determine if she was a hallucination, and said loudly, "I'm Admiral Carver of Space Command. Are you the crew of the GSC *Lisbon*?"

The outpouring of emotion occurred almost simultaneously among the stunned survivors as some began laughing hysterically and others dropped to their knees and wept. Some surged forward to touch her and assure themselves that she was real, but the Space Marines moved to protect her. The *Lisbon* crew stopped short when Admiral Vroman yelled, "Atten-shun!" Looking to him, they regained their composure, wiped their tears, and straightened up.

Admiral Vroman stepped towards Jenetta, now almost hidden behind the Space Marine guards who had moved to protect her when the survivors began to surge forward. But for her height, she would not have been seen. Jenetta put her hands on the shoulders of the two sergeants in front and gently moved them apart.

"Admiral Vroman, I'm delighted to find you alive and looking so surprisingly well after a year and a half on this dangerous planet." He was significantly thinner than the most recent pictures of him but appeared healthy otherwise. She extended her hand.

"Thank you, Admiral," he said, shaking her hand vigorously. "Welcome to Siena. I'm sorry for the condition in which you find us, but our uniforms wore out long ago and we've had to wear these homespun clothes."

"We have plenty of replacement clothing on board and you'll soon be back in real civilization."

"Allow me to introduce the officers of the *Lisbon*."

After introductions, Jenetta turned to the Space Marine Major and said, "Notify the ships to send down all their shuttles."

"Aye, Admiral."

To Admiral Vroman she said, "Have your people gather whatever possessions they wish to take with them and report to the shuttles for transport to our ships."

"You can't imagine how much I've yearned to hear those words."

Turning to Captain Lindahl, who was standing nearby, Admiral Vroman said, "You heard the Admiral; see to it, Captain."

"Aye, Admiral," he said, smiling.

In minutes, people were running for their shelters to gather up the few meager possessions or mementos they wished to bring back. Admiral Vroman turned to Jenetta and said, "Would you care for a tour, Admiral?"

"I'd love one."

"Let's start with the camp."

Admiral Vroman led Jenetta around the camp, with her security detail following at a tactful distance, while he explained the difficulties of starting life on a hostile planet with practically nothing. They toured the forge, mill, and cold storage warehouses, and walked to the North Pass wall. Admiral Vroman explained about the three dinosaur attacks they had repelled. He also told her of the other dangers outside the valley, such as the bearlons and the unknown creatures in the water that the first foraging expedition had observed.

On the way back to the camp he bragged about their projects, such as the farm, the new bridge across the river, and the development of black-powder rifles.

"It's amazing how well you've done here, Admiral," she said. "It's a real tribute to your leadership and organizational skills."

"Thank you, Admiral. There have been times when I felt a little like a king in my own kingdom, but a day hasn't gone by that I wouldn't have traded my kingdom for a ship."

A few hours later, all survivors of the *Lisbon* were safely aboard one of the two scout-destroyers. It would be a bit crowded on the return trip to Stewart, with crewmen bunking in holds and tripled up in crew quarters. Before leaving Siena, crewmembers freed the gelks in the corral so they could roam wild in the valley. With the two passes blocked, they should be safe from dinosaurs. The *Lisbon* crew hoped that, in the absence of predators, the gelks wouldn't overpopulate the valley and die from starvation, but nature had its own way of handling such things and they certainly couldn't take the animals with them.

The *Lisbon* crew took their first hot showers without time limits since their capture, and then the two dozen doctors Jenetta had brought checked them over from head to foot. The medical people treated them for all sorts of minor maladies for which their own medical people hadn't had medications. The crewmembers with unhealed injuries, either from the attack on the *Lisbon* or sustained while on the planet, received injections of nano-bots to assist in proper healing. Doctors would schedule reconstructive surgery for those serious cases that required it as soon as they reached Stewart. The next order of business was the transmission of vidMail messages to family and loved ones. After shaves, haircuts, and receiving clean clothes, the *Lisbon* crew was happy beyond words and regaled the crews of the scout-destroyers with tales of their life on the planet. Over the following days, they would get enough food to fill out their bodies, which looked much older than their years because of the hard work, sun, and vitamin-deficient diet.

"I can't tell you how good it is to be clean-shaven again," Admiral Vroman said to Jenetta, rubbing his face as they sat in the officer's mess hall enjoying mugs of coffee. "I'll never again complain about having to shave once a month."

Jenetta smiled. "We feared we might be too late to rescue you when we learned where you were."

"How did you find us?"

"During interrogation, a Milori prisoner told us about dropping you off in the Siena system. The rest was easy."

"The Milori," Admiral Vroman said as if he had a bitter taste in his mouth. "I think they're planning to invade soon. Why else would they have attacked the *Lisbon*?"

"They did attack, a few weeks ago. We kicked their butts again."

"How many ships did we lose?"

"None, but two were slightly damaged. We lost twenty-two crewmen."

"I'm talking about a full-scale invasion, Admiral, not a small skirmish. They'll be coming in force this time."

"They did. Following your capture, we hunted down and destroyed twenty-five ships that were hiding inside our borders. One other managed to escape, but it didn't represent much of a threat because we damaged it so seriously in the encounter. When the invasion force of four Milori fleets arrived, we destroyed three hundred eighty-eight ships, and, as far as I know, that accounts for every Milori ship in Galactic Alliance space."

"Three hundred eighty-eight, and you didn't lose one? That's incredible. I hope you'll find time later today to tell me about your victory."

Jenetta smiled. "Certainly."

"I always knew it would be you who found us, Admiral. I imagined you stepping out of a shuttle so many times that I almost thought I was hallucinating today. But why did you come in this small ship?"

"This is the *Colorado*."

"The *Colorado* that you set the speed record with?"

"The very same. The nearest ships to your location were still about forty-five light-years away when we learned of your whereabouts because I had had to recall all ships in preparation for the Milori invasion. Using the *Colorado*, I was able to get to you in two and a half days. We'll be back at Stewart before you know it."

258

"Two and a half days to travel seventy light-years? Unbelievable."

"We're going to make you a believer. We're currently traveling at Light-9790."

Admiral Vroman shook his head slowly and reached out to touch the bulkhead wall, checking the vibration. "Unbelievable."

"Are you hungry?" Jenetta asked, pointing towards the mess attendant. "Is there anything you'd like?"

"Yes, there certainly is."

Jenetta waved the mess attendant over. "Admiral Vroman would like to order something."

"Yes, Admiral?" the mess attendant said.

"I'd love a three-egg omelet with green bell peppers, cheddar cheese, and onions. I'd also like several pancakes with maple syrup, hash browns, a slab of ham, a side order of breakfast sausage, and four pieces of rye toast. Is that possible?"

"Can do, Admiral. It'll be about five minutes."

Admiral Vroman smiled like the Cheshire cat in Alice in Wonderland. "Carry on, son."

Jenetta grinned and took a sip from her coffee mug.

Over dinner in her quarters that evening, Jenetta recounted the details of the engagement with the Milori.

"You actually got them to simply sit there while you pounded their ships to pieces?" Admiral Vroman asked incredulously.

"Dwillaak ordered them not to fire, and they didn't. I relied on their conditioning to do exactly as ordered at all times. I'm sure he would eventually have countermanded that order, so it was necessary to take his ship out as quickly as possible. I only sent in my battle groups to mop up so as to maintain the illusion that we destroyed the Milori ships with just SC vessels. I know the news images will eventually get back to Milor. The Milori vessels had a little more life left in them than I expected and they managed to strike two of our ships with torpedoes. I wish now that I'd waited just a bit longer."

Admiral Vroman smiled sadly and shook his head gently. "You continue to live up to your reputation, Admiral. Space Command is fortunate that you were still in command at Stewart. I shudder to think what would have happened if I had been in command. I don't think I have the imagination to lead ships in battle the way you do."

"We all have different skills and different methods, Admiral. You did every bit as wonderful a job keeping the crew of the *Lisbon* alive during the past year and a half. Many officers could not have accomplished what you did."

"Thank you, Admiral. That's kind of you to say. May I ask a favor?"

"Certainly."

"Would you call me Thad? We do hold the same rank."

"Certainly, Thad. My friends call me Jen. I hope we'll be friends."

"That's my wish as well, Jen. Where's your next posting?"

"I'm not sure. I had expected to remain at Stewart for a couple of years until a replacement flag officer could be sent to assume command since we'd been unable to locate you, but that's all changed now. I have a little project in mind if I can get approval from the Admiralty Board."

"Such as?"

"I'd like to visit Milor and show Maxxiloth we're not going to stand for any more nonsense from him. While I'm there, I'll try to remove his power to wage war against his neighbors for many years to come."

"But it will take three years for a task force to get there and another three years to get back."

"But it would only take the *Colorado* and the *Yangtze* forty-five days each way."

"They must still have a formidable force in place. You can't seriously hope to take on the entire Milori fleet with just these two small ships?"

"Why not? We can always outrun them if we can't outfight them."

Admiral Vroman grinned and shook his head in amazement. "If it was anyone but you, I'd say that person was certifiably crazy, but I do believe *you* might be able to pull it off."

"We must take the fight to Maxxiloth, and we must do it before he has time to rebuild his fleet. The only way we can accomplish that is with these two small ships. We can move into orbit around Milor and dictate our surrender terms. If he refuses, we destroy his shipbuilding facilities, munitions plants, armories, and military installations from space. Right now he won't be expecting an attack, and his ships will be spread out, keeping the empire in line."

"That's an audacious plan, Jen."

"That's become my stock in trade over the years, Thad," she said, smiling.

Chapter Nineteen
~ June 18th, 2280 ~

The news media was waiting in eager anticipation on the docking platform when the *Colorado* and the *Yangtze* docked. Workers had erected a small rostrum in expectation that Admiral Vroman would say a few words. Jenetta made the introductions, then turned the podium over to Admiral Vroman.

"It's my great pleasure to reach Stewart at last, my destination before we were attacked by Milori vessels more than a year and a half ago. The Milori marooned us on a planet with a temperate climate but neglected to tell us that dinosaurs were part of the indigenous population. They left us weaponless. That we're alive to be with you today is a minor miracle. Too many of our number are not; they lost their lives in attacks by creatures similar to Cretaceous period monsters on Earth. I can't commend the crew of the *Lisbon* enough for their bravery, perseverance, hard work, and dedication to duty. They maintained their professionalism throughout our ordeal and enabled us to survive the nightmare.

"Thanks to Admiral Carver and her staff we've rejoined the Space Command family, and I look forward to beginning my tour of duty as Commander of this station and the sectors of space surrounding it. Thank you all."

The last bit of information hadn't yet been publicly released. Reporters immediately began shouting questions at Jenetta. She stepped up onto the rostrum.

"Yes, it's true. Admiral Vroman was sent here to assume command of this station. The changeover was to occur a year ago December when my five-year tour of duty was up, but the Milori upset that plan. I'll remain in command for a short time until Admiral Vroman has regained his full health and strength and feels ready to take on the job. My status after that is uncertain. The Admiralty Board will determine my next assignment or posting."

One of the reporters yelled out, "Is this a demotion, Admiral?"

"Certainly not. As I just said, I completed my five-year duty tour on Stewart and was due to be relieved. I had been eagerly looking forward to having a long overdue reunion with my family on Earth, and perhaps I'll have an opportunity for that now. That's all, folks. Thanks."

* * *

"Next up for discussion is the request from Admiral Carver to travel to Milor," Admiral Moore said. "Any thoughts?"

"I think it's far too dangerous, and far too typical of Admiral Carver," Admiral Hubera said. "She proposes to go to Milor and fight the entire Milori Empire with two tiny ships and three hundred seventy crewmen."

"We already knew *you* wouldn't like it, Donald," Admiral Hillaire said.

"That's not fair, Arnold. I'm trying to give her the benefit of the doubt, but taking on an entire war-mongering empire with just two tiny ships is tantamount to suicide. If she wants to kill herself, that's one thing, but I can think of no valid reason why she should be permitted to take three hundred seventy officers, NCOs, and crewmen with her."

"What about her very valid point that most of their remaining ships will be away from the home planet trying to hold the empire together following the loss of their five fleets. You know that a loss like that can cause a lot of civil unrest in a totalitarian society where people are just looking for an opportunity to rebel."

"Who says the people are looking for an opportunity to rebel? Cultures where the government has suppressed the citizenry for innumerous generations are unique in that they've only known one way of living. If you've never experienced freedom, you may not yearn for it, nor trust someone who offers it."

"Parts of it haven't always been enslaved," Admiral Bradlee said, "at least according to our intelligence information. The Milori seized huge sections of territory from the Hudeeracs and the Gondusans during past decades. Perhaps we could try to make contact with those civilizations and ask them if they wish to fight to regain their territory. We can promise them that if they do, we'll restore their territory to them after we're through with Maxxiloth."

"And if they refuse to support our effort and participate in the offensive?" Admiral Woo asked.

"Then we let them know their territory won't be restored to them. It will remain part of the Milori Empire," Admiral Bradlee said.

"If we undertake this offensive, it must be with the idea of dismantling the empire forever," Admiral Plimley said.

"Yes," Admiral Bradlee said, "but we don't have to tell the Hudeeracs and Gondusans that right away. Let them think that if they don't support us, we're not going to serve up their territory on a silver platter. Let them believe this will be their one chance to get it back. It will provide more incentive to join the effort and genuinely support it."

"We've never been in the business of toppling other governments," Admiral Hubera said, "no matter how much we dislike their leaders."

"But when that government attempts to invade our space, not once but twice, with the intention of overthrowing *our* government and enslaving our people, it needs toppling," Admiral Burke said. "This dangerous despot must have his reins of power cut. Leave him his planet but isolate him on it."

"How do we do that?" Admiral Raihana Ahmed asked.

"Cut his reins of power?"

"No, I mean, how do we isolate him?"

"I'm not sure what you're driving at?"

"I'm pointing out that in order to isolate him, we must have a continuing presence in the area. We must halt any attempt to build or buy ships immediately, or he won't remain isolated for long. A continuing presence means a base or space station, and how am I, as the Space Command Quartermaster, going to supply a remote base when each ship is required to pass through enemy-held territory?"

"What Raihana is saying is important," Admiral Platt said. "If we begin this, we must be prepared to follow through, but I can't see any other course of action than to begin it. We can't suffer through an invasion from Milor every five years, or whenever Maxxiloth thinks he's strong enough to attempt it again."

"So what we're *really* saying here is that we must annex the empire and make it a secure part of the Galactic Alliance," Admiral Hillaire said.

"God help us," Admiral Ressler said. "Their territory was the size of the present Galactic Alliance before they started the most recent expansion. When you add in all the territory they've laid claim to between us and their former borders, we'd be increasing our territory by almost two hundred percent."

"But we'd return the territory that belonged to the Hudeeracs and Gondusans," Admiral Woo said.

"That's less than ten percent of the total, Lon," Admiral Bradlee said.

"That territory is too large and far too distant to administer properly from the present Galactic Alliance space," Admiral Burke said. "It'll take many decades to establish bases and a responsive military bureaucracy. Meanwhile, we'll probably be facing unbridled lawlessness for much of that time. It would be as they intended for us. We'll need someone out there capable of dealing with that kind of situation while receiving only minimal support from Earth."

"Oh God, don't say it," Admiral Hubera said, covering his eyes with his hands.

"We don't really have to, but I will for the record," Admiral Hillaire said. "Admiral Carver is our most experienced front-line base commander and I believe she's the only flag officer with the necessary skills to take on a job like this. Besides, she sort of asked for the job by initiating this."

"We'll have to clear this with the Galactic Alliance Council before we say anything, but all in favor of engaging the Milori in their home solar system and, with their defeat, annexing the territory presently known as the Milori Empire, with Admiral Carver named as Military Governor, raise your hand." Everyone raised their hand, including Admiral Hubera, although the look on his face suggested he had been sucking on lemons all morning. "Let the record show that the vote carried by a unanimous show of hands. We must suppress any mention of what we've discussed here today. Even if the GAC approves the action, I think that knowledge of plans to annex the Milori Empire could have detrimental effects on the operation and adverse reactions from potential allies."

* * *

Arriving just after Jenetta had started her workday, the message from Admiral Moore was the first piece of business she addressed.

"Hello Admiral, I hope this message finds you well. The Board has given serious attention to your proposal that you enter Milori space with the intention of impeding Maxxiloth's ability to wage war. We unanimously approve your plan as a logical next step in response to his continued attacks. Both the *Colorado* and the *Yangtze* are assigned to you in support of this operation."

"The Board recommends that you immediately notify your Hudeerac contact of the pending action and enlist their aide in whatever capacity you see fit. We authorize you to promise them the return of their former territory if they join us in this struggle and to inform them that we will not return the territory if they fail to participate. We leave the handling of that matter entirely up to you.

"Space Command Headquarters is attempting to contact the Gondusans with a similar offer. If we're successful, their liaison will contact you directly to coordinate efforts.

"The action you've chosen to undertake is an extremely dangerous one, and we feel that crews should be limited to volunteers. Good luck, Admiral. You carry with you the prayers and hopes of the Alliance for a speedy cessation of hostilities.

"Richard E. Moore, Admiral of the Fleet, Supreme Headquarters, Earth, message complete."

Jenetta walked around her office for more than an hour deciding on a course of action before touching the ring from her left hand to the spindle in the media tray in her desk and tapping the record button on her com unit.

"To Vertap Aloyandro, Minister of Intelligence for the Hudeerac Order, from Admiral Jenetta Alicia Carver, Base Commander of Stewart Space Command Base.

"Minister, I'm sure you've received news of our victory over the invading forces from Milor and that you understand this war is far from over. I wish to establish a formal arrangement with your government for the creation of a coalition that will end Maxxiloth's ability to wage war on his neighbors. A Space Command task force will reach Milor on the 15th of September 2280 according to the Earth calendar.

"We realize that your ship technology may not be comparable to that of the Milori, but we ask that you commence attacks on any Milori targets of opportunity no later than August 15th. We've made a similar request of the Gondusans. These diversionary tactics should draw all forces, other than their home guard, away from Milor, but once we commence our attacks, the Milori should break off their pursuit of your ships and return to confront us.

"I've been authorized to guarantee that all Gondusan and Hudeerac territories usurped by the Milori Empire will be distributed to the participants of this coalition in appreciation for their cooperation. Because of the distance involved, our task force will be smaller than we would like, so it's imperative that we work together in this endeavor.

"Jenetta Carver, Rear Admiral, Upper Half, Commander of Stewart Space Command Base, message complete."

Jenetta encrypted the message and pressed the send button a scant second before the com unit displayed a message from her aide. She saw that Admiral Vroman had arrived.

"Send him in, Lori," she said as she closed the media drawer.

"Good morning, Jen," Admiral Vroman said as he entered her office.

"Good morning, Thad. You're looking better every day."

"And feeling better. Your chef is wonderful, and I've really enjoyed our meals in your private dining room."

"Soon to be *your* private dining room."

"Not just yet. I'm enjoying the rest I've been getting."

"It can't be helped, Thad. I've just received approval for my plan to tackle Milor."

"Really?"

"Really. Apparently the Admiralty Board agrees it's necessary to clip Maxxiloth's wings."

"When will you leave?"

"As soon as you feel ready we'll have a formal ceremony in the conference center where I'll relinquish command of Stewart. My departure will follow shortly after that."

"Then I'd better start getting a little more involved in the day-to-day stuff."

"It would be best. How about a full tour? We've never walked the entire base. Do you feel up to it?"

"Walk the entire base?" he asked skeptically.

"Just an expression. We'll use a cart on each level."

"That sounds better. I don't think I could walk the entire base after the breakfast I just ate. I'm ready when you are, Jen."

As Jenetta rose, her cats rose as well, thinking they were going along. "Cayla, Tayna, stay," she said softly, and the cats sank back to a reclined position.

"They're trained quite well," Admiral Vroman said.

"We've been together for quite a few years. At times it seems like we share one mind."

"That was the half of the base dedicated solely to military operations," Jenetta said as they returned to her office late in the day. "Tomorrow we can tour the warehouses, concourse, and new habitat."

"New habitat?"

"Yes, we've almost outgrown this one. Based on growth projections, and with the full approval of Supreme HQ, we began construction on an expanded habitat adjoining this one a few years ago. The new habitat will be four times larger than the existing one. It will double our vendor concourse size, triple our military operations space, and increase living quarters by a factor of five. We're also adding a hydroponics section that will provide fresh vegetables year round. The skeletal work is complete and we've nearly completed the outer shell. About eighty-five percent of the floor space is pressurized and interior work has begun."

"I see. You don't think small, Jenetta."

"We have to be prepared, Thad. All of our statistical forecasting says that we'll need a lot more space. Stewart has already become a small city, straining at the seams to become a large city. I foresee Stewart as playing an increasingly larger role in the future as it becomes the prime anchor point for operations in this part of space."

"It's too bad you won't be here to see it through."

"I've started the ball rolling. With your great organizational skills, I have no doubt the work will be completed and that Stewart will become a credit to Space Command and the Galactic Alliance."

"What's your plan for going to Milor? How will you handle re-supply for example? You certainly can't take all the ordnance you'll need in those two small ships."

I've already dispatched a dozen of our fastest warships towards the outer border. Every available space from bow to stern is filled with ordnance, supplies, and food."

"Before Space Command even approved your idea?"

"Because of the distance involved, I couldn't wait while they considered the plan. It will take the ships almost a year to reach the outermost border of the Buffer Zone. Officially, I tasked them to begin patrols in accordance with our mandate to protect Galactic Alliance space, so the fact that they're carrying an overabundance of food, ordnance, and military supplies doesn't violate any Space Command regulations or directives from Supreme Headquarters. If my plan had been rejected, the ships would simply perform their patrol duties and return here without the need to be restocked for an extended period."

Admiral Vroman smiled. "You're an organizer's organizer, Jen."

"What I really am is hungry. Are you ready for dinner?"

269

"You bet."

"Let me take Cayla and Tayna to my quarters and give them their dinner. Then I'll meet you in the dining room."

"See you there."

"Lori," Jenetta said to her aide the following morning, "as soon as Admiral Vroman takes command of the base, I'm going to be leaving."

"Where are we going, Admiral?"

"I've received permission to undertake an extremely dangerous operation, but the Admiralty Board has specified that all participants in the operation be volunteers."

"I volunteer, ma'am."

Jenetta smiled. "You don't even know what it is yet."

"I know that if you've proposed it, it's necessary and important for the safety of the Galactic Alliance. Whatever it is, I volunteer."

"Okay, you're my first crewmember."

"You're building a crew?"

"Two. The Admiralty Board has assigned the two scout-destroyers to me for this operation. Our problem now becomes one of how to put together two crews consisting only of volunteers for a highly secretive operation that could take us far from home."

"Milor?"

"Yes."

"We won't have any difficulty putting together a command for that, ma'am. Every Space Command officer, NCO, and crewman on this station will jump at an opportunity to take the fight to the enemy for a change."

"Perhaps, but we have to verify that before we leave, and we can't afford to have anyone learn of our real mission. I've considered starting a rumor that we're hunting for Raider bases."

"That sounds reasonable, Admiral. Everyone knows how much you dislike the Raiders. And why."

"But the problem remains one of recruiting two crews."

"Why not just start by asking the current crews of the two ships involved?"

"We reassigned most of the crew to other ships before the battle. Only sixty percent of the original crew remains. Still, it would be a start. Arrange for a shuttle and we'll go over there."

"Aye, Admiral. I'll have one ready to go in five minutes."

"Welcome aboard, Admiral," Lt. Commander Gallagher said, after completing the formal greetings in the shuttle bay of the *Colorado*.

"Thank you, Commander."

"I was surprised when I was told of your inspection tour. Since we were being held in reserve, we didn't suffer any damage in the fight."

"I know, Commander. I came aboard to discuss your status now that the threat from the Milori has been reduced."

"Reduced, ma'am? You thumped them!"

"Thumped, maybe, but not beaten. We're still at war with the Milori and must remain extra vigilant."

"Of course, Admiral."

"Let's continue our discussion in the captain's briefing room. Invite your second in command."

"Aye, Admiral."

Lt. Cmdr. Lori Ashraf, Lt. Cmdr. Peter Gallagher, and Lt. Maria Cruz all took their seats in the briefing room once Jenetta had taken hers. Gallagher and Cruz were noticeably stiff in the presence of the renowned Admiral Carver.

"When this ship was dispatched to Stewart, I'm sure both of you expected to join the crew of the *Prometheus*, or receive a similar assignment. Since the original crew had worked together for several weeks, I decided to keep a core group aboard this ship for a special assignment. However, my 'Madness Ray' plan worked so well, I didn't need to employ the strategy for which you had trained. In normal times, this scout ship would now join its battleship, but these are hardly normal times.

"As you might have heard, I'll soon be turning over command of this base to Admiral Vroman. I've proposed a daring plan to the Admiralty Board and they've given me a green light. They've assigned the *Colorado* and the *Yangtze* to me for the duration of the operation but imposed a requirement that all crewmembers be volunteers. This is not a short-term operation and, by requiring that the crew be limited to volunteers, I'm sure you understand that it's extremely dangerous."

Jenetta paused for a couple of seconds to let the information sink in as she stared into the eyes of each officer. "If you choose to remain at Stewart, you'll be reassigned elsewhere almost immediately and your decision will not adversely affect your career. If you choose to remain aboard the *Colorado*, you'll be reassigned new roles. You, Commander Gallagher, would become second in command, and you, Lieutenant Cruz, would become fourth. I will be assuming the role of Captain and Commander Ashraf will be the second officer since she is junior in seniority to Commander Gallagher. I'll need your answers by the end of the day because I have much to do and not much time to do it."

"I don't need time to think it over, Admiral," Lt. Commander Gallagher said, "I volunteer now. It will be an honor to serve as your first officer aboard the *Colorado*."

"I don't need time either, Admiral," Lieutenant Cruz said, "I volunteer for this operation, whatever it is. That's why I'm out here."

Jenetta looked into the eyes of each officer and saw the determination there. "Welcome to my team. I can't reveal the particulars until we're actually underway. What I need from you right now is to put the matter to each crewmember individually and determine their interest. If they choose not to participate, the personnel officer will arrange for their transfer to another ship tomorrow. If they choose to stay— and it must be entirely their choice— they may find their current statuses changing as other more senior crewmen are brought aboard."

"We'll start interviewing the crew immediately, Admiral," Lt. Commander Gallagher said.

"Thank you, Commander. Forward your report to Commander Ashraf by tomorrow morning."

"Aye, Admiral."

Jenetta and Lt. Commander Ashraf visited the *Yangtze* next and met with Lt. Commander Soren Mojica and his second officer, Lieutenant Adel Baran. Like the other two officers, they immediately volunteered for the mission, even with the knowledge that they would be stepping down in authority. Jenetta had already decided she must have a more experienced officer in command of the *Yangtze*.

Admiral Vroman was sitting in Jenetta's office talking with Captain Gavin when Jenetta returned.

"Good morning, gentlemen. Sorry to keep you waiting, Admiral. I had a couple of things to take care of."

"Good morning," both men said.

"No problem, Jen," Admiral Vroman said. "Larry and I have been catching up on old times."

"Hi, Larry. I suppose you've heard you're not getting the *Colorado* back right away?"

"Yes. I received a message from Supreme Headquarters last night. What's up?"

"The Admiralty Board has approved my plan to take the fight to Milor. The *Colorado* and the *Yangtze* will constitute my task force."

Captain Gavin smiled. "With all due respect to the Admiral, didn't someone once tell her that she had more guts than sense?"

Jenetta also smiled. "Commandant Bacheer said that to me after I took Stewart. Are you thinking he was right?"

"You're planning to take on an entire empire of 'nasties' with just two tiny ships. You tell me."

"A crippled empire, at this time. If we wait until our main force can travel there, we'll have to face many more warships than they can presently muster, so we must strike as quickly as possible before they have time to reconstitute their fleets. Also, they won't be expecting an attack right now because they'll believe it will take us several years or more to get there. If I accomplish nothing more than the complete destruction of their main shipbuilding facilities and the ships presently under construction, the operation will have been a huge success. My goal is to put the Milori military on the defensive and in disarray. We'll hit and run until we reduce their ability to wage war to near zero."

Captain Gavin looked at Admiral Vroman. "Do you support this action, Thad?"

"It's difficult to argue the merits of the action, Larry, although I wish we had more ships to send. Jen will have to travel all the way back to GA space to re-supply."

"I never have been able to establish a sustainable position against Jen's logic," Captain Gavin said, smiling, "even when she was first assigned to my ship as a recently promoted Lt. Commander. Okay, Jen, is there anything I can do to help?"

"Militarily, no. Even at Light-412, I'm afraid the *Prometheus* is just too slow to help this time. However, I need some good people to round out the crew of my two ships. I can't go into a situation like this with a sixty percent crew complement. They must be volunteers, and this must be kept as quiet as possible so we don't lose the element of surprise."

"I'll find you some, although my crew is still very understaffed."

"I understand. I also intend to contact the other captains and see whom they can offer. Right now, I need a good, experienced officer to captain the *Yangtze*. Any suggestions?"

"Commander Frank Fannon from the *Lisbon*," Admiral Vroman said without hesitation. "He's intelligent, tough as nails, and an excellent leader. I considered him to be my best man on Siena, although I had to rely on Captain Lindahl to handle most command duties because of his rank."

"But he's just returned from a grueling year and a half on a primitive planet. He needs time to recover and recharge his batteries."

"Don't use me as a comparison, Jen; he isn't eighty-two years old. I saw him in the gym this morning and he's already getting antsy from sitting around with nothing to do. He lost his post on the *Lisbon* when you re-staffed it to participate in the battle, and he's hoping the temporary reassigns are sent back to their original posts soon so he can return to duty."

"Thanks for the suggestion, Thad. I'll speak with him later today to see if he'd like to volunteer."

Commander Fannon jumped at the opportunity to join the volunteer effort. He correctly guessed the goal might be to take action against the Milori, even if he didn't know the particulars, and he was anxious to repay the enemy that had marooned him on Siena. He was further delighted to learn he would captain the *Yangtze*. It would be his first command, other than when the *Lisbon* had been in port and Captain Lindahl had gone ashore briefly.

Over the course of the following week, Jenetta filled the vacant crew posts with volunteers, as required by Supreme Headquarters. Perhaps most interesting was that not a single individual offered the opportunity to serve with Admiral Carver turned it down. Her reputation for always being in the middle of the action, her tactical abilities, and her well-known concern for the safety of her crews made everyone anxious to serve with her.

The two small ships were provisioned and armed while in orbit so spies on the station wouldn't be witness to the action. The spaces not filled with torpedoes were packed with food, clothing, spare parts, or medical supplies. Even the crew quarters were used for storage. Jenetta's quarters and her briefing room were both half filled with boxes and cases, and they would remain that way until the massive stockpile of torpedoes in the holds began to decrease. Each ship was carrying over six times the ordnance normally found on a full-sized Space Command destroyer.

Jenetta's last official act as the commanding officer of Stewart was to turn over her report on the *Lisbon* attack to Admiral Vroman. It would be Vroman's responsibility to pursue negligence charges against Captain Lindahl for his actions prior to the loss of the *Lisbon*.

What was originally intended as a small ceremony, mainly a photo op for the news media, turned into an event that had to be moved to the convention hall. It seemed that everyone on the station wanted to watch as Jenetta turned over command of the station to Admiral Vroman. He made a speech praising her contribution to the cause of peace and security in the region and listed her accomplishments since seizing the base from the Raiders. Jenetta spoke about what being the base commander had meant to her, praised her staff effusively, and then praised the governments and officials with whom she had dealt since becoming commander of the largest off-world base in Space Command. Following her speech, she received a standing ovation that didn't diminish until she left the stage.

When reporters crowded around her afterwards and shouted questions about her next command, she remained non-committal, but she had made sure that rumors abounded that she was embarking upon a search for Raider bases in the Frontier Zone because Space Command knew the Raiders had assisted the Milori in their invasion attempt. Those stories filled the papers and vid channels for the following week as speculation continued to grow.

* * *

"My Lord?" Exalted Lord Space Marshall Berquyth said.

"What is it, Berquyth?"

"We've picked up an interesting news broadcast from Galactic Alliance space."

"And?"

"Admiral Carver has passed command of the station to Admiral Vroman."

"I'm sick of hearing about Carver and her activities."

"The news media is reporting that she's embarked on a crusade to find and destroy Raider Bases in their Frontier Zone."

"Good. I hope she finds and destroys every one, the traitors."

"But it's good news, isn't it, my Lord? I mean, if she's looking for Raiders, she can't be coming here."

"She'll get around to us eventually. That's why we have to keep rebuilding our fleet with all possible haste. When they arrive, they'll be met with an armada so large they'll regret ever entering our territory."

"Yes, my Lord. I simply thought you should know what we picked up."

"Thank you, Berquyth, but it does little to cheer me up. I don't think I'll ever smile again until I have Carver's head on my wall."

* * *

Minister Vertap entered the King's chambers and walked to his desk. "Your majesty, I've received a communication from Admiral Carver. She requests that we join Space Command in bringing down Maxxiloth. Their task force will reach Milor in four full lunars. In exchange for our participation, all of our former territories will be returned to us once Maxxiloth is defeated."

The king looked at his minister. "She proposes to give us back our own territory in exchange for sending our people to die in her war?"

"It's not just her war, your majesty, and neither, technically, are the territories ours at present."

"The Royal Assembly has decided we'll let the Galactic Alliance fight the Milori, and then we'll step in after they leave."

"That may be unwise, your majesty. They are expecting us to participate in this action."

"Why? What can they do if we choose not to join her?"

"A similar request for assistance has been made to the Gondusans. The message from Admiral Carver seems to suggest that the Gondusans might be awarded our former territories if we don't join this coalition and participate fully."

"She wouldn't dare."

"If we don't participate, we might have little to say in the matter. We believe the Galactic Alliance to be too powerful for us to fight. Their victories against the Milori have been most impressive."

As the king threw down his pen and stood up, Vertap bowed his head. Striding to the window while clenching and unclenching one of his hands behind his back, Jamolendre said, "We are not yet ready to take on the Milori, even a *weakened* Milori military. We believed we had several years before we had to face this question. How could Space Command have come so far, so fast?"

"They must have dispatched their task force after the first attack by the Milori, knowing the Milori wouldn't honor the treaty and would invade again. It's the only thing that makes sense, unless..."

"Yes, unless what?"

"There is a persistent rumor they have developed a new spaceship capable of incredible speeds."

"How incredible?"

"Twenty times the speed of our fastest ships."

"Twenty times?"

"Yes, my Lord."

The King appeared thoughtful for a few seconds before saying, "I wouldn't put any stock in that, Vertap. Our scientists all say speeds in excess of Light-862 aren't possible, and speeds greater than Light-562 may not be feasible for hundreds of years."

"Yes, my Lord."

"What is your recommendation?"

"It's not my place to say, my Lord."

"Come, Vertap. I value your opinion. What would you do?"

"I would do whatever she asks of us. To refuse might instill bad feelings in the one person who might rid us forever of the Maxxiloth threat. We know the Galactic Alliance is a democratic confederation, guaranteeing freedom from outside oppression to all member planets. I can't imagine a more benevolent group with which to be affiliated. I would join the coalition."

"But we're not yet ready. Why did she have to come now?" the king said, hanging his head.

Chapter Twenty
~ July 30th, 2280 ~

As the *Colorado* left orbit around Stewart, Jenetta began to re-experience the exhilaration of captaining a ship in space. It made little difference that the two small ships each had a compliment of just one hundred eighty-five officers and crew. On the second day out, they overtook and passed the dozen warships filled with ordnance and supplies that Jenetta had dispatched a month earlier. The twelve M-designate ships, capable of Light-450, almost seemed to be standing still as the two scout-destroyers passed them by at Light-9790. The communication chiefs aboard the twelve ships were receiving messages from Jenetta reporting the passage of the *Colorado* and the *Yangtze* even as the DeTect systems were first notifying the tactical officers of their approach. With an estimated travel time to Milor at Light-9790 of just forty-six days, the two small ships would reach the enemy planet before the supply ships were a quarter of the way to the Frontier Zone's outer border.

Every military organization trained its people to collect military information when capturing enemy installations, vessels, and personnel, and Space Command was certainly no different. Many of the captured Milori vessels had yielded valuable data. Passwords and encryption algorithms were normally changed immediately when a ship was captured or lost, but maps and defense information could be invaluable. Perhaps the Milori had never lost a ship to an enemy before taking on Space Command, or perhaps they trusted their commanders to destroy all important files before the vessels were captured; whatever the reason, the files were largely intact and Jenetta was able to piece together an excellent picture of the enemy they were facing. She knew where all the spacedocks were located in the empire and the locations of munitions factories, military installations, and storage armories. There was no way of knowing how many ships would currently be defending the planetary, or off-planetary, resources, so the plan would have to be a bit fluid, but as Prussian General Count Helmuth von Moltke said in the nineteenth century, "No plan survives contact with the enemy."

Neither the Gondusans nor the Hudeeracs had thus far agreed to join the coalition, and it was beginning to look like Space Command would have to go it alone. "So be it," she said to her pets as she sat in her briefing room reviewing her plan repeatedly in her mind while looking for weaknesses.

Fourteen days into the trip, Jenetta halted both ships and ordered them linked via airlocks. Their position was just inside the outermost border of the Galactic Alliance's Frontier Zone and she wanted to have a staff meeting of senior officers before they entered either the Buffer Zone or Milori space.

Commander Frank Fannon and his first officer, Lt. Commander Mojica, joined Jenetta, Lt. Commander Gallagher, and Lt. Commander Ashraf in her briefing room aboard the *Colorado*.

"The shipbuilding facilities are our principal targets on the mission. We must prevent them from reconstructing their fleets. Should we fail in our overall mission, we will at least make sure Space Command won't face a larger force of Milori-built ships than that which presently exists."

"Is another Space Command task force being readied, Admiral?" Commander Fannon asked. "One with ships using a conventional FTL drive?"

"Not to my knowledge, but if we fail, such a mission will become a necessity. We know Maxxiloth has two primary warship construction facilities, one in orbit at each of the two planets neighboring Milor. The shipyard at the third planet builds battleships, cruisers, and frigates, while the yard at the fifth planet in the system concentrates on building destroyers. They appear to be about equal in size. The *Yangtze's* computer contains all the information amassed from the captured Milori ships, so you can study it when you return

280

and ask any questions you have. The *Colorado* will take the yard at the third planet, and the *Yangtze* will tackle the yard at the fifth. We'll coordinate our attacks and begin our first runs at the same time. I expect, but have no way of ascertaining in advance, that the yards will be unguarded or lightly guarded. Amassing the armada sent to Stewart had to have drained their resources to dangerously low levels. I'm sure Maxxiloth ordered that every available ship be sent against us after the embarrassing defeat of the first effort. And being eleven hundred light-years from Stewart would have made them believe they had several years to rebuild their fleet before we could respond if they were unsuccessful."

"They're in for a mighty big surprise," Lt. Commander Mojica said, smiling.

"Let us hope," Jenetta said. "Our goal at the shipyards is nothing less than total destruction. We'll start with the ships closest to completion to ensure the Milori can't deploy them against us if they're almost ready for space trials. We can't depend upon them being unarmed; just slam them and slam them hard. I expect the facilities will have laser weapon protection, but that doesn't concern us because we're impervious; however, we must be concerned with torpedo-launching capability and minefields. I'd prefer that we not split our force, but surprise will give us a substantial edge. If you run into serious trouble, such as an unexpected assembly of warships, break off your attack and make for our position. We'll do a lot better working together against a larger force."

"And where should we go after destroying the shipbuilding facilities?" Commander Fannon asked.

"Take up position around Milor outside the minefield."

"Minefield?"

"Yes, there's a minefield that completely surrounds the planet."

"How do we get past that?"

"We don't have to. It's never been my intention to invade the planet. For one thing, we're hardly equipped for such an endeavor. Between us, we only have a single company of Marines aboard. For another, it wouldn't buy us anything. Our goal is to bottle up the Milori, and a minefield is almost as much of an obstacle to escape as it is a barrier against invasion. We can still direct laser fire through the minefield and launch torpedoes against selected ground targets."

Commander Fannon smiled. "That works for me."

"As soon as we begin our attacks on the shipyards, Maxxiloth is going to start screaming for his warships to protect him from us. It'll be easier to let them come to us rather than us chasing them all over the grid. If they just come running without stopping to form a task force, we'll take them on as they arrive. If they come as a force, I'll make a determination whether to fight or cut and run."

"Run?"

"Temporarily. We'll disappear so fast they won't know what happened to us. We can circle around and come at them again when they disperse to protect different resources. I'd put our ships up against any Milori vessel, or even any five of them, but I hesitate to take on an entire task force by ourselves at this point."

"The Milori Empire is huge. It may take months, or even years, for all ships to return home."

"Yes, I don't expect this to be over in a couple of months; it'll probably be a long-term effort. I've prepared a list of targets that will receive our attention over the next few months as we get a better feel for the situation. There's still a lot we don't know, but I believe we all recognize and agree that shutting down his warship production is a vital first step."

Commander Fannon nodded.

"That's the general plan. I'll continue to refine it as we gather more intel. Any questions?"

"Do we know anything about the minefield around the planet?" Lt. Commander Mojica asked.

"The intel we've assembled from captured files tells us the mines are a standard, self-aligning type with the same payload as their standard torpedoes. When a ship receives permission to enter orbit, they deactivate the mines at the entry point and move them aside to create an opening. The process takes about ten minutes to open or close, so we'll know if any ships on the surface are preparing to come out after us in sufficient time to confront them."

The meeting came to an abrupt end with a ship-wide announcement of General Quarters. The senior staff of both ships rushed from the briefing room.

"What is it?" Jenetta said to Lt. Cruz, the bridge officer in charge.

"Contact astern, Admiral, coming directly towards us. I've ordered the ship sealed and the airlock retracted."

"The ships are separated," the tactical officer confirmed.

"Helm, bring us around," Jenetta said. "Com, contact the *Yangtze* and have them turn to face the approaching ship but hold their position."

"The contact is slowing," the tactical officer said.

"Can we identify it, tac?"

"It's large, either a freighter or warship. It's not emitting a Space Command transponder signature. It appears to be Milori. Confirming that. It's a Milori cruiser and it appears to be heavily damaged, Admiral."

"Hail it."

After several seconds, the com operator said, "It's not acknowledging our hail, Admiral."

Facing the front of the ship, Jenetta said, "Put me on."

"You're on, Admiral."

"Attention Milori cruiser. This is the GSC *Colorado*. You're in Galactic Alliance space. I assume you're the cruiser that managed to escape our ships last year. Turn your ship around and proceed to Stewart for war internment or face destruction."

The monitor image changed to show the image of a Milora. Damage to the bridge was evident behind him. "This is the *Xiouthet*, a proud ship in service to the emperor. We don't take orders from toy Space Command ships. Clear the way or we'll plow through you."

"I've been told that your species is intelligent, but it appears you don't learn lessons any better than the Tsgardi. You had your chance," Jenetta said to him, then looked at the com operator and gave a signal to cut the connection. "Tactical, put two torpedoes into his bow."

Two torpedoes rushed from the *Colorado*. The Milora may have regretted his bluster as he tried to avoid the torpedoes. With the ship so badly damaged he didn't have a chance of getting out of the way. His laser gunners tried to hit the torpedoes but didn't come close. Both torpedoes struck the bow and opened huge holes.

"Helm, take us around to his stern. Laser gunners, target his engines and temporal field generator. I don't want that ship ever going anywhere again under its own power."

As the *Colorado* moved around the cruiser, laser gunners on the *Xiouthet* targeted the *Colorado*, but the shots had no effect on the Dakinium hull. The laser gunners aboard the *Colorado* ripped the *Xiouthet's* temporal field generator and sub-light engines to pieces.

"That's sufficient," Jenetta said. "Hold your fire. Helm, move the ship a billion kilometers away, speed Light-37. Com, tell the *Yangtze* to follow so we can reestablish our link. I'm sure Commander Fannon wants to get back aboard his ship." She looked at the Commander, who smiled and nodded.

"What about the Milori cruiser, Admiral?" Commander Fannon asked.

"They're not going anywhere now and we don't have room for prisoners. They'll no doubt have a few shuttles and fighters on board, so they can evacuate the crew to a nearby planet if they can find a suitable one, but they'd only be marooning themselves. We'll be keeping the Milori so busy they won't have time to send any ships back this way. When our supply ships reach this point in eight or nine months, they can pick them up. If their ship won't hold atmosphere they'll have to use their escape pods and stasis beds. They had their chance to surrender. It's one less ship we'll have to worry about later."

"I meant won't they alert Milor about our presence so close to the border?"

"We're still in our own space, eight hundred light-years from Milor, and the cruiser hasn't observed anything unusual except the resistance of our hull to laser fire. We'll put some distance between us before engaging Light-9790. Do you have any other questions about the attack plan?"

"Nothing right now, Admiral. I'd like to have a chance to study the data about the target."

"Fine. Contact me if you have any further questions. We'll proceed together to the designated deployment point and then separate to proceed to our targets. That's all, Commander."

"Aye, Admiral."

* * *

A few days later, Jenetta arrived on the bridge in the morning and learned that an incoming message from the Gondusans was waiting for her. She walked directly to her briefing room, prepared a cup of coffee and sat down to view the message.

"Greetings, Admiral," a Gondusan said as soon as its image appeared on the screen. Although she'd heard they always carried their fashion to excess— and the more powerful the person, the more excessive the clothing— Jenetta was unable to suppress a smirk over the garish costume the message-sender was wearing. She was glad it was just a message. Almost as bad was the gaudy makeup that, to Jenetta's eyes, made the Gondusan look like a circus clown and left her wondering if the Gondusan was a male or female. Of course, they could be celebrating some sort of special event like Mardi Gras and, however unlikely, the message sender may not have had time to change before recording the transmission. As she watched the message, Jenetta wondered if the Milori hated humans so much because their territory was ringed by species having hominine characteristics. Gondusans were very much Hominidae in appearance. Even the baboon-like Tsgardi were closer to hominid form than a Milora.

"I'm Senator Prime Curlekurt Emmeticus. Our planetary senate has voted to join your coalition of partners in an effort to eliminate the Milori scourge from the galaxy forever. We have dispatched our fleet of warships with orders to attack the Milori defensive perimeter at a number of points. We trust this will result in Milor turning its attention in our direction and give you an opportunity to strike at their very heart. We cannot hold out indefinitely against the might of the Milori military and hope your attack will convince them to break off their assault on our ships before we are destroyed. We trust you to do as your government has promised and return our former territories once you've destroyed Milor.

"Curlekurt Emmeticus, Senator Prime of Gondusa, Planetary Senate, Gondusa, message complete."

Jenetta chuckled. She hoped she was never required to meet in person with Curly or a delegation from Gondusa. She might not be able to keep a straight face.

* * *

On September 1st, two hours before the third watch began, while the ship was still over three hundred light-years from Milor, the com operator contacted Jenetta in her quarters.

"Admiral, this is Chief Greenwalt. I've been listening to a Gondusan media broadcast and they just broke in with a special announcement. Their government is reporting that their military has attacked Milori bases and outposts at multiple locations along their border. The announcer says the government is vowing to take back the territory stolen from them by Maxxiloth and his great-grandfather."

"Really? See if you can find any confirmation of that announcement. And check the Milori military frequencies to see if there has been an increase in traffic."

"Aye, Admiral. Goodnight."

"Goodnight, Chief. Thank you."

* * *

Over the next few days, talk of war filled Gondusan broadcasts, but there wasn't a single acknowledging statement from the Milori. It's understandable that a totalitarian society already in an announced state of war with a powerful enemy might wish to suppress such information. Populations in such societies are manipulated by the careful dissemination of information. Also not surprising was the fact that traffic on the IDS frequencies used by the Milori military, although encrypted, increased by a factor of twelve.

Each day brought the *Colorado* and the *Yangtze* twenty-five light-years closer to Milor.

* * *

Perhaps it took them longer to get their forces organized and positioned, or perhaps it was fear that the Gondusans would be awarded their territory if they failed to participate, but the Hudeeracs finally commenced action against the Milori. On September 4th, the com operator picked up broadcasts announcing that Hudeerac forces had attacked Milori ships and outposts.

* * *

Maxxiloth smashed a gripper claw down onto the table. "What's going on? Why have these sheep suddenly decided to roar?"

"They've no doubt learned of our defeat by the Galactic Alliance and feel we've been weakened so much that they can push us back to the old borders," the Minister of Defense offered. He didn't add that it was what he had feared when Maxxiloth had insisted on sending every possible ship to Stewart.

"We must crush these attackers at once. Perhaps it's time to finally finish off the Hudeerac scum."

Exalted Lord Space Marshall Berquyth said, "We easily pushed the Hudeeracs back and annexed their territory, but there's nowhere left for them to run. Their backs are against the wall and they'll fight to the last warrior now. We've estimated that we'll lose between twenty and twenty-five ships if we move in to finish the Hudeeracs, which is why we haven't done it before. Controlling that one small solar system wasn't worth the loss."

"And now we're paying the price for that decision," the minister countered.

"We're in no position to sacrifice any ships," Berquyth said. "We must wait until we've rebuilt the fleet. In an annual's time we'll be in a much better position to finish them off, but for now we must simply fight a delaying action."

"And while we're doing that, the Hudeeracs will be destroying our bases and outposts."

"I remind you that of our six fleets, only one hundred twenty-three warships remain."

"I know. And eighty-eight of them can't get out of their own way. That's the only reason they weren't sent to fight

Space Command. At least the other thirty-five are newly commissioned ships from our latest designs."

"The eighty-eight may be slow, but they represent a formidable fighting force. Their laser weapons and torpedoes are every bit as powerful as those on our newest ships, and I guarantee that no Hudeerac or Gondusan is going to hang around for long when they show up."

"Enough of this quibbling," Maxxiloth shouted. "Order half our ships to put down the Gondusans and send the other half to squash the Hudeeracs."

"But my Lord," the Minister of Defense said, "that will leave the rest of the Empire defenseless. As it is, most of our ships are already hundreds of solars away. If you order all ships to the outer borders with the Hudeeracs and Gondusans, they'll be six to seven hundred solars away."

"In less than sixty solars we'll be launching almost two dozen new warships. They will provide protection for Milor and the heart of our empire."

"But what if we have problems between now and then?"

"Are you going to tell me now that the Tsgardi have launched an attack?"

"No, my Lord, but even that is possible. The jackals seem to be sniffing for blood."

Maxxiloth mulled the matter over in his head. "If we don't put down these rebellions, and put them down hard, the jackals will indeed attack. We must crush the attackers quickly and decisively. After one enemy falls, our forces will combine to crush the other. See to it, Berquyth."

"Yes, my Lord."

Maxxiloth stood and strode angrily from the room.

After the door had closed behind him, the Minister of Defense looked at Berquyth and said accusingly, "You didn't tell him."

"No, he has enough on his mind."

"You don't think it important that one of our cruisers was stopped and incapacitated by two small Space Command ships— ships seemingly impervious to laser cannon fire?"

"That occurred inside Galactic Alliance space over eight hundred solars from here at our top speed. Our ship was already badly damaged from its encounter with three SC warships and incapable of putting up a fight. After the attack, the small ships left at Light-37. You think they pose a danger to us here?"

"The important fact is that they're impervious to laser fire. What if all Space Command ships have this new outer covering?"

"They don't. You saw the image logs of the attack on the *Lisbon*. Like our ships, that ship had just two layers of tritanium plating."

"The *Lisbon* was an old ship from their rear areas. I've heard that their newer battleships have three extra-thick layers."

"But they can still be punctured by laser weapons."

"The fact that the Galactic Alliance has perfected almost indestructible hull plating is significant. The emperor must be told."

"He has enough to think about right now. He'll be told at a more appropriate time, and *I* will decide when that time arrives."

* * *

Jenetta ordered the *Colorado* and the *Yangtze* to a full stop when they were five light-years from the Milor system. They were ahead of schedule and would lay over there for a day. Everyone was told to get as much rest as possible, but nervous tension prevented most from sleeping soundly. They were about to launch an attack in enemy territory, eleven hundred light-years from the nearest Space Command base, and there was no one to come to their rescue if their ships were incapacitated.

Jenetta had decided there was nothing to be gained by dialogue with the Milori. The attacks were timed so that both ships would reach their target just seconds apart in the very early hours of the day according to Milori military time. Jenetta expected that the work force might be smaller and that those on duty might be sleepy. The two ships would leave their deployment points at the same instant and, if all went according to plan, their attack would be a complete surprise. As far as Jenetta knew, no one had spotted them yet, but she was aware that the Milori had thought their surprise was complete when they attacked Stewart. A spy in the Hudeerac or Gondusan hierarchy could have warned the Milori of the September 15th attack, which is why Jenetta planned her attack for the 14th.

After confirming that the *Yangtze* was ready to commence its assault, Jenetta directed the *Colorado's* first attack run immediately upon reaching the shipyards around the third planet.

The physical magnitude of the shipyard was staggering and dwarfed the Space Command facility at Mars. Five hundred spacedocks floated in orbit around the planet. All open docks contained ships in various states of completion— from bare, incomplete skeletons to ships that already wore their outer skin and markings. It was reasonable to assume the enclosed docks were likewise filled.

Jenetta was mistaken with her expectation that this would be the slowest part of the workday. She couldn't have known that the Milori worked full shifts around the clock.

The laser gunners aboard the *Colorado* targeted the Sub-Light engines and temporal envelope generators of the nearly completed ships tethered in open docks first, thus ensuring the ships couldn't move under their own power. As the attack progressed, torpedo gunners fired volleys into the bodies. With their engine sections destroyed, and huge, gaping holes in the mid-sections, there was little likelihood the ships would be going anywhere under their own power very soon. Next, they targeted the closed docks, blasting the structures to scrap and the partially completed ships with them. Lastly, they destroyed the open docks that contained the new keels and skeletons.

As the *Colorado* and the *Yangtze* conducted their attacks, laser cannons mounted on floating satellites opened fire on the two small ships. A scan of the area hadn't detected the presence of any mines, and the dense ring of defense satellites would be ignored unless one suddenly launched a torpedo.

The *Colorado* overflew the shipyards repeatedly while the gunners rained destruction down upon the enemy docks.

Small shuttles and single-occupant transports scattered in every direction as they tried to escape the devastation as quickly as their engines would take them. Complete pandemonium would not be an overstatement.

Lasting just eighteen minutes, the destruction was complete. What wasn't utterly destroyed was twisted and broken beyond any practical use. The *Colorado* had just set the Milori battleship and cruiser program back at least several annuals.

"The *Yangtze* reports mission completed, Admiral," the com operator said. "They're proceeding to Milor."

"Understood. Helm, take us to Milor."

* * *

"My Lord, wake up," Exalted Lord Space Marshall Berquyth said as he gently shook his emperor. The emperor's attendants had been too afraid to awaken him after they learned of the attack from the War Planning Chamber secretary.

"Wha— who is it?"

"It's Berquyth, my Lord. There's been an attack."

"Attack?" he said groggily. "Tell me about it in the morning," he mumbled as he rolled over and tried to fall asleep again.

"But it's the shipyards around Behrooth and Klessith."

The emperor stirred, then threw off the covers and sat up. "Did you say Behrooth and Klessith?"

"Yes, my Lord. Both shipyards were attacked."

"Was there any serious damage?"

"I'm afraid it's very serious. We're still trying to get an accurate picture, but it appears the yards have been completely destroyed."

The emperor bellowed at the top of his lungs and his attendants ran from the room. He was fully awake now and he fairly leaped out of bed as he screamed, "Who is responsible for this, the Hudeeracs or the Gondusans? I'll have the heads of all their leaders for this assault."

"We're not sure yet, my Lord. The attack ended just minutes ago, and we're still trying to piece things together. We're downloading all the security footage now. We should have an image of the ships soon and then we'll know who is responsible."

The emperor had pulled on a robe and was striding towards the doors with Berquyth a couple of steps behind him. The emperor's attendants huddled in the outer room, trying to appear invisible.

A group of very sleepy ministers and military leaders, still in their bedclothes, instantly sat up straight when Maxxiloth entered the War Planning Chamber beneath the palace minutes later.

"Have we identified the attackers yet," Maxxiloth screamed, "and have *all* the new ships been destroyed?"

"Our information is that the yards were completely destroyed," the Minister of State said. "What's left of the ships would require more repair work than the effort to build them new. The space docks are in a shambles."

"And who is responsible?"

"The technicians are still working to enhance the downloaded security logs. Here's the best vid of the bunch," he said as he pointed to the large monitor at the front of the room. A dark image appeared to streak by as explosions illuminated the background. "You can see the ship was painted black. It came in fast, with all exterior lights off, using the shadow from the planet to screen it. It was over the yard before anyone knew it was there. It made pass after pass, firing its torpedoes and laser cannons until every ship was destroyed and then sped off, disappearing into the blackness of space."

"A black ship— obviously designed for just this type of mission," Maxxiloth said thoughtfully. "Then it attacked the other yard?"

"No, my Lord, there were two of them. They followed the same plan of attack."

"So it was well planned, coordinated, and probably rehearsed," Maxxiloth said. "That would seem to point to the Hudeeracs."

The phone near the Minister of State rang and he answered it. "The technicians have completed their work," he said after hanging up. "The enhanced image will appear on the screen in a second. It shows a single frame from the log, with the ship clearly outlined by explosions behind it. Ah, there it is."

The black image of either the *Colorado* or the *Yangtze* materialized on the monitor. Appearing much like a silhouette, the outline was solidly defined, but the features of the ship were indistinct. The enhancement work had only been able to make it somewhat distinguishable.

"That's nothing like Hudeerac or Gondusan warships," Maxxiloth said.

"No, my Lord," Berquyth said, filled with dread, "it's a Space Command destroyer. I recognize the distinctive shape."

"Space Command?" Maxxiloth screamed. "How did Space Command destroyers get here?"

"They must have dispatched ships after the first invasion attempt and hidden them in our space, just as we hid ships in theirs."

"Obviously they're better at hiding ships than we are, Berquyth, since they found ours before we could attack the designated targets."

"My Lord," the Minister of Defense said, "ships matching this description intercepted and incapacitated the *Xiouthet* before it could leave Galactic Alliance space. The captain of the *Xiouthet* reported they were impervious to laser cannon fire."

Berquyth's eyes began shooting daggers of enmity towards the Minister of Defense.

"That's consistent with reports from the shipyards, my Lord," the Minister of State said. "They report the ships were struck thousands of times but never slowed or altered their attack. They never even fired at the ring of defense satellites and acted as if the laser strikes meant nothing."

"It sounds like that material we heard about several annuals ago," Maxxiloth said. "What was it called? Dakinium?"

"Yes," the Minister of State said, "Space Command was reported to be experimenting with it as hull plating for their ships."

"If their ships are now covered with this Dakinium, it could explain how they defeated our invasion force while suffering so little damage," the Minister of Defense said.

"We must get our hands on one," Maxxiloth said. "Recall all ships immediately. We must capture or destroy one of these ships at all costs so it can be studied."

"The nearest ships are fourteen solars away," Berquyth said, "on their way to fight the Hudeeracs and Gondusans. By the time they return, the Space Command ships can lay waste to half our planet."

Maxxiloth blanched.

"And what about the Hudeeracs and Gondusans?" the Minister of Defense asked.

"These Space Command ships represent a greater threat than all the ships in the Hudeerac and Gondusan fleets," Maxxiloth said. "I want them destroyed immediately."

"Let's send out our fighters," the Minister of State said.

"To what end?" asked Berquyth. "Fighters don't carry torpedoes, just small rockets. If the Space Command vessels are impervious to laser fire, they'll probably shrug off the rockets as well. We have no ships, my Lord, other than a few transports, shuttles, and space tugs. You ordered even our home guard to the borders."

Chapter Twenty-One
~ September 15th, 2280 ~

"Com, see if you can contact their military," Jenetta said as the *Colorado* took up a position well outside the planet's protective minefield, directly opposite the *Yangtze*, which had established an orbital track on the other side of the planet.

After a couple of minutes the com operator said, "I have a rather rude Milora on the com, Admiral."

"Put it up, Chief, and feed the signal to the *Yangtze*."

"Who are you and why are you using a military frequency?" the nasty-looking Milora said, although to human eyes it was difficult to find one that wasn't nasty looking.

"This is the GSC *Colorado*. We just destroyed your major shipyards and now I want to speak to your emperor. Put us through."

The Milora stared for a few seconds as if he couldn't believe his ears. He had undoubtedly heard about the attacks on the shipyards by now. "The emperor will be asleep at this hour."

"I doubt that, but if he is, wake him."

"Terran scum does not dictate orders to the Milori military."

Jenetta turned slightly to look at the com operator. "Com, tell the *Yangtze* to commence its attack. Torpedo gunners, you have your target lists. Commence firing." It hadn't been necessary for Jenetta to give the command to the com operator because the *Yangtze* was already seeing and hearing both sides of the communication. She did it for the benefit of the Milora. Facing front again, she said, "When your emperor is awake and ready to talk, you know what frequency we'll be monitoring." Looking towards the com chief, she gave the signal to cut the contact.

Jenetta sat back in her chair as the *Colorado's* torpedo gunners went to work. Special high-yield torpedoes threaded their way through the minefield before falling like rain upon the planet. Directed against weapon production facilities, ordnance depots, and military installations, each high-yield device sprouted a non-radioactive mushroom-like cloud where the target had stood unscathed just seconds before. As she watched the explosions from high above, Jenetta reminded herself that the Milori had intended exactly such death and destruction for Earth. The thought made it easier to deal with the death and misery she was sowing.

The *Colorado* had completed just one-half revolution of the planet before the com operator said, "I'm receiving a signal from the surface. They want to speak to the commanding officer."

"Put it up," Jenetta said.

Instantly, the image of Emperor Maxxiloth jumped into focus on the large screen at the front of the bridge. "You?" he screamed upon recognizing Jenetta.

"Yes, me. I understand you've ordered all your space marshals to bring back my head. I thought I'd give you a good look at what you won't be getting." She turned her head from side to side so he could see her profiles before she turned to stare at him again.

"I order you to stop this attack immediately!"

"I will, when I receive your unconditional surrender."

"Never!"

"I'm sorry you've taken that attitude, but it's hardly surprising."

"I'll have your head for this!"

"So you've been saying for years. But it looks like your head is the one on the chopping block."

"I demand you stop your attack immediately!" Maxxiloth was foaming a bit at the mouth by now. He wasn't used to having anyone ignore his ranting and refuse his orders. For the first time in his life, he was powerless to control all events around him.

"When you surrender unconditionally, we'll stop the attack."

"Never! I'll never surrender! We'll fight to the last Milora! You just wait until my ships get here. I'll have your head, Carver."

"You know how to contact me when you're ready to surrender," Jenetta said, giving the sign to the com operator to cut the connection.

"Think he'll capitulate?" Lt. Commander Gallagher asked from his chair next to Jenetta.

"No, not a chance. As he said, he'll fight to the last Milora. He cares nothing for his people; he only cares about power, and will sacrifice anyone and everyone to get it. I mentally prepared myself for this situation before we left Stewart. There're only two ways to bring about the fall of a tyrannical dictator like Maxxiloth. One is to destroy the empire's infrastructure throughout this sector and the other sectors he controls. We'll have to destroy all his ships and military resources, leaving him nothing to command. It's a daunting task for two small ships."

Lt. Commander Gallagher nodded. "And the other way?"

Jenetta looked at him. "Through a palace revolt or military coup when his subjects decide they wish an end to the death and destruction."

After a dozen orbits of the Milori home world, the two ships had successfully destroyed all of their primary targets and a few of their more important secondary targets. A few torpedoes had failed to make it through the minefield, so they simply destroyed the target on the next pass. The news media all over the planet was pleading for a cessation of hostilities and, as was to be expected in a totalitarian society, announcing enormous death tolls from the enemy's unprovoked and deliberate attacks on hospitals, schools, shopping centers, housing complexes, sports arenas, and other civilian locations. They uttered not a single word about the destruction of the two shipyards and kept narration about the attacks on military installations to a minimum. But the population wasn't blind, deaf, and dumb to the real carnage around them. Jenetta ordered the destruction to continue until they destroyed all designated secondary targets. If their media wouldn't report the stories honestly, she would see that they didn't report them at all. The secondary targets largely consisted of power plants, broadcasting facilities and towers, and telecommunications facilities. She purposely bypassed the communication satellites in orbit.

"Confirming all targets destroyed, Admiral," Commander Fannon said.

"Good work, Captain. We've completed our objectives as well."

"I would never have believed we would accomplish that without at least one warship making an appearance."

"It would seem Maxxiloth hasn't much of a military mind. He apparently sent *all* of his ships off in response to the diversion. If that's true, we'll have at least two weeks of uninterrupted activity. Proceed to the next group of targets on your list that are closest to our estimated position of their outbound warships and commence action. Then work your way down the list for as long as you're able. If you run into any serious problems, break off and proceed to the designated rendezvous point using a zigzag course so they can't plot your travel."

"Aye, Admiral. Good hunting. See you at the RP."

"And to you, Captain."

As the *Colorado* traveled to its next target, one that the outbound Milori fleet had already passed, Jenetta prepared and sent a report to Admiral Moore about the evening's activities, appending both the *Colorado* and the *Yangtze* video logs for the engagement period and the brief conversation with Maxxiloth. It would take more than three weeks for the message to reach Earth, given the distance involved.

She next prepared reports for the Gondusan and Hudeerac leadership, including video log data from the attacks on the shipyards. She knew the images would hearten their military leaders and show them they had chosen correctly when deciding to back the Space Command initiative.

* * *

As Jenetta had predicted, it took two weeks for the Milori ships dispatched in response to the diversions to return to the heart of the empire. The *Colorado* and the *Yangtze* had attacked targets nearest the outbound ships and then worked their way back towards Milor, destroying all targets as they moved and drawing the returning Milori ships after them. They continued with their attacks after passing Milor, and the Milori warships followed. Their ability to travel to each objective at Light-9790 always kept them well ahead of the Milori fleet. The Milori home guard, pursuing in the Empire's oldest and slowest ships, never had a chance of catching the small SC vessels. The *Colorado* and the *Yangtze* had ample time to destroy their targets without interruption.

The Milori may have felt they were driving Space Command out of their territory, but Jenetta's plan was simply to scatter the ships across the sector. She knew that Maxxiloth, having been attacked once at home, wouldn't permit all the ships to pursue Jenetta. He would hold back part of his force for home defense, not that there was anything left to defend except his own person. The Milori were struggling to cope with a world in darkness, having lost most of their power and telecommunications systems in the planet-ary attacks. Military, governmental, and public service facilit-ies, such as hospitals, had power available from emergency generators, but the civilian population was generally without power unless they were fortunate enough to live near small generating stations that hadn't been listed as a secondary target in the attack.

Following the initial attack on Milor, and allowing for the distance that the messages had to travel, Jenetta received word from both the Hudeeracs and Gondusans that the Milori had broken off their attacks as soon as news arrived about the attack on their home world. Both allies reported they were retaking their former territories from the Milori personnel who remained on bases and space stations.

Jenetta sent messages of appreciation for their support and congratulations on the successful reacquisition of their territory but warned them against sending any warships into the Milori Empire beyond their former territory because all Space Command warships had orders to destroy any warship, regardless of their allegiance. She hoped the warning would be enough to stop any attempts to grab territory that wasn't historically theirs.

At three hundred light-years from Milor, the military targets had thinned considerably. Jenetta had purposely not included outposts and space stations with only defensive capability on the target lists, and there was little else after that point. She destroyed armories at remote bases and space docks for the construction and repair of warships but left Milori transports and supply ships alone. She then ordered her small ship to the designated RP where the *Yangtze* was already waiting.

As soon as the two ships had linked up, Commander Fannon and Lt. Commander Mojica came aboard the *Colorado* and made their way to the Admiral's briefing room.

"Welcome, gentlemen," Jenetta said. "I commend you on a job well done. Supreme Headquarters is extremely pleased with the operation so far."

"Thank you, Admiral," Commander Fannon said. "It's been a hell of an exciting three months. We've left the empire smarting."

"Yes, but I think we're all a little tired and can use a good rest. This location is so remote and so far from our last known locations that we should be safe here. The bridge will remain at alert status, but all other sections can stand down so all off-duty personnel can catch up on their sleep, or whatever. How are your supplies?"

"Adequate, but we could use a few items that are low and our ordnance is also getting low. I was glad when my quarters were finally empty of crates, and I never thought we'd use all the torpedoes we brought, but I'd like to have an extra hundred in my holds right now."

"We'll compare stores lists and share what we can. Our torpedo stocks are also low, so I guess we should make a trip to our supply ships after a week layover here. We'll continue to have an opportunity to rest up because it will take a couple of weeks to reach our ships. They should still be a few months from the border, so we'll have to travel further to meet them for this first re-supply."

"Where do we go from there, Admiral?"

"Back into the fray. This break will confuse the Milori leadership. They'll be expecting us to pop up somewhere and attack, and the waiting will get on their nerves. Without a specific target to chase, they'll have to spread out their forces to search for us or to protect the bases we've bypassed.

* * *

"How did Carver get here so fast?" Maxxiloth demanded.

"We know she has two clones, my Lord. We're speculating that the one in the news broadcasts was standing in for her."

"Then how did she defeat our forces at Stewart?"

"Perhaps the one here, now, is a clone?" the Minister of Defense offered.

"And how many of these damned little ships are in our territory?" Maxxiloth screamed at his advisors as he looked at a map of the sector that highlighted all of the attacked resources. "Are they mere clones as well?"

"We don't know, my Lord," Berquyth said. "They don't identify themselves, and without any external markings, they all look the same. Based on the distances involved and the timing of the attacks, we estimate there must be about twenty, but there could be as many as thirty."

"And not one of our ships has caught sight of one?"

"No, my Lord. They have always remained at least a solar ahead of us as they moved back towards Alliance space."

"Are they retreating?"

"It would appear that way, but not because we've been able to do anything to force them back. They might just be continuing their path of destruction, having already destroyed everything in this direction."

"Yes, Carver would never retreat unless she was being forced back."

"Perhaps it's simply a matter of not wanting to engage the superior fire power of our ships?" the Minister of State said.

"Carver's not afraid of our ships, you fool," Maxxiloth retorted, "and she's not about to end her attack while we still pose a threat to the Galactic Alliance. No, she has something else planned; I can feel it in my bones. And now they've dropped out of sight completely." Slamming a gripper claw down on the table, he said, "Where have they gone?" The question was purely rhetorical, as no one at the table had, or was really expected to have, that information. After a minute of concentration, he said, "She intends to double back and attack us here again after drawing off our fleet! Berquyth, order all ships to return here at once. They're needed to protect our planet."

"My Lord, perhaps that's exactly what she wants you to do? You'd be leaving all the territories unguarded again."

"There's little left to protect on that half of the empire."

"At present, my Lord," The Minister of State said, "but cleanup and rebuilding efforts are already underway. If our people learn we've chosen to leave them unprotected again, it might damage morale and slow the efforts."

"How far away are our other forces?"

"Our best ships, the ones that were stationed in the border areas, are hundreds of solars away, but others should begin arriving in just a hundred solars."

Maxxiloth turned angrily and stormed out of the room.

* * *

"Well, Donald, what do you think now," Admiral Hillaire said after the Admiralty Board had watched the latest report from Admiral Carver.

"She's been lucky, so far."

"Lucky? She's destroyed their shipbuilding yards, most of the weapon factories and military production facilities on the home planet, and perhaps half of all principal targets on remote planets in the empire."

"She hasn't come up against their fleet yet. She's been lucky."

"Luck or not, it's time we put the full support of the Galactic Alliance behind this operation," Admiral Moore said. "Now that the Council has approved annexation of the former Milori Empire and the complete isolation of Milor, we'll begin moving assets immediately. I'm assigning all of the former Milori warships that Admiral Carver's command was able to repair and retrofit for Space Command use to her new command. They'll be fully crewed, stocked with as much food, ordnance, parts, and supplies as they can carry, and sent out as soon as possible. Any other ships we can spare without leaving our territories under-protected will also go as part of this fleet. The twelve ships Admiral Carver had the foresight to fill with supplies and assign patrol duties along the outermost border are to be immediately released to her command."

"Is Admiral Carver going to be able to sustain the operation while she waits years for these resources to arrive?" Admiral Burke asked.

"Because of the nature of the action," Admiral Plimley said, "I'd say yes. She'll retreat as needed, re-supply food and ordnance, and then move back in to carry on the fight with the hope that she'll eventually wear down the Milori. Without the ability to replace warships, each destroyed Milori ship will strike another serious blow to the empire."

"Although they can't build new ships, they can still acquire them from other species," Admiral Bradlee said.

"Maybe, and maybe not," Admiral Ahmed said. "I seriously doubt the Hudeeracs or Gondusans will supply them, for any price, and they've alienated the Raiders by attacking and destroying Raider Ten. The Tsgardis are dumb enough to supply ships to a race that would later subjugate them, but the quality of their ships is quite inferior, and at Light-225 they're the slowest military ships in the quadrant. Their best bet would seem to be the Uthlaro, who will build for anyone who meets their price. Of course, with a top speed of Light-262, their warships are considerably slower than the Milori ships and their hull plating is much too thin. That's why we've been able to destroy so many Raider ships."

"Our latest intelligence is that the newest Uthlaro warships are capable of Light-300," Admiral Bradlee said.

"Problems with speed and hull plating can be easily resolved," Admiral Woo said. "We have to face the prospect that the Milori might begin exporting their shipbuilding technology if they can make a deal with one or the other species to manufacture their ships."

"Perhaps we should inform both the Uthlaro and Tsgardi that selling ships or ordnance to the Milori will remove their neutrality status and identify them as being allied with the Milori, making them legitimate targets to all our warships," Admiral Platt suggested.

"But we can only do that within Galactic Alliance space," Admiral Ressler said, "unless we intend to start a war with those neighbors."

"If the encounter occurs within a declared war zone," Admiral Bradlee said, "such as the Milori Empire, they would probably be hesitant to begin an open conflict with us."

"So it would be like the Korean conflict in the twentieth century," Admiral Plimley said. "The Chinese planes ducked back across their border whenever things got too hot for their pilots and the US planes were expected to break off the engagement."

"That would be intolerable," Admiral Hillaire said. "If pursuit begins in a war zone, the ship must be allowed to continue pursuit, even if it means open warfare with the Uthlaro or Tsgardi."

"We're getting ahead of ourselves," Admiral Moore said. "We haven't even learned if the Uthlaro *would* supply ships in violation of a ship embargo by the Galactic Alliance."

"Such details as embargos wouldn't stop the Uthlaro," Admiral Plimley said, "as long as the client pays promptly."

"We shall see," Admiral Ahmed said. "Perhaps the Milori will not even want their ships."

"If they must choose between Uthlaro ships or no ships at all, the choice would be clear even to Maxxiloth," Admiral Moore said.

* * *

"Welcome aboard, Admiral," Captain Bonilla said to Jenetta as she emerged from the starboard bow airlock into the GSC Battleship *Pholus*.

"Thank you, Captain. It's good to see you again. How have things been going?"

"No problems, Admiral. The ship has been running fine and we haven't encountered any Milori vessels. I've arranged for a light breakfast in the bridge conference room. Commander Fannon is docking at our larboard bow airlock and will be escorted there when he comes aboard."

"Thank you, Captain. You know my aide and second officer, Lt. Commander Ashraf, don't you? And this is Lt. Commander Gallagher, my first officer."

Captain Bonilla welcomed both aboard. Gesturing to the two officers by his side, he said, "This is Commander Olympia, my first, and Lt. Commander Grogan, my senior tactical officer."

After handshakes all around, the small party walked to the lift that would take them to the bridge deck.

Commander Fannon, Lt. Commander Mojica, and Lt. Baran were already in the conference room. Captain Bonilla made introductions again. After everyone had helped themselves to the small breakfast buffet, they took their seats.

"I've received orders transferring my ship from Stewart Base command to your new command, Admiral," Captain Bonilla said. "How far outside of Galactic Space do you wish us to travel?"

"Your destination is a system called Quesann, three hundred eight light-years this side of Milor. The Milori files we retrieved from seized vessels indicated the fourth planet from the sun is an Earth Class paradise. We swung by there recently to confirm that assessment. I've designated that planet as also bearing the system name. The Milori began building a military base there about a dozen years ago on an island about the size of New Zealand near the planet's equator. They had made a lot of progress, but after the new commanding officer for the sector visited the location he ordered the construction halted and went in search of another planet."

"Why did he move the base?"

"According to the reports, he felt the planet was too cold. He wanted a place for his command where the average temperature was closer to forty degrees Celsius. The site selected for the base on Quesann is twenty-five degrees year round, which was too uncomfortable for him. The trip should take you about a year and a half, and you'll be traveling through hostile territory for most of it, so you'll have to stay on your toes.

"Supreme Headquarters has transferred all of the M-designate ships to my command in support of this operation and promised as many others as can reasonably be freed up. We've stung the empire hard and wiped out their warship production capability, but they still have a sizable fleet of older ships. I'm estimating its size at anywhere from one hundred to two hundred. Their shipbuilding capabilities were incredible and in ten year's time they might have been almost invincible. They had at least a thousand ships in various stages of construction, and I'm talking about destroyers, frigates, cruisers, and battleships. Transports, freighters, and other support ships were being produced at facilities located elsewhere."

The officers of the *Pholus* listened in rapt attention as Jenetta described the attacks.

"We destroyed all of their shipyards during our attacks, so the only ship construction programs they have now are whatever they manufacture on the planet's surface— most likely just space tugs, shuttles, fighters, and small transports."

"What will you do until our support gets here, Admiral?"

"We've primed the pump with our attacks, and the Milori warships have already begun flooding back in to protect the home world. Only by destroying the Milori fleet can we end this war, so we'll let them do most of the work by assembling their ships in one place instead of chasing them all over the territory. While we're waiting for our forces to arrive, Maxxiloth is also waiting for his.

"My plan is to hit and run, and try to drive the Milori crazy. Anything the *Colorado* and the *Yangtze* can do to whittle down his forces will help later. Who knows, we might get lucky and find a few ships traveling alone or in pairs. In any event, the final act in this show can't begin until Maxxiloth's ships arrive back home from the border areas."

Before heading back into the Milori Empire, Jenetta called a meeting of all twelve captains and briefed them on their destination and the progress of the fight so far. Held in a conference room aboard the *Pholus*, she answered as many questions as she could during the meeting. The officers felt good about the operation by the time they returned to their ships. Most had openly expressed their wish for speed comparable to that of the *Colorado* or the *Yangtze* because their journey was so protracted, while the two small ships could be there in weeks.

* * *

"I'm happy to report that the Milori have pulled out completely," Minister of Intelligence Vertap Aloyandro said to the Royal Assembly of noblemen in the government center. "When they withdrew, they removed all warriors from the occupied planets. They left their civilian overseers to their own devices and our citizens have dealt with *them* as *they* have dealt with us for decades. Intercepted communications show the ships' officers were in a state of panic and, in complying with their emperor's order for all ships to immediately return to the home world, assumed it was a complete withdrawal of all military forces."

The Royal Assembly erupted into thunderous applause that lasted for minutes after the minister took his seat. Finally, as it began to die down, one of the more powerful members of the Assembly, Lord Melendret, stood up. "Long have we suffered under Milori rule. Maxxiloth's great-grandfather took part of our territory when he ascended to power and Maxxiloth took the rest after he murdered his own father to become emperor. The great-grandson has proven to be worse than the great-grandfather."

A chorus of voices agreed with the statements and Lord Melendret waited until it had died down before continuing. "But we are under his whip no longer and we have regained all our territory without the loss of a single ship." Another round of applause halted his speech. "And now, the time has come for us to expand our borders, while we're strong and Maxxiloth is weak. There are Milori colonies rich in mineral wealth and others rich in food production that we can conquer as easily as Maxxiloth's great-grandfather conquered our peaceful ancestors. They can be our colonies now, bringing their wealth and bounty to us in tribute, instead of to Maxxiloth. What say you, my countrymen?"

The assembled group fairly shook the building with their yelling and clapping. Minister Vertap Aloyandro knew it would be fruitless, and perhaps political suicide, to try to dissuade them from this course of action, but they had grown mad with what they mistakenly perceived as their new military power. Vertap knew the Milori had left their territory because of Space Command, not because of anything the Hudeerac forces had done with their quick raids and even quicker escapes. Admiral Carver had distinctly warned them not to go beyond their original borders or her forces would fire on them. She had never lied to them before and he didn't believe for a second that she was being untruthful now.

"My Lord," Vertap said to his sovereign in the King's sumptuous private chambers after requesting and being granted an audience, "this course of action is reckless and fraught with danger. We must not venture beyond our original borders. Admiral Carver has specifically warned us against that, and to go against her warning would be most foolhardy."

"There's nothing I can do right now, Vertap, except register my opposition to this activity, and I have already done that both on and off the record. For a long time, it has been our intention to recover our territories and much more as just reward for what Maxxiloth's family has done to us. Hundreds of thousands of Hudeerac citizens died in defense of our realm, and their descendants are anxious for retribution. Our ambitious shipbuilding program required diverting enormous sums that would otherwise have gone into social programs. With each passing year, we grew stronger militarily and Maxxiloth grew more wary of trying to overrun this lone system. He knew they would lose many ships in the battle, so he left us alone. This opportunity has presented itself much sooner than expected and we aren't fully prepared to take advantage of Maxxiloth's downfall, but I can't hold back the forces that have been unleashed."

"Maxxiloth hasn't been defeated yet, my Lord. Space Command has him scared, but he still controls a vast fleet of warships. He could yet come and overwhelm us again, or our new ally, the Galactic Alliance, could overwhelm us if we go against them on this. If we work with them instead of against them, we'll be far better off."

"It's out of my hands, Vertap. I appreciate your counsel, but there's nothing I can do. What will be, will be."

Chapter Twenty-Two
~ June 18th, 2281 ~

Jenetta chose a location in space roughly one light-year from Milor to link the *Colorado* and the *Yangtze* together for a conference of the two senior staffs.

"We haven't seen a single warship since returning to this area," Jenetta said, "so it seems safe to assume they're all guarding Milor. It's time to pay Maxxiloth another visit."

"You want to take on the entire Milori force that Maxxiloth has been able to assemble around his home planet?" Commander Fannon asked incredulously.

"Something like that, but don't worry, I haven't suddenly developed a death wish." Jenetta paused for a couple of seconds for effect. "What do military ships do when stationed in close proximity to comrade ships for long periods of time?"

The officers appeared to be thinking about the question and Lt. Commander Mojica offered first, "Link up?"

"Exactly. We link up."

"But it only takes twelve seconds to sever a link and begin to move a ship," Commander Fannon said.

"Yes, if everyone is alert and if a junior officer is stationed near every open hatchway, as on Space Command ships. However, these Milori ships are parked in orbit around their home planet. They're probably there in significant numbers, giving them a false sense of security, and they probably haven't had any information about us in months. As far as they know, we returned home to Stewart after wreaking havoc on the Empire. I estimate it could take them as long as sixty seconds to sever the links and retract their airlocks, and we could have as much as three minutes before most of their gunners can reach their posts. That's about two minutes more than we'll need."

The officers were so intent upon listening to every word Jenetta spoke, it seemed as if they had stopped breathing.

"What I'm proposing is this. We approach the planet at Light-9790, getting as close as possible to Milor before we drop our envelopes. We accelerate to Plus-Ten speed, fire a volley of torpedoes, and then accelerate away as quickly as we can while we rebuild our envelope. We then use Light-9790 to leave the area. We should be exposed for only one hundred eighty seconds at most."

"One hundred eighty seconds?" Commander Fannon said thoughtfully.

"Yes. The Milori ships will still be linked when we appear in their midst and we'll use WOLaR torpedoes to target the center of the ship clusters. The *Yangtze* will complete a partial orbit of no more than one hundred fifty degrees around the planet in a clockwise direction, while the *Colorado* will orbit in a counter-clockwise direction, also no more then one hundred fifty degrees. As we complete our runs, we engage our Light-Speed drive and leave on a parallel course until we reach a new rendezvous point."

"It doesn't leave much time for our gunners to locate their targets, lock on, and fire," Commander Fannon said.

"An experienced gunner shouldn't need more than ten seconds. And to stay any longer would invite possible disaster. We can probably handle the torpedoes from four or five ships, but if thirty or forty ships are firing at us, the volume would probably overtax the Phalanx system and some would get through. We need to get in, shoot, and get out. The WOLaR torpedoes can destroy their targets without striking them as long as the gunners get them in close. We know who our best gunners are, so they'll be manning the weapons systems for this run. We'll use extra target spotters to help locate the ship clusters quickly. Any other concerns?"

"How will we confirm our kills, Admiral?" Lt. Commander Gallagher asked.

"We'll launch a couple of sensor buoys while we're there. If we're successful, it could be hours before anyone detects their signals and moves to disable them. They might even go undetected for days."

In what Space Command Academy instructors would forever refer to as a textbook attack, the two small ships suddenly appeared around the Milori home world, fired a volley of their WOLaR torpedoes, and disappeared from scanners long before Milori crewmembers reached their GQ stations. The Space Command vessels were fifty billion kilometers away when the torpedoes detonated.

Jenetta ordered both ships halted so they could intercept information from the sensor buoys, but both remained on high alert. Sitting in her command chair on the bridge, she watched the video log of the event on the large, front view-screen as it came in. There had been six clusters of ships stationed outside the minefield at key defensive points around the planet. The two small ships had each fired six torpedoes before accelerating away.

* * *

"Thirty-two ships!" Maxxiloth screamed at the ministers sitting around the table. "Twenty-six *totally* destroyed and six so severely damaged that they're practically useless! What kind of idiot Space Marshalls are you putting in command of our ships? Don't they know we're at war with the most dangerous enemy we've ever faced?"

"I'm sorry, my Lord," Berquyth said calmly, "but the Space Command vessels took us completely by surprise, and they didn't remain here long enough for us to get a lock on them. They came in fast, fired their volleys, and disappeared before their torpedoes had even reached their targets. And they didn't use standard torpedoes. They used the high-yield variety like those they've used for targets on the planet's surface."

"Enough! I don't want excuses. I want results! I want the heads of whoever is captaining these Space Command destroyers."

"Yes, my Lord. Shall I order all remaining ships to pursue the Space Command vessels?"

"Are you mad? They're needed here to protect the planet."

"Yes, my Lord," Berquyth said, casting his four eyes upward. "What *could* I have been thinking?"

312

"You sent for me, my Lord?" Berquyth said to his emperor's back the next morning as Maxxiloth stood staring out the window of his palace apartment.

"Yes, Berquyth. I've reached a decision."

"Yes, my Lord?"

"We can't beat the Galactic Alliance. It was a grievous error to invade their space and it's only a matter of time before they finish us off. I thought we could defeat them before they grew too powerful, but they were already too powerful and their technology too advanced."

Berquyth stood listening, fearful of agreeing or disagreeing with his emperor.

"I've decided we must form a new, closer alliance with the Tsgardi."

"The Tsgardi, my Lord? They are not trustworthy. They would as soon slit our throats as shake our hands. What could they possibly offer? Their ships are slow and easily destroyed."

"They offer numbers. They have hundreds of ships and hundreds of thousands of able warriors. Space Command would be so busy fighting them that it might give us time to breathe. If they agree to join with us, we'll give them technology to improve the plating on their ships and to increase their speed."

"But, sire, can they be trusted? We've always kept them on a very short leash. How can we know they won't turn on us at the first opportunity once they have our technology?"

"We have no choice. We must defeat Space Command at all costs. To destroy Carver I'd make a pact with the devil, or even the Tsgardi."

* * *

"We've received a message from Milor, Admiral," the com operator said. "It's encrypted, using an old Space Command code that was abandoned after the *Lisbon* was captured. It's addressed to you."

"Put it on the screen," Jenetta said as she shifted in her seat on the bridge.

313

The image of a Milora wearing the stately robes of a senior governmental official filled the large monitor at the front of the bridge. He appeared to be standing in front of a large tapestry.

"Admiral Carver, I am Exalted Lord Space Marshall Berquyth, chief minister to his most revered Excellency, Maxxiloth IV of Milor. I send you greetings."

Jenetta shifted in her seat and mumbled, "Greetings?"

"I'm contacting you this way in an attempt to end the hostilities between our peoples. We desire an end to the decades of war we've been forced to endure since his Excellency Maxxiloth seized power from his father, Gilbraxx, and a return to the peace with our neighbors that we knew under our previous monarch. I hope you will accept my offer to cease hostilities at once. We make no demands and will trust you to treat us with the same respect you show to planets within the Galactic Alliance."

Jenetta chuckled and wondered why Maxxiloth should expect such consideration after the acts he'd committed.

"I represent the ruling council of twelve ministers in this matter. After deciding to form a new, close alliance with the Tsgardi, a move that all twelve council ministers most strongly opposed, our beloved Emperor Maxxiloth suffered a fatal accident. It seems he fell on his sword— twelve times. Since none of his eight successive wives had produced an heir to the throne before their unexplainable deaths, the council of ministers has asked me to represent our government until a new leader is chosen. I've ordered all Space Marshalls to cease acts of aggression except in matters of self-defense, and I eagerly await your reply. The Ruling Council has empowered me to offer you Maxxiloth's head, but we request that it remain attached to his body until an appropriate state funeral ceremony has been completed.

"Exalted Lord Space Marshall Berquyth, Viceroy of Milor, Palace of the Emperor, Milor, message complete."

The bridge was deathly silent. The bridge personnel looked at one another and at Jenetta, while she just sat in the command chair thinking about the message. Was it genuine?

Or just a bid to buy time to gain advantage in a future confrontation? She wanted to believe it.

Jenetta broke the silence on the bridge with, "Com, monitor Milori media channels and see if they're reporting the death of the emperor. And send a copy of the message to Captain Fannon."

"Aye, Admiral," the com operator said.

After a few more minutes of stunned silence, the com operator said, "All Milori media channels are reporting the death of Maxxiloth IV from natural causes after a very brief illness and giving information about where and when the body can be viewed prior to the funeral pyre ceremony."

It could still be an elaborate ploy, but Jenetta decided to play along just in case it was true. She walked to her briefing room and recorded two messages. The first went to Berquyth, accepting his unconditional surrender and informing him that the Galactic Alliance was now officially annexing the territory of the former Milori Empire. She listed specific actions he must take and informed him that any further resistance would now be treated not as an act of war, but rather as an act of sedition. The penalties for sedition were, in most cases, far more serious than the penalties allowed for war prisoners under Galactic Alliance law. It was Jenetta's way of telling him that the surrender had better not be a ruse and she knew the language wouldn't be lost on a career bureaucrat. She declined the offer of Maxxiloth's head and suggested it be cremated along with the rest of his body. She further suggested, strongly, that Maxxiloth's renowned collection of trophy heads be returned to the governments they represented when alive.

Jenetta's second message went to Admiral Moore and the Admiralty Board. She reported weekly, so the Board had been kept fully informed of her actions even though the reports took three weeks to reach Earth. She appended a copy of Berquyth's message to the new transmission.

Lastly, she had the com operator contact Commander Fannon aboard the *Yangtze*.

"Is it genuine, Admiral?"

"It would appear to be, but stay alert. It could be an elaborate ruse designed to get us to let down our guard."

"What's our next move?"

"I haven't decided yet. Perhaps we'll just hang around here for a while and see what happens. I don't intend to approach Milor peacefully until we have a lot of backup. I've notified Berquyth that as Viceroy of Milor he should recall all his troops throughout the empire, except for the small detachments of warriors needed to prevent the takeover and destruction of established resources such as space stations and bases, if that hasn't already been done. I've told him to park his remaining warships at the space docks around the second planet, shuttle all troops to the home planet except for a small security force, and disband all returning forces except for the home guard. I've also informed him that all territory of the former Milori Empire is, with their surrender, officially annexed to the Galactic Alliance."

"Annexed?"

"Yes, Space Command Supreme HQ sent me notification that the Galactic Alliance Council ruled to annex all the territory of the empire if we were successful in our mission. That includes the five hundred light-years of space between their former border and ours. It's the only way to ensure that Milor cannot resurrect their expansionist plans again. I was to keep it a secret unless, or until, Milor surrendered."

"Wow! How are you going to deal with this?"

"That's a good question. How are we going to oversee a territory almost two thousand light-years across and located beyond our Frontier Zone? Where the Milori had hundreds of warships and millions of warriors to maintain their control, I have just two ships here, a dozen more eighteen months away, and fifty others more than two years away. This is a thousand times worse than the situation at Stewart when I assumed command *there*. I guess we'll just do the best we can with what we've got."

* * *

"I've received a response to my message to Admiral Carver," Acting Viceroy Berquyth said to the eleven other members of the council. "She has accepted our surrender and informed me that, with it, the Galactic Alliance formally annexes our territories. Our former empire is now to be known as Region Two of the Galactic Alliance."

"It is as we expected," the Minister of State said. "Are we to understand that all hostilities have ended?"

"Yes, provided we follow her directives, recall our troops, and dismantle most of our forces. We may maintain a home guard to protect our solar system, but they will treat any further aggressive acts outside our planet's atmosphere as sedition against the Galactic Alliance. If and when we've proved that Milor has changed its warlike ways, we'll be granted a seat on the Galactic Alliance Council with full voting privileges."

The ministers looked quietly at one another. No one spoke until the Minister of State said, "That's all? She isn't demanding that our heads, or at least *your* head, be delivered to her?"

"No, but she did stress most strongly that we should return the heads in Maxxiloth's collection to their home worlds."

"She's being far more generous than Maxxiloth would have ever been on one of his best days," the Minister of Defense said.

"Maxxiloth had to go," the Minister of Off-world Base Operations said. "He would have had us sharing our world and our technologies with the Tsgardi and would have dragged us down further and further until Space Command had no choice but to come here and finish us off completely. As it is, it will be another full annual before we can restore electrical power to a majority of our citizens."

"It's time for our people to come together and heal the wounds of war," Berquyth said. "Over a million warriors were lost in this insane conflict with the Galactic Alliance, and now we've lost our Empire as well. Maxxiloth shall have his place in our history, but not the one he envisioned."

* * *

"Incredible," Admiral Hillaire said immediately after the latest message from Admiral Carver had played. "She took down the entire Empire with just two scout-destroyers and three hundred seventy crewmen. What do you say now, Donald? Just pure luck?"

"What else can you call it *except* luck?" Admiral Hubera said. "Do you honestly think it involved some sort of skill? The Milori assassinated their own emperor and surrendered to her because they're tired of war."

"But they only became tired after Admiral Carver destroyed almost six hundred active-duty warships and their crews, demolished a thousand new ships still in their space docks, threw their planet into darkness, and wiped out half their bases. Would *anyone* not be tired of war after that?"

"I think it's safe to say that Admiral Carver has again proven herself to be one of our most competent military leaders," Admiral Moore said, "and *most* of us on this Board have recognized her abilities for some time. My father was fond of saying that luck is what occurs when opportunity meets preparation. The harder you work at being prepared, the better your luck.

Admiral Platt smiled and said, "Karl von Clausewitz, the Prussian military leader once said, 'If the leader is filled with high ambition, and if he pursues his aims with audacity and strength of will, he will reach them in spite of all obstacles.' No one here doubts Admiral Carver's audacity and strength of will, not even Donald."

"The fact remains that Admiral Carver is now in way over her head," Admiral Hubera said. "She can't possibly supervise a territory that represents two-thirds of all Galactic Alliance space with just two small ships. It will take us years to get enough ships out to this remote territory and there's no way she, with all of her *preparation*, *audacity*, and *strength of will*, can prevent its collapse into complete anarchy. We knew we didn't have enough ships to cover Galactic Alliance territory before this latest expansion."

"We've sent her the sixty-two M-designate ships she restored to service," Admiral Bradlee said, "and a dozen more ships built at the Mars facility, plus all three of the new battleships that were recently launched. It will take time for her to get everything organized, but I'm confident she can do it. We know we can't stop the intermediate breakdown into

318

lawlessness. History has shown us that time and time again. It's happened to almost every conquered society during the transition period from one governing power to another when the ruling hierarchy is completely replaced. Someone will always be looking for ways to exploit others and build their own power base in the absence of a strong government presence."

"Yes, we must turn our full attention to the immediate development of a complete bureaucratic structure in the new territory," Admiral Platt said. "It can't be handled slowly, as with the last expansion where the Galactic Alliance simply pushed out its borders and began to bring order to an area of space that formerly had no order. We'll need everyone, from the newest recruits for manning bases to commanding officers as high in rank as Rear Admiral, Upper Half. The Milori established bases throughout the territory and we should be able to move right in, although some adaptation to our physical differences will be required, as was done with the vessels Admiral Carver restored. Recruitment on Earth is going extremely well, but recruitment on Nordakia is lagging behind. We're going to need substantially more forces than we have at present."

"There are any number of worlds in the Galactic Alliance where we've never actively recruited," Admiral Ressler said. "Perhaps it's time we looked to all members of the Galactic Alliance with seats on the Council for far greater military support."

"Most worlds lag far behind Earth and Nordakia in technology and education," Admiral Hubera said. "Can you imagine a Cheblook, Eulosian, or Wolkerron at one of the academies? We might as well open them to Pledgians."

"Perhaps most are not ready for the Academies," Admiral Woo said, "but they could serve as crewmen on bases or ships while their cultures develop the educational programs found on the more advanced worlds. I support Shana's suggestion that we begin active recruitment efforts at all Galactic Alliance planets, with the possible exception of Milor for the time being."

"In simple terms, we're faced with the problem of expanding the present Space Command by two hundred percent," Admiral Moore said. "That was the number discussed by the Galactic Alliance Council when they approved annexation of the new territory, but I believe a more realistic target would be an increase of four hundred percent. However, it's one thing to say and quite another to actually accomplish. We began shifting forces when we faced the prospect of an invasion by the Milori and must now step up those efforts. Let's inform every base commander that they will be losing half of their forces and begin reassigning them to the new territory. I just wish we had more ships with Light-9790 capability."

"They're coming, Richard," Admiral Plimley said. "Every new warship and transport coming out of the Mars dockyards will have an outer hull made of Dakinium and their engines will utilize the new design. In addition, the construction of new facilities dedicated exclusively to the retrofit of existing ships is proceeding according to schedule, so within a few years we can look forward to having all older ships capable of at least Light-450. All *Prometheus* class battleships and *Kamakura* class cruisers will have their outer skin removed and replaced with Dakinium while their power plants are being retrofitted.

"It can't come soon enough," Admiral Ahmed said. "The new transports may be the only way I can hope to supply bases that are three thousand light-years from Earth."

* * *

Jogging around the running track in the hold was still Jenetta's favorite morning exercise, and she had been running for over a half hour with her cats by her side when she received a message through her CT from the com operator on the bridge.

"Admiral, you've received a message from Admiral Moore's office in Supreme headquarters."

Pressing her Space Command ring, she asked, "Is it a Priority message?"

"Negative, Admiral," the com operator said.

"Thank you, chief. I'll view it when I come on duty."

"Aye, Admiral."

"Carver, out."

Jenetta finished her run and took a shower before eating the enormous breakfast that was delivered to her quarters. She arrived on the bridge ten minutes early, and after cheerfully greeting the bridge crew with a "Good Morning," she accepted Lt. Commander Ashraf's status report and relieved her. Rather than settling into her command chair, she turned the bridge over to Lt. Cruz, the ship's fourth officer who had also arrived early, and walked to her briefing room.

Sitting down behind her desk, she selected Admiral Moore's message from the queue and tapped the play button.

"Hello, Admiral," Admiral Moore began. "On behalf of myself, the Admiralty Board, the Galactic Alliance Council, and all the peoples of the Galactic Alliance, I congratulate you on your incredible victory. As always, you've demonstrated that the trust we've placed in you has been well deserved.

"We've begun the massive task of transferring equipment and personnel to the new command. Most existing bases will lose up to half their forces so we can begin to fill the needs of the new territory. Your first task must be to identify which former Milori bases will become GA bases and communicate that information to us so the proper routing of transports can take place. Your recommendation that the base on Quesann serve as the Space Command Headquarters for Region Two is acceptable and your headquarters staff will be directed there."

"*My* headquarters staff?" Jenetta said aloud.

"Since you'll be setting up dozens of new bases, and many will have StratCom-One and StratCom-Two designations, the Galactic Alliance Council has approved the creation of an appropriate number of new Lower Half and Upper Half flag officer positions. Moreover, for the first time in GA history, a new position above the rank of Upper Half has been created where the flag officer is permanently assigned outside Supreme Headquarters on Earth.

"Congratulations, Admiral Carver. By recommendation of the Admiralty Board, and with unanimous approval of the Galactic Alliance Council, you have been promoted to the rank of Admiral, a rank commensurate with your new responsibilities as Commander of the Second Fleet and Military Governor of Region Two. Admiral Platt's title has been officially changed to Commander of the First Fleet."

Jenetta's jaw was hanging down by now and she had stopped breathing. She had been so relieved when she wasn't promoted to Vice-Admiral and now she had been promoted to the even higher rank of Admiral.

Admiral Moore's message continued. "Thank you, Admiral, for everything you've done, and will do in the future. You are the only one I would trust to prevent that territory from sinking into complete anarchy. Your job will not be an easy one, and there will be days when you'll want to throw up your hands and resign, but you will stay and do your duty as you always have. And I know that the job will be done as well as— or better than— it could have been done by anyone in Space Command. As always, you have my full faith and confidence."

Jenetta released her breath and closed her mouth. Actually, her face was frowning with displeasure.

"By the way, I know you'll have trouble getting the proper insignia out there, so no one will criticize you if you vary slightly from regulations by simply doubling up your existing two-star insignias. Congratulations, Admiral Carver."

"Richard E. Moore, Admiral of the Fleet, Supreme Headquarters, Earth, message complete."

Jenetta put her hands to her face. Admiral Moore had hit the right buttons in talking about duty. If not for her sense of duty, she wouldn't be out here at all. If not for her sense of duty, she would have resigned her commission when they promoted her to flag officer. And now, because of her sense of duty, she was going to be the best damned Commander of the Second Fleet that she could. However, in five or six years, she'd better get her own battleship, or she would have to reevaluate her continued service in Space Command. A thought suddenly occurred to her. Could she resign from Flag Officer rank without leaving the service or leaving a blemish on her record? Because her two stars had been brevet rank, she hadn't seen a problem before, but full approval by the

Galactic Alliance Council made this a permanent promotion. Could this be the reason for the condition placed on her receiving the battleship? Had they planned this all along, knowing that her rank would prevent her from reporting to the Mars facility to pick up her ship?

Jenetta returned to the bridge and climbed into the command chair. The bridge crew noticed she was unusually self-absorbed, and everyone wondered what calamity could have occurred that would change her mood so dramatically.

In early afternoon, the com operator said, "Admiral?"

"Yes, chief?" she replied.

"We've received today's com traffic from Supreme Headquarters."

"Fine, chief. Log it as received."

"Admiral, a report announces that you've been promoted by order of the Galactic Council, effective three weeks ago, as of the date the report was sent out."

"Yes, chief. I know."

"Aye, Admiral."

The bridge crew didn't miss the brief conversation, and those at stations with com screens discreetly called up the daily report and read the announcement. Those who didn't have a com screen got the information from the others at their first opportunity.

When Lt. Commander Gallagher reported for duty just before the second watch, he came to attention and saluted Jenetta. Jenetta returned his salute as she stood up.

"Congratulations, Admiral," he said, as he held out a small box. "I can't think of anyone more deserving."

Jenetta accepted the box and opened it. Inside, she found two improvised insignias with four stars each. As Gallagher and the bridge crew applauded, she said, "Thank you, Commander. Thank you everyone."

"It was the best we could do on the spur of the moment, Admiral, but the engineering staff will have regulation insignia made up by tomorrow."

Jenetta smiled. "Thank you, Commander, and my thanks to everyone who assisted in the preparation of the insignia. I'll wear these proudly."

Congratulation messages began flooding in the next day as word of the surrender, annexation, and promotion had been spread first through Space Command communications and then through the news media. Everyone back on Earth and in the sectors adjoining Earth had known for weeks already. As on such occasions in recent years, Jenetta prepared a universal thank you message for replying to most senders and then recorded individual replies for the others. Her mom had been so choked up that the message from her was almost unintelligible. It had begun normally enough.

"Hi, honey. I'm speechless. I was stunned when you made lower half, and then astounded when you were promoted to upper half, but now I'm utterly speechless. I mean, I've always known how very special you are, but no parent *really* expects the rest of the galaxy to appreciate their child's abilities. And now you're the military governor of an area twice the size of Galactic Alliance space, or at least half again as large since your territory is now part of ours. I mean it's one big territory and you're the commander of more than half of it— the far half— the more dangerous half. You're always in the far half and you're always in the more dangerous half. You'd think I'd be used to that by now, but I'm beginning to wonder if you'll ever get home again while I'm still alive. Each posting has taken you farther away from home for longer and longer periods, but I certainly never expected you to be posted two thousand light-years away from home."

With each minimally coherent sentence, Annette Carver had moved closer to tears. Jenetta could feel the anguish coming through and it stirred her own emotions. She had promised her mother that she'd be home for a visit as soon as she could and then she'd asked for this assignment to bring the war to Milor. As the first tears appeared on Annette's face, Jenetta felt tears streak down her own cheeks. For the first time she was glad they didn't have a direct connection. She would at least have a chance to dry her eyes before preparing her reply.

After the message ended, Jenetta took several minutes to compose herself and then recorded a message in response. She tried to make it very positive and mentioned again how she had been promised a ship in about six years, and if she didn't make it home before then, she would at least make it at that time, regardless of what calamity had befallen the GA in the meantime. She made sure that a smile graced her face during the entire message. She signed off still smiling.

Messages from Hugh, her brothers, sisters, and sisters-in-law were considerably more cheerful. Hugh joked about becoming one of her aides and the boys all pretended to be shocked that the Admiralty Board could appoint their baby sister to such a responsible position while dredging up embarrassing childhood incidents as proof of Jenetta's inability to command the Second Fleet and function as Military Governor to two-thirds of all Galactic Alliance space. Nevertheless, Jenetta could see that they were all extremely proud of her. The messages from Eliza and Christa were humorous, almost comedic, as they pretended to scold her for allowing the Admiralty Board to isolate her even further behind a desk, or an entire barricade of desks. Both joked that they would become a ship's captain before she did, although they knew of the Board's promise for one of the next crop of battleships. Her sisters-in-law, neither of whom she had met in person, just expressed their awe of Jenetta and the things she had done, and sent her their love.

Jenetta viewed the message from her father last. She rather expected it to be quite a bit more somber than the others. As it appeared on the screen, her father's face was soft and friendly.

"Hi, sweetheart. Congratulations on your promotion and your successful prosecution of this war. Everyone here is celebrating your victory, *our* victory really, and for the first time in decades, we're hopeful that the Galactic Alliance can enjoy a period of peace and prosperity without seeing the dark clouds of war hovering on the horizon. *You've* made that possible. *You've* made the difference. I can think of no finer legacy for any military officer. Whatever happens for the rest of your life, you'll be forever known as the one who defeated the Milori Empire and brought us peace. Every parent hopes that his or her child will go on to greater heights than themselves, and there's no doubt you have. I'm so proud to be your father that I can't adequately put it into words.

Her father's expression then changed completely. "But I'm also furious with you. Are you crazy? How could you let them promote you to permanent four-star rank? They'll *never* give you a ship now. Four-stars fly desks, not ships. Oh, sure, your mother's happy because four-stars rarely see any action, but I know *you* won't be happy. Our problem now is what to do about it. I've asked a buddy of mine in JAG to look into the regs and find out if and how you can revert to the rank of Captain without damaging your record so bad they won't give you a ship, but his first impression was that it just isn't possible. He said you can resign your commission, but he's never heard of anyone in Space Command resigning flag officer rank to become a commissioned officer again. Even in the Terran militaries on Earth, he couldn't recall any occasions, except for brevet or battlefield rank where the promotion hadn't been made permanent or where the flag officer lost his flag as the result of a disciplinary action. I'll let you know what he finds out as soon as I hear." His face softened again. "In the meantime, you be the best damned four-star in the service, and be careful out there.

"I love you, baby, and I *am* so very, very proud of you.

"Quinton E. Carver, Captain, GSC cruiser *Octavian*, message complete."

Jenetta sighed. She'd have to think for a while before responding to her father's message, and there were many more messages waiting.

She moved on to the messages from close friends and lastly to the ones from VIPs. As she had risen in rank, the list of VIP's she knew had grown considerably. One person who qualified both as a friend and very important person was Admiral Holt, the commanding officer of Higgins Space Command Base, and she replayed his message so she could tailor her response to what he said.

Jenetta smiled as soon as she saw his cheerful face appear on the com unit.

"Hello, Admiral. Congratulations on your recent promotion and on your new posting as Commander of the Second Fleet and Military Governor of Region Two. You know how much I've always enjoyed reading or hearing the reports of your adventures, and whenever I hear your name, I can't help but remember the young ensign who nervously appeared before me and seemed so shocked when she learned she was being promoted. It isn't so hard to visualize because outwardly you haven't changed a bit, and also because it wasn't all that many years ago. I recall telling you on that occasion you'd go far, but you've exceeded even *my* expectations."

Admiral Holt's expression turned serious, as he said, "I expect that your shoulders are drooping a bit by now from the weight of the responsibility that's just been heaped upon them. You're certainly no stranger to responsibility, but those two extra little stars add the burden of hundreds of populated worlds and trillions of sentient beings to your load, not to mention the hundreds of thousands of Space Command personnel that will soon become part of the Second Fleet. I know this job isn't the one you've wanted, but it's critically important and I know you'll do it well."

His face returned to its usual affable look as he said, "I haven't yet collected on my bet with Admiral Hubera, although he hasn't denied you were the first from your class at the Academy to make Captain, and now, at just forty-five, you're the youngest four-star in Space Command history by thirty some years." Admiral's Holt's expression turned mischievous as he said, "I'm sure you're still a bit overwhelmed, so I have to wonder if you've yet realized that only one officer in all of Space Command outranks you? Something to think about, eh Admiral?

"Good luck, Jen, and take care of yourself. I hope you'll stop by to visit next time you're in the neighborhood.

"Brian Holt, Rear Admiral, Upper Half, Base Commander, Higgins Space Command Base, message complete."

Until Admiral Holt mentioned it, she hadn't really thought about there being only one individual who outranked her. Of course, there were four other flag officers holding the rank of Admiral and their length of service made them all senior to her, but she was now one of the top six officers in Space Command. A smile spread across her face as a thought occurred to her.

"Not bad for someone voted 'least likely to succeed' while at the Academy," she said aloud. "Not bad at all."

~ finis ~

*** *Jenetta's exciting adventures continue in:* ***
# Against All Odds

Appendix

This chart is offered to assist readers who may be unfamiliar with military rank and the reporting structure. Newly commissioned officers begin at either ensign or second lieutenant rank.

Space Command	Space Marine Corps
Admiral of the Fleet	
Admiral	General
Vice-Admiral	Lieutenant General
Rear Admiral - Upper	Major General
Rear Admiral - Lower	Brigadier General
Captain	Colonel
Commander	Lieutenant Colonel
Lieutenant Commander	Major
Lieutenant	Captain
Lieutenant(jg) "Junior Grade"	First Lieutenant
Ensign	Second Lieutenant

The commanding officer on a ship is always referred to as Captain, regardless of his or her official military rank. Even an Ensign could be a Captain of the Ship, although that would only occur as the result of an unusual situation or emergency where no senior officers survived.

On Space Command ships and bases, time is measured according to a twenty-four-hour clock, normally referred to as military time. For example, 8:42 PM would be referred to as 2042 hours. Chronometers are always set to agree with the date and time at Space Command Supreme Headquarters on Earth. This is known as GST, or Galactic System Time.

Admiralty Board:

Moore, Richard E.	Admiral of the Fleet
Platt, Evelyn S.	Admiral - Director of Fleet Operations
Bradlee, Roger T.	Admiral - Director of Intelligence (SCI)
Ressler, Shana E.	Admiral - Director of Budget & Accounting
Hillaire, Arnold H.	Admiral - Director of Academies
Burke, Raymond A.	Vice-Admiral - Director of GSC Base Management
Ahmed, Raihana L.	Vice-Admiral - Dir. of Quartermaster Supply
Woo, Lon C.	Vice-Admiral - Dir. of Scientific & Expeditionary Forces
Plimley, Loretta J.	Rear-Admiral, (U) - Dir. of Weapons R&D
Hubera, Donald M.	Rear-Admiral, (U) - Dir. of Academy Curricula

Ship Speed Terminology	*Speed*
Plus-1	1 kps
Sub-Light-1	1,000 kps
Light-1 (*c*) *(speed of light in a vacuum)*	299,792.458 kps
Light-150 or **150 c**	150 times the speed of light

Hyper-Space Factors	
IDS Communications Band	.0513 light years each minute (8.09 billion kps)
DeTect Range	4 billion kilometers

ii

Strat Com Desig	Mission Description for Strategic Command Bases
1	Base - Location establishes it as a critical component of Space Command Operations - Serves as homeport to multiple warships that also serve in base's defense. All sections of Space Command maintain an active office at the base. Base Commander establishes all patrol routes and is authorized to override SHQ orders to ships within the sector(s) designated part of the base's operating territory. Recommended rank of Commanding Officer: **Rear Admiral (U)**
2	Base - Location establishes it as a crucial component of Space Command Operations - Serves as homeport to multiple warships that also serve in base's defense. All sections of Space Command maintain an active office at the base. Patrol routes established by SHQ. Recommended rank of Commanding Officer: **Rear Admiral (L)**
3	Base - Location establishes it as an important component of Space Command Operations - Serves as homeport to multiple warships that also serve in base's defense. Patrol routes established by SHQ. Recommended rank of Commanding Officer: **Captain**
4	Station - Location establishes it as an important terminal for Space Command personnel engaged in travel to/from postings, and for re-supply of vessels and outposts. Recommended rank of Commanding Officer: **Commander**
5	Outpost - Location makes it important for observation purposes and collection of information. Recommended rank of Commanding Officer: **Lt. Commander**

Sample Distances

Earth to Mars (Mean)	78 million kilometers
Nearest star to our Sun	4 light-years (Proxima Centauri)
Milky Way Galaxy diameter	100,000 light-years
Thickness of M'Way at Sun	2,000 light-years
Stars in Milky Way	200 billion (est.)
Nearest galaxy (Andromeda)	2 million light-years from M'Way
A light-year (in a vacuum)	9,460,730,472,580.8 kilometers
A light-second (in vacuum)	299,792.458 km
Grid Unit	1,000 Light Yrs² (1,000,000 Sq. LY)
Deca-Sector	100 Light Years² (10,000 Sq. LY)
Sector	10 Light Years² (100 Sq. LY)
Section	94,607,304,725 km^2
Sub-section	946,073,047 km^2

The following two-dimensional representations are offered to provide the reader with a feel for the spatial relationships between bases, systems, and celestial events referenced in the novels of this series. The mean distance from Earth to Higgins Space Command Base has been calculated as 90.1538 light-years. The tens of thousands of stars, planets, and moons in this small part of the galaxy would only confuse, and therefore have been omitted from the image.

Should the maps be unreadable, or should you desire additional imagery, .jpg and .pdf versions of all maps are available for free downloading at:

www.deprima.com/ancillary/agu.html

The first map shows Galactic Alliance space after the second expansion. The white space at the center is the space originally included when the GA charter was signed. The first outer circle shows the space claimed at the first expansion in 2203. The second circle shows the second expansion in 2273. The 'square' delineates the deca-sectors around Stewart SCB, and shows most of the planets referenced in Books 4 through 6 of this series. The second image is an enlargement of that area.

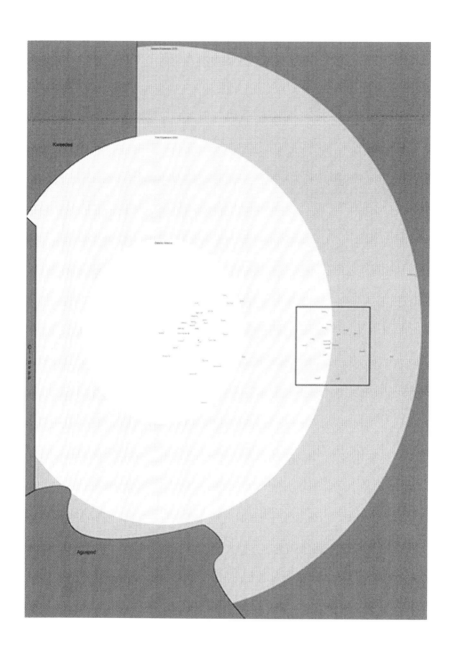

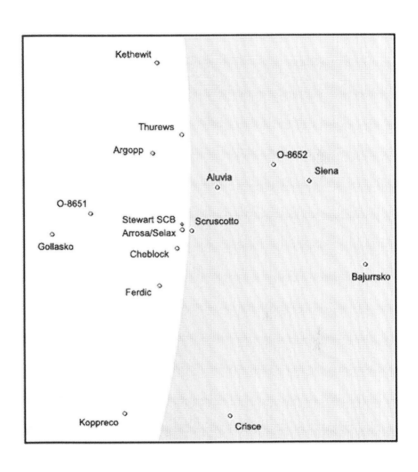

3929341R00192

Printed in Great Britain
by Amazon.co.uk, Ltd.,
Marston Gate.